QUEST FOR HONOR

QUEST FOR HONOR

DAVID TINDELL

Mr Matt,
Pil Sung!
Dave Tindell
9/20/14

ISBN: 978-1499198454

Cover art by Damonza, www.damonza.com.

Book trailer by Jim Tindell.

www.facebook.com/DavidTindellAuthor

*To my father, James J. Tindell, and grandfathers,
Alvin Carpenter and James L. Tindell, who showed us
how to live a life of honor.*

The credit belongs to those who are actually in the arena, who strive valiantly; who know the great enthusiasms, the great devotions, and spend themselves in a worthy cause; who best know the triumph of high achievement; and who, at worst, if they fail, fail while daring greatly, so that their place shall never be with those cold and timid souls who know neither victory nor defeat.

Theodore Roosevelt

Honor is the inner garment of the soul; the first thing put on by it with the flesh, and the last it layeth down at its separation from it.

Akhenaton

CHAPTER ONE

JULY 2011 – SOMALIA

EVERY NIGHT, HE saw the children. No matter how tired he was, no matter how preoccupied he was from the events of the day, no matter anything, he dreamed. And in his dreams, they came for him. Pain and supplication filled their eyes; a shadow, dark and menacing, loomed behind them. Sometimes he could hear its wicked laughter, smell its fetid breath.

On this hot night, he woke up screaming. "No! Save them! Save them!" Bolting upright, the bedclothes fell away, drenched with his sweat. He was panting. The shadow had gotten close to him, as the children milled around, and he felt its cold tendrils snaking around him, drawing him closer…

There was a knock at the door, then a muffled voice. "Yusuf! Are you all right?"

He didn't answer, and the door edged open. The face that peered in was that of Amir, his most trusted lieutenant. *Did the man never sleep?*

"Are you ill, Yusuf? May I get you anything?"

Yusuf shook his head, banishing the last wisps of the faces, knowing they would be back, perhaps as soon as he nodded off again. "Thank you, Amir, but I am fine. A bad dream, that is all."

"Shall I prepare some hot tea? It often helps me sleep."

Yusuf started to object, but said, "That would be good. Please, bring it to the library, and join me."

He rose, pulled on a dry robe, switching on the light. The lone overhead bulb sputtered but stayed on. At least the electricity was running, he thought. Otherwise it would be candles and lanterns, as it was some nights. How could this truly be part of the land of Allah's people if it could not consistently provide even the bare necessities? Ah, but what necessities are we thinking of, Yusuf reminded himself. The ones you enjoyed back in America, at university? Or the ones the true believers scraped and scavenged for every day, here in the barren countryside, the crowded cities, that made up the lands of the Prophet, blessings be upon him?

In the library, which was little more than a room with some shelves laden with books, a desk and his precious computer, Yusuf sat on one of the pillows along the walls as Amir joined him with a steaming pot of tea and two cups. They sipped in silence for a few minutes, and then Amir cleared his throat nervously. He was always so respectful, rather surprising for a Libyan; as a rule, Libyans tended to look down on central Africans, like Yusuf.

"What is it, Amir?" Yusuf said. "You may speak freely, my friend."

"I—well, these dreams of yours, Yusuf, they must trouble you. I frequently hear you cry out." Amir lowered his eyes. Men did not often speak of such things, especially the proud and, let's face it, the arrogant men Yusuf worked with and led. In spite of himself, Yusuf smiled, his white teeth showing

2

starkly against his black skin. He reached over and clapped Amir on the shoulder.

"Amir, you are my brother, do not be embarrassed. It is proper for brothers to speak of such things with each other. Privately, of course." He chuckled, and Amir, relaxing, did as well. Yusuf sighed, took another sip of the sweet Turkish tea, and said, "It is the same dream. It is about Katabolang."

"Ah," Amir said. "The children. Yes, it was bad. But they were martyred and are in Paradise now. We must believe that," he said fervently.

"I know they are," Yusuf said, but in his heart of hearts he didn't really believe that anymore, did he? "I wish, sometimes, that we had been able to do it differently, so that the children may have been spared. They might have grown up to be strong fighters," he hastened to add.

Amir drank from his cup. "It was a good plan," he said, believing it to be so, Yusuf knew, because Amir had helped draw it up. "The Americans had to be drawn to the mosque without knowing about the children, Allah be praised, and our brothers in the ranks of the lackey Kabul army were successful in falsifying the intelligence. The video of the bodies after the American attack was very effective."

"Yes, it was," Yusuf agreed. Once it had aired on al-Jazeera, the images of the broken and burned little bodies succeeded in drawing many contributions to the madrassas, funds which helped finance the cause. And who knew how many new fighters were inspired by the pictures? In America, the crusaders' always-helpful news media made much of the slaughter, although they were careful not to blame the policies of their new president, whom they adored. Still, the crusaders' cause had doubtless been hurt severely. The operation was truly well-planned, it was well-executed—

Executed. That was an appropriate word, Yusuf thought. Twenty-three children were killed by what appeared to be American tank shells, but before that they'd been kept there for three days by Yusuf and his men, while a larger force outside held the villagers at bay, waiting for the Americans to come. Yusuf's engineers carefully planted the explosive charges, designed to be set off by any incoming American heavy fire, or by remote-control if necessary. In the final hours, they tied up the children, then gagged them as their pitiful screams rent the night. Some of his men, yielding to the intense pressure, beat those older ones who attempted to escape, defying Yusuf's explicit orders. Things were getting out of hand, discipline was breaking down. Yusuf had started to think about releasing the children, which would have been in defiance of his orders, but the Americans arrived, and the slaughter began.

Then came their own escape from Afghanistan, evading American and lackey patrols as they moved over the mountains into Pakistan. Reporting to the Sheikh himself, and Yusuf recalled the scene in the mansion in Abbottabad where the tall bearded man with the still-fierce eyes embraced him, calling him a hero of Islam, for his fine work in Katabolang, promising there would be more work for him, more chances to strike the infidels. Always he referred to Yusuf by his code name, *Sudika*, a name that was already known, and feared, in the Horn of Africa. Then they were sent back here, to Somalia, a place even more desolate than Afghanistan, where Yusuf and his men had done much good work in the past, with more to come.

He had barely settled back into the life of the remote outpost when the shocking news of the Sheikh's death had flashed upon his computer screen, and with Amir and dozens of their fighters, they watched the satellite TV screen in amazement as the American president arrogantly announced the news to the world. Could it really be true? How could this have happened?

Over the next few weeks, Yusuf struggled to hold the camp together. Some of the foreign fighters gave up and left for home, but most had stayed. They were heartened when the American president announced late in June that he would begin withdrawing his troops from Afghanistan. "We must hold on, brothers!" was heard often in the camp over the next few days. Yusuf did nothing to temper their expectations, but tried to keep them on an even keel. He knew what they did not: the Taliban were nearly exhausted and on the brink of defeat. The Americans had proven to be a much more formidable foe than the Russians had been. For one thing, the Americans were technological wizards. The *mujahedeen* lived in constant fear of attack from the devilish drones that could be lurking overhead at any moment. The American soldiers were well-trained and courageous, and they were formidable fighters who were highly motivated. Most especially, the Americans were making inroads with the population, giving them education and medical treatment, helping with their agriculture and building infrastructure.

The Russians had been different, caring little about the innocent Afghans around them. Most of their soldiers were conscripts, with little stomach for fighting an elusive and deadly enemy so far from home. The Russian Special Forces troops, the *Spetsnaz*, were an exception, as Yusuf had found out personally on more than one occasion, but fortunately there had not been enough of them to make a difference.

Success would all depend on how quickly the Americans left. Yusuf had read that the president's generals all opposed the withdrawal plan, but the political realities of a difficult re-election campaign trumped their objections. If the Taliban re-took the country after the American withdrawal, that would be a problem for the next president.

The real threat to the Americans was one that few of them yet perceived, and those who did were often discounted within their own government, as far as Yusuf had been able to tell. The Arabs still looked for leadership from the Sheikh, and now from his anointed successor, but Yusuf was one of a very select few within the leadership of the movement that knew what was really going on. His work in the Horn and elsewhere for jihad had not gone unnoticed, not just by the Sheikh, but by others, the ones who had provided al-Qaida and other jihadi groups with much of their funding and weapons.

Yusuf remembered the day he was summoned to Tehran, five years before. He spent two days in his hotel, meeting with a few very important men. Then someone very high up indeed must have made a favorable decision, for he was whisked away in a small motorcade to an air force base, and from there in a small jet to a remote airfield well to the east, and finally overland to a place in the Aladagh Mountains, east of the Dasht-e Lut basin, one of the driest places on Earth. There, he saw with his own eyes what the future of the jihad would be.

Just a few weeks ago, Yusuf had received a coded message, brought to him personally by courier. Using the code he had been given in the Aladagh, he deciphered the message. It was the one he had been awaiting for half a decade. *Maintain order and discipline in the ranks. The events which were foretold to you are about to come to pass. Expect new orders soon.* The message was signed simply, "al-Qa'im".

Yusuf nearly shivered when he had completed the decoding and read the full message. He was excited, to be sure, but unsettled as well. Could he be in line for another mission like Katabolang? He prayed to Allah that it would be something different, not involving innocents this time. But over the next few weeks, his soul was increasingly troubled. More often now he thought of his time in the land of the Great Satan, his days at university in that small town in their province of Wisconsin, and the friends he'd made, the times he drank beer with them and laughed and studied together, and even the times he attended their Christian churches with them, with the joyful singing and the words of love and kindness...

Yusuf's hand trembled as he placed the cup down, and he heard it rattle against the saucer. Amir looked at him with concern. "Are you all right, Yusuf?"

"Just a brief flash of the nightmare, Amir. It has passed." He rose, as did Amir. "Thank you for the tea. I will retire now, and I believe I shall sleep soundly. Thanks to you, my friend." He clapped Amir's shoulder. "Good night."

In his bedroom, with the light off, Yusuf Shalita, once known to his friends in his native Uganda, and to his friends in America, as Joe, lay back and stared at the dark ceiling. He reached a decision. The next day was July fourth, a date that had no meaning here, but in America, it was their Independence Day. Tomorrow, he would begin his quest for his own independence, freedom at last from an ideology that had eaten away at his very soul. He would begin to work out the details, but he knew without question, in his heart of hearts, that he could no longer do this work. It was wrong. It was—evil. Yes, he had to finally admit to himself, it was evil. How could Allah, blessed be his name—how could God, by any name, consider such things to be acts of good, of love?

No. He would stop, and what's more, he would stop the others, as well. He had committed many crimes, caused the deaths of many innocents, and for those crimes the Americans had hunted him for years, and perhaps they would show no mercy on him, even if he renounced his past, even his very faith. Yusuf Shalita trembled, because he remembered his read ings of the Christian Bible, and the fate that awaited men who performed such evil deeds.

Perhaps, though, there was yet a way. First, he would have to somehow convince the Americans to give him sanctuary, protection. They did it for their own criminals all the time, didn't they? Yes, but those criminals always had something to trade with: information. He had a great deal of that, didn't he? Information was a commodity, after all, and the Americans knew all about the value of commodities. Yes, it might be possible, especially since he held within his head what was perhaps the most valuable piece of information in the world, a piece only a handful of men knew:

He was one of a handful of people outside Iran who knew about al-Qa'im, and where to find him. He knew what al-Qa'im was planning, and how he could be stopped. A great many American lives could be saved with that information, and if there was one thing the American politicians valued, it was the lives of their people. The cynic in Yusuf said that was because those lives meant votes to keep the politicians in power, but the realist in him knew that the great majority of the politicians did indeed care deeply for their people and their country. He had become convinced of that during his time among them. They were a proud people, fiercely patriotic, and although they often squabbled among themselves, they did not hesitate to rally together when threatened. That was their greatest strength. They would do whatever was necessary to defeat their enemies and protect their country. In his lack of understanding of that basic fact, the Sheikh himself had seriously underestimated the Americans. Now, with the Sheikh gone, the movement was in the hands of al-Qa'im, a man whose understanding of the Great Satan was much more complete. This understanding had led to the plan he had for the next great strike against the Americans, a plan he had broadly outlined to Yusuf in the Aladagh.

Yusuf did not know what his own role in that plan would be, but what he did know left him cold. Katabolang would seem as nothing compared to what was now being put in motion from deep in the mountains of eastern Iran. But without al-Qa'im, the plan would not come to fruition. That much was clear to Yusuf.

And Yusuf could deliver him to the Americans.

Surely the Americans would be willing to bargain for that. His life, for that of their newest and most dangerous enemy. They would offer money, as well, but he cared not a whit for that. His life, that was what he cared about, and the chance to repent.

He would have to be very careful. Which of his men could be trusted? None of them, that much he knew, even Amir, his most loyal, who had been by his side for twenty years now. Worse, al-Qa'im now had his own eyes and ears in the camp. No, he would have to be very clever, a challenge very great, even for a clever man such as himself. But it could be done. For the next hour he turned the problem over in his head, and finally an idea came to him. It was dangerous, and perhaps the longest of long shots, but it might work. The success or failure of it all would depend on one man. Yusuf didn't know where the man was; he hadn't seen him in nearly three decades now, since university. Was he still around that town? Was he even still alive? There was only one way to find out.

He slept, and he did not dream.

CHAPTER TWO

WISCONSIN

THE ENGINE ROARED as the driver slammed the accelerator to the floor, and Jim Hayes had to hold on to the handles of the machine gun as their modified Humvee raced through the streets. Images flashed past him on the right: the faces of the Iraqis, some frightened, some angry, some cloaked in scarves. Those were the ones to watch out for, because they always had an RPG or an AK-47 ready to fire. They hadn't been quick enough to trigger the IED right under the vehicle, but the sound of the blast was still ringing in his ears. They were in it now, and only their skill and some luck would get them out.

There, at two o'clock, two guys with an RPG, standing up on the roof of that building! Jim swung his weapon up and pressed the trigger, holding on tight as the machine gun roared, and he fought to bring it to bear on the target. He was a bit low, and the snout of the damn RPG was lowering toward them. He yelled up at his partner on the top turret gun: "Billy, at our two, RPG, help me out!" But the kid was too slow, and

Jim saw his tracers arc far to the left of the target. Jim fought the urge to duck and instead struggled to keep his breathing steady. He sighted his weapon and fired. The two men went down, the rocket still in its launch tube.

"Two miles to go!" the driver screamed, wrenching the wheel to the right, throwing Jim back into his seat. He cursed as he tried to right himself. Where did this clown learn to drive anyway? Not for the first time, Jim wondered how the hell he'd gotten assigned to this crew for the patrol. Two miles would be an eternity here, and the way things were going, they just might not make it.

But they did. There were a couple more close calls, but they got clear of the village and the Humvee careened to a halt. Jim sagged back in his seat and wiped away the sweat on his forehead. A face appeared at the window, a young guy with a high and tight haircut, wearing Army camo. "How'd you like it, sir?"

"Pretty neat," Jim said. "Thanks." He knew he was dating himself even more by not using "cool", but what the heck.

"Need a hand getting out, sir?"

Jim shot the kid a look, trying to keep it friendly. What was he, about twenty-five? That made him half Jim's age. The gray at his temples must've given him away. "No thanks, Sergeant," he said, noticing the stripes on the soldier's front tab. Three up, none down. Jim let him open the door of the Humvee and he unfolded himself with only a little cracking in the knees. "They don't make these for real tall guys, do they?"

He laughed. "No sir, they don't." When Jim stood straight next to him, he topped the soldier by about two inches, making him about six-one. "Did you serve, sir?" he asked.

"No, I didn't, I'm sorry to say." That was his stock answer, but it was sincere enough. "Blew my knee out playing ball.

Even in those days, they wouldn't take a guy with a bum knee. I have a younger brother in the Army, though."

"Is that right?"

"Yes, he's a lieutenant colonel, commands a firebase over in Afghanistan."

The young sergeant perked up. "Which one would that be, sir? I just finished my last deployment three months ago."

"Camp Roosevelt, but I forget what province it's in. He said it was close to the Pakistan border." Actually, Jim couldn't remember much more. Mark's emails were infrequent and those that he did bother to send weren't very descriptive.

"I wasn't there, but I've heard of that outfit. The Rough Riders. If your brother's the C.O. there, sir, you should be proud."

Jim just grinned, but not as broadly as he might have. He offered his hand. "Thanks for the ride, Sergeant. Good luck, and thanks for your service."

The soldier's grip was pretty strong. "You're welcome, sir, and thanks for your support. Tell your brother the guys back home give him a big 'Hooah!'" A shout from the top of the vehicle drew their attention. The twelve-year-old kid who'd been manning the .50-caliber machine gun had barked a shin as he was being lifted out by another soldier. The sergeant smiled. "He had a little trouble with the .50," he said, then he looked back at Jim. "But you handled that M60 nicely, sir. I would've bet you were a veteran. Persian Gulf, maybe." Well, at least he hadn't said Vietnam. Jim didn't want to feel any older than he was.

The simulation called for four people to man the vehicle. There was a driver, a guy on top with the M2 heavy weapon, and one on each side with window-mounted M60 7.62mm machine guns. In real life, there would be no side-mounted weapons, according to what he'd been told by a soldier while he was waiting in line outside the simulation tent. "I wanted the .50 but the kid was too fast for me," Jim said. The sergeant laughed.

Outside, the sun was shining, breaking through the morning clouds that had almost kept them home, thinking rain might wash out the air show. But Jim had been waiting to see the Blue Angels for years and was willing to take the chance the weather would break. Annie hadn't been quite as confident as him and wouldn't have minded staying home, but he had the feeling she would've preferred that regardless of the weather.

"Have a good time?" she asked. He noticed that while he'd been on the sim run, she'd changed out of her jeans into shorts. More than a few other men noticed that, too, judging by the heads that were turning as they walked by.

"It was great," he said. "They had big screens on three sides, and the vehicle was on a platform so you really got a feeling of movement."

"Kill anybody?" Her eyes were hidden behind her sunglasses, so Jim couldn't tell for sure whether she was being playful or slightly sarcastic. Knowing Annie, it was probably sarcasm, but he let it pass.

"I think I got a couple," he said. He checked his watch. "Showtime in a half-hour. Want to get something to take back to our chairs?"

"Sure."

He'd thought that watching the blue Navy jets screaming through the sky, with gorgeous, blonde Annie sitting next to him would have made him forget about the date, if only for a little while. He always wound up sitting around moping on this day, but then he heard about the air show here in Madison and figured it was time to do something different. Six years had passed, after all, and some said that even the most traumatic memories start fading after less time than that. Jim was still waiting for that to happen.

There were a lot of couples out here today, not too many teenagers, and a fair number of seniors. Everybody appeared to be having a good time, enjoying the weather, glad the threat of rain had passed. Just in front of them was a couple a few years younger than him, a married couple judging by their rings. How long had they been together? No way to tell, of course, but they had that easy familiarity of a couple long together. He didn't have that with Annie, not yet, and he was beginning to think he might never have it. That was too bad; he'd enjoyed being married to Suzy, twenty-two of the best years of his life. All ended so suddenly, six years ago tomorrow. He glanced at his watch. Right about this time, in fact, when the gun had fired—

Stop it. He didn't want the memory to spoil this day. That wouldn't be fair to Annie. The memory was always there, always would be, but he'd learned to deal with it, pushing it back into a little corner of his mind, the corner where it always stayed. Until it came creeping back out at him, usually at night, but sometimes during the day, and almost anything could trigger it, or nothing. Memories were like that, at least according to the grief counselor he'd met with for a while.

The pilots assembled in the reviewing area, lining up in perfect precision, wearing blue jump suits and khaki garrison caps, standing at parade rest as they were introduced over the public address systems. They got a big hand from the crowd and then headed to their planes, which were already warming up, the thrumming of the engines rising very gradually until

Jim could almost feel the sound waves. The pilots boarded, put on their helmets, and then the canopies came down. The six blue and gold F/A 18 Hornets moved gracefully out onto the runway and took off with terrific roars.

Jim thrilled at the display as the jets soared and knifed through the air. What discipline! He thought about those six pilots, four Navy, two Marine Corps. Most likely they were all married, or had been, and dealt with challenges in their lives, too, perhaps even tragedies. Yet here they were, doing what nobody here on the ground could ever dream of doing. Whatever had happened in their lives, they had overcome the challenges to get here, to the very apex of their profession. Nothing had stopped them.

He was a long way from them, but Jim felt the tenuous strands of a kinship. He knew a thing or two about overcoming challenge. There had been some times, some dark times, after that day six years ago, times when he didn't think he'd make it, but the counselor had hung in there with him, and Jim had somehow found the strength to persevere. That was one of the five tenets of *taekwondo,* after all. He recalled them now as easily as he knew his own name: courtesy, integrity, perseverance, self-control, and indomitable spirit. Four months after the sessions started, Jim told the counselor he had decided not only to resume his martial arts training, but in fact wanted to step it up, and when he told the man why, Jim could tell from his reaction what he thought of that. Jim walked out of his office that day and never looked back. What did he know, anyway? Some egghead prof who lived a nice secure life in academia, where the most dangerous thing he might encounter would be a balky lawnmower. What did he know about a man's desire to avenge his wife? What did he know about becoming a warrior?

Jim reflected later that he hadn't really been fair with the man. He'd helped Jim deal with Suzy's death, and especially the manner in which it happened, and for that Jim was thankful. The next several months after that terrible July day had not been pretty, and some parts were downright scary in retrospect, but he came out of it in one piece, still had his health and a job and hadn't gotten hooked on drugs or porn or liquor, like so many men did when they lost their wives way too early. There were some close calls, but he'd made it out of that emotional cave, at least out of the worst of it. The darkness still called for him now and then, but not so much anymore.

The counseling helped, and he got back in touch with the religious faith of his youth, but what really had saved him was his martial arts training. Two hours after leaving the counselor's office for the last time, he was on the mat at his *dojang*, stretching and feeling the tightness in his muscles that he'd have to work through in the days and months ahead. The tightness in his heart would take a lot longer.

The jets came screaming overhead, nearly at the speed of sound along the runway, the engines drowning out the cheers of the crowd. The skill of the pilots was almost unbelievable. Jim could hardly imagine the training they must go through to get picked for this team. Did his brother ever go through that kind of training? Well, of course not, he was an Army infantry officer, not a pilot, but certainly he'd been through the wringer many times. There was West Point, and how many overseas deployments? Jim couldn't remember them offhand, but that was probably because he and Mark, well, they hadn't been talking that much in recent years, had they?

Six years. He could've stopped the guy. He was *right there...* It took him months to pull himself out of the muck, but he finally decided that rather than let that failure destroy him, he would rise above it. He had to. There was no other choice, not really. He had not been strong enough, fast enough, proficient enough to save Suzy.

That could be fixed. He dedicated himself to become the best martial artist he could be, to push his middle-aged body as far as it could go, and then to go farther still. He pushed himself in the dojang, got his black belt, and expanded his horizons, discovering a world of vast depth and possibilities, a world filled with men and women of discipline, courage, honor.

What did it really mean, to be one of these kinds of men? What kind of philosophy, what kind of ethos, did they have? It was more than just training. It was knowledge, discipline, and tying it all together was a sense of honor. He had to learn how to live that kind of life. When he got home, he started reading every book he could find about warriors, past and present. He re-discovered the writings of his boyhood hero, Theodore Roosevelt, and soon his ever-expanding library shelves were overflowing.

He would become a warrior. He was too old to go into the military himself, so he would never come close to his brother's level, but he would get as close as he could. And the next time, he would be ready.

They packed up their camp chairs and started winding their way through the crowd as the Blue Angels soared into their finale. When they got behind the seating area, toward the concession stands and static displays, Jim said, "Let's hold up here and watch the finale."

He could hear a little sigh from her, but she turned around to watch the jets along with him. It was worth it, as far as Jim was concerned, and when the Hornets made their final pass in an amazingly tight six-plane Delta Formation, screaming over the airfield and peeling off to a huge roar, he felt a surge of exhilaration. It was worth the wait all morning long, worth the heat and the crowds and the long walk back to the car, just to see that discipline and precision.

"Wow, wasn't that terrific?" he asked, almost giddy.

"Pretty cool," Annie said. "Well, let's head back." She hoisted her folded-up camp chair and slung it onto her back. "Shall we?" She had that time-to-move-on look, something Jim had not learned to deal with quite yet. But he didn't object.

"Yeah, sure."

Wherever Anne Boswell went, she turned heads, and Jim watched them now. Teenagers with sideways ball caps and droopy pants, twenty-somethings showing off their tattoos with muscle shirts, family men with their own wives and kids in tow, they all looked. Some of them looked at him, too, and he saw that familiar envy in their eyes. Being with Annie was a rush, and not for the first time he caught himself thinking that was the main reason he was with her, because it made him feel good about himself, perhaps even satisfied, for the first time in…well, about six years.

She was forty-two, looked ten years younger, and still had the toned body of the college volleyball star who worked as a figure model for a time before her first marriage. By the time Jim met her at the health club in Cedar Lake just after he moved to town, she'd already been through one husband and had two kids in college. A year ago she'd been divorced from number two, and now they'd been dating for several months. Jim didn't really have a sense of where it was going, but he was in no hurry. Neither of them had mentioned marriage, and the question of children had never come up, and never would. Been there, done that for both of them. His daughter Michaela would turn twenty-five this fall. The son he never got to hold would've been six next winter. He liked to think it would've been a boy, anyway. Suzy had been only two months along...

He shook his head, trying to push the thought out. "Something wrong?" Annie asked.

"Just thinking about those pilots," he lied. "Unbelievable." Annie knew about Suzy, but she didn't know about the significance of this day. He wanted to keep it that way.

He doubted whether Annie would ever really understand. She'd taken what she could out of her marriages: from the first, to a computer wizard, the IT business she ran out of her downtown Cedar Lake office, and from her second, a wealthy banker, the log home out in the country and the Jaguar in the garage. She was focused on her work first and her home second, with Jim somewhere a distant third. He knew she grudgingly respected his martial arts training, but the one time he'd told her about why he was really doing it, showed her his ever-growing library, he could tell she was not too impressed. Still, things were good with her, most of the time. Yes, he got a rush from being with her in public, and sex with her was an awesome experience.

But there had to be more than that, didn't there?

The crowd was starting to move toward the exits now, at the back end of the large observation area on the airport grounds near the cargo terminals. Jim and Annie were in the first few ranks and as they came around a corner of a hangar, he saw the protestors on the other side of the gate.

"What's going on up there?" Annie asked, suddenly interested.

Jim squinted to make out one of the signs they were carrying. "'Stop the war now'. Ah, hell, here we go." He should have expected this. They were in Madison, after all, one of the most liberal cities in America, a place where aging lefties still got misty-eyed about the anti-war demonstrations they'd had on campus during the Vietnam years, and it wasn't from remembering the tear gas. People elsewhere in Wisconsin tended to call Madison "an island surrounded by reality."

"I'd heard they might be out here," Annie said.

He looked at her. They were about fifty yards from the gate now. "What do you mean?"

"Well, hello, Jim, they're anti-military, and what do we have here today but the ultimate example of the military?" "Those guys fly those planes to keep it safe over here, so that these yahoos can raise hell," he said grimly. Once or twice during the show, as the fighters came screaming low across the field, he'd wondered if that's how they looked from his brother Mark's perspective over in Afghanistan, when he and his troops were pinned down and needed help from the skies. Now he looked at Annie carefully for any reaction, but she kept quiet. They'd discussed politics just enough for him to know that she was left of center on almost everything, and one time she'd accused him of being somewhere to the right of Attila the Hun. Rather mild, really, for a woman who had a tee shirt showing Dick Cheney as Darth Vader.

There were about thirty protestors, about evenly mixed between men and women, ranging in age from early twenties to mid-sixties. "They must be upset because the president hasn't run up the white flag yet," Jim said, drawing a sharp look from Annie. The only real argument they'd had, so far, had been about the war, with Annie arguing passionately that the troops should be brought home right away, regardless of the consequences, and Jim just as adamant to keep them over there till the job was done, even if it meant his brother would be in danger. He knew from Mark's infrequent emails that he felt the same way.

There were policemen at the ready, but not decked out in any special gear that Jim could see. His training kicked in and he automatically scanned the protestors for any sign of possible weapons or other trouble, just as Major Kemerovo had taught them at the Systema camps he'd attended, and he felt his breathing slow and deepen just a bit as his senses sharpened and his body relaxed. The typical Madison lefty was about as dangerous as a summer breeze, but you never knew. There was a time, after all, when they'd rioted and bombed and generally raised hell on campus and elsewhere. Until the draft had been abolished, anyway.

The cops and a handful of airport personnel were funneling the air show crowd through three gaps in the makeshift gate that led to an access road and the parking lot. The protesters were on the right, and Jim and Annie were going through the right-side gap in the gate. Had he subtly steered them in that direction? The protestors were chanting "Stop the war now!" and waving some signs, none of which dared criticize the president, who was still their hero, but there were more than a few slogans slamming the military in general and the Blue Angels in particular.

Jim was wearing an Army ball cap he'd picked up at one of the souvenir stands, even though he knew Annie hated ball caps, but he'd forgotten to bring his straw fedora from home and it turned out to be a sunny, warm day. One of the protestors zeroed in on the cap, just as Jim was coming through the gate.

"Hey, Army guy!"

The man looked to be in his forties, thinning gray hair pulled back into a ponytail, goatee, and wire-rimmed glasses, and from the size of his paunch he hadn't seen the inside of a gym for a long time. He was carrying a professionally-printed sign: WAR IS A CRIME. BRING HOME THE CRIMINALS.

Jim was within about six feet of the man now. Annie, on his left, tugged at his arm. "C'mon, Jim, ignore him." "Army guy! How'd it feel to shoot kids over there?"

Jim stopped and looked at him. "I wasn't over there, sir. I wear this hat to honor my brother. He's over there now, helping to protect us here. Even idiots who don't deserve it."

Behind the glasses, his eyes were wide. Was he on something? He took a step forward and leaned closer to Jim, and there was spittle at the edges of the man's lips. Behind him, a mousey-looking woman in braided hair tried pulling him back. "Your brother's a criminal!" A chubby finger poked Jim in the chest. "He's no better than—"

"Don't touch me again."

The man reached out and poked, harder. "Why?" Poke. "Not?" Poke. "Army guy with the criminal brother?" Poke.

"Because now I get to do this."

CHAPTER THREE

AFGHANISTAN

THEY SHOWED UP as green apparitions in his night-vision goggles, picking their way along the rocky path. Lieutenant Colonel Mark Hayes counted them: eight, nine....no, ten, here came the last one. At least two of them were carrying long thin tubes, hard to make out because the tubes weren't radiating heat, but they had to be RPGs, old Soviet-made rocket-propelled grenade launchers that could turn a soldier's day from bad to worse pretty damn quickly.

It was unusual for the Taliban to move at night, but lately they'd seen more evidence of enemy night patrols, the better to evade American drones. The UAVs didn't care whether it was night or day, of course, as the bad guys were starting to find out. A drone had observed this group mustering across the border in Pakistan the day before, and rather than take them out right there, somebody upstairs had decided to let them cross the border and let Mark deal with them.

This bunch was making decent time, which was a bit surprising. The Taliban didn't have NVGs except for the few they'd captured or stolen from the Afghans, or bought on the black market, and Mark doubted if this bunch had more than one pair, if that. They'd be on the guy in the lead, now about eight hundred meters from their position and closing. But maybe, for once, their intel had been accurate, and this was the Taliban force that was moving on the village about ten kilometers to the north. The village only had a small platoon of Afghan troops guarding it, with no armor. The nearest air support was a good half-hour away, making the village a prime target. The local *malik* had thrown in with the government and the Americans some time before and that put him at the top of Mullah Omar's hit parade, along with the other locals who had gone over to the infidels and their lackeys. Of course it was the infidels who dug a new well for the chief's village, who rebuilt the school and opened it to all the children, even the girls, who brought medical and dental care to the malik's people. Mark had seen what the Taliban had done to other villages, and it wouldn't happen to this one, not on his watch. They'd already attacked it once, and three little girls were now getting treated in an American military hospital because of it. They'd live, although their faces would be scarred for life. Maybe the SOBs who'd done that deed were in this group now, coming his way. Mark hoped so.

The intel didn't always come in soon enough for Mark to mount an effective operation, but this time it had, and he had time to mount up a platoon from his nearest forward operating base, FOB O'Neill, about ten klicks away, and hump over the ridges to the ambush site in time to set up just before sundown. Mark had ten men with him on this side of the valley and his lieutenant, Frank Johnson, had another dozen on the other, and between them they had a good enfilading field of fire set up. Now it was just a matter of waiting for the insurgents to get close enough.

Keep coming, boys, it's almost time for your surprise.

Mark brought his M-4 up to his shoulder and sighted on the target near the middle of the enemy column, the one between the guys carrying the RPGs. Taliban squads in the field didn't utilize formal Western-style rank as such, but there was always one of them who was in charge, and typically he was in the middle along with the heavy weapons. He would have to go first. Even without leadership, the insurgents could be counted on to fight hard and sometimes quite effectively, if you gave them the chance. That was one of the things that had surprised many of the Americans who first came downrange in late '01 and early '02. Not Mark. He read up on these characters, studied their history all the way back to their campaign against Alexander the Great, even talked to ex-Soviet Spetsnaz vets who'd fought here twenty years ago. And the message was loud and clear: Do not underestimate these people. They looked like a bunch of raggedy-assed scarecrows, but they could pull a trigger, they could launch a mortar, plant a roadside bomb. There were plenty of reasons not to give them any chance when you got the drop on them. Out here there was no such thing as a fair fight. You wanted to make it unfair in your favor, as much as possible. No one-on-one Rambo crap was allowed. That only led to dead soldiers and Mark did not enjoy writing those letters home.

Time seemed to slow down. He calculated the distance, measured the slight wind, took everything into account to set up his shot, and then it was just a matter of waiting till the shot presented itself. The waiting was the worst part.

He'd done his share of that downrange, for damn sure. His third tour here, along with a couple in Iraq, meant Mark Hayes had spent precious little time back in the States since the balloon went up on 9/11. He must be in the running for some kind of medal. Did they give out anything for Most Time Spent in Hellholes Chasing Bad Guys? Well, it wasn't as if he had a lot

25

waiting for him back home. His folks were both gone, he hadn't talked to his big brother in months. But there was his boy, in middle school back in Virginia, growing up with an absent father, like so many Army kids these days. Every now and then he thought about retiring, going back home. His roommate from West Point had put in his papers a couple years ago and now had a thriving corporate and personal security firm back in the States, and Mark had a standing offer from him to come aboard. It would be interesting work, with pretty good pay and benefits. It was tempting to think about that, especially on the days when the paperwork was piled up on his desk, on the cold winter nights when he was out checking the perimeter.

Next to him, Sergeant Waters whispered, "How's it look, Colonel?"

Mark lined it up again. "Another minute or so...Spread the word, fire at will upon my shot."

"Roger that, sir."

Eddie. He thought of his son at the oddest times. Mark missed him, sometimes desperately, and then he would curse the Army that had kept him away from being the dad he'd always wanted to be, from repairing a marriage that had fallen apart. But he loved it, God help him. He loved the Army, and his fellow soldiers, and that's why he'd held off on pulling the pin as a lieutenant colonel in '07, twenty years after his graduation from West Point. He was due for a tour at the Pentagon, and it was tempting to quit before having to deal with all the political bullshit, but he figured he needed at least another year there and maybe another combat tour to get to full colonel. Retirement would be a lot better if he went out with eagles on his tabs. Besides, what else did he have to do?

Mark had never liked pushing paper, and sometimes a staff officer's work consisted largely of covering his boss's ass. That had been the case in his last billet at the Pentagon, and when push came to shove over a major screw-up by his commanding officer, Mark had told the truth in his report. He wasn't going to sugarcoat the man's incompetence and he sure as hell wasn't about to take the blame and fall on his own sword. The result had been the general's early retirement, but he didn't leave before making sure that Mark's own career took a hit, keeping him a light colonel well past the usual time for promotion.

Once again, he considered hanging it up, but his staff work must have impressed someone. When an important billet opened up on the staff of Commanding General, International Security Assistance Force, Mark's name was mentioned and he jumped at the chance to get back into the field, his third tour in Afghanistan. It meant leaving his son behind for another year or so, but that wasn't enough to make him want to resign. Not quite yet, especially since the General had called him into his office four months ago and asked him to take command of a battalion that had been going downhill under a do-nothing desk jockey. Out here, at last Mark had the chance to put into practice all he'd learned, and he was enjoying the hell out of it.

Just another couple dozen meters. Come to papa, Achmed, or whoever the hell you are, and get ready to cavort with the virgins.

The gravity of what he was about to do started pulling at him. He'd taken more than one man's life during his time in the Army, and given orders that had taken many more, and most of the time he didn't lose any sleep over it. Was that wrong? He knew guys who'd seen a lot less action than him, good men, almost paralyzed by PTSD, and the sounds of men immersed in nightmares were common in the hooches on his base and the FOBs. What gave him bad dreams, though, were the things he'd seen the gomers do. The beautiful twelve-year-old girl with her nose cut off, punished for attending school. The seven-year-old boy swinging from a tree, hung by the Tals because the boy's grandfather had defied them. The three girls from the nearby village, their faces permanently scarred by the acid thrown at them as they walked to school. The...

They were stopping. Somebody had called a halt down there, and the insurgents hunkered down. The two with the RPG tubes swung them around, one pointing ahead to the left, the other to the right. Had somebody up here made a sound, maybe somebody over in Johnson's position? Dammit! Mark froze, and so did his men nearby, hardly breathing. They were a good hundred meters away and well-concealed, and the moon had gone behind the clouds. The Taliban held their position for a full minute, then the officer made a motion. Mark heard a voice drifting up here on the breeze, but couldn't make out the Pashto. Must've been an order to move out, because they got to their feet and started walking again, this time more slowly. The RPG tubes were still scanning for targets. Mark wanted to wait till they were safed. If one of those rocketeers reacted to Mark's shot by firing off a panicky round, it might hit something it shouldn't.

The gomer in the lead was traversing the kill box now. Just a few more seconds and Mark would have them where he wanted them. He wondered how many were Afghans, and how many were fighters from other countries? He'd run into the whole gamut of them over here: Pakistanis, Chechens, Saudis, Palestinians, a few more. Since the Islamists had started throwing their weight around in Egypt, he'd seen a few more of them, too. The intel people said the bastard who'd led the Katabolang strike was from some central African country, he couldn't remember which one. Mark wasn't in on that action, but he'd been there with the General a couple days later, and like every other soldier involved, he wanted to get his hands around the neck of that son of a bitch.

Mark sighted on the gomer who looked like he might be the leader. When they'd planned the ambush, Mark once again allowed the top marksmen in the team to draw lots for the privilege of taking the first shot. To his surprise, they insisted he take part in the lottery. He was qualified, after all, having proven it on their makeshift range, and hey, it was his birthday coming up, they reminded him. Yeah, he would be forty-six in a few days, but he could still shoot with the best of them.

He pulled the trigger on his weapon.

It was over in minutes, and when none of the enemy fighters were moving anymore, Mark gave the radio signal to advance. Frank and his men would stay in place, just in case, while Mark's squad checked out the bodies. They did it very cautiously, because it wasn't unknown for the enemy to booby-trap one or two of their own, but these guys were clean of bombs. A couple of them weren't dead yet, but the medic said they were too far gone to save and Mark didn't question the man's judgment. In the early days the Americans would've worked hard to save Taliban lives, even brought in medevac choppers, but then a few of those got rocketed and some good men died trying to save these sorry bastards, so there wasn't much room for mercy after that. Very few of the survivors ever produced usable intel anyway. The leaders, the big shots who were the brains behind the outfit, they weren't out here, oh no. They were back safe and sound in some Pak village, or maybe a cave near the border if they had a big op going on or wanted to stay clear of the Pak soldiers who occasionally went out looking for them.

And once in a while, Americans went over the border, too. It was all top secret, but in his time at Camp Roosevelt, Mark had provided some logistical support for two different Special Operations teams going into Pakistan. Very close-hold stuff, orders directly from the General detailing what Mark was to do—and what he could not do, such as going along. Not that Mark would've been much of a hindrance. During his time downrange he'd worked with several different teams all over the country. His regular duties for the General required him to work with most of the different nationalities stationed here, and he'd been with Brits and Canadians, Germans and Poles, Belgians and Bulgarians. The time with the British unit, just before taking over the Rough Riders, was especially fortuitous because that's where he met Sophie, a BBC embed, and they'd been able to spend some time together in Kabul and one great weekend in Mumbai.

As he moved down the hillside toward the kill zone, Mark tried to get his mind off the carnage for just another minute or so, and thinking of Sophie was a good way to do that. He would send her an email when he got back to the base. Last he'd heard, she was due back in country soon.

Without wasting any time, Mark had his men search the bodies for any documents, and they found a few in a pouch carried by the commander, but they might have been letters home for all Mark knew. He'd become conversational in Pashto during his time in-country but this stuff was in Arabic, and his was rusty with his last Iraq deployment five years ago now. It'd give the intel weenies back in Kandahar something to do, at least, so he put the pouch in a vest pocket and gave the order to sanitize the kill box and bug out. They gathered the enemy's weapons and Sergeant Kittoe, the combat engineer, took them behind some rocks and set up a small C-4 charge with a five-minute fuse. Mark and his men were half a klick away when the charge went off with a loud bang. Frank and his men rejoined their column as they humped out toward the landing zone.

It had looked like most of the insurgents were Afghans or Pakistanis, although many times you couldn't really tell. The documents would probably shed some light. Word had come down that the Iranians were getting more active, and not just in the south, near their border. ISAF higher-ups wanted to know right away if any Iranian special operators were killed or captured, but Mark and other field commanders had been told specifically not to share any of that with media people. That could mean a lot of things, but to Mark and many of his fellow officers, it meant that the politicians back home didn't want that word to get out, maybe because it would upset the applecart of whatever negotiations were going on with the mullahs in Tehran over the nuclear issue.

Of all the gomers Mark had run into over here, the worst ones were the Iranians. Maybe your average Iranian grunt was no better or worse than anyone else, but their Special Forces guys, the Takavaran, were real bad actors. Before coming to Roosevelt he'd spent a week with a French Foreign Legion outfit for a hair-raising mission along the Iranian border. He'd been able to get up close and personal with some Takavar operators, and it was satisfying to send those arrogant bastards to Allah or whatever awaited them. Mark had to respect their abilities as soldiers, but where was the honor of being a soldier if your mission was to reinstate a regime that brutalized its own people, the way the Taliban did?

The Afghan people, for the most part, didn't much care for these foreigners, but there had been foreigners marching through this godforsaken country for more than two thousand years. The Afghans had an understandable dislike for the invaders, even those who were Muslims, but they were fatalistic about it. What could be done? It was only in the last couple years that Mark had seen a change. It was slow, it was here and there, but it was real, and growing. They were starting to see that the Americans weren't here to conquer them, but to help them, and the Tals and their Islamist allies had other goals in mind.

Mark gave the order to call the chopper for evac, and as the sun rose on this Sunday morning, some of the men broke march discipline a little and started talking about what the cooks might have for breakfast, how long they had till they were rotated home, whether the Packers could win it again this year, assuming the lockout didn't wipe out the NFL season. None of them talked of the firefight; that would come later, over Rip-Its and NA beers back at the firebase, when it started to sink in and most men felt the need to talk about it, almost like being in the locker room after a football game. Right now the small talk was soothing for Mark, who tried to put out of his mind the fact that he had just participated in the killing of ten men, some of them as young as his own son, men who hadn't been given much of a chance to fight back.

By the time they got back to the firebase, the morning's divine services would be over. Mark would be grabbing some breakfast, do a debrief with Frank and then chopper back to Roosevelt. Even though it was Sunday, he would have to tackle at least some of the paperwork waiting for him, but maybe he'd have time to look up the base chaplain. Jeff Eisele was a good guy, on his third tour downrange, and they'd already had some good talks since Mark had taken command of the battalion. They were due for another one, and this Sunday evening would be a good time to have it.

CHAPTER FOUR

IRAN

"*SEHE...DOH...YEK...*" FLAMES ROARED from the engine of the missile and the noise drowned out the last words of the countdown. With a guttural rumble, the missile broke free from its mobile launcher and rose into the azure sky. All eyes were on the Shahab 3, in its olive drab, unmarked elegance, gaining altitude rapidly and tilting gracefully to the southwest.

"Where will it land, General Fazeed?"

The Pasdaran general turned to the man who had asked the question. He looked like the other mullahs in the viewing area, except for the Ray-Ban aviator sunglasses. He also appeared to be younger. His beard was jet black, but of course it could be dyed. Fazeed didn't think so. This man carried himself like a younger man, and he was clearly in charge. The four other men were older but deferred to him. "The target is in the Arabian Sea, about two hundred kilometers off the coast. The port of Bandar is the closest city."

"How far from here?"

"Nearly one thousand kilometers."

The man's left eyebrow raised above the Ray-Bans. "And what is the range of the missile, General?"

"This model is the Shahab 3B, imam. The range is nearly two thousand kilometers."

"It could reach Israel?"

Fazeed hesitated, then glanced at a man in a tailored Italian suit. The man, a senior official in the Ministry of Defense, nodded slightly. "Yes, imam," the general said to the man in the Ray-Bans.

"Tell me about the warhead."

Another nod from the man from the ministry. What was his name? Jafari. This imam must truly be important, the general thought. Very well. "It can carry a single warhead of nearly a thousand kilograms, or it can be configured for five cluster warheads. Each can be targeted separately within a few hundred kilometers of the main destination of the missile."

"We would only need two," one of the other mullahs said to the man in the Ray-Bans. "Tel Aviv, Haifa. We would have to spare Jerusalem."

"No, my friend. The first strike would have to target the Zionists' missile sites. Would that not be so, General?"

"That...would be logical, imam," Fazeed said. He knew much about the pre-selected targets for the Shahab regiment, but he would not give this man any of that information without a direct order from his superiors, the man from the Defense Ministry be damned. How did he know this man in the sunglasses was not a Zionist spy? Everyone knew Tehran was crawling with operatives from Mossad and the various Western intelligence services. He had been ordered to allow these mullahs to observe the launch, but nothing more.

The imam gazed back into the sky at the contrail of the missile. "It is very fast," he said.

"Over five thousand kilometers per hour," the general said. He was not revealing anything classified. The Americans and the Israelis already knew everything there was to know about the Shahab, which was an improved version of the Nodong 1, built by the North Koreans. The Americans had no doubt observed the launch with one of their many satellites and were tracking it all the way to its destination.

"So the Zionists would have very little warning," the imam said.

"From launch to impact, at maximum range, perhaps twenty minutes," Fazeed said. He assumed the man could do the simple arithmetic in his head. It was a moot point anyway. There would almost certainly be much more time available to the enemy. The underground bunkers would conceal much of the preparations necessary to launch the missile regiment, but there would still be signs, and the Americans knew all of them. They had spent half a century watching the Russians, after all. Nothing the Iranians could do would fool them, and there would be no way to conceal the launchers when they rolled out, pulled by heavy-duty semi-trucks. So, if it actually came down to it, they would play a game with the Israelis and the Americans. What did they call it? He believed it was "chicken".

The problem with that game, the general knew, was that someone was likely to be killed. Did these fools have any concept of the magnitude of what they were obviously contemplating? The general had made it a point to familiarize himself with the studies that projected the devastation of a nuclear exchange. If he was going to command the missile regiments that would rain destruction upon the enemies of his country, he wanted to know—felt it was his duty to know—what the scope of that destruction would be. Plus, what would happen to his own country as a result of the inevitable retaliatory strike. It would not be pretty, that much would be certain.

General Fazeed considered himself to be a patriot. His father had served under the Shah, following the honorable path of military service, and nearly paid for that with his life following the revolution. But he managed to persuade the new rulers that he could be trusted, that they needed him and many of his fellows to defend the nation against the many outside forces that wished to destroy the new regime. And so the son followed in his father's footsteps, but not in the regular armed forces, but in the Pasdaran, the Revolutionary Guards, the elite services tasked originally with the protection of Iran's Islamic authorities. Known in the West as the Iran Revolutionary Guard Corps, or IRGC, it had grown into a mighty force of over 125,000 men, with ground, aerospace and naval forces, not to mention Quds Force, the shadowy and much-feared Special Forces. Fazeed worked hard and rose in the ranks, ultimately to this posting, which held power far in excess of any his father, blessed be his memory, had ever held. But with such power came responsibility, and the general took that very seriously. He had built these missile regiments to defend his nation, but he worried constantly that the political leadership would throw everything away by launching a first strike against Israel.

Some of the mullahs in Tehran could be trusted. They were pragmatists, above all. Yes, they wanted to establish the great caliphate of Islam, but not at the cost of their own nation. What had his father told him once about the Russians? They wanted to rule the world, but not a radioactive world. Their pragmatism kept them from striking directly at the Americans. They pushed, here and there—Berlin, Cuba, Vietnam. Sometimes the Americans pushed back, and ultimately the Russians were done in by their own inefficiency. Even as their regime crumbled, though, the pragmatists never allowed the fanatics to get too close to the button. The men who safeguarded the arsenal survived to start the long process of rebuilding their nation.

But Iran in 2011 was much different than Soviet Russia had ever been. The general's concerns now were with those influential mullahs who were fanatics, and especially the clown who held the presidency of his nation. Now, he wondered just what side this group of mullahs in front of him was on. He had not been told their names, and although he thought he recognized one or two of the older ones, the man in the Ray-Bans was a mystery to him.

It was time to wrap this up. "Do you have any more questions, gentlemen?"

One of the older mullahs, the one who had talked earlier about targets in Israel, spoke up. "When will the missiles be fitted with the nuclear warheads?" This drew a glance from the man in the Ray-Bans, who then turned back to the general with an indulgent smile.

"Please forgive my enthusiastic colleague, General. I am sure that information is highly classified."

"Indeed it is, imam," the general said, looking at the man from the Defense Ministry. "But I can assure you that we stand ready to defend our nation against any aggression. Any attack upon our people would be met with swift and devastating retaliation."

The mullahs nodded. Fazeed gave them a confident smile. It was all he could do to keep from laughing at them, but his iron discipline held his real thoughts in check. What they'd said to him was illuminating: they were not within the inner circle around the *Rahbare Mo'azzame Enghelab,* the Supreme Leader of Iran, Ali Khamenei. Only a handful of people in the entire Islamic Republic knew the real truth about the Iranian nuclear weapons program. The president, Ahmadinejad, claimed to know everything, but the general knew this was not true. When he was elevated to command of the missile regiment two years ago, Fazeed was given what he felt was a full briefing on the status of his country's military forces, and he had paid close attention ever since, especially to the progress of the nuclear program.

He had been surprised to learn that the program was much more advanced than what he had heard. Enough disinformation was spread by the government's counterintelligence services to preserve the fiction that was widely believed in the West, that they were several years away, and the president, to his credit, did his part, constantly repeating the mantra that Iran's nuclear program was designed for peaceful purposes. Fazeed had long ago stopped being amazed at how the gullible Western media believed what lies they were told. Their politicians huffed and imposed sanctions, which the regime diligently worked around. The people grumbled, but for the most part did as they were told.

Fazeed and his colleagues didn't allow themselves to be fooled, though. The Western military and intelligence services, especially the Israelis and the Americans, certainly were not fooled. There was the constant threat that the Israelis, or perhaps both in concert, would attack in an attempt to delay the program. The general's duty was to organize a missile regiment that would provide a deterrent force against such attack, preparing for the day when the conventional warheads then available could be replaced with nuclear payloads, giving Iran a much more powerful means to deter aggression...or to enhance its own.

That day was close now, very close. It had always been only

a matter of time, and of course the big question was whether the Israelis would give them that time. Fazeed doubted that they would. Were he a betting man, he would've given even money that an Israeli attack would happen within the next twelve to eighteen months. Such a scenario had been war-gamed several times, and the most favorable outcome his colleagues had come up with was discouraging: they could at best count on shooting down perhaps half of the attacking Israeli planes. Enough would get through to cause serious damage to his country's nuclear facilities, delaying the program at least five years. If the Zionists attacked with their Jericho missiles, Iran's only option would be to launch a retaliatory strike—if there was anything left to retaliate with.

There was a way around that problem. Everybody knew the Israelis would never attack without American support. But if such support were withdrawn, that would be a different matter altogether. Various projects were underway to achieve that end, but the general had always doubted whether any of them would be successful. Using disinformation and subterfuge to turn American politicians and public opinion away from Israel was one way. It had been done before, not too long ago, but Fazeed knew this time was different. Israel was not South Vietnam, and frankly he doubted whether the mullahs framing this policy were as clever as the North Vietnamese and their Soviet KGB advisers had been, although it did appear they'd achieved some success in making the Western media sympathetic to Islam and thus hostile to Israel. Despite that, he was certain that his country's intelligence services would never be able to recruit the sorts of helpful stooges on American college campuses and in the ranks of Hollywood elite who had been so instrumental in propelling the North Vietnamese to victory.

Then he was told about one project that most definitely held great promise, not to mention great danger. For six months now, he had devoted increasing amounts of his time toward that end. He tried not to think about the danger. He was a military man, after all, whose profession by definition was dangerous. Yet, sometimes late at night, as he lay in bed with his wife gently snoring beside him, the thoughts crept back to him, and on those nights he had difficulty getting to sleep.

The reception for the mullahs was held in the officers' dining room. The general had invited his staff to attend, and he saw them mingling diplomatically with the guests. A table had been filled with delicacies and tea was served in small cups. The military men seemed rather taken aback by how much the mullahs ate, especially the one who had requested *kahle pache,* a traditional Persian breakfast soup of sheep's head, brain and hooves. Fazeed had consumed it on occasion as a child but now preferred more modern fare, although of course he never ate bacon.

The man from the Defense Ministry appeared by his side. "This has gone very well, General. My compliments to you and your staff."

"You are welcome, sir. The test was indeed flawless." He had received a report from the ship in the target area: the Shahab-3's dummy warhead had impacted right on target. The general decided to venture a question. It was a bit risky, and he had learned from his father that a general always had to consider political implications when dealing with Tehran, but he felt himself to be on fairly solid ground, considering how the test had gone. "Mr. Jafari, I noticed when the guests arrived, there were no introductions. Some of these gentlemen I recognize, but some I do not. The man in the sunglasses, for example."

Jafari looked away, toward the mullah in the Ray-Bans, who was picking a piece of bread from a basket as he held a teacup in the other hand. "With respect, General, our guest has requested that his identity remain confidential. For the time being."

"I see." The general decided to take another step. He could almost hear his father recommending caution. "I heard one of the mullahs call him 'al-Qa'im'. Does that mean what I think it means?"

Jafari was silent for a moment, and Fazeed knew he had cut very close to what he suspected was the truth. "You may draw your own conclusions, General," the Defense Ministry man said. "That does not mean they would be correct."

"I see," the general said.

After a moment, Jafari looked at his watch. "I'll be escorting our guests back to Tehran shortly," he said. "Might I have a word with you in private? I have an update on a subject of... mutual interest."

The general knew exactly what he was talking about. "Of course. Let's go to my office." That was only about twenty steps away, and with every step Fazeed fought harder to keep his anxiety level under control. He had thought that after six months, he would be able to discuss this topic without apprehension, but that was not so, not yet. They reached his office. Once inside, they sat in adjacent chairs next to the coffee table. The general's desk dominated the other end of the room. As they sat, the general looked up at the portrait of his father that hung proudly on one wall, and he prayed to Allah for some of the old man's strength.

"The ships are ready to sail," Jafari said without preamble, and the general could not suppress his intake of breath.

A half-hour later, the general shook hands with the mullahs

and Jafari as they prepared for the short ride to the airstrip. The Defense Ministry official's grip was firm and his eye contact said much more than the platitudes they were exchanging. As the general watched the two Land Rovers drive off, he reflected again on what he had been told in his office just a few minutes before. Part of him was filled with pride, for his role in the mission, delicate and hazardous as it had been, was now successfully completed. He was also concerned for his old friend and colleague, a Navy admiral who now was in charge and who now would have to rely on the professionalism and skill of his sailors, the hand-picked crews of the two ships, to bring the mission to a successful conclusion. Of course there were others on board, the security troops from Quds Force and the technicians in charge of the weapons, but they would be little more than passengers until the ships reached their destinations. It was the Navy's job to get them there. The general said a quick prayer for the admiral and his brave men.

He prayed for their success, and the success of the other men on board, for if they failed, it could mean the end of everything...for the general, his family, his country.

Everything would be riding on PERSIAN METEOR.

CHAPTER FIVE
WISCONSIN

ANNIE WAS PRETTY quiet on the drive from the air show back to her place, giving him time to think about what had happened at the gate. The rush of the confrontation was wearing off now, and so was the thrill of seeing the protestor's eyes go wide with surprise and pain. It was a good thing the cop had come by to break it up when he had, or the guy might've gotten seriously hurt. Yeah, that clown had started it, with his insults and taunts and his damn finger poking Jim in the chest, but still...

When they came to a stop in her driveway, she said, "I could whip up some dinner, if you're interested."

"Sure." He'd just assumed they'd be coming back here anyway, having dinner and then spending the night together again, as had been their routine on Saturdays for the past few months. They alternated between her place and his, although if truth were to be told, he preferred her place out here in the country to his little house in town, and once or twice—well, okay, more often lately—he'd wondered if he might someday be asked to move out here permanently, and if he'd accept the invitation.

One thing about Annie he definitely liked was her cooking, and even something quick and simple turned out to be quite good. He helped out by making the salads while she busied herself with the main course, a chili macaroni dish recipe she'd seen in his latest issue of *Men's Health*. She talked a little bit, too, but it was small talk, about their kids mostly. Nothing about the air show, or what had happened at the gate.

"Very good," he said when he put his fork down after the last bite. "More wine?"

"Sure," she said, and he poured her half a glass of the Riesling, leaving enough for him to have about a half-glass himself. She'd put away a couple already, and that was unusual. Annie didn't drink very much and usually had a one-glass limit on wine.

"Listen, about what happened…"

"You didn't have to break the guy's finger, Jim," she said, with a flash of those eyes that he knew could very well mean trouble.

"I didn't break it," he said. "Dislocated, maybe, but it wasn't broken."

"He could press charges, you know."

"I doubt that. The cop was right there and he didn't take my name. He saw the guy do what he did. He started it, after all. I just finished it." Jim felt himself getting defensive, but he didn't care. Sometimes Annie liked to push people's buttons, and that was one thing he didn't like about her. Then again, she was more right than wrong about this one, wasn't she?

"You could've walked away. Right from the start. Just ignored him."

"The guy insulted my brother, he insulted me, and he insulted the United States Army."

"Just words, Jim."

He set the wine glass down with a little more force than he needed to. "No, not just words. There's a lot more to it than that. Those characters come out to events like that air show and wave their idiot signs and call people criminals and nobody ever calls them on it, then they go back to their cocktail parties and brag about how tough they are. They have no idea what toughness really is. Well, now there's one guy who found out."

"Yeah, you showed him, Mr. Tough Guy. Did it feel good?"

Jim remembered the man gasping in pain as his finger was bent backward, then his wide-eyed amazement as his arm was wrenched upward and over his shoulder and then the fear and pain as he was bent over backward with Jim's elbow at his throat. Jim could've taken him to the ground but that's when the cop came over and broke it up.

"Maybe I took it a little too far," Jim said, "but yeah, it felt good. The guy was a bully. He's probably been bullying people for the last thirty years. Somebody had to shut him up and today that happened to be me."

"What do you mean, a bully? He didn't hit you. Didn't even really threaten you."

"A bully can use words, Annie. He doesn't have to be the kind who pushes you around physically. These guys pretend they're tough by what they write and what they say in their lectures in their classrooms. I had a few of them back at Platteville and you sure as hell had them in Madison."

"Come on, Jim, they're harmless."

"I disagree. They influence people. They do it now, they did it then. Forty years ago they were the ones spitting on the veterans when they came home from Vietnam. Now they don't have the guts to do it to guys like my brother when they come home, because the rest of the country won't put up with that crap anymore. But they still feel the same way. That was pretty obvious, wasn't it?"

"And you're gonna set 'em straight, right? The martial arts master's gonna teach the big bully protestor a lesson." Annie had a funny look in her eyes. She was provoking him, giving him more than just the little needling she'd used before when the subject of politics had come up. But he wasn't really in the mood for playing games tonight.

"I'm not a master, I'm just a student," he said. "My sensei is a master." That thought led him to wonder what Sensei would have said about this confrontation. Probably not much. Ah, hell, why couldn't he have just walked away?

"What do you care what they say about your brother, anyway? You said you haven't talked to him more than once or twice in years."

That did it. "Maybe I'd better be going," he said. He pushed his chair back and stood up.

"Yeah, right. Eat and run. Or you could stay and fight, tough guy." She stood up, too.

"I think you've had a bit too much wine, Annie."

"Now you're telling me how much I can drink? Gonna break my arm if I have some more?"

He shook his head and started walking toward the front door. He had his hand on the doorknob when he felt her pulling at his arm. "Don't you walk out on me!" she said angrily.

He turned, smoothly removed her hand from his bicep and started to twist it, but held back. Her eyes went wide as she realized what might happen. The look cut Jim to the heart. He didn't want to hurt her, had never hurt any woman, but she had kept pushing him, and he didn't like being pushed. "Be careful, Annie," he said.

She was breathing a bit more heavily now, but her eyes changed, from fear to something else, a look that usually excited him. "So you think you can handle me, big guy?"

Jim had seen her like this once or twice, when their foreplay got a little rough. Annie had always taken the lead in terms of sex, right from the start, on their third date. She was aggressive, dominant, and a match for him physically. That had made for some interesting times indeed, and more exciting, to be honest, than anything he'd ever had with Suzy. But while there was passion with him and Annie, there was little of the tenderness he'd known with his wife. Like every other part of her life, Annie considered the bedroom to be a place of competition, where winning was the only option. He had never really been sure how he felt about that, but he was now.

"Yeah, I can handle you, Annie," he said, letting go of her hand, "but that's not what I want to do." He kissed her on the forehead. "Good night."

Back home, Jim fed the cat and fell into bed, suddenly exhausted, asleep almost as soon as his head hit the pillow, a rarity for him. He dreamed about Suzy, flitting from seeing her on campus in college to their first house together and then...

"No!" He forced himself to wake up, pulling himself out of the dream before it got to where he had never wanted to go ever again, and sat up in bed, eyes wide open. Next to him, Spike stirred and started purring. The clock showed 4:13. He could press a button on it to show the date, but he knew what it was: July the tenth. Exactly six years since that day.

It was better to think about the years before July 10, 2005. They had been good years, very good. Start with that day in the fall of '80, when he was sitting in his English class at college in Platteville and she walked in. Susan Mitchell had lustrous black hair and dynamite legs, and he couldn't believe his luck when those legs walked over to the empty desk next to his. She beamed him a smile that lit up his world. Two days later they had a cup of coffee after class, and then their first date on Saturday night. He quickly forgot about trying to rehab his knee enough to get back on the basketball team.

More good memories: graduating in '83, getting engaged and starting their careers, him in marketing at a cable-TV company in Dubuque, Iowa, just across the Mississippi, and Suzy teaching elementary school in Potosi, a small town on the Wisconsin side. They married in '84, and Michaela was born two years later. In '90 he had a great job offer from a company in Milwaukee, and even though she didn't want to go, wanted to raise their daughter in a small town just like she had been, she came along, of course she did, because she loved him. They settled in a nice suburb, and even though two miscarriages marred their happiness, they got through them, which made her surprising pregnancy in the spring of '05 all the more special.

Then she got word in early July that her favorite aunt had died back in her hometown of Mount Sterling, so they went to the funeral on a Saturday, and her cousin Edie asked them to stay the night. How could he say no to that? Suzy and Edie had grown up together here among the ridges and valleys of Crawford County. Even though Edie was mourning her mother, she was thrilled to hear Suzy's news about the pregnancy, and now Jim remembered through tears the sight of the two women embracing and crying, sharing the joy. Sure, they would go to church with Edie and her family the next morning, then hit the road for home.

Now he knew what he had to do. For six years he had avoided it, pushed it aside, denied it, but it always came back. He had to face it. He got up and headed to the shower.

The church looked just as it had six years ago. That morning was sunny and warm, too, and he remembered hearing the greetings passed between the adults as they walked from their cars to the front door, the little kids running ahead, laughing with excitement, just like now.

He sat in the car, watching. The last of the worshipers had gone inside, the bell rang out, and then he heard the sound of the organ, the voices raised in song. He took a deep breath, and allowed it all to come back.

He and Suzy were sitting with her cousin's family in a pew about three rows from the back of the small sanctuary. About a hundred people were in attendance, enjoying the special music for the day, a father on guitar accompanying his teenage daughter on "In the Garden". He must have rustled in his seat because Suzy looked at him and whispered, "Are you okay?"

"Have to use the rest room," he said. He squeezed her hand and got up. The singer began the final verse as he opened the right side of the sanctuary's double doors, with the ushers sitting to their right. He closed the door behind him. Where was the bathroom? Oh yeah, he'd seen people using it earlier, and it was over there to the right, around the corner by the coat rack.

It must've been right about then that the rusty old Chevy Lumina pulled up outside. He didn't hear the driver's door open, didn't see the man getting out, didn't see the .45 handgun he was carrying, didn't see him approach the door of the church. Jim went into the bathroom, but before he could close the door he heard the front door of the church opening, heard the heavy footfalls on the stairs, a sound that didn't belong here. The hairs rose up on the back of his neck. Jim glanced back out of the bathroom toward the stairs and saw the man and knew immediately he was trouble.

He steadied his breathing, just as his taekwondo instructor had taught him. There was a Bible lying on a chair next to the bathroom door. He picked it up.

The man with the gun was just topping the staircase and stepping onto the main floor. He was a white guy in his twenties with a two-day growth and wearing fatigue pants stuffed into his combat boots, a black tee shirt with some sort of heavy-metal band's logo on the front, and on his head was a black baseball cap with the bill turned backward. He had his weapon pointed straight ahead, toward the doors of the sanctuary, and Jim looked that way automatically and saw one of the doors opening, the same one he'd just used. Suzy was coming through, and she looked at him with a quizzical expression, always thinking of him, surely wondering if he was feeling all right, and then she took a second step into the narthex, the door swinging shut behind her, and saw the gun.

Time seemed to slow down for Jim. He shouted and threw the Bible with a backhand toss straight at the man's head, and started running. The punk's head turned his way and his eyes went wide as he saw the book flying at him, and he squeezed the trigger and the muzzle blazed a split-second before the Bible hit him in the face. Jim saw the gun come around toward him as the guy staggered backward. Jim's training came flashing back to him: *Fight the man, not the weapon.* He came in at an angle, out of the line of fire, and things happened fast now. The end of the gun blazed again and Jim sensed something hot rocketing just past him, a moment before he brought his left hand down to grip the top of the gun and his right fist crashed down onto the gunman's forearm, right onto the LI-7 pressure point. That brought a shriek from the guy and caused his hand to release the gun.

Jim drove his right elbow around into the man's jaw, knocking him off-balance even further. With the gun in his left hand, Jim fired a front kick into the man's solar plexus, driving him backwards and crashing into a cart full of books. Jim set the gun carefully on the floor and took another two steps to the guy who was rolling off the toppled cart, moaning. He came down with his right knee into the man's exposed left rib-cage and he heard ribs crack as the guy screamed in pain. He pushed the man onto his stomach and brought his left arm up into a chicken wing hold, pinning it in place with his knees. "Turn your head away!" Jim screamed. "Cross your ankles! Put that arm out straight!" The guy was slow to comply, so Jim cranked his pinned arm enough to feel something tear in the shoulder, and then there were other hands reaching down to help him.

For the first time Jim became aware of the pandemonium surrounding him, men yelling, women screaming, feet pounding. A red-faced man knelt down beside Jim. "I've got him! Go to your wife!" Jim released his grip just enough for the other man to take over and then stood up, looking back toward the sanctuary doors.

Jim sat in the car now, sweating and crying and pounding the steering wheel. He cursed himself for coming back here, but at the same time he knew it had to be done, this one time, and it would be over. He fought to get his emotions under control, and his Systema training came back to him now, saved him, brought his breathing back down and cleared his mind. If he'd only had that back then, he might've been able to move faster, more efficiently, to save Suzy, but he hadn't started that training until '06, a year too late to help her.

He wasn't aware that another twenty minutes had gone by. He stared at the front door of the church, where the man with the gun had gone inside that day. A psycho, they said later, privately, some yahoo whose girlfriend had broken up with him a week before. She attended that church but hadn't even been there that day. He didn't know that, but he went there looking for her and he was going to take her out and a lot of other people, too. The cops found two full magazines in his pants pockets. But Jim had been there to stop him. He saved maybe dozens of people that day. Only one died, because he wasn't fast enough, well-trained enough, strong enough. He'd failed.

The memories flooded back over him again. His wife, her face pale and eyes wide with pain and confusion, looking up at him one last time as he held her close, feeling the life drift out of her, watching the red stain grow on the front of her new white blouse. The screaming and wailing of the other churchgoers, with the pastor kneeling down beside Suzy and blessing her with a trembling hand. The phone call he had to make to his daughter, back home on summer break from college, and hearing her hysterical sobbing on the other end of the line. And later that night, sitting out on Edie's front porch, gazing up at the stars, seeing a meteor blaze briefly across the sky, and wondering if it might be Suzy's immortal soul, going wherever souls go, without him. He wanted to beseech God to take him too, so he could be with her in eternity. He wanted to curse God for not taking him instead. But he did neither. He simply sat there for the longest time, staring at the sky, feeling a hole open deep within the pit of his own soul, a dark abyss that had never closed.

The church bell rang. Jim started the car and drove away, heading east, to Cedar Lake, and his empty house.

CHAPTER SIX

SOMALIA

"YOU WILL DO exactly as I say, and you will tell no one. Is that clear?" Yusuf gave the boy his hardest stare, the one that had cowed even hard-core Arab fighters in the past.

"Y-yes, sir," the boy stammered. Only sixteen, and he looked four years younger. Yusuf wondered again if this youth was the right choice for the mission. But he had precious few options. The boy's very youth would be to the Ugandan's advantage in this case; he had not been part of the group of fighters for very long, had not had time to come under Amir's spell, and as a Somali he was looked down upon by most of the other fighters, only a few of whom were Somali.

"Tell me again what you will do."

The boy reached into the pocket of his robe and pulled out a piece of white chalk. "I will go to Mogadishu, to the Hotel Shamo. After nightfall I will use the chalk to make a mark on a telephone pole." The boy hesitated, trying to remember.

Yusuf forced himself to be patient, but he didn't have much time. The mosque would be calling the men to prayers in just a few minutes, and Amir would be making sure there were no stragglers. "What telephone pole, Ayan?"

"The one near the entrance to the hotel...?" The boy looked up at Yusuf hopefully.

Yusuf nodded and smiled. "That is correct. And what mark will you make?"

"The mark of the infidel cross, with a circle around it."

"Show me, in the dust there." He pointed at a film of grit on the wall.

The boy reached up and traced the sign, then looked hopefully at him again. "Very good," Yusuf said, and he rubbed the mark out of existence with the flat of his hand. "And what is your task after that?"

"I will go to the home of Aziza, on the Jidka Walaalaha, and ask for shelter during my stay. I am to tell her Sudika sent me. She will give me a note. At dusk, I am to go back to the hotel. In the telephone booth across the street, I will use a screwdriver to open the base of the telephone. I will place the note inside and replace the cover."

"Very good indeed. And finally?"

"Two nights later I am to go back to the hotel. I am to go to the telephone booth and open up the telephone again. Inside there will be a folded paper. I am to bring it to you."

"Yes, and remember to put the telephone back together before you leave."

"I will, *hogaamiye*," the boy said, addressing Yusuf as "Chief", as the Somalis liked to do. The other fighters always used the more formal Arabic, *Ra-iss*. "And I am to show the paper to no one else. If anyone asks me, I am to eat the paper."

Yusuf nodded, patting the boy on the shoulder. "You will do well, Ayan. You will leave after morning prayers tomorrow, on the bus." The rattletrap Italian-built bus carried men from the village to Mogadishu, fifty miles away. Yusuf gave the boy a fifty-shilling note and a few coins, enough to pay for the bus and bribe anybody who tried a shakedown on the way. "Please give my blessings to Aziza and tell her I will visit her soon."

"Yes, *hogaamiye*," the boy said. "I will not fail you."

Yusuf looked out his window to see men walking toward the mosque. The call to prayers would come very soon. "Very well. Go now. I will see you in three days." The boy bowed and walked swiftly out of the room. Yusuf took a deep breath, smoothed down the front of his robe, and looked out the window once more.

There was Amir with two of his trusted sergeants in the company of a pair of foreign fighters, one a Jordanian, the other a Chechen. Yusuf suspected their loyalty was more to his lieutenant than to him. He would not care to have Ayan taken by them and questioned. An even worse fate would be for the boy to be taken by the Iranian, Heydar. Yusuf did not see him now, but he was around. Technically, he was an "adviser", provided by the Sheikh himself through the courtesy of their allies in Tehran. Heydar had spent much time in Lebanon and Syria, working with Hezbollah, and with Hamas in Gaza. Yusuf suspected that he was an officer in the much-feared Iranian Quds Force. It was said he had personally killed six Israeli soldiers and had led the raid in Karbala, Iraq, in 2007 that resulted in the capture and execution of four American soldiers.

Yusuf thought the Karbala story was credible, but doubted the one about the Israelis. He had known a few IDF soldiers and they were not men who were easily killed. Heydar was a physically powerful man, a world-class martial artist who had competed in taekwondo at the Olympics in Sydney, but that was one thing. Being strong enough to kill six Israelis in hand-to-hand combat was quite another. Still, Heydar was not a man to be trifled with, and if the truth were to be known, Yusuf was a little bit afraid of him. He had pointedly declined Heydar's invitation to train in the makeshift gymnasium the Iranian was using to instruct some of the fighters in taekwondo and some rather exotic martial arts weapons.

It was most unfortunate, but now Yusuf knew that he could trust no one, not even Amir. Well, that was not quite true, he corrected himself. He had to place his trust, at least for the next forty-eight hours, in a pair of Somali teenagers and an Ethiopian woman. The first boy, a cousin of Ayan's, had been sent to Mogadishu the day before with a coded message for Aziza, whom Yusuf knew to be an agent of NISS, the Ethiopian intelligence service. She would make sure Ayan got the message to the CIA dead drop. If the boy came back with the response Yusuf hoped to see, perhaps he might be able to put his trust in a certain man he had not seen in almost thirty years. It was almost too much to hope for, but then he remembered the screams of those Afghan children. How many more children would die if he failed?

The Chechen was joined by one of his countrymen, a hulk of a man who looked more like an ethnic Russian. He was a new arrival at the camp, and Yusuf had not yet had a chance to interview him. The man turned his head and Yusuf saw a glimpse of his face. For a moment, Yusuf thought it was the man from—

No, that could not possibly be. That man was an American, and it was long ago, but Yusuf had never forgotten him. It was at the campus night club, one night shortly after Yusuf's arrival at the college in America. Yusuf knew nobody, the fall term had just begun, and he thought there might be other foreign students at this place. As he stood there, minding his own business, he was bumped by a large white man, and Yusuf's

Coke spilled from the plastic cup onto the shirt of the man. He towered over Yusuf and glared down at him, then started yelling. Yusuf's English in those days was far from fluent, but he did recognize one word, *nigger*. The man was very angry, probably drunk, and Yusuf suddenly was in fear for his life. He looked around, but nobody wanted to intervene, to challenge the bully. Yusuf was wearing a cap, a brimless *kufi* that was his favorite cap from Uganda, and the man arrogantly plucked it off Yusuf's head and tossed it on the floor.

Then another tall white man, this one more slender, stepped forward. "Pick it up and give it back," the man said to the bully, who responded with an epithet, and the next thing Yusuf knew the bully was on his knees, one arm pinned awkwardly behind him, obviously causing him much pain. With his free hand he picked up the cap and handed it back to Yusuf. Then the bully was back on his feet and the other man, Yusuf's savior, was walking him to the doorway, giving the arm one more twist as he propelled the drunk out the door. Many people applauded. The slender man walked back to Yusuf. "Are you all right?" he asked.

"Yes," Yusuf said, almost stammering, his fear starting to go away. "Thank you."

"You're welcome," the man said, sticking out his hand. "My name's Jim Hayes."

Yusuf's thoughts snapped back to the here and now as the two Chechens walked toward the mosque. Yusuf followed, knowing that his prayers to Allah this evening would be, at least in his heart, quite different than those of the men beside him.

CHAPTER SEVEN
AFGHANISTAN

MARK DIDN'T NORMALLY go on the supply choppers that made weekly rounds of the forward operating bases, but today he decided to hitch a ride on the run that would end at FOB Langdon, the battalion's newest and most dangerous forward operating base in the valley. Maybe it was that book he'd been reading, *The Boys of 98*, about the original Rough Riders. The last survivor was Jesse D. Langdon, who died on June 28, 1975, and it was ironic that Mark finished the book just a couple weeks ago, on the thirty-sixth anniversary of the old trooper's death. Work on the outpost was just about completed then, and the lieutenant he'd put in charge asked him to suggest a name. The other six FOBs in the battalion were all named after Rough Riders, so Mark suggested Langdon to keep the tradition going. It seemed appropriate, as this was likely the last base they'd be building in the valley. The battalion was on the verge of being stretched thin.

Not that there wasn't plenty to keep him busy back at the main base camp, but the hard work they'd all put in meant he could afford to take the day for this jaunt. Four months now since he'd taken command, and things were shaping up nicely. It had been a struggle, because many of the officers left behind after their commander was sacked weren't used to working very hard. Mark kicked several asses, rotating a few back to the rear or stateside just to get them out of his hair, and he tapped into his extensive network to find competent men to replace the dead weight. Fortunately, the non-coms got the message and he'd had little or no trouble there. The troops fell into line quickly and morale started to rise. Like most of the soldiers the Army had left in country, these were largely men who'd had one relatively quiet tour of Iraq and were here to get some action before it was all over. Many of them were still lacking the coveted Combat Infantryman's Badge, and while that was a worthy thing to have, Mark made sure the men knew the way to get it was not to get all cowboy out here on the line and make mistakes. He didn't want to have somebody back home sewing the CIB on a dress uniform that was headed for a casket.

The howitzers of his artillery detachment were tuning up for the day's first fire mission when Mark took one last look at the paper littering his desk. He always visited the gunners right after breakfast and then toured the perimeter. On top of his IN box was a flimsy from his overnight staff. The lieutenant at Langdon was reporting fresh intel of a possible enemy attack against the nearby village, about three klicks from the mountainside where Langdon commanded a strategic view of the southern end of the valley. When they'd built the base, someone said it was like they were giving the Tals down in the valley the finger. Was it the lieutenant who'd said that? Something about this guy's name....He read it again. *Solum.* That rang a bell somehow.

He'd met the lieutenant in question, of course; Mark had made an effort to get to know each of his officers, not to mention as many of the enlisted men as he could. With over seven hundred troops under his command, that was exhausting work, but it enabled him to give his command a more personal touch, and the men got to know their C.O., which was always helpful. What about this guy? Mark took a minute to find the man's file. Just a one-page entry, as it was for most of his officers. There it was. Kenneth Solum, twenty-six, graduate of the University of Wisconsin-Stevens Point, went through ROTC there, hometown was Rice Lake, Wisconsin. That was it. He remembered the name now, from a story his father had told him and his brother years ago. Could his lieutenant be related....? No, too big of a coincidence, but the geography fit. He made a decision.

In the outer room of what passed for his headquarters, Mark saw Captain Bill Richards, his adjutant. "Bill, isn't there a chopper going to Langdon this morning?"

"Yes, sir, about a half-hour from now. Langdon's the last stop on the run." Richards, a tall, angular Texan with a drawl that confused the locals here but, Mark suspected, charmed the women back home, checked the clock on the wall. "Make it twenty minutes. Going along, sir?"

Richards had an instinct about these things, and that made him a particularly good adjutant. "I think so. Where's Major Ruiz?"

"Already out with the battery, sir, prepping the fire mission." Ruiz was Mark's 2IC, second-in-command, and a damn good one he was turning out to be. This morning Mark's battery of four 155mm guns was getting ready to fire in support of FOB O'Neill, which had taken three mortar rounds from the nearby mountainside about twenty minutes ago, an annoying

CRIMSON TIDE

interruption of morning chow. This wouldn't be their last mission of the day, probably; in the hundred and twenty-five days Mark had been in command, his battery averaged nearly four per day, firing over fifteen hundred rounds. The loud crack of the big guns was a common sound around the base, and the farmers and villagers down below hardly paid attention anymore. Mark had seen them more than once, going about their daily business just as they had been doing for generations, ignoring the one-sided duels between the heavy weapons of the Americans and the lighter, less-accurate mortars of the insurgents. Even when the stray mortar round landed in their fields, the Afghans rarely complained. What good would it do? It was how life was in Afghanistan. He'd asked a village chief about it once. "Before you Americans," the chief said wearily, "it was the Russians. Before them, the British. Before them, someone else. After you leave, someone else will come. It will never stop."

"We'll see about that," Mark had said, and his Afghan National Army interpreter had struggled with that one, finally coming up with something that sounded like the Pashto version of "*Inshallah,*" the Will of God.

It would be a short hop to Langdon, but not necessarily a safe one, so Mark was glad to see the Blackhawk helo was fully armed and manned. In a real hot zone he'd have an escort of one or two Apaches, but this would do for now. The warrant officer pilot snapped off a salute when Mark approached. "Need a ride somewhere, Colonel?"

"You can drop me off at Langdon, Mr. Witz."

"Roger that, sir. Step inside and the flight attendant will show you to your first-class seat. Keep your tray in the upright position until we reach our cruising altitude, and have a safe flight."

Mark was helped aboard through the port side door by the gunner and strapped himself in to the only empty seat. Mark could remember a time when sacks of mail would fill supply choppers, but now there was only one small sack that looked like it had some packages. Most of the troops relied on email, which they could access when they rotated back to Roosevelt. Along with the mail, the bird would carry other, more vital supplies to the twenty men at Langdon: food, bottled water, spare parts, and some ammo crates. Mark would be the only soldier getting off at the last FOB.

The crewmen were finishing up the loading when Mark suddenly remembered when he'd first heard the name Solum. He hadn't thought about it since leaving his office, but that's how it worked sometimes. This particular memory was nearly forty years old, but now it came back to him with near-perfect clarity. He remembered his father speaking the name....

"You okay, sir?"

Mark blinked away the tears that were about to come, seeing the door gunner looking at him through his shaded visor. "Yeah. I'm fine."

He remembered the day: Memorial Day, 1972. Sunny and warm, and his dad, Ed Hayes, had taken him and Jim to the veterans cemetery near County Stadium in Milwaukee. Dad was quiet on the drive from their house in the suburb of St. Francis, and that was unusual for him. He always had the radio on, always a ballgame or a country station, and he would sing along, although not too well. Ed Hayes was a carpenter, not a singer. He was a baseball fan, too, and had taken his boys to the ballpark a few times to see the Brewers. But the team was out of town that day, so Mark was puzzled when they drove past the stadium with its vast empty parking lot. In a few minutes they parked along a side street and walked a block to the first cemetery Mark had visited since his grandfather's death, four years earlier.

He remembered the lush green grass, and all the crosses, hundreds of them, all over the rolling hills. Mark was only seven at the time. Jim was eleven, old enough to remember Grandpa Hayes's funeral. "They bury dead people here," Jim said to him, "like they did Grandpa."

There were a lot of people there that day, and Jim said it was because it was a special day, they'd talked about it in school on Friday. All these crosses were for guys who died in wars, he said. Vietnam for sure, and there were big ones a long time ago.

"Dad was in one," he said. Jim was whispering, because Dad was walking ahead of them, slowly but purposefully, and this seemed like a place to be quiet, even though Mark heard birds singing like they always did on sunny days.

"He was? Was it Vietnam?" Mark wasn't really sure where Vietnam was, but there were people on TV who talked about it all the time and usually they were yelling.

"No, the one before that. Korea. I saw his medal."

"Yeah? Where is it?"

"In his foot locker, down in the basement." Mark didn't know how that could've happened, because there was a big padlock on it, but Jim must've found the key. He was pretty smart.

Dad stopped, looked closely at the row of headstones to their left, and started down the row, the boys following. They passed some people. There was a woman about the age of Mark's second-grade teacher back at Willow Glen School, and she was kneeling in front of one of the crosses, crying. A little boy stood next to her. Farther down, there was an old gray-haired woman leaning on a cane, with a long-haired young man wearing a grubby jacket with that one sign on it, like a rocket in a circle, standing next to her. She was putting some flowers down near a cross, and the long-haired guy was looking away, up at the clouds, but Mark thought he saw his chin trembling.

Dad finally stopped before one of the crosses, and after a few seconds he got down on one knee and touched it. Mark saw his father's shoulders start to shake. He peered past him to see the words on the front of the cross:

MICHAEL T SOLUM
PVT CO C 1st BN 1ST CAV
5 JULY 1931 – 1 NOV 1950

The boys stood silently behind their father. After a couple minutes, he stood up, took a deep breath, and said, "Come on, boys. There's a bench over here."

Around the perimeter of the graves were several stone benches, and Dad found the nearest one and sat down. Jim sat on his left, Mark on his right. After a moment of staring back at the grave they'd visited, Dad began to talk. Nearly forty years had gone by, but Mark could remember almost every word.

I was in the Army, First Battalion, Eighth Regiment, First Cavalry Division. We'd fought our way up from Pusan, over the thirty-eighth parallel, into North Korea, and it was late October 1950 and we were in Pyongyang and thought for sure we'd be home for Christmas. Didn't even have winter uniforms yet and it was cold as a bitch up there.

I was there when MacArthur flew in. Nobody knew where Kim Il Sung was. He was the North Korean dictator. "Where's Kim Buck Tooth?" MacArthur says, and everybody laughs. Then he flies back to

Tokyo that night. You know, he never spent even one night in Korea with us, always flew in, flew out, same day.

The ROKs, the South Koreans, they couldn't fight their way out of a paper bag in those days, but we'd sent them up ahead, toward the Yalu, chasing the rest of the North Koreans, and the word came down about maybe some trouble up there, so we saddled up and headed north.

We got up to this place called Unsan and we dug in, and the word was that some Chinese had come over the river, but all the officers told us the Chinese would never come across the border, so we thought it was just bullshit, but then by God I saw a patrol bringing in a couple guys in these heavy, baggy uniforms and they didn't look like any North Koreans I'd seen.

It was the first of November, about ten at night, we're about four hundred meters from the town and trying to stay warm and then we hear these weird sounds, almost like music, but no music I'd ever heard, and it was damn scary, and later we found out it was the Chinese with their bugles, that's how they signaled on the battlefield, and here they came, goddamn waves of them.

I'm in a foxhole with Mike Solum, kid from near my home town up north. Had a new bride back home, a baby on the way. We'd gone through boot camp together, and there we were, a couple of Wisconsin kids way the hell up at the goddamn ends of the earth in North Korea, best buddies, and the lieutenant yells for us to fall back. Mikey's banging away with his Tommy gun, and then it jams and here comes a Chink right after him with a bayonet, and I shot the guy point-blank with my carbine, blew his face right off.

We get back to the rear and nobody knows what the hell's going on, there's no armor, no air support, Chinese everywhere and those damn bugles, and the lieutenant tries to rally us, but then he took a round in the throat, and he was gone, and it was every man for himself, so we headed down this gully near the road with about a half-dozen guys, trying to make it out of there.

Mikey, he'd taken a round in the leg, and I was helping him walk but he's losing a lot of blood, and it sounds like the Chinese are get ting closer, but if we can get back to this one road that's where we knew there was some armor and we could hear some artillery open-ing up, so we had maybe a mile or two to go, and Mikey tells me that he's almost gone, I gotta leave him there and get out. And I said no, I'm not leavin' you here. But he's bleedin' out, and he says for me to tell his wife back home, Julie, that...that he loves her very much. And then he dies right there in my arms. Another guy tells me to get movin', the Chinese are coming, and so I lay Mikey down and take his dog tags, and I make it outta there, and about a hundred meters out we're on a bit of a rise and I look back to Mikey, and in the moon-light I see the Chinese around him, using their bayonets on him, over and over.

War is goddamn hell, boys, don't you ever forget it. Sometimes it's gotta be done, we had to save those South Koreans, and we did, but I wish to God I hadn't had to do some of the things I did.

Mark had thought often about that day, and what Ed said to him and his brother. He knew it scared Jim, could tell it even then, and Mark suspected that had played a large part in how Jim had lived his life since then. Jim had a lot of potential, and he proved it in the classroom and on the basketball floor, but other than throwing a few elbows in a game now and then he was one of the most passive guys Mark had ever known. Maybe that had changed recently, since his wife died, and he'd gotten into martial arts, but Mark had seen his big brother only a couple times since her funeral, so it was hard to say.

For Mark, it was different. He was too young to really understand Ed's feelings about combat, but it sounded pretty darn exciting, and as he grew older he became fascinated with

the military. He read everything he could find about it in the
school library and then the city library yielded even more trea-
sures. By the time he was in eighth grade he knew he wanted
to be a soldier, a warrior, someone even greater than his father
had been. He set his sights on West Point and hit the books,
and he also dedicated himself to excellence on the football
field, because he knew that would help his chances. He was
right. After his junior season at St. Francis High, an assistant
coach from the Point said he would see about helping Mark get
the necessary congressional appointment. Athletes had to meet
the academic standards just like everybody else, but if you had
a great time in the 40, that would help. It did. Mark got his
appointment and headed off to the Point after graduating high
school and he never looked back, never once regretting the life
he'd chosen.

His father had talked to him about it only once, the night
they got the phone call from the Academy telling him the
appointment was his if he wanted it. In Mark's mind, there
was no question about it, but he respectfully listened to the
old veteran when Ed took him out into the garage. They sat in
the car and talked about it, and Ed told him some things about
Korea that he'd left out of the story at the cemetery, sobering
things that Mark took seriously, but they didn't change his
mind. Finally, he said, "Dad, I understand. I really appreciate
you telling me this. But I'm going."

Ed stared out the windshield at the tidy workbench along
the back wall of the garage. Then he said, "Okay, son. We won't
need to talk about this again. Your mother will need some
more convincing but I'll talk to her." He looked over at his
son. "I pray to God you will never have to go through what I
went through, but sure as hell the shit's gonna hit the fan again

someday and that's when this country will need good officers in the Army. Maybe you can be one of them. It's up to you."

"I'll make it, Dad. I won't let you down."

For the first time that evening, Ed Hayes smiled. He put his hand on his son's shoulder. "You'll do just fine, son. I'm proud of you."

The voice on the helmet intercom broke through Mark's reverie. "Coming in now, sir. Make sure you're buckled in, might get a little rough. The gomers have been pretty active out here lately."

Good. It was time to get back to work.

CHAPTER EIGHT

WISCONSIN

THE *BO* WAS almost a living thing in his hands, an extension of himself, his will. The six-foot oak staff, tapered at both ends, ripped through the air with an audible hum, helicoptering overhead, then slashing with a backhand side strike, a perfect *ichimonji-mawashi.* He followed with a forehand strike to the midsection, then an extended *nagashi-zuki* thrust as he lunged forward, left leg extending back behind him, his weight perfectly balanced, upper body in the vertical as the bo speared upward at a forty-five degree angle, and the loud *kiai* spirit yell almost leaped of its own accord from deep within him. He held the pose for a second, then brought the bo back in a perfect *yoko-uke* sweep and block as he stepped back into a cat stance, held it another split-second, and went into his close, the *musubi-dachi* ready stance, bringing the bo to his side, closing with the final bow, and taking a half step to his left into what his brother would term a parade rest position., bringing the bo around to his front horizontally with an over-hand under-hand grip. He was panting, his headband dripping sweat, his *gi* soaked through.

"Very good, Mr. James. A very respectable *Shushi-No-Kon-Sho kata*." The sensei stood up with a fluid motion that never ceased to amaze Jim. He didn't really know how old Yamashita Sensei was, but he had to be in his early sixties, at least. Yet the man moved with the grace of someone decades younger. It was something Jim knew he could never fully achieve himself, no matter how much stretching he did every morning.

"Thank you, Sensei. It's not the easiest kata to perform."

"Indeed. How many moves?" The Japanese-born master led the way to the edge of the mat. Jim followed at his side, but respectfully a step behind.

"A hundred fifty."

"Ah. Would you like some tea?"

"Very much so." Jim toweled his head and neck as the sensei went into his small office and retrieved two bottles from his refrigerator. He handed one to Jim, who twisted the cap off and took a healthy swig. "Hits the spot," he said.

"I must thank you for introducing me to this Honest Tea," Nakamura said. "It is quite good."

"Best there is for bottled tea," Jim said. He'd read about it somewhere, and it quickly became his beverage of choice. How long had it been since he'd had a can of pop? He couldn't remember.

The master sat on one of the chairs in the waiting area, and Jim took the seat next to him. There were a dozen chairs in the small lounge, with a half-wall separating it from the training area. The dojo was tastefully decorated with Japanese artwork, including some *bonsai* plants that Sensei carefully cultivated. Bonsai was an art Jim had taken up recently and he was proud to have a nice plant in his own home. Fortunately the cat left it alone.

Jim had found Rising Sun Martial Arts on his first visit

to Cedar Lake, five years ago when he came to town for his interview at Tri-County Telecom. A month after making the move from the Milwaukee suburbs, he joined the dojo and started training in *isshin-ryu* karate and *kobujutsu,* the study of Okinawan weapons. The training was a lot different than tae-kwondo in many respects, but Jim found himself enjoying it. For one thing, it was easier on his legs than the Korean art, which emphasized a lot of kicking. He especially enjoyed the weapons training. Sensei also brought in guest instructors for occasional day-long seminars in judo, Brazilian *jujitsu,* and Hardened Target combatives, and Jim used his Systema contacts to arrange yearly seminars in the Russian art.

It didn't take Jim long to find himself immersed in the training. He was at the dojo three or four evenings a week, some-times also on Saturdays, and he also maintained a membership at a gym a few blocks away, where he kept up his weight training. He maintained his aerobic fitness with bicycling through the countryside in the summer and fall, and with the machines at the gym during the winter and early spring. One or two mornings a week he would swim at the town's indoor pool. Once he'd actually tracked how much time he spent in training for an entire month, and he was astonished at how quickly it all added up. But he was in great shape, and what's more, the training had helped satisfy the deep-set urge he'd felt since Suzy's death, to push himself toward his elusive goal.

The camaraderie was in many ways the best thing about it all. He'd become friends with several of the men who trained at the dojo, and he found that they understood what he was doing, because they were doing it themselves, in varying degrees. They had all discovered that outside the walls of the dojo, people didn't know about these things, didn't understand that there was so much more to martial arts than what they saw on television. It really was a way of life, and Jim found that it suited him perfectly. He advanced through the ranks quickly and now held black belts in both of the disciplines taught by Yamashita Sensei.

The private training was what Jim enjoyed the most. About a year ago, the master surprised Jim by inviting him to stay after class one night and work on something. Jim couldn't even remember what it was now, but the one night turned into two, and then it became a regular occurrence, so that Jim would now routinely spend a half-hour or more after the evening's final class, working with Sensei on one aspect or another of the arts. Tonight, it was the bo.

"Are you going to the tournament this weekend?"

Jim snapped his thoughts back to the present. "I had thought about it. It's a long way, but I think I just might." A month earlier, a flyer announcing an open tournament in Rice Lake, up in the northwest corner of the state, had been posted on the dojo's bulletin board. Jim competed in five or six tournaments a year; his most recent had been the Badger State Games in Appleton at the end of June, where he'd won gold medals in sparring and weapons in his division. The Rice Lake event wasn't one he'd considered when he first saw the flyer, but now, the way things were going this week, he thought that getting away for a weekend might be just what the doctor ordered.

"You have seemed a bit preoccupied in class this week, Mr. James. How are things going for you?"

Jim had long ago ceased to be surprised by his master's instincts. In truth, the Japanese sensei was one of the most remarkable men Jim had ever met. "Well, I've had better weeks," Jim said now. His argument with Annie, coupled with his somber trip to the Mt. Sterling church, had set the tone. Things hadn't gotten much better.

"You focused quite well on the kata just now. Perhaps if you direct your energies toward the tournament, it will help your focus outside the dojo as well."

"I think you might be right about that, Sensei."

"May I make another suggestion?"

"Of course."

"Do not use the bo in the tournament. Use the *sansetsukon*. The kata you performed with it last night was quite good. I doubt if they have seen that weapon very much."

Jim thought about that. The weapon was a three-section staff, sometimes called the "coiling dragon staff", with each section about three feet long and connected with short chains. It was very difficult to master and thus rarely seen in tournaments, but Jim had started working with it several months ago and lately had put together a kata that he thought might be competition-ready by the time of the Diamond Nationals, the big tournament held every October in the Twin Cities. Jim had been there twice, had yet to win an event, and he really wanted one of those big trophies. "Do you think the kata is ready for that, Sensei?"

"There is only one way to find out."

Jim took Friday afternoon off, packed an overnight bag and his competition gear, and hit the road. The five-hour drive gave him a chance to do some serious thinking.

There'd been a message waiting for him on his home phone when he got back from Mt. Sterling the previous Sunday. It was Annie, wanting to talk. He was a bit surprised Annie hadn't called him on his cell, because she had the number, but he was sort of glad she hadn't. On the way home he had time to think about the events of the day and evening before. It was the first time he'd ever turned down sex with her, and he wondered what that meant.

Maybe, he thought, that was a sign of something. He returned her call, but he held something back, and she could tell, so when they hung up after five minutes of small talk there wasn't a promise to get together later in the week. Surprisingly, he was okay with that.

The work week hadn't started off too well the next morning. He went through his usual routine of stretching and calisthenics before his shower and shave, then popped open his laptop computer at the kitchen table as he ate his breakfast omelet. Spike the cat, contented now after having his own breakfast, curled around his legs and went off to find a sunbeam for a nap. *The Milwaukee Journal Sentinel's* website was one of Jim's regular stops on his morning surf, and today the third entry in the News section caught his eye: "Anti-war group looking for air show assailant." A bit of a chill ran through him as he clicked on the link.

The story was brief, but now he knew the name of the protestor: Carleton Higgins, a sociology professor at UW-Madison, who was claiming he'd suffered two broken fingers and a sprained wrist "when he was assaulted by a man leaving Saturday's air show at the Dane County Airport." According to Higgins, the attack had been completely unprovoked.

There was a photo, taken by someone in the group of protestors, evidently with a cell phone. Jim couldn't help holding his breath as he examined it. The camera had been about eight feet away and to his right, he estimated, and fortunately for him, it didn't show his face very clearly. His back was partially turned toward the camera, as he'd been shifting his upper body to the left as he used his left hand to remove Higgins' right hand and twist it downward and to his left. The shot didn't show the grip, but it caught the look of surprise and pain on the professor's face. Jim looked closely, but there didn't seem to be anything that would clearly identify him. Annie was not in the shot at all.

Well, it could've been worse, somebody on the other side could've taken the photo and gotten a clear view of his face. Or it could've been a video, showing the entire thing. There was the chance somebody else with evidence like that could come forward, of course, but Jim figured he was probably in the clear. There'd been police nearby, after all, and none of them had done anything. It had happened pretty quickly, and by the time any of the cops got around to talking to Higgins—he said in the story he'd given a statement to the police—Jim and Annie had been well away from the scene, in the parking area and lost among the people heading for their cars. Fortunately, none of the protestors had been thinking clearly enough to follow him. No surprise there; they certainly didn't have any kind of training in responding to such situations.

That sort of set the tone for his week at the office. Despite the progress he and his team had been making on their major summer project, revamping the telecom's website and its associated multimedia marketing campaign, his supervisor, Lori, was all over him about it. Every morning there was an email in his inbox with another picayune question, and every afternoon he could expect to have her "drop by" his office to "see how things are going." By Thursday he was dreading the sound of her heels clicking their way toward him on the tiled hallway.

The highway sign said he was passing Tomah, with another hour or so to Eau Claire. He'd leave the interstate there and head north another hour to Rice Lake. He kept it at sixty-five, which was the limit but seemed kind of slow, compared to the traffic. His Hyundai Genesis could keep up with anything on these roads, but Jim wasn't in any hurry. Behind him now, he saw a red sports car coming up behind him, then swerving into the left lane. As it cruised past, Jim glanced over and saw the driver, a severe-looking blonde in large sunglasses, staring straight ahead, ignoring him. For a brief, jolting second he thought it was Lori. He forced himself to get a grip. The blonde's Porsche Boxster accelerated ahead.

Jim liked to think that nobody could intimidate him anymore, but Lori Atwood could get to him. Part of it was her position, of course. As manager of the telecom's business section, Lori had the power of life or death over about two dozen jobs, including his. She'd demonstrated more than once how she was willing to use that power, sometimes on what appeared to be just a whim. By what he heard around the office when she wasn't around, most of the women felt the same way about her. Jim liked to visit Plant, where the all-male crew of technicians hung out, and they all thought she just needed to get laid more often. Divorced a few years earlier, no kids, Lori was said to be dating a guy from Madison. Even if that was true, nobody had yet come up with a way to thaw out the Ice Princess.

It made him wonder if he could survive another ten or twelve years there. He could always check out another job. It wasn't as if he had any strong ties to Cedar Lake, especially with things apparently cooling off with Annie. He'd hate to leave the dojo, but there were lots of good dojos out there. But as he got older, retirement was something that crossed his mind now and then. That was a lot more attractive than another job search, another move.

Well, he would just have to hang in there, keep his head down around Lori and hope for the best. Ride it out and take his retirement when he was ready. But somehow that didn't feel right. He was just on cruise control, and he'd never really done well just cruising along in his life. Not anymore. Since Suzy's death, he'd overcome some big challenges, and found out a lot about himself. He'd avoided challenges, for the most part, in the old days. Basketball came easy for him in high school, but it was tougher in college, so he just gave up on it, using his knee injury as an excuse. Yes, he'd tried to get into the military, twice in fact, but the rejections hadn't surprised him. They wouldn't take anyone with his knee problems, and although it was disappointing, in a way wasn't some part of him, back then, actually relieved about it? So he just sailed onward, with his wife and daughter and their comfy little life, and it was good while it lasted.

Six years of training and study had toughened him, though, and now he didn't want to just sail along anymore. He wanted to climb the mountain. Maybe that would mean a new job. He'd have to look into that. Maybe it would mean a new woman in his life, too, although he didn't particularly feel like hunting for one. But he knew he'd have to find himself a goal, something to shoot for, beyond going to the office every day and training every night, even beyond the Diamond Nationals.

Jim left the interstate at Eau Claire, heading north. The sign said it was about sixty miles to Rice Lake. He'd made good time, so he thought ahead to the rest of the evening. He'd check into the hotel, grab some dinner and maybe see if they had a movie theater in town. The new Captain America picture was out, and ever since he was a kid, Jim had been a comic book fan, reveling in the adventures of heroic men and women. The comics were a lot different today than they used to be, of course, but he still trekked to Madison once a month or so to haunt the comic book stores. Batman and Superman were his all-time favorites, but seeing Cap on the big screen would be fun.

It had been a long ride but it gave him a chance to think, and he came to a decision about Annie. It just wasn't going to work with her. Now it was just a matter of mustering the courage to tell her that. Damn, why did he find himself so passive around women? It had been that way forever, way back to junior high. Just when he started noticing girls, they started noticing him, too. But while he noticed their evolving curves and breasts and legs, they noticed his tall, gawky frame, his glasses and his acne. How many times had he gotten the cold shoulder at school dances? Too many to count. That really didn't change much till he got to his junior year of high school, when his body started filling out and his play on the basketball floor got their attention. But up until then, it was a lonely time.

His mother always knew, though, always understood. Once or twice she'd found him sniffling in his bedroom over the latest slight or insult, and she always had a kind word, a hug, a kiss on the forehead. Alice Millman Hayes was the perfect mom, as far as Jim was concerned. From those embarrassing middle-school misadventures with girls to that day during his senior year, at the state basketball tournament, and beyond, she'd supported him unequivocally. He could still see her sitting in the stands at the arena, clapping and shouting encouragement to him as he walked back to the bench after missing the free throws that would've won the championship. Dad was sitting next to her, arms crossed, looking away from him.

God, how he missed her.

He wiped the tears from his eyes. He missed his dad, too. Things had gotten better between them after high school, and Jim was there by his side the night his mother died, and he was in the hospital room with him when the final heart attack came.

Although his dad had never said it out loud, Jim believed that his father truly loved him, was proud of him, just as his mother was. He wanted to believe that, had to believe that Dad had loved him just as much as he loved Mark.

There was the sign for the Rice Lake exit. The GPS in his smart phone dutifully reminded him to get off the freeway here, and his hotel was only a mile or so away. Still not five o'clock yet, so had time to unwind a little bit. He'd hit the sack early, compete the next day and hit the road for home, hopefully with a trophy or two in hand. This seemed like a nice town, but he couldn't think of any reason why he'd want to stay an extra night. He'd get home kind of late, but he could sleep in Sunday. Maybe he'd give Annie a call, talk things over. Make a clean break of it.

Of course, he could always stay a second night. Why make the long drive home any sooner than he had to? It wasn't as if he had a whole lot else going on.

CHAPTER NINE
DJIBOUTI

OFFICIALLY, TOM SIMONS was the Special Assistant to the Ambassador for Cultural Relations. Since the United States didn't have much in the way of relations beyond economic aid and military support with the small Horn of Africa backwater of Djibouti, Simons didn't have a lot to do in that capacity. The great majority of his time, therefore, was devoted to his real job, that of Chief of Station for the Central Intelligence Agency.

Simons was fifty-three years old and left his family's Indiana farm for the Marine Corps the day after he graduated from high school. The Corps was good to him, and after twenty-two years he retired with the rank of sergeant major. His experience working military intelligence, not to mention his combat record in Desert Storm and other places he still wasn't allowed to talk about, opened a door at CIA. He worked his way up through the ranks to the COS level, much to the surprise of some stuffed shirts who said a former non-com could never do it, and requested a posting anywhere there might be some action. After 9/11 that meant anywhere from

North Africa through the Middle East, Central Asia and all the way to Indonesia and the Philippines. The posting at Djibouti came open and Simons jumped for it, much to the consternation of his second wife, who would've preferred someplace a bit more civilized, like Europe or at least South America. She soon became Simons' second ex-wife.

Djibouti had indeed been the place to be for a COS wanting some action, especially for an ex-marine who was only three pounds heavier than he was when they pinned the globe and anchor on him at Parris Island. His hair had some gray on the sides now, and he couldn't hide it now that he had to let his hair grow out a bit from the Corps' regulation high-and-tight. The former sergeant major's daily runs and workouts with the martial arts trainers on the nearby base kept him in top condition, and more than once he'd gone into the field himself, sometimes in search of the elusive Sudika, "the Thunderbolt", the highest-ranked al-Qaida officer in the Horn. Simons had never found him.

Until now, perhaps.

He stared at the note in his hand, and had the feeling that everything he'd worked for, in uniform and in mufti, might just be coming down to this. He forced himself to take a deep breath, and then turned back to the younger man sitting across from his desk.

"What do you think, Phil?"

Phillip Klein was Simons' assistant chief and had been in Djibouti fourteen months now, compared to his boss's three years. With his rather nondescript appearance, average height and thinning hair, Klein didn't look anything like a spy, which was one reason he was a pretty good one. "We've never had any contact with Sudika before, have we? How would he have found out about this dead drop?"

"After we pulled out of Mogadishu in '93, it took us a while to re-establish some contacts over there," Simons said. "Didn't really get going until we moved into the Lemon in '01." "The Lemon" was the local nickname for Camp Lemonnier, the former French Foreign Legion base that was taken over by the U.S. Navy and was now home to the Combined Joint Task Force-Horn of Africa. "We put the word out that anybody from the other side who wanted to come over could contact us through this particular dead drop."

"Sounds a little risky. The other side could use that to set one of our people up."

Simons nodded. "Everything's a risk in this business, Phil. We can't just drop a business card off at every mosque in town, now, can we?"

"Has it been used before?"

"To my knowledge, only four or five times in the past six years, and never by anyone with, shall we say, the stature of Sudika." He picked up the file on his desk and flipped through it again. It was about a half-inch thick and contained virtually everything Western intelligence services knew about the Ugandan al-Qaida operative who called himself Sudika. Most of the intel was CIA-generated, but some significant data came from Israel's Mossad and the French DGSE. "If this is legitimate, it could be big. Pretty damn big."

"Nobody from The Contractor's inner circle has ever come over. Voluntarily, anyway." Klein's eyes glinted with a glimmer of excitement. "The Contractor" was the CIA's nickname for Osama bin Laden. In the months since the Navy SEALs had sent The Contractor to his final reward, many more of his associates had been rolled up, the result of the intelligence bonanza that was the other great prize of the raid. Sudika was perhaps the highest-ranked al-Qaida chieftain who wasn't dead or in

Gitmo by now, although there were rumors about someone else rising to the top. To flush out Sudika, and perhaps even this newest and potentially greater threat, would be an intelligence coup indeed. "He could very well have important intel."

"He could at that," Simons said. He looked again at the message, which had been picked up from the dead drop that morning. It appeared to be a series of gibberish words, hand-lettered in English, but the accompanying paper was the decoded translation his staff had finished just minutes ago. Sudika had used a rather simple code known as the Caesar cipher. Not the hardest cipher to break, by any means, but one that could be used to provide at least a modicum of security in a message. The fact that the terrorist had not used a more complex code told Simons that he was under pressure, probably operating against some sort of deadline. Reinforcing that impression was the insistence that a response had to be received by sunset two days later. That gave Simons just over twenty-four hours from now to get his answer back to the dead drop.

"I assume we want to respond right away?"

"Yes," Simons said without hesitation. "Use the same cipher. Tell him we agree to the meet. But let's not let him run the entire show. Tell him we must have a response by August first."

Klein made a note on a pad. "A little more than two weeks from now. Creating a little urgency, are we?"

"Why not?" the COS said. "Let him know we're not going to screw around. I would imagine he doesn't want to, either. This guy's pretty sharp, by all accounts, and I think he might be under some time pressure."

Klein made a note on his ever-present pad. "Didn't he go to college in the States? Minnesota, wasn't it?"

"Close," Simons said, standing up. "Wisconsin."

CHAPTER TEN
AFGHANISTAN

FOB LANGDON GOT hit the day after Mark's visit. Five mortar rounds dropped into the hillside compound just after sunrise, and by the time Solum's own mortar team was able to respond, two soldiers were wounded and one was dead. Corporal Pat Tracy, a twenty-three-year-old farm kid from Nebraska, was the fourth KIA in the battalion since Mark had taken command. That was four too many as far as he was concerned.

Mark choppered in that afternoon to see for himself. The outpost had taken some damage, but the men were quickly repairing the breaches in the HESCO barriers that formed the perimeter and had cleared away the remains of the destroyed hooch, where Tracy had been writing a letter home when the round came in through the tin roof. The psychological damage to the men who had survived would be tougher to repair, but getting that job underway was Mark's responsibility.

Solum was handling things about as well as could be expected, considering that one of his men had just died. He was all business, making sure the repairs and cleanup work got done, evacuating his wounded and the body of his fallen soldier. Mark's helo arrived shortly after the evac bird left. The men were grim faced, but they were holding it together. It would sink in later, and there would be tears shed in the hooches this evening.

Solum laid out a map of the valley on the table in the cramped hut that doubled as his HQ and his own hooch. "Our intel from the village says the Tals are staging out of this compound," he said, pointing to a small cluster of buildings about five kilometers west of the nameless village. The outpost overlooked the Afghan town that was about an hour's trek away. Solum and his men hadn't ventured further west since setting up the base. Two klicks past the compound was the Pakistan border

"How solid is the intel?" Mark asked.

"Pretty good, Colonel," Solum said. "The chief in the village tipped us off right away to a couple arms caches. I've had mounted patrols going out regularly since we set up shop here. I'm a little worried about this village, though. It's been a week since we've been there. I had a patrol scheduled to go through there tomorrow."

That didn't sound good to Mark, either. What was now FOB Langdon used to house a platoon of Afghan Border Police, a notoriously corrupt outfit. Appeals from some of the maliks in the valley led Mark to use his influence with ISAF; the ABP's were moved elsewhere and Mark sent Solum and his men in to take over their post and convert it into the battalion's most distant outpost. The enemy pretty much had their way while the ABP unit was around, but that was changing. "The chief seems to be reliable, then?"

Solum nodded. "He lost a grandson to the Tals in Kabul

before we moved in. They hung him from the diving board of that swimming pool the Russians built."

Mark remembered seeing that grim site when he arrived in the capital during his first tour. The Olympic-sized outdoor pool was built by the Soviets during their occupation of the country, but the Taliban drained it and used it for a gallows. Sometimes they didn't bother to hang the victim; they just pushed him off the diving board to the concrete floor ten feet below. Bound and gagged as they were, not too many survived the fall. Those who did were shot where they lay.

"Maybe it's time to pay that compound a visit, Ken."

"My thoughts exactly, sir. I've got a mission planned for this evening. Care to come along?"

"I'll promise not to get in the way. You'll be in command."

"Thank you, sir. We move out at 1600 hours. We'll go through the village on the way. I plan to hit the enemy compound at 2030." He folded up the map, then his shoulders dropped a bit and Mark heard a sigh.

"You all right, Ken?"

"Tracy…he's my first KIA," the young lieutenant said softly. He looked over at Mark with eyes that were raw, pleading. "That letter is gonna be the toughest I've ever had to write."

Mark nodded, remembering the day in 1991 when he had to write one of those letters for the first time, from a dusty tent in southern Iraq. "It won't be easy, Ken, but you have to do it. I wish I could tell you it'll be the last one you'll ever write on this job, but we both know it probably won't be."

"How do you deal with it, Colonel?"

Mark looked away for a second, remembering Specialist Eric Meyers, a gung-ho young infantryman from Arizona who had taken an Iraqi bullet in the first hour after Mark's unit came over the border from Saudi. There had been more since then. Would it ever end? Would they ever be able to beat their swords into plowshares?

Only if the other guys agreed to do it, too, which meant it would probably never happen. There would always be work to do for Americans like Meyers and Tracy, dirty, nasty work, dangerous work in places like the one they were in now. He looked back at Solum. "You just do your job, Ken. That's all you can do. Keep your men sharp, stay alert, and you'll bring most of them home. That's all we can ask of ourselves as officers."

The lieutenant nodded. It was times like these Mark felt his heaviest responsibility, but he drew on the lessons he'd learned along the way, good and bad. It had been that way in this man's Army since George Washington took command at Cambridge Common, July 1775. Mark remembered reading about that event at the Academy and had visited the marker in the Common near the Harvard campus. With a bit of a shock, Mark realized that Washington was only forty-three years old at the time, three years younger than he was now.

"By the way, Colonel, I heard from my uncle back home about that soldier you mentioned the other day, the one who was with your dad in Korea."

"Oh?" Mark had told Solum about old Ed's buddy. The young lieutenant said he thought he remembered the name and would check it out.

"Yes. Michael Solum was my great-uncle. My grandfather's younger brother. I sent an email to my father, and he said Mike was his uncle. Dad asked me to give you his address so you can write him; he has some stories for you that he got from his father. From what he said, my great-uncle and your dad were pretty tight."

Mark had to collect himself for just a moment. He'd been

thinking of his own father quite a bit lately. "I'd like that," he said.

Solum handed Mark a folded slip of paper. "That's my father's email address. He lives way up in Bayfield now, retired there a couple years ago. Doesn't mind the winters."

Mark remembered the beautiful little town on the shores of Lake Superior, with the Apostle Islands dotting the surface of the lake. "I've been up in Bayfield, but not in the winter. Your dad didn't go south when he retired?"

"No, he said he had enough heat and humidity in Vietnam to last him a lifetime."

The platoon started to mount up in mid-afternoon. Mark would be riding shotgun in Mustang Three, the third Humvee in the five-vehicle convoy, with Solum in the second, following the point vehicle. A last check in with Mark's intel people back at Roosevelt, known collectively as "Prophet" due to their ability to monitor enemy radio traffic and distill credible intelligence from the transmissions, revealed that the Tals had been on the move that day. They were overheard boasting of their mortar attack on the FOB. Solum made sure the men in the column knew the enemy was celebrating the death of one of their brothers. The news did not go over well, but Mark was pleased to note that the men were keeping it together as they prepared their vehicles and weapons.

He would've preferred to hit the Taliban compound with a tactical air strike followed by a company-strength infantry assault supported by armor, but the official Rules of Engagement that had been "modernized" a year or so earlier meant that he and Solum had no tac air and no armor. What they did have was about two dozen troops, nearly three-quarters of Langdon's complement, and they had to wind their way down the mountainside on a road that was barely wide enough to accommodate the Humvees.

They kept it slow, always on the lookout for possible IEDs At that pace it took an hour to reach the village, but there was still plenty of daylight left. Enough for them to see that nobody was out walking around, and that by itself was unusual. The lead Humvee came to a sudden halt.

"Look alive, gentlemen," Mark said. In the turret behind him, the soldier on the .50-caliber machine gun readied his weapon.

Over the company radio net, Solum's voice crackled, "What do you see up there, Smitty?"

"Movement in that large hut at our two o'clock, sir. Looked like a kid."

"All right, One and Two dismount, let's check it out. Everybody else, stay alert."

Mark saw Solum and another soldier getting out of the second vehicle. He saw the building now, about twenty-five meters away, and there was movement in the open doorway. The approaching soldiers had their rifles at the ready. Mark noticed with approval that the turret gunners in the lead two vehicles were keeping their weapons trained at their ten o'clock and two o'clock, just in case.

Solum peeked into the hut, then stepped inside, followed by one of his men. After a moment, the lieutenant's voice came back over Mark's radio. "Colonel Hayes, we need you in here, sir."

There were four children in the hut. Two of them were still alive, but Mark almost wished they weren't. The girl, who couldn't have been any older than eight, sat on the dirt floor, her bloodied, toothless mouth gaping open, raw empty sockets where her eyes had once been. On the tattered bedding next to her, a boy of maybe five lay with open wounds covered with flies.

They found some adults, all of them frail and gray haired, cowering in one of the huts. The Taliban had swept through the village that morning. Somehow they found out, or guessed, that the chief had informed on them to the Americans. As punishment, they brutalized the children of the village, forcing their parents and grandparents to watch. The girl was raped, her teeth broken with the butt of a rifle when she hesitated to obey the order to fellate her assailants. When they finished, they gouged out her eyes. The chief, who was the grandfather of the girl, was beheaded. A dozen or so younger men and women were carted off.

Mark had seen some pretty goddamn awful things in this country but this was right up there with the worst. Solum had wisely decided not to let anybody else into the hut except the medic, to treat the injured children as best as possible, but word quickly spread among the troops. Mark heard the muttered curses, and before they moved out the two officers went to each vehicle and ordered the men to stay focused. There would be a reckoning, and it was coming very soon. The engines of the Humvees roared as the convoy moved out.

The mountains seemed to close around them as they rolled through the valley. Mark used his field glasses to sweep the mountainsides, hoping without much confidence to see any sign that they were being watched. The Tals almost surely had spotters up there, well-hidden, with their own binoculars and radios. Solum was monitoring the enemy frequencies. Neither side was going to have the element of surprise in the coming engagement. Once again Mark considered calling in an air strike, maybe with some Apaches instead of fixed-wing fast-movers, but even that request would have to go up to Brigade and then he'd run into those stupid ROEs again. Helluva way to run a war, but as the General had reminded him more than once, they were here to win hearts and minds, and you couldn't do that by hosing down a compound that probably had women and children inside. Too bad the other side didn't play by the same rules.

Well, there was only one thing to do about that. Get inside that compound, and then it would be their men against his, straight up. Mark liked those odds.

The first warning shout from the spotter up on the mountainside came over the radio when they were half a klick from the compound. "Okay, guys, punch it!" Solum ordered, and the engines roared as they picked up speed, closing on the target. No sense giving the enemy a chance to zero in their mortars or bring RPGs into play. Within two minutes they were dismounting at the south wall near the main gate. Solum waved Four and Five to stake out the rear of the compound, where there might be another gate besides the ones on the south and east walls, and watch for enemy coming over the wall, trying to escape.

The compound was average-sized by Afghan standards, roughly square and about a hundred meters on each side, surrounded by an eight-foot wall of sun-baked mud. Their most recent aerial photos showed thirteen structures inside, with six or seven likely to be individual homes. They would have to go house-to-house.

From inside they could hear sounds of movement, some shouts, and the unmistakable, all-too-familiar sound of AK-47 bolts being slammed into place. Solum hustled over to Mark. "Only way in is the two gates," the lieutenant said, breathing a bit hard. Mark tried to remember the man's file; was this going to be his first firefight? Mark hoped not. "Colonel, could you take half the men and cover the gate on the east wall? I'll come in first from this gate." Solum was excited, which was okay, to a point, but he was getting a little too wired.

"Ken, look at me."

"What?"

Mark took him by the shoulder and turned him away from the men. "Stay focused, Lieutenant. You've gotta keep it together. Stay calm."

"Yeah. Okay."

"Take four men, two to this corner, two to the opposite corner," Mark said, pointing first to the southwest corner of the compound to the left of the main gate. "One man gets boosted up on each corner. They can eyeball the gates. None of the buildings inside are higher than the wall, so our guys on the corners can spot any enemy on the rooftops waiting to pick off the assault teams. They can lay down covering fire when we come in."

"Good. Good idea." Solum appeared a bit more in control now. "Sergeant Powers!"

"Right here, sir." The tall, North Dakota-born Sergeant First Class, Langdon's ranking non-com, hustled over. Solum rattled off orders for Powers to pick and deploy the men who would get up on the corners to cover the assault.

"Corporal Swanson! Your squad is with the colonel."

"Roger that, sir." Swanson waved an arm at the men behind him, bringing six up close but hugging the wall. "Where to, Colonel?"

"Follow me. Stay sharp, watch out for bad guys on the wall." Mark led the squad off at a run, hanging a left around the southeast corner. The secondary gate was in the middle of the east wall. Ahead of them, Mark saw one soldier boosting another up to the top of the wall at the northeast corner. The soldier scrambled up to the top and lay prone, rifle extended, then reached his left hand down with a thumbs-up signal.

Mark edged closer to the double-doored gate. The wood was roughly hewn and didn't look too terribly solid, but was probably barred on the inside. Mark motioned Swanson over. "Who has the C-4 to breach the door?"

"Uh, nobody, Colonel. But Weeden here brought a sledge."

Mark couldn't believe it. They were on a mission to assault a compound and they hadn't brought explosives? Solum would hear about this, assuming they lived to talk about it. Fortunately, the big Nordic-looking soldier with the sledge-hammer looked like Thor holding his hammer. "All right, Swanson, half your men on the other side, half with me. We'd better hope this damn door isn't barricaded from inside." He sized up the men with him. Some faces showed fear, others a sense of calm. Those would be the veterans, he knew. "Any of you guys been in Iraq?" Four men nodded, including Swanson. "All right, this is gonna be just like that. We clear the build-ings one by one. Two-man teams. Get your buddy right now. Anybody with a gun in his hands, you shoot. Unless it's a kid or a woman, got it? Take down the women and kids hand-to-hand." Mark knew that the smart thing would be to spare nobody, that anyone with a gun should go down, but after Iraq, he couldn't bring himself to give that order. He knew he was ratcheting up the risk to himself and his men, but so be it.

The men took their positions. From the south wall, Mark heard one of the soldiers yelling in Pashto, demanding that the gate be opened. They had to identify themselves as American soldiers, but Mark figured that probably wasn't a surprise to anybody inside. The response was a shout of "*Allahu akhbar!*" The soldier on the southwest corner opened up.

"Take that door down, Weeden!" Two powerful strikes with

the sledge did the job. "Go go go go!" Mark yelled, and he led the troops through the gate.

The men moved with trained efficiency through the compound. Mark felt his senses expand, taking in everything around him. The fading daylight lent menace to the shadows. He smelled the peculiar Afghan aroma of cooked food, human sweat, and goat excrement. He heard shouting in English and Pashto, the crying of a baby, the screams of women, the crash of wooden doors being broken, the popping of the soldiers' M-4's greatly outnumbering the distinctive rattle of AK-47's.

The moment the gate was breached, time seemed to slow down for Mark. His long years of training and experience took over the moment the gate was breached, and despite the fear and the chaos around them, Mark felt calm, and he sensed, rather than saw, that his men were in the same zone as he was. They were soldiers in the United States Army and they had a job to do, and in only minutes it was done.

Mark's closest call was in the second building. The first had been a storeroom, empty except for some rugs, scattered cans of food and baskets of grain. The second was the armory. Two men were inside, grabbing for weapons from a crude stack of submachine guns and old bolt-action rifles. One of them swung around to face the door, bringing an AK up, and he went down with two rounds into the chest from Mark's M-4, and at a range of only six feet the rounds lifted the man off his feet and he crashed backward into a row of rocket-propelled grenade launchers leaning against the wall. The second man, younger and more nimble, dodged the body of his comrade and pulled a knife from his belt and came at Mark, screaming, bringing the knife back with his right hand to slash. Mark stepped in toward the man, thrusting his rifle up and out to slam the Tal's forearm. The man's scream changed to one of pain and the knife flew out of his hand. Mark finished him with a sharp thrust with the butt of the rifle into the man's throat, crushing his windpipe. The man sagged to the floor, eyes rolling backward.

The sound of an explosion rattled through the room. Mark's partner, a private from Minnesota named Roberts, crouched in the doorway, peering out. "What's going on out there, Roberts?"

"Jesus, Colonel, looks like one of the gomers took a grenade."

Roberts dragged the unconscious insurgent out the door as Mark moved on into the courtyard. There was no more shooting, just shouts as the Americans herded the Afghans into the open. Solum had deployed some of his men for perimeter security, with the rest surrounding the Afghans, weapons leveled.

"Any casualties, Lieutenant?"

"Just one, Colonel, a crease on his leg, not serious," Solum said, and Mark noted with some relief that the young lieutenant's eyes and breathing were normal. He'd come through. "About five enemy KIA, a couple wounded."

"What happened over there?" Mark pointed to the large home where the explosion had ripped off the door. Blood and human remains stained the mud-brick sides and the dusty floor.

"Gomer came out with a couple grenades, must've had the pins pulled because when one of my guys nailed him, they dropped and went off. I've got a couple men inside—"

A soldier appeared at the blasted doorway. "Medic! Medic!" He motioned frantically to the officers. "Lieutenant! Gotta see this!"

Mark and Solum hustled over to the doorway. "What have you got, Johnson?"

The trooper's eyes were wide, contrasting with his dusty, black features. "There's a tunnel in here. Somebody bugged out for sure."

Mark ran back out into the courtyard. The soldiers who had been on the parapets were still there. "You men up there! Keep a lookout for squirters popping out of a tunnel!"

"Roger that, Colonel!" yelled the man on the southwest corner. Probably an Iraq vet; he recognized the term American troops used over there to identify insurgents escaping from buildings. Mark turned to look at the man on the northeast corner, who waved at him, then suddenly raised his rifle and aimed to the north. The soldier fired two shots.

"Got him! Comin' up outta the ground!"

Mark pointed at Swanson. "Corporal, take three men out there and get him. Watch out for more of them in the tunnel."

"I'll go down in the tunnel, Colonel. My old man did that in 'Nam, told me all about it."

"All right, go." Mark trotted back to the main house as Swanson and his team rushed for the east gate where they'd come in.

Inside the front room, Langdon's medic, a ruddy-complexioned veteran from New York who'd joined the Army after 9/11, was hunched over a small figure on the floor. Two other soldiers were assisting him. Solum was coming into the room from a side room. Mark edged closer, making sure to allow enough room for the medic to work. "What have you got, Tranelli?" Then he saw, and his heart sank.

The medic was working on a girl of about four lying motionless on a rug. He'd removed her shirt, showing a bloody entry wound in the right side of the abdomen. The girl's eyes were glassy, but she was breathing.

"Took shrapnel from the grenade, sir." He applied a field

dressing. Another soldier put a small pillow under the girl's head and gently stroked her forehead. Tears ran down his face. Tranelli glanced at him. "Keep her still, Evans." The medic listened to the girl's chest with his stethoscope. "I think her right lung is collapsing." He rummaged through his medical kit.

"Come on, Doc, for God's sake, you gotta help her!"

"Easy there, Evans. Let the doc work," Mark said.

"Sorry, sir. I got two girls at home, no older than this one here."

"I know. Keep it together. She needs your help now."

Tranelli took out a small tube with a three-inch needle attached to it. "Gotta do a needle decompression. Bleeding's not too bad, but we have to get the lung to expand again. Colonel, we're gonna need a medevac for this kid." He inserted the needle just above the wound, then attached a short catheter.

Solum gave the order to his radioman. "Should have a chopper here in about twenty minutes, Doc."

"Tell the doc at Roosevelt to get prepped for this one. I'll get on the horn with him in a couple minutes." The soldiers watching the procedure were breathing heavily, but a couple had turned away. Evans was calmer now, gently stroking the girl's forehead and cheeks, whispering to her in English. "Okay, that should hold her for a bit. What about that chopper?"

"Medevac's about fifteen minutes out," the radioman said.

"Tell him to land just outside the south gate," Solum said. "Anything else we can do, Doc?"

"A prayer or two wouldn't hurt," Tranelli said grimly.

Mark stepped outside, and Solum joined him. "Looks like this place was home to a pretty big fish," the lieutenant said. "Found some documents in the other room, a couple maps, some radios. I'm having it all gathered up for the intel guys."

"Was that the gomer who sent himself to the virgins with the grenades?"

"No, he was just providing cover. Looks like the head honcho was the guy in the tunnel making a break for it." He motioned over to the south gate. "Here they come now."

Swanson and his team were carrying an Afghan man. "This guy's wounded!" Swanson yelled as they hustled the prisoner over to the officers.

"The doc's busy inside with a patient," Mark said. "How bad is this guy?"

The Afghan was laid down on the dirt floor of the compound. The troops had already field-dressed his legs. "He'll live, I think," Swanson said. "Esser up there on the wall put a round in each leg. Mighty fine shooting."

Mark looked up to the northeast corner where the soldier was standing, his rifle at the ready. He gave Esser a thumbs-up, and the soldier waved back. Mark made a mental note to look up the man's service jacket later. He suspected he'd find some impressive marksmanship records. He also thought the man would be in line for a commendation.

The Afghan was about forty, with streaks of gray in his thick beard. He was conscious and glared defiantly at the Americans surrounding him. One of the soldiers pointed his rifle at the wounded man. "This guy the motherfucker who hurt those kids in the village? We should waste him right now."

"Secure that weapon, soldier," Mark said firmly.

"Sir! After what he did—"

Swanson stepped up to the soldier. "Stand down, Private. This bastard will get what's coming to him." The soldier stepped back, holding his weapon at port arms, breathing heavily.

Mark gave him one last hard look, then knelt next to Afghan. "What is your name?" he asked in Pashto.

"Sta plar...nikkan sara..yo kam...sudui bachiya." The man's eyes showed pain, but also hatred.

"What'd he say?" one of the soldiers asked.

"'I equate your fathers and forefathers, son of a pig.' He says he'll kill my family." Mark leaned closer and whispered in the man's ear, then stood up as the man glared at him.

"What'd you say to him, Colonel?" Swanson asked.

"I paraphrased Patton. 'May Allah have mercy on you and your kind, because we won't.'"

Mark was having late chow with the rest of the troops at Langdon. Men decompressed from a mission in different ways, some better than others, but one thing Mark had found helpful was having a meal together. Plus, they were hungry. Chow at the FOBs was a bit less refined than at Roosevelt, but it was still good.

Solum approached him when Mark was disposing of his trash. "Colonel, do you have a minute?"

Outside the large hooch that served as the mess hall, the night was chilly. Mark flipped up the collar of his jacket and pulled his patrol cap down a little tighter. Down in the valley, there were no lights on in the village. The only sounds from outside the hilltop base were the whistling of the wind, carrying the occasional bleat of a goat from the valley floor.

"Man, I can't get over the stars," Solum said. Above them, the heavens were alive with uncountable millions of lights. "Seems like so many more than back home."

"A lot less ground light over here," Mark said. He knew the young man wasn't out here to discuss astronomy. "What's on your mind, Ken?"

"Colonel, I…well, I guess I wanted to know what you thought of the mission."

"We'll have a formal debrief in the morning, before I go back to Roosevelt."

"I know, sir. But, well, I was hoping you could…"

"You did fine out there, Ken." He'd bring up the C-4 during the debrief.

He heard the younger man exhale, just a bit. "Thank you, sir."

They were silent for what seemed like a full minute, then Solum said, "I was scared, sir."

"We all get scared, Ken. If you don't have fear, there's something wrong with you. It's how you deal with it that counts. How you help your men deal with it."

"I know, sir, I heard that more than once back at CFT."

"You were ROTC, right? Back in Wisconsin?"

"Yes, sir."

Another link fell in place for Mark. Solum's jacket had indicated he was one of his battalion's top students, but Mark must've missed the CFT notation. Cadet Field Training was a course for top ROTC sophomore cadets over eight weeks in the summer, most of them at West Point's Camp Buckner. Leadership skills were one of the things cadets learned there. "I taught one year at the Point," Mark said.

"You did, sir?"

"Yes. It was before your time," Mark said with a grin. "One of the reading assignments I gave my students was a book called *Never Without Heroes*, about Marine Force Recon troops in Vietnam. The writer had something very interesting to say about how you feel in combat. He talked about combat in terms of engaging the enemy, but also engaging ourselves."

"How so, sir?"

"He described it this way: 'The conflict that pits courage, duty and responsibility against fear.'"

The men were silent for a moment. Mark could almost hear Solum processing what he'd heard. "The men were talking about how you took out those two gomers—I mean fighters, in the assault," the lieutenant finally said. "One of them came after you with a knife?"

"Yes," Mark said, remembering the moment. He hadn't thought about it till he'd seen a woman weeping over the body of the man with the knife. He'd died, choking to death on his own blood, before the medic could get to him. It occurred to Mark that he had killed two men that day. He looked up at the stars, wondering if God would forgive him.

Solum wasn't done. "Once we got inside, I wasn't afraid anymore. Things just sort of clicked." Mark nodded ever so slightly. The kid was starting to understand. His training had been good. So many of the instructors back home were veterans now, significantly improving the quality of the training. "Colonel, I got one of the KIAs at the compound. First guy I saw when I got through the gate. Guy was running right at me, bringing up his weapon. I just reacted, brought my weapon up, squeezed off two rounds. Right in the chest."

Mark didn't say anything. He knew exactly what the young lieutenant was feeling right now. Something like this changed a man forever. How the man handled it from here on made all the difference.

"I never killed a man before," Solum said softly. "Plenty of deer back home, but never a...." He looked at the older man, and in the dim light Mark could see the glint of moisture in the eyes. "I'm not sure how to think about that," Solum said. "When we were done, I felt...well, I felt relieved. My first firefight, and I made it through. My men made it through. Is that the way I should feel about taking a human life, Colonel? I didn't feel anything more about that man than I felt back home about a door. I was the hunter, he was the prey."

Mark thought back to that night in Iraq, and a talk he'd had with a man who'd survived three tours in Vietnam. "Yes," Mark said. "You have it exactly, Ken. You're here to do a job. You won the fight. Everybody on your team made it home safely. You removed some real dangerous characters from the war. This one goes in the win column. Like an old veteran told me many years ago, winning beats losing every time."

Solum nodded, then looked back out into the valley. "That was a helluva thing, in the village," he said.

"Yes, it was." Mark tried to think of something that would help the younger man process that horror, but he couldn't come up with anything. How could you explain that? He couldn't, no more than he could explain what he saw in Kuwait back in '91 after they drove the Iraqis out, things like torture chambers where naked men were strapped to bare bed springs, doused with water and then jolted with electricity.

Solum spoke again, and Mark could hear the anger in his voice. "What the fuck kind of people do those things? To kids? Sometimes I think we should just nuke the whole goddamn country."

"We could do that, Ken, but then we'd have to nuke the next one, and the next. Where would it end?"

"I don't know," Solum said, his anger subsiding. "Maybe we should just do Iran. They're behind a lot of this, aren't they?"

Mark knew a fair amount about that, but there was little he could tell the lieutenant. He thought back to one particular highly-classified briefing at ISAF HQ a few months earlier, about a potential Israeli strike against Iran's nuclear sites, and also increased activity by Iranian special forces throughout the region. The General felt there was a connection, and Mark was pretty sure he was right about that. But what he said was, "That kind of thing is pretty far above our pay grade, Ken."

They were silent for another minute, and then Solum asked quietly, "Were you scared today, Colonel? If you don't mind me asking."

Mark looked at the young lieutenant, and saw himself a quarter-century earlier. He thought of his father, frightened and cold that night in Korea when he had to leave this kid's great-uncle behind to be killed by the Chinese. "Damn right I was scared, Lieutenant. But I learned a long time ago not to let fear overwhelm those other three things I mentioned. When that happens, you're dead. Or worse yet, your men are dead."

"Roger that, sir."

CHAPTER ELEVEN

IRAN

A S A GUEST of the Islamic Republic of Iran Navy, General Fazeed couldn't very well escape from the launching ceremony and the ensuing receptions, at least not until a respectable amount of time had passed. He had to admit, though, that the new guided missile frigate, *Jamaran*, was an impressive vessel. Along with several other high-ranking officers, both in the regular military forces and his own Revolutionary Guards, he had been given a personal tour of the ship by her captain, as Admiral Sayyari, the commanding officer of the Navy, beamed and thrust his heavily-medaled chest out a little further every minute. Fazeed expected to see buttons and pins flying at any moment.

It was another hot day, but fortunately here in Bandar-Abbas the sea breeze kept things reasonably comfortable. Still, Fazeed was perspiring in his dress uniform, and he was glad when they went below into the air conditioned interior of the ship. The narrow passageways immediately gave him a feeling of claustrophobia, and he came close to barking his shins on the hatchways more than once. The first time, he felt a hand at his elbow, providing a discreet means for him to regain his balance and his dignity.

"Thank you, Rostam," Fazeed said, nodding to his friend, Admiral Ralouf. The head of the IRGC Navy returned the nod and added a knowing smile.

"Not like your missile bases, is it?"

"No, it is not." That was an understatement. Ninety-five meters in length, only about eleven meters across at the beam, the ship was designed for a complement of a hundred forty sailors. Fazeed had thought the barracks his own men stayed in on the base were cramped, but they were almost luxurious by these standards. Still, the ship was spotlessly clean and obviously well-organized. When the group reached the Combat Information Center, the cabin from which the captain and his men would direct the ship during combat operations, Sayyari invited his guests to ask questions.

The first one, from a regular Air Force general, was obviously a plant; Fazeed knew the man was a close friend of Sayyari. "Captain, this is most impressive. How does your ship stack up against the Americans?"

"We are prepared to defend our nation against any aggressor, General. The Americans would find themselves in the fight of their lives if they challenged my ship."

At the back of the group, Fazeed leaned slightly toward Ralouf and whispered, "How long would he last?"

Ralouf offered a small shrug. "Oh, perhaps twenty minutes." From the other side of the group, Sayyari frowned at them. The rivalry between the regular forces and their IRGC counterparts, which included Fazeed and Ralouf as well as three other men in the tour group, was well-known. The regulars had the bulk of the hardware and the troops, but the Pasdaran had the most important missions, and they had the trust of the nation's highest leadership, which was critical when it came to funding and political support. Fazeed likened it, in his private moments, to the relationship in Nazi Germany between Hitler's SS and the *Wehrmacht*.

The questions continued for several more minutes. Fazeed wondered if Ralouf was being completely fair to Sayyari and his captain. After all, this was a modern warship, armed with missiles, cannon and torpedoes. He had no reason to doubt the efficiency of the Navy's training. The only problem was that Iran's sailors had really not been tested in combat for many years, whereas the Americans had been conducting combat operations in the Gulf and nearby waters almost continuously for more than two decades. They also had the advantage of more than two centuries of tradition, from which today's officers could draw inspiration. It was impossible to underestimate the value of experience and tradition, especially among the officer corps. While he had no doubt that Sayyari's sailors would fight bravely, Fazeed held no illusions about the outcome of a conflict between Iran's navy and America's.

Well, with any luck at all, he thought, we will not have to find out.

The tour concluded with a polite round of applause for Sayyari and his men. The admiral invited them all to a reception at his quarters, to be followed by a formal dinner. For the next two hours, Fazeed made the rounds of the assembled officers, many of whom had brought their wives, and the conversation was lively and collegial. Morale was high among the sailors at the base. Well, why wouldn't it be? The government had spared no expense to expand and modernize the facilities here. Even as the Westerners' sanctions tightened their grip on the country, squeezing the civilian population, the military was well-funded.

Finally, Ralouf nodded to Fazeed from across the room and they made their apologies to their host, citing pressing business elsewhere on the base. Sayyari bade them farewell and invited them to come back anytime. He was obviously proud of his fleet and his men, and from what Fazeed had seen this day, he had a right to be. No doubt the admiral was waiting for the day when he would receive the order from Tehran to sail his fleet against his nation's enemies. He did not know, at least as far as Fazeed could tell, that Ralouf had already received that order. Thus their departure from the dinner party for a roundabout trip by car to a distant part of the base.

It was fully dark when they arrived at the gate, and Fazeed was pleased to see that security was tight. IRGC troops manned the post and a pair of armored vehicles flanked the entrance on the inside. Fazeed knew that Ralouf had been able to appropriate this portion of the base many months ago. His forces had bases on four islands off the coast of Iran, but none of them had the infrastructure required for this particular project, especially the necessary security. Once they were waved through the checkpoint, Ralouf's driver took them a quarter-kilometer further and then stopped.

"On foot from here, my friend," Ralouf said.

"That's fine, it's a nice evening for a walk." Leaving the car and driver behind, they set off toward the quay, where bright spotlights were lighting up a shape at one of the piers. As they approached, Fazeed recognized the outline of a nondescript cargo ship. Twice on the way there, the strolling officers were intercepted by security patrols, who demanded at gunpoint to see their credentials.

"Your men are very efficient," Fazeed said when they were finally on their way after the second vehicle had let them pass. "My compliments."

"Thank you, but Colonel Zadeh is in charge of security here."

"Ah," Fazeed nodded acknowledgement of Ralouf's knowing look. Zadeh was the commander of the *Ansar-Ul-Mehdi* Corps, the Followers of the Twelfth Imam. This division of the IRGC provided security for the nation's top civilian and military officials, as well as some counter-intelligence and covert operations services that not even Fazeed knew about. Having Zadeh's troops here emphasized the facility's importance. The general was impressed.

They were within about fifty meters of the quay when they had to pass through another security checkpoint, and they were joined here by a man in civilian clothes and a hard hat, who nevertheless saluted Ralouf. "Admiral, it is good to see you, sir."

Ralouf returned the salute and then shook the man's hand. "And you, Captain Nariman. May I introduce my colleague, General Fazeed?" More salutes and another handshake.

"This way, gentlemen," Nariman said. The captain led the way to the bustling quay. Fazeed noticed immediately that he and Ralouf were the only men in uniform.

"My friend, the *Lion of Aladagh*," Ralouf said, sweeping his hand forward. The ship was a nondescript freighter, by Fazeed's estimation, but it appeared in fine shape, freshly painted and now almost crawling with sailors.

"I must say, she does not appear out of the ordinary," Fazeed said, and then he realized he may have unintentionally given offense to her captain. "My apologies, Captain Nariman. I am sure she is a fine vessel."

"No apologies are necessary, General," Nariman said with a proud smile. "I understand completely."

"She was chosen specifically because she is rather ordinary," Ralouf said.

"Of course," Fazeed agreed. He knew the mission parameters well enough to know that discretion was of the utmost concern. "Captain, I was most intrigued by what the admiral told me of your, ah, delivery system. Did you have any problems with the installation?"

"No, sir. The Russian engineers we hired were most helpful. They designed it, after all."

"Ah, of course. When will the other ship depart?"

"*Star of Persia* will sail five days from tomorrow," Ralouf said. "By then, Nariman and his ship will be rounding the tip of India."

Fazeed recalled the timetable, so carefully planned for so long. "You sail tomorrow, Captain?"

Nariman checked his watch. "In about ten hours, General, about two hours after our cargo is secured aboard."

Fazeed's heart beat a little faster at the mention of the "cargo". It was what he had come here to see. The tour of the new frigate was just a pleasant diversion.

"The transfer of your special cargo is about to begin," Ralouf said. "Your people delivered it here last night in excellent condition."

"Is Major Paria here?" Fazeed asked. Paria was the specialist he had chosen to go on the mission. No one knew more about its operation than he did. If all went according to plan, Paria's name would be hallowed by his countrymen for generations to come. If it didn't...well, it would. It would have to.

"Waiting for you in the warehouse," Ralouf said. "Shall we, Captain?"

"Certainly," Nariman said. "Follow me, please, gentlemen."

An hour later, Fazeed shook hands with Nariman and Paria

one last time. He took one final look at the cargo, enclosed now in its special shielding, designed to look as much as possible like a typical, everyday maritime cargo container. Loading the cargo onto the ship at night was designed to foil the American spy satellites as much as possible, but still they would take great pains to disguise the true intent of their task. Fazeed had been allowed to see it, though, before the final hatch was closed. Paria had even said it was perfectly fine for the general to touch it, but Fazeed couldn't quite bring himself to do so. None of them could, really. Paria and his men would have to do so when it was safely stowed in the hold of the ship, of course, but that would be something Fazeed would not have to participate in.

On the ride back to his guest quarters, the admiral and general were both silent. Fazeed's thoughts were more troubled than he thought they would be at this point. Throughout the months of planning, the preparation of the two special cargoes for their shipment to Bandar-Abbas, he had gone about his work with his typical strong sense of duty. Yet there were times, late at night usually, when he wondered about the mission. He always pushed those doubts aside, but they came back. One of these days, perhaps very soon, he would be forced to confront them.

Fazeed bade his comrade farewell when they reached his stop, at the rather sumptuous home the Navy provided for visiting flag-rank officers. Ralouf would be returning to the IRGC section of the base to oversee the final preparations for sailing. It would be a long night for his old friend, but Fazeed had done more than a few of those himself. The two officers shook hands and then embraced.

"Rostam, thank you for the tour. It was most enlightening."

"You're welcome. Please pass my gratitude along to your men at your base. They were first-rate in preparing the cargo."

"I will be happy to." Fazeed paused, the doubts once more burbling up inside. Did Rostam share them in any way? He had known Ralouf for years, but they had not yet discussed certain aspects of PERSIAN METEOR. Fazeed felt a sudden strong urge to talk to his old friend, to unburden himself. But now was not the time.

"Is there something else, Arash?" In the dim light from the porch of the house, Fazeed thought he saw Ralouf's eyes narrowing, but perhaps there was something more there.

"No. May the blessings of Allah be upon your men tonight, and on their voyage."

Ralouf hesitated. "They will need them. We all will."

CHAPTER TWELVE

WISCONSIN

THE FIRST TIME Jim stepped into a sparring ring for real, he knew fear. It was at his very first tournament, back in his college days, a big event in Dubuque. He had just passed his first belt test and wore his orange belt tied around his freshly-laundered *dobok,* which didn't take long to become saturated with sweat once he put on the *hogu* vest. Jim remembered that he was actually trembling a bit as he was called into the ring by the referee. Facing him was a fighter wearing a yellow belt, one rank above his, and the logo on his dobok jacket said he was from a club in Peoria, Illinois. To Jim he looked like an experienced fighter, moving very smoothly, and in fact he'd won his forms division earlier in the day, with Jim finishing fourth, out of the running for a trophy.

Could that really have been thirty years ago? Jim thought back to that tournament as he stretched, working out the kinks as he prepared for the sparring competition in Rice Lake. Some days he felt every one of those thirty years, but truth be told, he was probably in almost as good physical condition now as he was then. He was about twenty pounds heavier, but he'd been pretty slender coming out of high school, and in those days they didn't do much weight training, even in college. Being lighter back then didn't help him in the ring that day, but being lucky did. The guy from Peoria landed a side kick right away that rocked Jim and put him behind 1-0, but then he got a little too cute and left himself open for Jim's right roundhouse kick to the head. The knockout surprised Jim even more than the guy on the receiving end. Jim's luck ran out in the semifinal bout, which he lost badly, but he came back to win the third-place bout in overtime and went home with a nice trophy. That trophy was packed away in a box somewhere, but the memory of winning it, and the feeling of pride and satisfaction he had then, were still there.

Today's competition wouldn't involve any knockouts, at least not intentionally. Since starting his training in isshin-ryu five years earlier, Jim competed only in karate-style point sparring, not the full-contact taekwondo variety. After competing in a couple dozen full-contact events, Jim certainly wasn't scared of that style, but he didn't feel like tempting fate too much, either. He was at the age now where he competed in "senior" divisions, and in taekwondo that might mean fighting guys as young as thirty-five. For a guy who'd just turned fifty, that was asking for trouble in full-contact. Point sparring allowed only light contact and emphasized speed and quickness, and frequently the larger tournaments had fifty-plus age divisions. This one today wasn't large enough for that, but he'd sized up the field already and although there were a couple guys who appeared to be around forty, he figured his chances were good.

Jim hadn't been this far north in Wisconsin for some time, and this was his first visit to Rice Lake, a town of about nine thousand, halfway between Eau Claire and Superior in the northwest corner of the state. He'd met the host, a high-ranking black belt named Anthony Bronson, on the tournament circuit a few years ago and got on his mailing list. Finishing up his stretching now, Jim wished he'd gotten his usual eight hours of sleep instead of only seven. The little things made a difference in competition.

Despite that, things had gone pretty well so far. His three-section staff kata earned him first place in his weapons division, and he finished second in the empty-hand forms competition. After that came a couple hours of helping to judge the color-belt rings, and now finally the black belt sparring was beginning. There would be four other fighters in Jim's senior division, the youngest about forty. The winner would fight the young-adult winner for the grand championship. If everything moved along smoothly, they'd be done by about three o'clock and he could be on the road and home by nine.

"Excuse me, it's Jim, right?" He recognized the Italian accent, got a whiff of the intriguing mix of perfume and perspiration, and turned around.

"Yes. Hi, Gina."

She was about forty, her dark shoulder-length hair tied back in a ponytail, and her gi fit snugly enough to reveal a nice figure, with the brown belt accentuating a trim waist. Jim had been one of the judges for Gina's rings, and she'd done well, displaying excellent balance and technical expertise. What put her over the top was the confidence she showed in the ring. She won the empty-hand competition and finished a very close second in weapons with her kata featuring the *tonfa*, a weapon resembling a police baton that was not often seen in tournaments.

She flashed a dazzling smile. "I just wanted to thank you for the scores you gave me, and the tip from Green Bay."

"No problem," he said. Four months ago, Jim had judged

Gina's ring at the Harris Memorial, one of the state's premier events, and mentioned after her event that she seemed a bit tentative. Obviously, she'd taken that to heart.

"Your weapons kata was terrific," she said. "How long have you been working with the three-section staff?"

"About a year," he said. He didn't agree with her openly, but he knew that he'd really nailed the kata today. This was the first time he'd used this particular weapon in competition, and everything clicked. "I thought I might have a decent chance if I didn't brain myself with it," he added with a smile.

"It's the first time I've ever seen anybody use that weapon at a tournament. It looks difficult."

"It's a challenge," he said. Then, thinking why not, he said, "Maybe I could show you a couple things with it later."

The smile came back. "That would be great. Well, good luck in the sparring." She bowed, and he returned it. As she walked away, she looked back and smiled again.

Jim finished putting on his sparring boots and was working on his forearm guards when Anthony Bronson came over. Jim had competed against him before, but today, as host, Tony was sitting out the competition. That was good; Bronson was well-known as one of the top senior karate fighters in the state. "I see you've made Gina's acquaintance," he said with a grin.

"Yes, she's a nice gal. From Ashland, isn't she?"

"That's right," Tony said. "Master Lewitzke has a nice club up there. Ever been up that way?"

"Close. When I was a kid, we came up to Bayfield for a week one summer. Went through Ashland, I think. Pretty remote country."

"Yes, it is, but it has its charms."

"Gina is definitely one of them."

"You should ask her out. She's single, I hear."

"Is that right?"

The senior division sparring came down to Jim and a fighter from St. Paul named Bill Rich, shorter and about ten years younger, wiry and very active in the ring, favoring hand strikes, worth one point. Jim's height and his taekwondo background led him to prefer kicks, worth two. He'd watched Rich's semi-final bout closely, and when Tony, acting as center judge and referee, called the two of them into the ring for the title bout, Jim was focused and ready. Just as Rich had done in his first bout, he started this one with a leaping lunge for a hand strike to the head, but Jim dropped to one knee, raised his left arm in a high block and shot his right fist into Rich's chest. "Point!" Tony yelled, and the fighters separated. The four corner judges agreed, and Jim was up 1-0.

When the bout resumed, Jim took advantage of his lead and went for a kick. Rich easily evaded Jim's right roundhouse kick to the head, but Jim anticipated correctly that he would move backward, toward the side of the ring, and Jim followed with a left turning side kick that landed squarely in Rich's abdomen. "Point!"

Trailing 3-0 now, Rich had little choice but to be aggressive. The first fighter to five points would win the bout. In karate point-sparring, Jim had found, few bouts ever lasted the two-minute distance. Full-contact taekwondo sparring was usually a battle of attrition that went the full two rounds, four minutes of hard fighting, but karate bouts were fast, with explosions of high-energy strikes and blocks separated by lulls when one fighter would stalk the other. Jim had been able to transition easily into this style and his dojo was one that spent a lot of time sparring. It paid off again today. Rich got a point with a hand strike to Jim's side, but Jim finished him off with a right roundhouse to the side of the head, with just enough contact to score, after feinting a roundhouse to the side to draw Rich's guard down.

Jim's knee was starting to feel the strain of the competition, but there was one more bout to go, this one for the grand championship, matching him against the winner of the younger men's division, a lanky, blonde-haired college student from Eau Claire named Derek Saunders. Jim had never seen the kid fight before today and from what he'd seen, he knew he'd have his hands full. The kid had a cocksure attitude and he backed it up with a very aggressive fighting style.

Tony pulled out all the stops for the climactic event of his tournament. Jim and Saunders entered the center ring as the roller rink's light show bathed them in swirling colors and the speakers blared the theme from *Rocky*. Tony himself acted as the referee, and the four corner judges were some of the highest-ranked instructors from northern Wisconsin, all of whom Jim had met at various stops on the tournament circuit. Jim glanced over toward the scorekeepers' table and caught a glimpse of Gina, holding a stopwatch as the timekeeper. She gave him a smile and a quick thumbs up. Tony came over to him and put the red ribbon around Jim's belt in the back. Each judge had a six-inch square of red cloth in one hand and a white one in the other, which they'd use to signal when they awarded points. "Be careful with this guy," Tony whispered. "He gets a little frisky."

"I noticed," Jim said, and the fighters came to the stripes marked on the mat, facing each other.

"Grand championship bout!" Tony shouted. "Fighters, face me, *kitsukay*." Jim and Saunders bowed to Tony, then bowed to each other with the next command. Jim sank slightly into his fighting stance, left foot forward, leaning back slightly on his right foot, hands up.

He kept his breathing steady. He had a shot at his first-ever grand championship, and this was no time to be nervous.

"Hajimay!" Tony yelled, and as he brought down his right arm in between the fighters, Saunders attacked. The kid was lightning quick, unleashing a flurry of kicks. He was wearing a black gi and boots, making it tougher for Jim to track the legs, but he was able to block the first, the second, the third, and then Jim barely had a split second to register a fourth, a backspin whistling in toward the right side of his head. Jim tried to bring his right arm up in a high block but he was a millisecond too slow, and Saunders' booted heel slid across the top of Jim's forearm and crashed at nearly full speed into Jim's helmet above the right temple.

It was like an artillery shell went off inside his skull. Jim staggered to his left and had to go down on one knee. He shook his head, and his vision cleared, enough to see Tony pushing his right fist into his left palm, the signal for excessive contact.

"No points!" He turned to Saunders, who was dancing lightly. "Excess contact. This is a warning. Next time there's a point deduction."

Jim slowly stood up, shaking his head again. Across the ring, Saunders waited, loose and confident. Tony came over to Jim, asking, "Are you okay?"

"Yeah, let's go."

"Back to the center, fighters!"

There was no sign of apology from Saunders, which was unusual. Sportsmanship levels were always high at these tournaments, but every now and then a hotshot thought he was above the rules. Jim knew he'd have to be careful with this guy, but he also knew he couldn't afford to show any sign of weakness.

"Hajimay!"

Saunders danced in, bobbing and weaving, while Jim held his ground. Saunders lashed out with a left side kick which Jim evaded by stepping back, and then he ducked just in the nick of time as Saunders rocketed a right backfist at the spot where Jim's head had been an instant earlier. Even with his helmet on, Jim heard the swish of air as the gloved hand whipped overhead. Jim pivoted on his left foot and put everything he had into a right turning side kick, loosing a loud *kiai* yell as he launched the kick. His heel connected solidly with Saunders' exposed abdomen. The air whooshed out of the kid's lungs as he collapsed around the kick and was lifted half a foot into the air before landing hard on his rump. The crowd issued a collective groan but there were also more than a few cheers.

"No points! Excessive contact!" Tony gave the signal and then went over to Saunders, who had rolled over to his hands and knees, wheezing. Damn, Jim thought, he'd lost control with that one. A shot like that might get him disqualified. He had to stay focused.

Saunders got slowly to his feet, holding the right ribcage with his left hand. "Can you continue?" Tony asked.

The kid looked over at Jim, then nodded. Beneath the mask, though, his eyes looked a little different than they had at the start of the bout. Fear, maybe? Well, Jim thought, perhaps it was about time.

"Okay, guys, let's dial it down, all right?" Tony said. "Fighters to the center. Hajimay!"

Saunders was cautious now, and Jim sensed it was time to take control of the fight. The kid was protecting his midsection, and Jim took advantage by faking a right roundhouse kick to the kid's side, pulling it back at the last split-second as Saunders came down with a double forearm block and striking instead to the head. The toe of Jim's boot ticked against Saunders' forehead. "Point!" Every judge held up two fingers and pointed at Jim. "Two points red!" Tony shouted to the scorekeeper. "Fighters to center. Hajimay!"

Saunders came over the top with a lunging right jab at Jim's head. Jim parried with a left high block and lashed out with a left side kick, connecting lightly on Saunders' right ribcage. The kid winced and clutched himself again as two of the corner judges yelled "Point!"

"Two points red!" Tony yelled. He looked at Saunders, who nodded gamely that he was ready. He wasn't bouncing around anymore, though. Tony looked over at Jim. "I almost called excess contact on that one, Jim. Take it easy."

"Barely touched him," Jim said. "Let's go." He had a 4-0 lead now and the grand championship was only one point away.

Saunders showed he wasn't in as much pain as he'd let on, scoring with a hook kick that clipped Jim on the side of the helmet, then with a nifty counter, faking a backfist to the head and sneaking a punch into Jim's midsection. Now it was 4-3. "Thirty seconds!" Gina yelled from the scorer's table.

Jim made a quick decision. The kid was gaining confidence now; if Jim was too aggressive, he might make a mistake and give the kid an opening to tie the match. If it went to sudden-victory overtime, anything could happen. Jim's knee was starting to weaken, and he didn't dare trust it too much longer. He needed to force the kid into a mistake. Jim started moving backward, dancing away lightly, making it look like he wanted to stall out the rest of the bout.

Saunders saw his opening and went for it, launching a right

roundhouse kick that Jim evaded, following with a spinning left backspin kick. Jim ducked underneath it and saw his opening. He launched his left leg from the rear, but instead of firing a front kick, he pulled it back slightly and twisted his body in midair around to his left, whipping his right leg up and around in a tight arc, sending the toe of his boot into Saunders' face mask. Jim crashed to the mat as the crowd cheered and three corner judges screamed "Point!" He rolled over onto his back. Saunders was staggering backward, arms splayed out, and Tony was pointing two fingers at Jim. "Two points red! Match!"

Jim could hardly believe it. He hadn't planned that kick; he'd seen the opening and just reacted. All the training in the dojo back home, all the sparring rounds with Sensei and the other black belts, it had all come down to one moment on the mat, in a town he'd never set foot in before. He rolled onto his back, arms and legs splayed out, savoring the moment, almost in disbelief.

"Hey, champ, you okay?" It was Tony, leaning over him and grinning.

"Yeah. Give me a hand, will you?"

Tony helped pull him to his feet. All of a sudden, Jim felt as if every muscle ached, and his bad knee was throbbing. What might turn out to be a monster headache was beginning to throb. His gi was drenched in sweat. He could barely raise his arms to pull off his helmet, but all that was forgotten when he looked at the scorer's table and saw that beautiful trophy, a stylized eagle with wings spread. It would look very pretty on his mantle back home. Standing next to the table was an even prettier sight. Gina was applauding and flashing a dazzling smile.

There were handshakes all around, including one from

Saunders. "Sorry about that first shot," he said. "It got away from me."

Jim rather doubted that, but instead he said, "No problem. Nice bout."

"See you next time, sir." They bowed to each other and Jim watched him leave the mat and get a hug from a perky blonde wearing a gi from the same club and a brown belt. He'll get some consolation when he gets home tonight, Jim thought, and I'll have a long, lonely ride. He'd already checked out of his hotel. Maybe that hadn't been such a good idea; the hotel had an indoor pool with a Jacuzzi and that was mighty tempting right now.

"Congratulations!" It was Gina, beaming up at him.

"Thanks," he said, shaking her hand and exchanging bows. "I'll pay for it tomorrow, though."

She cocked her head a bit. "You need to sit in a Jacuzzi for a while. That'll make you feel better."

"You know, I was just thinking the same thing. My hotel has one, but I already checked out."

There was the briefest of pauses, and then she smiled. "I was planning to stay another night, and I think we're at the same hotel. Why don't you join me?"

He settled down in the four-person pool and let the water embrace him. Even without the jets turned on, it felt great. In the nearby swimming pool, a few kids were splashing, with their parents lounging alongside. Jim was glad none of them wanted to use the Jacuzzi. It would just be the two of them.

There'd been a bit of an awkward moment when they arrived, but Gina solved that by offering to let Jim use her bathroom to shower and change. When he emerged wearing his trunks, which he'd thanked himself for remembering to bring along, she was sitting at the desk, wearing a hotel robe and tapping on her laptop computer. Below the robe, her calves hinted strongly at the promise of very nice legs indeed.

"I'll see you down there," he said, and she smiled at him

Now he lay back and enjoyed the warm water, trying not to think too far ahead. Just let it play out, he said to himself. But there would be one important piece of business he'd have to settle right away. He hadn't seen a ring on her finger, but it never hurt to ask. Tony might not have the latest on her.

He saw her walking toward the pool, carrying a towel and wearing a green two-piece suit that was a bit too conservative to be called a bikini, but still revealing enough to display her well-toned body. She'd put her hair up, and her skin was lustrous, with a Mediterranean shade that spoke to her Italian heritage. "How's the water?" she said, with another dazzling smile.

"Terrific," he said, "and it's about to get better."

CHAPTER THIRTEEN
MOGADISHU, SOMALIA

I T WAS EIGHT minutes to ten, according to his watch. Three minutes later than the last time he'd checked. Simons wondered again if this was the smartest career move he'd ever made, or the stupidest. The problem with stupid career moves in this business was that you often didn't get a chance to make more than one.

He fought to keep himself calm. It was a typically hot night, but fortunately there was a bit of a breeze coming in from the ocean. The main benefit of the wind was to dilute the stench of the city; any relief from the heat was just a welcome side effect. The Mog hadn't changed much since Simons had last been here. He'd come ashore in December '92 with Battalion Landing Team 2/9 as part of Operation Restore Hope. The memory of the name made him chuckle. Some politician had come up with that one, no doubt. Ten minutes after your boots hit the dirt in this rat-hole, you knew there would be precious little hope restored here.

"We have movement on the perimeter, sir", a voice

whispered in his earpiece. "One vehicle, approaching from the northwest."

"Copy that," Simons responded in a barely audible voice. The hidden button-sized mic would have no problem transmitting the words to the security team. He'd brought a dozen men with him on this op, Delta Force commandos from the Lemon's detachment of Special Forces. There were a good number of them on the base, but even Simons didn't know how many. He did know that in addition to the Delta detachment, there were Army Green Berets, Navy SEALs, Air Force Special Tactics, and some British SAS and German KSK, not to mention French Foreign Legion troops. The Deltas had brought two of the Germans with them on this mission, in fact, and somehow that made Simons feel good. His granddad would've been proud; old Reinhart Marske, God rest his soul, had fought as a *Fallschirmjäger* for Germany in World War II before being captured. Two years as a POW in America convinced him to come back in '52 when the promises of the Worker's Paradise in East Germany had started to dim. He brought along his wife and teenage daughter and found work in a factory in Fort Wayne. Hilda Marske wound up marrying Ted Simons, the star quarterback on her high school football team. Tom came along a few years later.

They were about a half-mile from the Hotel Shamo, and by day this would have passed for a commercial area, but the vendors had long since packed up and headed for home. Not much was done at night in the Mog, although Simons knew there were a few areas where fearless—or careless—Westerners could find a drink and agreeable, if costly, companionship in what was nominally a devout Muslim city. The warlords who controlled the Mog were just as interested in making a few bucks as anybody. Simons had been all over the world and that was the one constant he had found. Whether it was dollars, euros, rubles, or Somalian shillings, it was always the same.

"Should see his headlights turning onto the street, sir." Simons looked to his right, and three blocks down the street he saw the glow, then the arc of the lights as the car turned onto the street and headed toward him.

"Anything else moving inside the perimeter?" Simons asked.

"Negative, sir. Only one vehicle, the one coming toward you, no foot traffic."

The Deltas had set up a three-square-block perimeter around his location and could see anything that moved, thanks to their night-vision scopes. Ready to lend a big assist was the modified MD4-200 surveillance drone they were ready to deploy from a nearby rooftop. The yard-wide, German-built four-rotor helicopter had been brought along just in case Simons would be taken someplace else for the meet, something the station chief fervently hoped to avoid. Mogadishu was a big city and he wasn't all that confident about the drone keeping up with a speeding car, if it came to that. The Delta commander had assured him they'd move instantly to cut off any vehicle's escape if Simons found himself in trouble.

The car was a hundred feet away now and moving toward the curb. A name raced through Simons' mind: *Buckley Buckley Buckley*. He forced the name away. William Buckley was the CIA station chief in Beirut in '84 when Hezbollah snatched him from the curb in front of his apartment building. Three subsequent videotapes delivered to the CIA by the terrorists had shown Buckley being tortured in gruesome detail. His body was never recovered.

The car pulled to the curb in front of him, engine chugging sluggishly. Simons could see it was a Nissan, at least ten years old. The left rear door opened up and a short Somali stepped out. "Mr. Simons?"

"Yes?"

"Sudika sends his greetings and felicitations," the man said carefully in English.

"I thank him for his hospitality," the CIA agent said, completing the coded acknowledgement.

The Somali stepped aside and motioned to the dark interior of the car. "Please, come with us. It is just a short drive."

Simons took a breath, calmed himself as much as possible, and folded himself into the car. Just before sliding in, he thought he caught a glimpse of a dark shadow flitting somewhere overhead, but the sputtering car engine kept him from hearing the rotors of the drone.

When the blindfold was removed, he was sitting in a bare room, with the only light coming from a lamp on a side table. In front of him was a rickety wooden table, with another chair on the other side. Moving his head slightly as if to loosen his neck, he used his peripheral vision to glimpse each of the armed men standing behind him and to either side.

He had been blindfolded in the car and they'd driven for about seven minutes, according to his watch. The Deltas were on top of things, though; twice the commander had whispered into Simons' earpiece, assuring him the drone was on the job and they were keeping pace in their own vehicles. He'd acknowledged them with a couple of coughs. When he'd been helped from the car, he was casually frisked, but he'd brought no weapon, and they missed the button mic, which looked like every other button on his white shirt. Now he just had to wait, and he was able to relax a bit. Had they intended to kill him, he'd be dead by now; if they'd been sent to kidnap him, he'd either be on his way to some nameless dungeon or the Deltas would've intervened.

The door in the wall facing him opened, and a Somali woman entered with a pitcher and two glasses, which she set on the table. Without making eye contact with Simons, she turned and shuffled back through the door. The next person to step through was a black man of medium height, wearing a dark shirt and slacks. His close-cropped hair and beard were flecked with gray, and he wore black horn-rimmed glasses. His features were more central African than eastern. He sat down in the empty chair.

"Good evening, Mr. Simons," the man said, in English with a hint of a Swahili accent. "Thank you for agreeing to this meeting."

"I presume I am speaking with Mr. Yusuf Shalita, otherwise known as Sudika," Simons said.

Shalita smiled. "Yes, that is my name. As to the nickname, I think that was invented by some creative Western reporter some years back."

"What can I do for you, Mr. Shalita?"

The Ugandan looked past him at one of the guards and said something in Somali. Simons sensed movement behind him, then the opening and shutting of a door. He risked a glance behind him, and the guards were gone. "They are right outside the door," Shalita said. "A word from me and they will be here in two seconds."

"I'm sure that won't be necessary," Simons said.

The Ugandan narrowed his eyes. "Your country wants me in custody, or dead, Mr. Simons. You might possibly be able to kill me with your bare hands before the guards could stop you."

"It would be a suicide mission, and we don't do those,"

the CIA agent said. "You should also know that if I do not emerge from this room in perfect health, you will never leave Mogadishu alive."

Shalita smiled. "I think we understand each other. Well, to business, then. Are you familiar with the Katabolang mosque incident in Afghanistan?"

Simons felt a bit of a chill. "I would consider it more than an 'incident'. I would call it a massacre of innocent children."

"The children were killed by American tanks."

"Let's not play games, Mr. Shalita. Your people set that up. Our troops didn't know there were noncombatants inside. The video of the bodies was on the Internet almost before we finished counting them."

"I know. I was in command of that operation."

Simons leaned forward, putting his hands on the table, trying to control his anger. "Did you think you'd fool anybody with that stunt?"

Shalita shrugged his shoulders. "There were enough who believed it happened the way we wanted it to appear. Many young men joined our jihad after that video was posted. Some of them may have questioned our version of the incident, but they came anyway. Many of your journalists apparently believed our version as well, from what I read in the days to follow." He casually poured water from the pitcher into each of the glasses, setting one of them closer to the American. "Please, I know you must be thirsty." Shalita took a healthy swallow from his glass.

Simons leaned back, folding his arms, resisting the urge to lunge across the table. "Did you bring me here to brag about that...*incident*? I have better things to do with my time."

Shalita leaned forward, folding his hands on the table in front of him. He glanced downward for a second, then his eyes met the American's. "You may not believe me, Mr. Simons, but I have deep regrets over that incident now. Very deep regrets indeed."

Simons said nothing.

Shalita averted his eyes after a few seconds, then bit slightly on his lower lip, sighed, and blinked his eyes a few times. He's trying to compose himself, Simons thought. If it's an act, it's a good one.

Then the Ugandan looked back at his guest. "I will come to the point, Mr. Simons. In recent months, since Katabolang, I have thought much about that incident, and about my role in it, in this endless jihad. I have prayed every night to Allah for guidance, and for his forgiveness."

"Good for you." Simons immediately regretted the words. This was not the time to antagonize this man. Something was happening here.

"I understand your skepticism, but I would ask you to believe me when I tell you this: I have decided it is time to end my role in the jihad. I have done many things, Mr. Simons, for which I have deep regrets. Whether Allah will someday forgive me, I cannot say. But before I meet him, blessed be his name, I wish to make things right, as much as I am able."

"Go on."

Shalita took a deep breath. "I am willing to give myself over to American custody. I am willing to tell you everything I know about al-Qaida, which I can assure you is a substantial amount of information. I also know a great deal about al-Shabaab, and about the various pirate groups that prey on your shipping off the coast."

Simons fought to keep his features impassive. The mother lode of intelligence was within his grasp. Not just al-Qaida, but al-Shabaab, the Somali terror group. Throw the pirates in for good measure, and it was a potential treasure trove of incalculable value. What he said in the next few minutes might lead to an end to what was becoming known within the Company as "The Forever War", but which the new administration in Washington, increasingly distancing itself from reality, now called "overseas contingency operations". "I am...intrigued, Mr. Shalita," he finally said. "I'm sure my government would be most interested in your offer."

"I have some, ah, requirements, in order to secure my cooperation."

"I assumed as much. And they are...?"

Shalita sat back in his chair, hands still folded on the table. Simons flicked a glance at them; they were perfectly still. "Immunity from prosecution, in civil court or by military tribunal, by any nation."

"I will pass that along to my government. But we may not be able to guarantee the cooperation of other governments. Some of them may wish to extradite you for trial on charges stemming from crimes you committed on their soil."

Sudika waved a hand dismissively, then his eyes narrowed. "Before I surrender myself, I must see in my hand a letter, signed by your president, guaranteeing this immunity and also promising that I will not be subjected to...what did your former vice president call them? Oh, yes: 'enhanced interrogation techniques,' or something like that."

Simons couldn't suppress a smile. "I'm sure you've heard that our government has publicly renounced those kinds of things," he said.

"I have indeed heard that," Shalita said, "and we both know, Mr. Simons, that it is still happening, in your prisons in Afghanistan and elsewhere. If your news media finds out about it and asks questions, your president and his people will say they knew nothing about it, they will solemnly condemn it, they will blame the previous administration, and promise a vigorous, transparent inquiry. Then they will proceed to cultivate whatever intelligence was gleaned by these techniques. They will fire a few underlings and promise never to let it happen again. And it won't, until the next time."

"I think we both understand how this game is played, Mr. Shalita. Now, do you have any other conditions that I can take to my government?"

"Yes, I do," Shalita said. "But I am very serious about that letter, Mr. Simons. When I have that letter in my hand and have satisfied myself as to its authenticity, I will surrender myself into your custody and give you a piece of information that I am sure you will be most interested in."

"And what kind of information would that be?"

"I know the location of the man who is now the de facto leader of the jihad. I can tell you how to defeat his security precautions, which are much more elaborate and lethal than what your SEALs found in Abbottabad."

"If you are speaking of Ayman al-Zawahiri, I'm sure we would be interested in learning more about him."

Shalita shook his head. "No, not him. Someone far more important. This man is beyond your reach at the moment. But I can tell you where he is. Then you will have to decide whether or not you wish to go there and get him."

The CIA station chief narrowed his eyes. Who could Shalita be referring to? If not al-Zawahiri, then who? His mind raced. Ilyas Kashmiri, who planned the 2008 commando attacks in Mumbai and had been planning similar strikes in Europe, was taken out by a U.S. drone in Waziristan back in June. Al-Zawahiri was announced as al-Qaida's new leader only days after the Kashmiri hit. The CIA was hunting him at this very moment, and Simons had no doubt about their ultimate success. Yes, it would be nice to get him right away, but...

Wait a minute. There had been scuttlebutt in the past couple years about someone else, a man whose existence was fiercely debated within the Western intelligence agencies. Simons had just been talking with a colleague from the Baghdad station a few weeks ago about the rumors..."Are you referring to someone who is known as 'al-Qa'im'?"

Their eyes locked for a few tense, silent moments. Then, Simons saw a very minute change in those brown eyes.

The Ugandan spoke. "I will give you two items for free, Mr. Simons, as a sign of my good faith. Yes, al-Qa'im exists. That is the first item. The second is this: Hamas is preparing a strike in Israel in three days. This is an operation planned and supported by al-Qa'im. A test run, so to speak. The target is the town of Ashkelon."

Simons knew the town. It was on the Mediterranean coast, just south of Ashdod, only a few miles north of Gaza. "What, specifically, is the target in Ashkelon?"

Shalita shook his head. "That is all I can tell you. The date is three days from now. I am sure your Mossad friends will be able to figure it out from there. But if successful, it is a harbinger of things to come from al-Qa'im. If you wish to find out more, you must agree to my conditions."

"Why would Hamas want to attack Israel now? The Palestinians are seeking recognition as a state in the United Nations. Why would they want to jeopardize that?"

Shalita shook his head and frowned. "You have not been listening to me. You assume that Hamas is under the control of Abbas and his regime in the Palestinian Authority. Where does Hamas get its funding? Its weapons?"

"They get most of their money and weapons from...." It hit

Simons like a thunderclap. Two and two suddenly added up to four. *Iran.* How could he have been so dense as to miss that right away? "I see," he said, nodding. It took all of his Marine Corps discipline to control his growing excitement. "That is most interesting indeed," he said finally. "What are your remaining conditions?"

"I spent a few years in your country, Mr. Simons, when I was a young man. I came to admire you Americans in many ways. But I also learned, in the years after I returned to Africa, that most of you cannot be completely trusted. Americans, by and large, are selfish and greedy. Many of them are naïve about the world. Your new president has made a big show of going all over the world and apologizing for his own country. He bowed down to the King of Saudi Arabia, a ruler who has turned a blind eye to the money flowing from his country's madrassas to fund our jihad. Yet surely you know that the men of jihad laugh at your president. In the end, he will be like every other American, out to protect Number One, as you so often say. So, my one remaining condition is this: I will surrender myself to one American, and one American only. He is the only one I remember from my time in your country that I found to be an honorable, trustworthy man."

"And who would that man be?"

"He was a fellow student of mine, at the University of Wisconsin at Platteville. His name was James Hayes. I will surrender to him, ten days from now."

"Assuming we can find him, what if he refuses to cooperate?"

"It was a long time ago, Mr. Simons, but if James Hayes is anything like the man I once knew, he will help you. He was a man of honor."

"What if he's dead?"

Shalita's eyes narrowed. "He is not. He has a page on Facebook, and he posted a message there just two days ago. In seven days I will send further instructions to you about our next meeting, the one in which you will be accompanied by Mr. Hayes, to a place of my choosing."

Simons spread his hands. "I will do what I can."

Shalita stood up. "See that you do." He leaned on the table. "You can be assured of this, Mr. Simons. If you do not bring James Hayes to me, I will disappear. You will never find al-Qa'im on your own. He is far too clever for you." He turned to go, then stopped and faced Simons again. "I know that many in your country now feel you won your war against us, now that Osama is dead. But know this, Mr. Simons. Our cause is more than just one man. There are over a billion Muslims in the world. If only one in a hundred supports us, that is ten million people. Ten million. How many Americans are willing to put their lives on the line to defeat us? Not very many."

Simons fought against his temper again, forcing himself to stay impassive. "The few that we have seem to be doing pretty well against you so far."

Was that a slight nod of grudging respect from the Ugandan? Simons allowed himself to breathe a little bit. Shalita stood and leaned forward on the table. His eyes were hard.

"Yes, your soldiers and Marines are formidable fighters, Mr. Simons. Al-Qa'im has much respect for them, which is why his plans are designed to attack your weaknesses, not your strengths. Our jihad will continue, and we might very well win. We Muslims are a patient people, Mr. Simons. You think in terms of days, even hours; we think in centuries. Will the black flag of Islam fly over the ruins of the White House one day? You and I might not live to see that, but our grandchildren might. Do you want to see your granddaughter wearing a *burqa*? I thought not." He stood up straight, eyes blazing. "One week, Mr. Simons. Find James Hayes and prepare to bring him to me." He raised his voice and issued an order in Somali. The door opened behind Simons and hands gripped him under the arms, lifting him roughly to his feet.

Sudika gave him one last look, then turned and left the room.

CHAPTER FOURTEEN

SOMALIA

YUSUF WAS LEAVING the camp's makeshift mosque the next morning after prayers when Heydar approached him. The Iranian offered a friendly smile and asked, "May I have a word with you?"

He'd had only a few hours' sleep in his own bed, so Yusuf was not feeling very alert this morning, but he was alert enough to notice that Heydar had once again failed to address him as "brother", which was common among the senior leadership in the camp. The more junior fighters always used the Arabic "Ra-iss", and the Somalis who were contracted to do the menial chores, considered beneath the dignity of the foreigners, always used the traditional "hogaamiye". Heydar, however, had subtle ways to remind everyone that he was not only the equal of anyone else in the camp, but first among equals.

"Of course, brother," Yusuf said, slightly emphasizing the last word. He was fluent in Arabic, which was the common language used in the camp among the foreigners, and he was conversational in Somali. He had been pleased to find that his English was still very good. "We can have privacy in my office."

The trip to Mogadishu and the meeting with the American had exhausted him. The temptation to simply surrender to the CIA agent had been almost overwhelming, but Yusuf summoned his willpower and stuck to the plan. Besides not trusting the CIA, it was entirely possible that neither one of them would have been able to leave the building alive. The security detail he'd taken to the capital was a mix of some of his own men from the camp and local Somalis, and who knew how many of them could be trusted?

I am getting paranoid. But, as the Zionist leader Golda Meir had once said, even paranoids have enemies. He remembered reading that when he was at university in Wisconsin, studying the Arab-Israeli conflicts in a history class. The American students had engaged in lively discussions about the Palestinian question. Yusuf rarely said anything. What did any of those fools know about the suffering of the Palestinians, not to mention his own people in Uganda? The people he associated with, when he met with them over coffee in the commons or in the evening at the campus bar, did not even consider that he might be a Muslim. With one exception, he reminded himself; among his silent prayers to Allah this morning was a prayer of hope that this man would be willing to help him now.

His quarters came into view as they turned right down a narrow "street". The camp was housed in a large walled compound, very similar to the many Yusuf had seen in Afghanistan, but with more modern amenities, or at least as many as Somalia could provide. Generous financial inducements to the proper authorities ensured that the compound would have reliable electricity and was left alone by what passed for a government in this wretched country. With about two hundred fighters in the camp, Yusuf had a formidable force, more than enough to discourage all but the most foolhardy challengers who might decide to alter the status quo. In this land that was ruled by gangsters, nobody was that foolish. To attack the camp would have been bad for business. Yusuf's superiors, after all, spent a considerable amount of money to support their operations in Somalia, and if the Somalis for some insane reason were to cause trouble for Yusuf, there was always Sudan. Perhaps even his homeland, which he had not seen in ten years.

Ah, Uganda. Sometimes he caught himself longing for the streets of his old neighborhood in Kampala. His father had been a highly-ranked official in Milton Obote's government, wealthy by African standards, so much so he was able to send his only son to university in America. Yusuf thought often of the family's villa on Lake Victoria. He tried to remember it as it was in the heyday of his youth, a place of beauty and laughter and music. The last time he'd seen it, the villa had been neglected, its once-sumptuous lawns and gardens overgrown with weeds. He had not been able to bring himself to go inside. His parents fled to Kenya when Obote was overthrown in 1985, and they now lived on what money Yusuf could send to them in Nairobi. He wished that someday he could bring them home, but that was impossible as long as the current dictator, Yoweri Museveni, was in power. Museveni had overthrown the general who had overthrown Obote, and had not relinquished power in a quarter-century. He would likely live longer than Yusuf's parents, unless the Lord's Resistance Army got him first. Yusuf had once been offered an important position in that group, which had been fighting Museveni in the north of the country for years and coveted al-Qaida support, but Yusuf would have nothing to do with them. They enslaved children and had murdered and displaced thousands of his fellow Ugandans. Of course, what had al-Qaida done to his fellow Muslims? It struck Yusuf now that it had all led here.

His quarters was a simple four-room building that had the only bathtub in the compound, a rare luxury Yusuf indulged in as he dared, never wishing to give his men reason to be jealous. There was his bedroom, a small kitchen, and his office, plus the small anteroom that functioned as a guest room of sorts, where Amir frequently slept. Furnishings were sparse, but his needs were few. He had grown up in Kampala in relative comfort, thanks to his father's position in Obote's foreign ministry, and his student lodgings in America were simple for that time and place but luxurious by African standards. Sometimes he wondered what it would be like to live in a large, comfortable house, with lights that never dimmed, and hot water out of the tap whenever you wanted it.

He led the way to his office. "Can I get you some refreshment?" he asked the Iranian.

"Thank you, that would be most appreciated." They made small talk as Yusuf brewed some tea. Heydar could be charming when it suited him, which was most of the time. He never lacked for female companionship, that was for certain. Yusuf strictly enforced the rule that forbade his men to fraternize with the few unmarried women in the camp, but Heydar had found ways to get around that, and Yusuf had chosen not to challenge him on it. He regretted that now, regretted the several instances where he could have stood up to the Iranian and put him in his proper place. It was too late now, perhaps. But perhaps not. Yusuf knew he must be careful. He could exile Heydar from the camp, but without very good cause, that would come back to haunt him. The mullahs in Tehran wielded considerable influence, far more than they should have, in his opinion, but he had to deal with reality. In America he had learned that he who writes the checks makes the rules. That was true everywhere.

They took seats in Yusuf's cramped office. "What can I do for you today, my friend?"

"I received a private communication last evening from Tehran, and I wish to share it with you."

"Indeed." This was unprecedented. Yusuf knew that Heydar was the only other person in the camp who had access to the internet, and he assumed he received his instructions from his superiors via encrypted emails. Yusuf and his al-Qaida brothers had learned some time ago that this method could not be trusted, as the Americans were quite clever in their code-breaking abilities. Most of his own orders came via courier. It was slower but more secure.

"I am informed that you will be receiving similar orders in a day or so by courier," Heydar said.

"But you wish to give me advance notice? That is most... interesting, Heydar."

"I understand your skepticism, ra-iss," Heydar said, and Yusuf did not miss his use of the honorific. Oh, but he was a smooth one. "I hope you understand that I am not your enemy. I am here only to provide assistance. My government is a strong supporter of your movement."

"Even though your leadership is Shia and mine is Sunni?"

"We have a common goal: to crush the Zionists, to throw out their crusader allies, and to establish the caliphate. Is this not so?"

"That is true," Yusuf said, choosing not to let this devolve into a theological discussion. It all came down to politics, anyway. Yes, the caliphate was the ultimate goal: a Muslim state, stretching from Morocco to Indonesia, over a billion people strong and armed with a mighty arsenal of nuclear weapons.

Then they would move on Europe and India, and eventually America. China and Russia would be more difficult, both huge nations with nuclear arms, but even now they were making inroads in the more remote provinces of those countries. The big question, of course, was who the caliph would be. Osama had seen himself in that role, but now he was enjoying his virgins, or so many of his followers thought. In his heart of hearts, Yusuf was not so sure about that.

The Iranians believed that the caliphate would be led by the Twelfth Imam, Muhammad ibn al-Hasan al-Mahdi, a descendant of the Prophet himself who was born in 869 A.D. and did not die, but was hidden by Allah, an action known as the Occultation. He would emerge in the future to bring peace and justice to the world, and he would do so by the sword. As a Sunni, Yusuf had been taught that the Mahdi has not yet been born, but was coming, and when he grew to manhood he would lead the faithful, as the Shia believed too. The big difference, it seemed to Yusuf, was that the Iranian rulers professed to know that the Mahdi was about to emerge from his Occultation. Their president, Ahmadinejad, claimed to have been in personal contact with the Mahdi and was ordered to prepare for his arrival. At one time Yusuf had thought that was hogwash, but since his trip to the Aladagh, things had changed. Not his own religious beliefs; not for one second did he believe that the man he had met in those mountains was indeed the Mahdi. He had his doubts as to whether the man himself believed it to be so.

But if the Iranians believed it, that was all that mattered, wasn't it? Yusuf recalled his history classes from university. Nobody outside Germany had believed Hitler would do what he said he would do, but the Germans believed, and that proved to be decisive. Yusuf had studied that movement very carefully. In many ways it was very similar to the jihad of the Islamists. And how close did Hitler's jihad come to achieving success? Very close indeed He led only a relatively few million followers, and they did not have nuclear weapons, yet because of the Germans' iron discipline and meticulous planning, combined with their awesome conventional military strength, their jihad nearly triumphed. Today, the Islamists did not have any real kind of armed forces in the traditional sense, but times were different than in Hitler's day. Victory could be achieved in ways that did not involve overwhelming military power.

With the Mahdi, the Iranians might now believe they had found that way. It was a thought that had crossed Yusuf's mind many times in the past few years, and the more he thought about it, the more he feared it. He hoped that Simons was taking his offer seriously. The strike on Ashkelon was now only two days away.

Heydar was talking, and Yusuf forced himself to concentrate. His mind had been wandering a lot recently, and that was dangerous. "Your leadership has requested our assistance for a mission that you and your men will undertake in a few weeks' time."

"Indeed?"

"I would assume that you and your men have not had much experience in maritime operations?"

Yusuf couldn't help but grin ironically. "We do not exactly have the facilities here to practice our swimming skills."

Heydar chuckled. "That is certainly understandable," he said. His tone of voice could have been interpreted as fraternal, or perhaps patronizing. Yusuf would give him the benefit of the doubt, for a while longer. "Our target will be at sea. In August, a British cruise liner will be moving up the eastern coast of Africa. The ship begins its voyage in Lisbon, Portugal, and will sail around the Cape of Good Hope." From a shirt pocket he produced a map of the continent, spread it out before Yusuf on the desk, and traced a course southward, along the Atlantic coast. "The itinerary includes several stops, including Cape Town and Durban in South Africa. Then it sails northward, stopping in the Comoros, then Dar es Salaam, Tanzania. From there, to the Seychelles. Its ultimate destination is Mumbai, India. On the eighth of August, it should be here." His fingertip came down on a spot just across the equator, around fifty degrees east longitude.

"You refer to it as '*our* target', my friend. Does that mean you will be accompanying us?"

"Yes, I will," Heydar said. His dark eyes betrayed a slight hint of excitement.

"Well, that is intriguing," Yusuf said. Heydar had been attached to his camp for almost a year, and the three operations Yusuf's brigade conducted during that time had all been without the Iranian's direct participation. He was involved in the planning and training, of course, but when the time came to "ship out", as the Americans would've said, Heydar always stayed behind. There was some grumbling about that among the men, Yusuf knew, and he did nothing to really discourage such talk. "I assume you have had some experience in these types of operations?"

The Iranian nodded. "I have," he said. "To assist us, a small group of my countrymen will be arriving in two days' time. There will be six of them, and they have considerable experience in planning and executing these kinds of missions."

Yusuf assumed the visitors would be members of Iran's Quds Force, as was Heydar. As the special operations arm of the Pasdaran, Quds Force operatives had been active for years in support of groups like Hamas and Hezbollah, not to mention al-Qaida. The IRGC also had a naval unit, Yusuf knew, which had been involved in missions in the Persian Gulf, relatively close to the Iranian coast. Four years earlier, IRGC boats seized a dozen or so British sailors and marines in the Gulf and held them for two weeks before they were released. Yusuf had not heard of any operations conducted as far away from Iranian waters as the tip of the Arabian Peninsula.

But of course this would not be an Iranian mission, would it? Yusuf doubted that any of the Iranians, except Heydar, would actually be going on the mission. In the event the mission failed and his men were captured, the Iranian government would not want to be put in the awkward position of having to explain something like that. Yusuf assumed Heydar would not allow himself to be taken prisoner. But could it be possible that all of the Iranians would go? Yusuf had a hard time believing that his men, as experienced and dedicated as they were, would be able to handle the challenges of this type of mission without direct assistance. If the Quds Force commandos were going along, that was ominous indeed. It would represent a significant escalation of Iran's involvement. Was there a connection to the Ashkelon strike? He suspected that was so. Then he recalled the date Heydar had given him for the mission. Something clicked in his brain. His trip to the Aladagh…

Yes, it was beginning to make sense now. His new friend Simons would certainly find this interesting. But he would have to think about that later. For now, he had to play along with Heydar. "I have two immediate concerns," Yusuf said. "First, the timetable. We have less than one month to get ready. Second, the location." He found the spot on the map where Heydar had indicated the seizure would take place. "This appears to be about a thousand kilometers off the coast of Somalia. That is a very long distance."

"Both of your concerns are quite valid, my friend. The training itself will be intense. That is why my men will be here, to assist you. As to the location, we have arranged for some of your friends in al Shabaab to provide a vessel that will be quite capable of making this voyage. It is one they seized earlier this year."

Yusuf sat back in his chair, steepled his fingers in front of him, and gazed at the map. The logistical challenges of such an operation were huge, but not insurmountable, for men properly trained and equipped. Very risky, of course, but their business was all about risk, was it not? Without great risk, there could not be great reward.

"I tell you this because it is possible the men will arrive here before your own orders do," Heydar said. "I have been authorized by my superiors to give you this advance notice."

Yusuf nodded his thanks, already thinking of the immediate, practical considerations. He would have to assign Amir to prepare for the Iranians' arrival. Quarters would have to be prepared, and so forth. But such details were not Yusuf's biggest concern. The target was, and the implications such a target brought with it.

"A cruise liner, you say? That is most interesting," he said.

"Yes," Heydar said. "Approximately seven hundred passengers, crew of one hundred seventy-five."

Yusuf stroked his short beard thoughtfully, contemplating the tactical challenges of such an assault. "This will require a significant force of men," he said.

"About fifty," Heydar said.

Yusuf raised an eyebrow. "Fifty men, to control nearly nine hundred hostages? We will need at least twice that number to have a chance."

Heydar shook his head. "If our goal was to seize the ship

and its personnel and hold them for a period of time, yes," he said. "But we will not be doing that."

"Please explain," Yusuf said, although he suddenly knew where this was going.

"We will attack the ship, disable it and board it. Then we will sink it."

Yusuf stared at the man hard. "What of the passengers and crew?"

Heydar shrugged his shoulders. "If they can swim, they might have a chance."

CHAPTER FIFTEEN

TEHRAN

THE SECURE CONFERENCE room deep inside the Ministry of Defense was about half-full. General Fazeed recognized nearly everybody there, and had been able to have a quick word with Admiral Ralouf when he arrived. They exchanged pleasantries, inquired about each other's families, and of course stayed away from the topic of the meeting. The presumed topic, that is; nobody had been informed of the subject matter, only that their presence was required for a discussion of matters of strategic interest.

Not even the ubiquitous Mr. Jafari would enlighten them. He had greeted Fazeed and then Ralouf warmly. Since their meeting at the base two weeks earlier for the missile test, Fazeed had done some discreet checking on the Defense Ministry official, who turned out to be not from the Defense Ministry at all, but from VEVAK, Ministry of Intelligence and National Security. That was not a great surprise, but it was another reason for Fazeed to be cautious.

"Gentlemen, the President of the Islamic Republic."

Fazeed faced the doorway and came to attention. Mahmoud

Ahmedinejad entered the room, smiling, greeting the first men he encountered. The president was wearing his usual business attire, a light-colored linen suit, white shirt open at the neck. As always, he was bearded, but Fazeed could never tell whether it was a beard cropped very short or a few days' growth left untended. He was not, the general had concluded long ago, an impressive individual. He was wily, shrewd, devious, and not as naïve as the West made him out to be, but he was not the kind of impressive leader his nation needed.

Then again, who was? Leadership was an elusive trait. Many desired it, many thought they had it, few did. Not for the first time, he wondered what would happen if this operation, the one he presumed they were here to discuss, failed. How many of the men in this room would survive?

"Gentlemen, the Supreme Leader of the Islamic Republic."

Ayatollah Ali Khamenei entered the room, imperious and condescending, engulfed in his robes and turban, his wire-rimmed spectacles edging toward the end of his large nose. Unlike Ahmedinejad, he did not greet anyone, did not offer his hand. Khamenei took the seat at the end of the oval-shaped table, and the president sat to his right. "Please be seated, gentlemen," Ahmedinejad said.

Fazeed sat to the Supreme Leader's left, on the same side as the military men, all of whom were from not the regular armed forces, but the Pasdaran. That was interesting. To Fazeed's left was Ralouf, who headed the IRGC's Navy, then Major General Suleimani, the head of Quds Force. Opposite them were the civilians: the president, the defense minister, and then Jafari.

The president looked at Khamenei, and nodded. "You may begin, General," Ahmedinejad said.

Suleimani stood and bowed to the men at the head of the table. "Supreme Leader, Your Excellency Mr. President, welcome. This briefing is classified as Most Secret." Using a remote control, Suleimani dimmed the lights slightly, and a flat-screen television on the wall lit up with the seal of the Islamic Republic. "The operation is code named PERSIAN METEOR. You are familiar with the history of the project. With your permission, Excellency, I will briefly review events of the past few days."

Ahmedinejad nodded his assent. Khamenei sat silently, hands clasped across his ample stomach, occasionally stroking his long white beard. Fazeed noticed he had pushed his glasses up. The lenses reflected the screen as the code name appeared in Farsi.

"Before updating you on the status of PERSIAN METEOR, I will brief you on two preliminary operations being conducted in conjunction with our allies." Suleimani clicked his remote, and a map of Israel came up on the screen. Fazeed heard muffled curses from some on the civilian side. He didn't dare turn his head to look at them.

Suleimani's laser pointer landed on the port city of Ashkelon. "Operation KAFTOR RISING. The Hamas strike team is in place and will launch its operation tomorrow. The team commander on the ground is confident of success."

"Is he one of our people?" Jafari asked.

"No. It was decided that this operation would be carried out entirely by one cell from the Izz ad-Din al-Qassam Brigades. Our advisors have been working with the cell in Gaza, helping prepare the strike. None of our people will be crossing the border."

"Very good," Ahmedinejad said. "Much better than shooting off their rockets."

"You mean, *our* rockets," Khamenei said with a chuckle.

"What is the source of the code name?" Ralouf asked.

Fazeed had a pretty good idea, but was surprised that his old friend, a student of ancient history, did not know the answer already.

"Ashkelon was one of the five city states ruled by the Philistines in ancient times," Suleimani said. "Gaza was another. Some sources say the people may have called themselves the Kaftor. The Hamas leaders chose the name, recalling the glory of their ancestors." Fazeed had been right, but he did not point out that those glorious ancestors saw their mightiest warrior, the giant Goliath, brought down by a single Jewish teenager with a slingshot. The Jews the strike team would confront in Ashkelon would be armed with weapons considerably more lethal.

"And the other operation?" Fazeed asked. He had heard rumors of increasing Quds Force activity against the Zionists, but until now had not known any particulars.

Another click, and this time the Horn of Africa was displayed. "This one is about to start the planning and training phase. The code name is ARTEMIS DAWN." Next to Fazeed, Ralouf grunted and offered a small smile. Fazeed knew enough ancient Persian history to recognize the name, too. Artemisia of Caria was a renowned naval commander under Xerxes in the fifth century B.C., even though she was a woman. It was Artemisia who had counseled Xerxes against massing his naval forces in one great attack against the Greeks in 480. Xerxes ignored her advice and sent the entire fleet into battle at Salamis. Despite the resulting defeat, Artemisia fought bravely. To this day, many Iranian children had a poster of Artemisia and Xerxes on their bedroom walls. Many assumed Artemisia was Xerxes' queen.

For the next fifteen minutes, Suleimani went over details of the mission. The more Fazeed heard, the more his unease grew.

Training al-Qaida terrorists for a naval mission? Assaulting a cruise ship many kilometers out to sea, and then scuttling her, all to distract the Americans and British?

"This is to take place when?" the defense minister asked.

"August eighth," Suleimani said. "The timing of the mission will become clear as we proceed in our review of PERSIAN METEOR."

Fazeed could not help himself. "It is most risky, is it not, General, to include your own men on this mission? NATO has many naval units in those waters. What if, in spite of your men's best efforts, something goes wrong and they are captured?"

Suleimani gave Fazeed a condescending smile. "There is always risk, General. But this unit will be composed of some of my best men. They will not fail. In any event, even if they are captured, it will quickly become irrelevant, as we shall see."

The two men stared at each other for a few seconds, and then Ahmedinejad cleared his throat. "General Suleimani, perhaps the details of this operation could best be discussed another time. Shall we proceed to the main topic of our meeting?"

The Quds Force general bowed slightly to the president. "Of course, Excellency." He turned to the screen and clicked the remote.

"July fifteenth. Unit One is successfully loaded on the merchant ship *Lion of Aladagh* and the ship sets sail from Bandar Abbas twelve hours later." The screen showed the cargo vessel Fazeed and Ralouf had seen a week ago. The next photo showed a ship that could've been its twin. "July twentieth. Unit Two is loaded successfully on the *Star of Persia*. She sails eleven hours later. This map shows their current positions."

Fazeed leaned forward slightly. The icon showing *Lion of*

Aladagh, sailing eastward, was rounding the northernmost point of the Indonesian island of Sumatra, about to enter the Strait of Malacca, with the Malay Peninsula ahead, Singapore at its tip. Far to the west, *Star of Persia* was off the southern coast of the Arabian Peninsula, about to enter the Gulf of Aden, entrance to the Red Sea. "What are their itineraries?" the defense minister asked.

"I will defer the question to Admiral Ralouf."

"*Star of Persia* has two ports of call," Ralouf said. "Jeddah, on the Red Sea coast of Saudi Arabia, and Casablanca, in Morocco just past Gibraltar. From there it sails into the Atlantic. Scheduled destination is Puerto la Cruz, Venezuela."

"And the other ship?"

"Singapore, then Tokyo, Japan. From there, eastward across the Pacific, scheduled to end its voyage in Manzanillo, Mexico."

Ahmedinejad raised a hand. "Admiral, refresh my memory, please. What is the purpose of these intermediate stops? Why not sail directly to their true destinations?"

"The ships are registered with our own Islamic Republic of Iran Shipping Lines. It is highly unusual for this line to send ships across these waters. It was our conclusion that to enhance security, we should include routine ports of call on the itineraries."

"I see. And their scheduled destinations?"

"Our people in Venezuela and Mexico have made all the proper arrangements, including news releases to the local media that will be published on August seventh, heralding their scheduled arrival several days later. It will be the start of a new era in trade relations between our country and theirs," Ralouf said. "I should say, General Suleimani's people, in conjunction with my own." The admiral nodded at the Quds Force general.

"Very good." The president nodded at Suleimani to continue, but Fazeed cleared his throat to get their attention. Ralouf might have been inclined to be diplomatic; Fazeed was not.

"You have a question, General Fazeed?" Suleimani asked.

Fazeed brushed aside his irritated tone. Inter-service rivalries were petty when the stakes were this big. "Yes, as to the ports of call. What are the chances that the ships will be searched by local security forces? Is that not fairly common?" It would be impossible to hide the ships' most important cargo even from a cursory inspection, or so Fazeed assumed.

"Actually, no," Ralouf said. "Port security in almost every port in the world is surprisingly lax, except on rare occasions when threat levels are high. When we devised the itineraries, we deliberately chose ports in nations that are not only receptive to trade with us, but rather unremarkable when it comes to their security measures, with the possible exception of Singapore, although we expect no problems there."

With an annoyed glance at Fazeed, Ahmedinejad said, "I am satisfied, General. Please proceed."

"The two vessels will be in the open ocean when they divert from their scheduled courses," Suleimani said. One click of his remote brought up the Atlantic, with the route of *Star of Persia* moving westward from Morocco, then angling to the northwest. Another click showed the Pacific, with *Lion of Aladagh* describing a parabolic route from Japan through the northern latitudes and then swinging down toward North America.

"If both ships remain on schedule, they should be on station no later than August eighth. We are allowing a few days to account for weather or other unforeseen circumstances, such as mechanical problems."

Rafsanf spoke up, anticipating the next question. "Both ships are in excellent condition, and their crews are our best men. Although nobody can predict the weather for certain, we anticipate no problems meeting the timetable."

Khamenei stroked his beard. "It is, perhaps, a pity that we could not have this done on September the eleventh. It would be fitting, would it not?"

"Ten years to the day since the first attacks," Ahmedinejad said.

Jafari spoke for the first time. "The Americans would be on high alert that day. It was decided to not take that risk. As it is, August ninth is the anniversary of their nuclear attack on Nagasaki, Japan, in 1945. There will be several demonstrations around the country, with our propaganda teams providing assistance. Another distraction for their leadership."

The Supreme Leader nodded. "I understand completely. In any event, PERSIAN METEOR will be much more, shall we say, effective, than what was accomplished by our late friend Osama, may he be with Allah in Paradise." Some of the other men murmured assent.

Suleimani brought up a new slide, showing a map of the continental United States, with one pulsing dot off each coast. "On X-Day, *Star of Persia* is here, approximately thirty-eight degrees north latitude, sixty-three degrees west longitude, about eleven hundred kilometers off the coast of Delaware. Washington D.C. is a little over a hundred kilometers further inland. In the Pacific, *Lion of Aladagh* is about eleven hundred kilometers west of San Francisco, at thirty-seven degrees north latitude, one hundred thirty-two degrees west longitude."

"How precise do those coordinates have to be?" Jafari asked.

Suleimani nodded to Fazeed for the answer. "Not very precise, but relatively close," he said. "The strikes are designed to detonate about eight hundred kilometers inland. For the best possible result, our scientists determined the warheads should explode at an altitude of about four hundred kilometers."

"Can your missiles achieve this, General?" Ahmedinejad asked.

"Yes, Excellency," Fazeed said.

"And the weapons, they will be large enough?"

"They are the largest we have available to us now, approximately four hundred kilotons as measured in destructive power. By comparison, Excellency, the weapons the Americans used in 1945 to incinerate Hiroshima and Nagasaki were only about twenty kilotons each."

Khamenei shifted in his seat, stroking his beard. "It seems to me these weapons would be more useful striking actual targets on the ground, would they not? I have seen pictures of the Japanese cities. Surely weapons twenty times more powerful would decimate even the largest American cities. General, I defer to your expertise, and forgive an old man for being somewhat forgetful, but why explode them so high above the ground?"

"Not at all, Imam. You are correct in assuming that these weapons, targeting the cities of, say, New York and Los Angeles, would be quite destructive. Perhaps ten to twenty million casualties total. I believe General Suleimani has some slides that will illustrate our points." The Quds Force general clicked his remote, and a photograph of what appeared to be the sun, breaking through dark clouds over a city, appeared on the screen. Fazeed continued. "Gentlemen, this is a photograph from a test the Americans conducted in 1962 called Starfish Prime. They detonated a device measuring close to one and a half megatons in the atmosphere, at an altitude of four hundred kilometers, over Johnson Island in the Pacific. This photograph was taken from their island of Oahu, in the Hawaiian Islands. The test was just before midnight."

There were some slight intakes of breath around the table. "That is not the sun you see," Fazeed said. "That is the explosion of the weapon, nearly fifteen hundred kilometers away."

Ahmedinejad broke the silence. "And the results?"

"Much more devastating than the Americans had predicted. The explosion created an electromagnetic pulse, which spread out in all directions, even into space. Radio transmissions were disrupted for several hours. There was damage to many electrical components in Hawaii. Several American and Russian satellites were damaged or destroyed as well."

Suleimani, with a glance from Fazeed, clicked the next slide onto the screen. It showed two pulsing shapes over the United States. "Gentlemen, it is important to remember that the Starfish Prime test was nearly half a century ago. Electrical components were much simpler then, but in fact were more resistant to the effects of EMP. Our scientists conservatively estimate that our weapons, detonated at the proper altitude and at the locations shown on the screen, will have enough power to bring us very satisfying results."

"How satisfying?" Ahmedinejad asked, his voice almost hushed.

Fazeed met the president's eyes. "The entire electrical grid of the United States will be shut down. Permanently."

On the screen, pulsing waves moved outward from the detonations, quickly covering the entire nation, reaching north into Canada and south into Mexico and the Gulf.

Jafari cleared his throat after a moment. "My intelligence analysts have just completed a study of the EMP strike's after-effects," he said.

"Please proceed," Ahmedinejad whispered.

"The explosions themselves will cause relatively few immediate casualties. But virtually all machinery relying on electricity will become useless. Perhaps some of their oldest vehicles will survive, but not many. All vehicles on their roadways will stop, most of them by crashing. Commercial aircraft will all come down. These initial events will cause well over one hundred thousand casualties."

"There will be chaos everywhere," someone said. Fazeed thought it was Ralouf, next to him, but he couldn't take his eyes away from the screen, watching those waves pulsate over their enemy's continent.

"Their entire society is held together by electricity," Jafari said. "Once the grid fails, it will cascade through every system. Food processing, storage and delivery. Water and sewage treatment. Heating and air conditioning. Transportation. Communications. In only a few hours' time, their society will regress two hundred years. Their people will not be able to cope. Without communications and vehicles, government will be paralyzed, at all levels. It will not take long for anarchy to rule their streets."

"And the long-term effects?" That was Khamenei.

"Imam, our analysts predict that within twelve months, two-thirds of the American population will be dead."

The enormity of the attack was such that the men in the room were rendered speechless for a few minutes. Fazeed wondered why the civilian leaders were so stunned. It was not as if this

had not been discussed before, but perhaps not in such exqui-
site detail.

The meeting recessed for a few minutes, then resumed. The
screen was blank now. The military men were not immune to
the scope of the operation, of course, but they were used to
dealing with casualty figures and war-gaming scenarios. The
civilians were not always prepared for something so...stark.
Well, Fazeed thought, perhaps it is time they understand what
it is they are about to implement.

There was more discussion about the particulars of the
mission. Could the Americans intercept the ships? Of course
they could, but there were hundreds of ships at sea all over
the world at any given time, and the American Navy, mighty
as it was, had only so many ships available. They would have
to know exactly which commercial vessels were the threats.
Suleimani was confident in the security of the mission. Of
the ships' crews, only the captains had known their itineraries before they sailed. At their ports of call, the captains and
a few trusted officers, and nobody else, would be allowed to
leave the ships. Could the missiles be shot down after launch?
Yes, the Americans had the technology to do that, but it had
never been tested in combat. A successful anti-missile defense
relies on being able to identify the threat in time, and having
necessary assets available. If the Americans knew an attack
was imminent, and from where, they might be able to react in
time to have a decent chance of interception, or better yet, they
could attack the ships from the air before launch. As Fazeed
and every missile regiment commander knew, the best way to
deal with an ICBM strike was to hit first with a pre-emptive
attack. If you had time, and the nerve.

"Can they retaliate against us?" Ahmedinejad asked.

"The plan was designed to greatly reduce that risk,"

Suleimani said. "If we were to hit just two of their cities, the destruction and loss of life would be great, but retaliation would be inevitable. If the entire country is the target, however, that is a different story altogether."

"They could still strike back," Fazeed said, becoming a bit exasperated, but hiding it well. "Their political leadership will be paralyzed by the attack. All military units within the country, including their ICBM regiments, will be useless." Privately, Fazeed had some doubts about that. There were rumors that the Americans had been hardening their military communications circuits against EMP, but he would save that flimsy card for later. "However, they will retain enough military assets outside the country to retaliate."

"Such as?"

Ralouf took that one. "The American Navy has eighteen guided missile submarines, Excellency. At the time of our attack, at least half of them will be at sea, well away from the effects of EMP. Even one of those submarines has more than enough weapons to destroy our nation completely."

"But they would not launch on us, would they?" asked the defense minister.

"Probably not at first, Minister. Their armed forces that are deployed outside their continent will not launch any kind of retaliatory strike until they are instructed to do so by their civilian leadership. The American military officer corps is well trained and highly disciplined, especially at their highest command levels. They will defend themselves, of course, but they will not attack unless and until they are ordered to do so."

"Admiral," Khamenei said, "are you saying that your Navy cannot protect us against one submarine?"

Ralouf stiffened slightly. Fazeed saw that, and knew the civilians had pushed his friend too far. Ralouf composed himself, then spoke with defiant confidence. "With respect, Imam, that question would more properly be directed toward my good friend Admiral Sayyari, but I believe I can safely say that there is no such thing as an effective defense against the American submarines. They can be stopped only if they can be found, which is extremely hard to do. The Russians have the only force which comes even close to the Americans, and even with all their assets and their experience, they have had little success in finding and tracking American missile submarines at sea. Each one of them carries up to twenty-four Trident missiles, and each missile has multiple warheads, which can be independently targeted. They can strike from more than seven thousand kilometers away. I say to you frankly, gentlemen, our Navy has no chance against them. None at all."

That seemed to set Ahmedinejad back a bit, but Jafari was not giving up. "They will not attack," he said again, more forcefully this time.

Fazeed felt his temper start to rise. "Not right away, at least," he said, forcing himself to stay calm in the face of such foolishness. "It will all depend on when their leadership comes to an understanding of what has happened, and is able to re-establish communications with their overseas units."

"With any luck at all," Ahmedinejad said, "their president will be in his aircraft when the bombs detonate."

"The Americans have contingency plans for that," Fazeed said. "Their vice president is rarely in the air at the same time as their president. If Air Force One goes down, control of the government and military switches immediately to his successor. They have trained for virtually every possibility."

"Not this one," Suleimani said.

"Even assuming they recover quickly," Jafari said, "which

is a big assumption, an American nuclear strike against us has a very low probability, according to our studies."

"I disagree," Fazeed said. "If the Americans are attacked, and they find out who did it, they will strike back. They have always done so."

That brought a glare from the intelligence officer. "Of course, nothing can be ruled out," he said, "but we consider it much more likely that within a day or so of PERSIAN METEOR's success, the Israelis will panic and launch an attack on us."

"Which would have the same results as an American nuclear strike," Ralouf said. "We would be destroyed. The Zionists have a large nuclear arsenal. Not as large as the Americans have, but large enough."

"Useless to them if we strike first," Jafari said.

"General Fazeed, are your forces prepared to implement SWORD OF PERSIA?"

Fazeed turned to the ayatollah. He had known this was coming, but there was no way to avoid it. "Yes, Imam. We would prepare three missiles with nuclear payloads upon receiving the proper authorization. We would require only perhaps twenty-four hours' notice."

"And your targets?"

"Two multiple-warhead strikes on their Jericho missile regiments, and one on Tel Aviv. To deal with their political leadership, which is in Jerusalem, we will use three missiles with conventional warheads to target the Knesset and the prime minister's residence." That drew smiles from the civilians. Fazeed had to remind them of one important fact. "You should know, gentlemen, that the weapons we would use in these two operations are the extent of our current inventory. It would take our production facilities several more months to manufacture new warheads, assuming the facilities would still be in existence." He did not add that the political decision to rush the existing weapons into service had skewed the production schedule drastically. They were truly rolling the dice After these missions, Iran would not have a nuclear deterrent force available for some time, if ever. Even if the Americans and Israelis were out of the picture, they would still be endangered by potentially hostile nuclear-armed neighbors: India, Russia, China, perhaps even Pakistan. All of those states possessed hard-core Islamist minorities, and those governments would quickly become very nervous about Iran. That was not a desirable state of affairs at all. A regional nuclear war was a strong possibility, Fazeed now realized, and that was a war Iran would lose.

It was clear, though, that the civilians weren't thinking about that. Khamenei was stroking his beard again. "It is written in the Holy Qu'ran, 'Fight and kill the disbelievers wherever you find them, take them captive, harass them, lie in wait and ambush them using every stratagem of war.' From the ninth Sura."

Fazeed was not going to get into a theological argument with his nation's Supreme Leader, but he was becoming increasingly nervous. Did these men really have so little understanding of what they were going to do? Of the hundreds of millions who would perish? "Imam, we of course defer to your wisdom in these matters. But we—I—would be derelict in my duty to the state and the people if I did not point out the obvious. If something should go wrong with PERSIAN METEOR, the Americans would almost certainly make war upon us."

"They do not have the nerve," Ahmedinejad said. "They are pulling out of Iraq. They will soon withdraw from Afghanistan.

They do not have the stomach to fight us. Their president certainly does not."

"I am not suggesting they would invade our country," Fazeed said, fearful that he was getting himself in too deep, but the memory of his father drove him onward. "They would not have to. I have complete faith in Admiral Ralouf's brave sailors and General Suleimani's equally brave soldiers who are going to launch the weapons, but things could go wrong through no fault of our own. The Americans are not complete idiots. We should not underestimate them, as Saddam and Osama did." This brought stares from the civilians, not friendly ones at that. "Gentlemen, I merely urge caution. We should not take this step unless we are assured of the highest probability of success, and that it is the right thing to do for our people."

"The people want to see the caliphate restored," Khamenei said. "They want to destroy the infidels, and spread the faith throughout the world. That is our destiny."

Fazeed wondered about that. The average Iranian probably wanted the same thing the average Afghan or Iraqi did, or for that matter the average American or Israeli: to live a life of peace so he could raise his children and make a living.

Fazeed glanced at the wall, but the map of America was no longer there. That gave him another thought: Did these men have any idea of what would happen to the world if the Americans were suddenly gone? Did they have any concept of the impact on the world economy? If the Israelis no longer had the Americans to hold them back, what would they do? SWORD OF PERSIA might succeed, or might not. If it didn't, tens of millions of Iranians would die horrible deaths. It was likely, in fact, that at least a few Israeli missiles would survive the strike and be launched at Iran. Israel had some submarines, too, armed with cruise missiles.

But Israel was a very small country, and Iran very large. Two or three nuclear detonations in Israel would devastate their country. One or two in Iran would be very serious, of course, but the nation would survive, until an American submarine showed up. Iran would be utterly defenseless against such an attack, which would complete the job the Israelis had begun.

Next to him, he sensed Ralouf's discomfort. He glanced at Suleimani, who looked nonplussed. No, he was with the civilians. Fazeed looked back at his president. Ahmedinejad's eyes were bright. "The time of the Twelfth Imam is upon us," he said. "Allah's will be done." Khamenei nodded his head.

Fazeed knew at that moment that his life would soon be forfeit. He would be incinerated by an American or Israeli nuclear warhead, or he would die before a firing squad. One way meant he would have followed his orders and helped cause the deaths of untold millions. But the other way, by doing something to stop these fanatics, that might mean that only a very few people would die. Perhaps only one.

CHAPTER SIXTEEN
AFGHANISTAN

THE VILLAGE, LIKE most of the others he'd seen on his tours, probably hadn't changed in decades, maybe even a century or two. Once again, Mark Hayes marveled at the differences between this country and Iraq. Over there, in what the troops called "The Sandbox", you could see signs of the twenty-first century in nearly every village: motor vehicles, satellite dishes, cell phones, laptop computers. When you visited an Iraqi tribal chieftain, he might be in traditional robes but would be wearing a digital Swiss watch, take a call on his cell phone, have an assistant pecking away at a laptop. Even there, though, conditions were sometimes beyond belief for the Americans. Mark remembered the overpowering stench of Fallujah, where sewage ran through the streets and high-rise buildings had "shit pits", open chutes that emptied into holes.

Like virtually every Afghan chieftain he'd ever met, the man sitting on the mat across from Mark had none of those modern accoutrements. He had the traditional clothes, which here meant the low cloth cap, the shirt and jacket, the worn pants and boots. He wore a scruffy beard, dyed red to signify his leadership role, and he might've bathed a week or so earlier. The mud-walled compound he and his extended family lived in had no running water or electricity. Mark and two of his officers were sharing tea with the man and his only son, who was his nominal second in command. For Mark, it was a courtesy call to discuss the latest news, go over the progress of the construction projects in the village—a road, a school, and a medical clinic, as usual at the top of the list for American and UN aid for any Afghan community.

This particular village was at the opposite end of his command area from the village he and Solum's company had been through a week earlier, but word had spread. Once again, Mark was impressed by how quickly these people received news from some distance away, without the aid of telephones or radios. It was an ability that American intelligence operatives were finally figuring out how to use to their advantage.

Mark had picked up a fair amount of Pashto during his tours and was able to hold a decent conversation with the chief, who reciprocated by using some English. As always, though, Mark brought an interpreter along, an Afghan National Army lieutenant who was detached to the base. The 'terp was young, eager and new; Mark had been forced to arrest his predecessor when they discovered he'd been leaking intel to the Taliban. That guy was now in the Kabul prison, where he was awaiting a trial that might be a long time coming, if it ever came. The Afghan criminal justice system was rough around the edges, compared to its U.S. counterpart. Mark remembered discussing it with some civilians back home, after his first tour downrange. One of the civvies, studying for his master's at Georgetown, had remarked on how primitive the Afghans were. Mark replied that they had a lot fewer people in prison than America did, even considering the population difference, so maybe they were on to something.

Dealing with the Afghans was an acquired taste. Americans tended to be straightforward, getting to the point quickly, but the Afghans could spend an hour just discussing the weather. The lying was something that had taken Mark a long time to get used to. Lying is part of their culture, he was told on his first deployment, and all these years later there hadn't been much change. But this malik was more progressive than most of his peers, and Mark thought they had finally reached an understanding. Today they opened with the usual pleasantries and small talk before getting down to business. Over the weeks Mark had developed a healthy respect for the chief, who seemed to be genuinely concerned for his village and tribe. In addition to an eighteen-year-old son, he had four daughters and was determined to see them get an education. Six months earlier, two of his nieces had been scarred for life when two Taliban on motorcycles had run them down on their way to school, throwing acid in their faces. One of the first patrols Mark led after taking over the firebase tracked the two men down and dealt with them and their buddies personally. That particular firefight was one of the most one-sided, and satisfying, of Mark's career.

"Tell me, Colonel," the chief said through the interpreter, "what news do you have of the medical clinic?"

"Good news, sir," Mark said, smiling. "The UN doctors will be returning in two weeks' time. First a team will come to fix up the clinic building, then the doctors and their nurses. Your people will have the best medical care once again." Mark had been working hard the past several weeks to cut through the red tape and get the clinic back. Two years earlier, Taliban attacks forced the UN to pull out of the area. Now, Mark had convinced them he could provide them with security.

The chief nodded, but his son was not pleased. He barked something at the 'terp, who started to translate, then stopped. "What did he say, Lieutenant?"

The young Afghan swallowed. "He asks, Colonel, if the UN doctors will be treating the women of the village and the surrounding area."

"Of course," Mark said. He looked back at the chief's son, and said in Pashto, "Women and men."

What was this kid's name, Dawud? He had a ratty, teenager's beard and his father's gray eyes, but none of their wisdom and maturity. This one's eyes blazed with the fury of the true believer. He fired back at Mark in rapid Pashto, too quick for Mark to pick up completely, but he did catch something he thought translated as "men command". "Lieutenant?"

"He quotes from the Holy Quran, Colonel. The fourth Sura, which begins, 'Men are in charge of women.'"

"Ask him if the Holy Quran specifically forbids women from receiving medical treatment." Mark knew the answer to that one already. There was nothing in the Muslim holy book that said a woman could not see a doctor, yet on his first deployment Mark had witnessed a horrifying scene, when a group of Afghan villagers who had been mortared by the Taliban allowed their wounded daughters to die while bringing the boys to the Americans for treatment. Sometimes, in his nightmares, Mark still saw the eyes of the eight-year-old girl who had bled out in his arms after he rushed into the family's hut to save her.

The chief answered before the translator could finish. "The chief asks that we excuse his son," the lieutenant said. The old man's words came more harshly this time. "He is still a boy in many respects."

Mark knew it would not be a good idea to get into an argument with the kid. Instead, he nodded his head at the chief. "I understand completely," he said. "The young men in my country often speak before they think." The chief nodded and smiled at the translation.

Would the doctors really get to treat everybody in the village? Mark had heard about problems in other districts. Trying to educate these people in basic hygiene and nutrition ranged from relatively easy to almost impossible, depending on where they were in the country and how much influence the Taliban still had. Afghan doctors, trained by American and European aid workers and physicians, sometimes disappeared, only to be found days later, in pieces. All for trying to help heal the sick, prevent disease. It was tragic; no, that wasn't the right word. It was barbaric. Growing up in placid, modern Wisconsin, with a clean and efficient clinic in almost every town, Mark would never have believed such things happened in the world.

He knew better now.

"How'd it go, suh?" Sergeant Major Elkins asked when Mark led the ANA lieutenant back out to the waiting vehicles. Elkins had played football at Mississippi State twenty years ago and was still built like the All-SEC linebacker he'd once been. A blown knee ended his NFL career after two years, but it somehow hadn't kept him out of the Army. The enlisted men thought he was the best sergeant in the Army and it hadn't taken Mark long to conclude that they might very well be right.

"Okay. Is Doc back yet?" Staff Sergeant King, one of the company medics, was making the rounds of the village, treating what he could. He always had patients, and lately they'd become more eager to see him. Mark took that for a good sign. Whatever the chief's son had going on, and Mark suspected it had something to do with Taliban cells in the area, it wasn't cutting much ice with the locals.

"Here he comes now, suh."

With two female specialists in tow, King snapped off a quick salute to Mark. "All set, Colonel."

"Any problems?"

"Nothing out of the ordinary. That woman I told you about, the one ready to deliver? Well, she did. We got here just in time."

That explained the happy glow on the faces of the lady specs. "A boy, sir," one of them said, Quarters, he thought he remembered the name. "Six pounds, two ounces."

Mark cracked a smile. "A keeper."

"Yessir," the other woman said. "The umbilical cord was wrapped around his throat. Might not've made it if we hadn't been there."

"Good work," Mark said. "Okay, people, let's mount up."

"Oh, by the way, suh," Elkins said, "got some commo from the base. Word came down from Division. Congratulations, suh, you are now a full bird colonel." The sergeant snapped an order to the other soldiers. "Ten-SHUN!" The fifteen troopers fired off parade-ground salutes in perfect unison.

Mark smiled as he returned the salutes. He was pleased and a bit surprised at the promotion, and he suspected the General might've had something to do with that, crossing one more thing off his list as he was preparing to turn command over to his successor and head back home to begin his new duties as head of the CIA. Mark made a mental note to give him a call when they got back to the base. "Okay, people, let's mount up and go home. I'm sure my paperwork load has just gone up."

Mark's Humvee driver had just started the engine when a man came running down the street toward them, waving his arms and yelling. "Cut the engine," Mark ordered as he dismounted. The ANA officer hustled out onto the dirt street to join him.

The Afghan looked a lot like the chief, and Mark rapidly tried to place him. Wasn't he the chief's younger brother? The man was frantic, jabbering at him, his eyes wide with fear. Mark held up his hands, saying "Slow down!" in Pashto.

With an effort, the man tried to catch his breath. He was panting, and not just from running down the street. Something was very wrong. Mark quickly waved to the rest of the troops. "Dismount! Form a perimeter!" Elkins appeared beside him, his M-4 at the ready, scanning the rooftops.

The 'terp calmed the man down and asked him to tell them what was going on. His eyes still fearful, the man rattled off several words.

"He says that they have taken his son."

Mark glanced at the interpreter. "Who took him? How did it happen?"

More Pashto was exchanged between the two Afghans. "His son is eight years old. He was out tending the goats. He went off to catch a goat that had strayed away. Three men came in a pickup truck and took him."

Oh, shit, Mark thought. "How does he know this?"

"The boy's older sister was there and saw it. She ran back to tell their father."

"When did it happen?"

The man jabbered back at the interpreter. "Not too long ago. Maybe twenty minutes."

Mark turned to Elkins. "Sergeant, take some people and a

couple vehicles, take this man out to where it happened. See if you can find anything."

"Yessuh." Elkins quickly picked a squad and they roared off, the ANA lieutenant and the villager with Elkins in the lead Humvee.

Mark looked at King and his assistants. "How good is your Pashto?"

"Not bad, sir. Getting better."

"Okay, come with me. We're going to find someone and have a little chat. Somebody here knows what went down and I think I know who it is."

They found Dawud at the wheel of a battered Toyota pickup, cursing at the engine as it failed to turn over. The chief had one of the few vehicles in the village, but apparently his son hadn't been keen on keeping it serviced. Mark came up from behind on the driver's side, his M9 pistol at the ready. He saw the young man's eyes flick to the side mirror and go wide.

"Get out! Hands where I can see them!" Mark shouted it in English, but he knew Dawud would get the meaning. Just to make sure, King was covering the kid with his rifle through the passenger window. Mark knew he was taking a chance by treating the son of a chief this roughly, but he didn't have time to screw around.

Dawud stepped down out of the cab, hands in the air. He did his best to look defiant, but Mark could see his hands trembling. The chief broke through the cordon of troopers and confronted his son, berating him in rapid-fire Pashto. Mark could follow some of it, and it wasn't pretty. No doubt the chief had gotten the word at the same time they had.

The chief finished his tirade and waited for his son to say something, but Dawud was silent. Mark ordered one of his men to frisk the kid. "He's clean, Colonel." Holstering his side-arm, Mark approached him.

"Do you know what happened to the boy?" Mark asked in Pashto.

Dawud's eyes flicked away, then back to Mark's. "No."

"You are lying."

"Tell the colonel what you know!" the chief yelled. "They took your cousin!"

Dawud looked away. Mark knew they would have to get something out of this kid quickly if they had any chance to save the boy, but his options were limited. He knew what he would like to do; what he was allowed to do would be something very different, and not as effective.

"In the name of the Prophet! Tell the truth!" the chief shouted. There were gasps from some of the villagers who had gathered to watch. To invoke the name of Muhammad was most serious, and the devout Muslim was required to respond.

Dawud swallowed. "I....I did not know they were going to take Atash," he said, voice trembling.

"Where did they take him?" Mark demanded.

"I am not sure...."

"Where do they go?" the chief said. "Where do they meet?"

"I think...I think they use a farmhouse, about five kilometers to the south," Dawud said. He looked back and forth between his father and Mark, his eyes pleading. "I am not one of them! I swear it! They have tried to get me to join them, but I—"

"That is for you and your father to discuss later," Mark said. "Is this farm on the main road?"

"Five kilometers south, then one to the west."

"I know the place, Colonel," King said. "We were there a month ago, inoculating the family. There'd been some talk that

174

the two older sons had joined the insurgents, but the family clammed up."

"Mount 'em up, Doc," Mark ordered. King was the highest-ranking noncom he had after Elkins on this mission. To the chief, he said, "We will leave you now, sir. We will try to rescue your nephew."

"May God be with you," the chief said, his eyes a mixture of anger and sadness.

Elkins and his men had gotten a heads-up from Mark over the radio and were five minutes ahead. Mark saw them a couple klicks down the road, through clouds of dust. Normally they would be going a lot more slowly, on the lookout for IEDs, but not this time. It was a gamble, but Mark knew this road had been cleared of bombs just the day before and he doubted—prayed—the Tals hadn't had time to set any new ones, especially since they'd snatched the kid only a short time ago.

Elkins and his trailing vehicle came to the side road and took the turn with rocks flying. Mark radioed permission for the sergeant major to engage upon arrival at the target. Bouncing along behind them, Mark's vehicles were at maximum safe speed, but he figured they'd still be on target about two minutes behind Elkins. By then it could be all over, Mark thought grimly. He knew Elkins had four kids back home. The sergeant major wouldn't be looking to negotiate anything on this mission.

What the hell was the matter with these people? The thought had crossed Mark's mind so many times during his deployments that it had become second nature to him. For every act of kindness and decency he saw from the Afghans, and there were many, there seemed to be one of cowardice, brutality, even what some would call evil. Were they really any different than anyone else, though? Adults tortured and murdered children everywhere. But over here, it seemed to be part and parcel of what the enemy was doing. Mark had dealt with more than one suicide bombing clean-up detail back in Iraq, and the sights of dismembered children were ones he'd never forget. Mark quickly learned that one of the best ways to deal with the horror was to find the perps and send them on the way to face God's judgment, or whatever the hell Muslims had to face from Allah.

The radio crackled as Elkins' vehicles pulled up to the perimeter of the farmhouse and he deployed his squad. Shots rang out, the distinctive flat crack of the AK-47, answered immediately by the deeper sound of the M-4. As Mark's two Humvees approached, he saw Elkins crouched behind one of his vehicles, waving them around the perimeter. Like they'd done many times before, Mark's two vehicles split off, one heading to the left, Mark's driver to the right, flanking the single-story, mud-brick farmhouse. Goats and chickens scattered.

There was a tall poplar tree behind the farmhouse. "Get us around back!" Mark yelled. Bullets ricocheted off the armored sides of the vehicle. From the top turret, a corporal returned fire with the fifty-cal, raking the side of the house. They were only about thirty meters from the side of the building. The driver swung the Humvee around and the tree came into view. A man was throwing a rope over one of the large branches, with two other men standing nearby, holding AKs. One had a hand clamped on the back of the neck of a small, terrified boy.

"Stop!" Mark yelled, and the driver braked hard, swinging the wheel around so that the Humvee faced the tree. Mark estimated the distance at about fifty meters. "Hold your fire, Wilson!" Mark shouted to the corporal manning the fifty.

"Goddamn motherfuckers gonna lynch that kid!" Wilson screamed.

"Hold fire!" Mark knew that a burst from Wilson's fifty would take out the boy. His training and experience carried him now, calming his breathing, his actions coming almost without conscious thought, as they had so many times in his career, in so many firefights that he'd lost count long ago. He jumped out of the vehicle and knelt down on his right knee, brought his weapon up, sighted on the insurgent to the left and pulled the trigger.

Time seemed to slow down. His shot caught the gunman square in the chest, knocking him backward as a puff of red sprayed out. The Humvee driver on the other side of the vehicle squeeze off a round, and the insurgent with the rope suddenly lost the top of his head. Mark was bringing his carbine around to sight on the remaining gunman when his eyes registered the flash from the AK's barrel and something next to his head exploded. His world went white, and then very dark.

CHAPTER SEVENTEEN

WISCONSIN

J IM OPENED UP his personal email when he got back from lunch and the inbox had its usual collection: updates from *Men's Health* and *Black Belt* magazine, a couple of discussion alerts from one of his favorite sites, Art of Manliness. An old high school classmate was inviting him to be her friend on Facebook. Assorted junk. Nothing yet today from Gina.

Jim sat back in his chair with a little sigh and looked out the window. It was Friday and plenty of people in the office already had the weekend jitters. Some of them were bailing out early, but he'd decided to stick around till the end of the day. He only had so much leave time to use, after all, and taking an hour here and another hour there pretty soon added up to a day or so of vacation he couldn't take later. Not that he had much use for his vacation time anyway. In the past year, he'd taken two weeks off, one at a time. For one of them, he just stayed home, put in some extra training at the dojo, relaxed a little bit, caught up on his reading. The other was more of the same, except that he allowed himself to go visit Mickey in Milwaukee for a couple days.

But there was something to be said for taking a break. During his last week off he'd been puttering around in the back yard and decided to turn one part of it into a Japanese garden. He knew nothing at all about gardening but he got himself a couple books, talked to a few people and got after it. Now he made a point of getting out there every day or so, weeding and tending the plants, tinkering with the stone path and the water feature he'd installed. It was soothing, and he found it helped him clear his mind. He was a little worried about how the garden would last through the winter, but he would just have to prepare it and hope for the best.

Well, he had about a week built up again, and he thought now about taking a few days and maybe driving up north. He seemed to recall that Bayfield had a festival of some sort, and Gina was only a few miles away in Ashland.

He was surprised and not a little concerned by how much he missed her. The tournament was six days ago, and after all, he'd only spent a few hours with her. After the hot tub, one thing led to another and they hadn't gotten out of her room until about eight o'clock to get a late dinner at a nice little bistro down the road called Adventures. Jim remembered the name with a laugh. Yes, the weekend had certainly provided a few of those.

He stood up and walked over to the window. His second-story office overlooked a strip mall, and beyond that, the town ended and the countryside began. Like so much of Wisconsin, with rolling farm fields and wooded hills, it beckoned him with a timeless temptation of adventure. Some of his fondest memories from childhood were of the visits he made to his Uncle Chuck's farm near Palmyra, where he and his brother and cousins would hike through the woods to the swimming hole, fish the trout streams, and explore the caves on the hillsides.

He should get out and do some hiking, maybe head over to Kettle Moraine State Park. It wasn't much fun going alone, and he was pretty sure Annie wouldn't want to go with him anymore. In fact, he knew now he wouldn't want her to go. It was time to bring down the curtain on that one. He hadn't returned her call from the other night, but that would have to be done. Tonight.

Down on the street, a woman rode past on a bicycle, heading into town. He recognized the coppery-red hair. It was Jessie, the rural mail carrier, she of the trim figure and lustrous complexion. He saw her frequently at the gym, lifting weights, running on the treadmill. Mid-thirties, with a couple of kids, and she was married. That was too bad…

Women. Sometimes Jim felt they were his only weakness, although objectively he knew that wasn't true. He had worked hard the past six years to get his life under control, and he was almost there, although he wasn't too terribly sure exactly where "there" was. But he was close, he could feel it. There were all the workouts, the training, his bookcase groaning with biographies and novels about men and women who'd made a difference. He had built himself a life of discipline, and always tried to conduct himself as a man of honor and integrity. It was not the easiest path to take in life, that was for sure. It was hard, and sometimes he felt lonely.

At first it was a matter of survival. The only way he could deal with Suzy's murder was to train, train as hard as he could, so he'd be ready the next time. But the martial arts did more than just get him fit and ready; his training and studies opened up an enormous new vista to him, impacting his life in every way. It was more than just learning how to fight, so very much more. It was a philosophy, a way of life, and it led him to delve even deeper into the concept, the ethos, of the warrior. What did it mean to be one? What made those men, and those women, stand apart from the herd? He didn't have all the answers, but what he'd found out so far was that it took discipline, integrity, and a determination to live a life of honor. He was on a journey, and he found himself wanting to share that with someone.

It was hard, because there were so many temptations to relax, loosen up, take it easy. Especially from women. They were everywhere, on the TV, on the internet, and every now and then he slipped, clicking the TV remote to catch a skin flick on one of the premium channels, or letting his fingertips type out the Web address of a porn site. He never watched those movies all the way through, never paid a dime for online porn, but now and then he would weaken and sneak a peek or two. Later he would curse himself for his weakness, vow never to do it again, and that would hold for a month or two, sometimes more. He was getting better on that score, going on six months now since he'd last fallen off that wagon. There was no avoiding the women he encountered in real life, though. They were out there, and more often than not they were sending signals.

It wasn't their fault, of course; the signals that came in loud and clear nowadays were ones he'd never read when he was married to Suzy. There were no more temptations out there now then there had been before, but the difference was that now he was paying attention. That had gotten him into trouble once or twice, when he got involved with women he shouldn't have. He'd left his job in Milwaukee for this one in Cedar Lake when one brief relationship with a co-worker turned sour very quickly, but he should've seen that one coming. If she'd really been separated from her husband, like she said, why was she still wearing her wedding ring? An unsettling phone call from the husband one day set him straight on that score.

He'd been here nearly five years now. Met Annie shortly after arriving, but hadn't started dating her till just last year. In the meantime there were a few others, none serious. Jim never considered himself to be any kind of swordsman, or playa, or whatever they called those types of guys these days. For one thing, he now scrupulously avoided entanglements with any of the women he worked with. There were plenty of other fish in the sea.

Now, there was Gina. Of the women in his life the past six years, she had rapidly climbed to the top of the charts. Physically, she was breathtakingly toned and comfortable in her body, her movements fluid and confident. That had to be from her martial arts training, and Jim presumed, with his relatively limited experience, that would be pretty common among martial artists and athletes. Certainly Annie, a college volleyball star who had stayed in great shape, had the same qualities, although her aggressiveness and attitude set her apart, and not necessarily in a good way. Gina was different. The physical side of their evening together had been more than satisfying, but there was an emotional connection too, something he'd not had with any other woman, except Suzy. While that thrilled him, it was also a bit scary. Could he be falling in love with this woman, after so little time together? Was that possible?

That wouldn't necessarily be a bad thing, come to think about it. Gina had a lot going for her. She had the looks, of course, but a lot more beyond that. Jim was able to find out quite a bit about her, and there wasn't much there not to like. Married at twenty-one to a U.S. Air Force officer stationed near her home in Ravenna, Italy, she emigrated to the States and lived the life of a military wife for the next fifteen years, raising twin boys while her husband flew fighter jets. He survived combat tours in Desert Storm and the Balkans, only to go down in a training accident in 2004, leaving her a widow at thirty-nine. She raised her boys alone through their difficult teenage years and it wasn't easy, but they both graduated high school with honors and went on to college.

"How did you ever wind up in Ashland, Wisconsin, of all places?" Jim had asked her over dinner.

"That was my husband's hometown," she said. "He was going to retire from the Air Force in another year or two, after his tour was over." Lieutenant Colonel Larry Curtis, serving as a training supervisor for Air National Guard bases in Wisconsin and Minnesota, went down over Lake Superior on a cold winter day when his F-16's engine flamed out and his ejection seat malfunctioned. Gina had shed a tear as she told the story, and Jim reached across the table, covering her hand with his.

"I know what it's like to lose someone you love," he said gently, and then he told her about Suzy.

His cell phone chirped, and he saw Gina's face on the screen. Things were looking up. "I was just thinking about you," he said.

Her laugh was like feathers touching his skin. "I'll bet. I know I've been thinking about you."

"Obviously." This was the third time they'd talked on the phone since Sunday morning. The call the other night had lasted an hour.

"How's your day going?" she asked.

"Pretty good. It's Friday afternoon, for one thing. What're you doing this weekend?"

"It so happens I'm going to Marshfield for a conference tomorrow," she said. Gina was a nurse practitioner with a clinic in Ashland, part of a network that was headquartered in Marshfield, in the center of the state.

"Is that right?"

"Yes, and it adjourns at four o'clock."

"I've never been to Marshfield. Anything to do there on a Saturday night?"

There was that laugh again, and he felt a shiver. "I know a place or two."

Jim hesitated. Yes, he wanted to see her again, wanted that badly, but he knew that if he did, he might very well fall head over heels for this woman. His head wasn't sure about that, but his heart seemed to be pulling him along.

What the hell. "Tell you what. Find a place where a guy can treat a girl to a romantic dinner, and I'll—"

The phone beeped. He pulled it away and glanced at the screen. INCOMING CALL flashed with another beep, and the next words almost knocked him out of his chair: US ARMY 445IR 3BN.

Wasn't that Mark's unit? "Gina, sorry, but I just got a beep, might be an emergency. I'll call you right back."

"Okay, Jim."

He touched the screen. "Hello?"

The voice sounded a bit hollow, but not that far away. "Is this James Hayes?"

"Yes, it is." Jim held his breath.

"Hold one, please, for the colonel." Then, another voice, and even though Jim hadn't heard it in nearly a year, he knew it well, and he started breathing again. "Jim? Are you there?"

"Mark! Are you all right?"

"Well, I took a round today, but I'm okay."

Jim straightened up even more in his chair. Lori passed

by his open door and glanced in with a frown, but Jim barely noticed her. "What do you mean? Are you hurt?"

"Just a pretty bad headache. I wanted to call you before you read about it in the paper. We have a reporter from *USA Today* embedded with the battalion."

Three minutes later, Jim sank back in his chair. "So the bullet hit your helmet?"

"Yeah, well, glanced off the side, you might say. Still packed a punch. Good old Army-issue Kevlar comes through again."

"Well, I'm glad to hear you're okay."

There was silence for a few seconds. Jim could hear the hiss on the line. "You there, Jim?"

"Yeah. I'm here, Mark."

He heard something that sounded like a cough, then, "Listen, I can't stay on the line very long, but, ah....God, this headache's a bitch."

"You should probably get some rest. What time is it there, nine, ten o'clock?"

"It's, uh...just after eleven. Jim, I've been thinking about Dad. Thinking about a lot of things, really. I'll shoot you an email, okay?"

"Yeah, sure, Mark. But you get some rest." Then, he added, "When you get home, we can get together, catch up."

"Sure, okay. Say hello to Mickey from her long-lost uncle."

"Sure will." The line went dead.

Jim put his phone on his desk, then got up and walked over to his window. He looked westward, following the town's main street as it changed into County Road T and meandered off to the west through the farmlands. It was so placid, far removed from the mountains of Afghanistan. Jim wondered for the umpteenth time how he would've held up over there. He suspected he might've had a hard time, certainly harder than Mark, who always seemed to take physical challenges in stride, from high school football to mountain combat.

Yeah, it was always easy for Mark. It always seemed that way, anyway; Mark had never told him anything different. But really now, had Jim ever bothered to really reach out to his little brother? Maybe it was time to change that, set things right.

He called Gina back, told her about Mark, then said, "About tomorrow night..."

"Yes?"

He paused. "Listen, I want to see you, very much. But, well...maybe we shouldn't take things too quickly." Damn, why did he say that? Now she'd think he was backing off.

She was quiet for a second. There was a bit of a sigh, then, "Jim, you should know something. About last weekend, well, I don't normally do that with a guy I just met. In fact, I'd never done it before. First date, I mean." Was there a hopeful tone in her voice?

"I'm flattered," he said. "And, well, it's like that for me, too." He had to laugh. "Man, I feel like I'm in high school again."

She laughed with him. "Well, we're all grown-up now, so we can do grown-up things. Can you come to Marshfield? It can just be dinner, if you want."

"Tell you what. I'll bring my toothbrush anyway, just in case."

CHAPTER EIGHTEEN

WASHINGTON, D.C.

WAITING TO SEE the President of the United States was never relaxing, although sitting in the Roosevelt Room was better than cooling one's heels anywhere else outside the Oval Office. Denise Allenson was making her first visit to the building, and trying to hide her nervousness. Things were moving rapidly. This morning, she had come to work at Langley looking forward to another day of preparing for her next overseas assignment, then a relaxing weekend. That had changed fifteen minutes after she sat down at her desk in the section of CIA Headquarters devoted to the National Clandestine Service. Starting her day with a summons to the office of Director-NCS was something that had never happened to her, and the whirl of activity in the next several hours had left her scrambling to catch up, feeling just a bit flustered.

Denise wasn't used to being flustered. From that day on the Vanderbilt campus when she'd taken a dare by a sorority sister to hand her resume to the CIA recruiter at the job fair, things had fallen into place for her. She hadn't exactly started out to be an intelligence operative, but she found it be a lot more exciting than following in her parents' footsteps and becoming an accountant. Dad had been disappointed when his daughter told him she wouldn't be joining the family firm, but now he got a rush when he was asked at cocktail parties about his little girl's occupation. He was only allowed to say she worked for the Federal government, but that was enough, since he usually added, "I can't tell you any more than that," with a raised eyebrow.

There was some luck involved, of course, but hard work and dedication had brought her to this room. In her fifteen years in CIA, her work had taken her all over the world, and she never dreamed that her most recent posting, in Djibouti, would amount to much. But she was one of the few available operatives who had recent experience in the Horn of Africa. Besides, the chief of station down there had specifically asked for her. She knew that had to be due to the quality of work she'd done at that posting, and not because Tom Simons thought she had great legs, although she suspected he did. He'd been one of the few men she'd worked with who hadn't actually said so.

The two men in the Roosevelt Room with her were Director-NCS and the Director of Central Intelligence himself, whom she had met for the first time just a few hours ago. DCI was a short, courtly gentleman who reminded her of her late grandfather, a history professor at Vandy. Just a few days ago, the Senate had voted unanimously to confirm the Director as the new Secretary of Defense. That meant this operation would be one of his last as DCI. She wasn't comforted by the thought that she might have a hand in shaping his legacy.

A man whom Denise recognized as the president's chief of staff stepped into the room. "Director, the president will see you and your people now." Denise stood and gave her two-button jacket one last quick adjustment, thanking her stars once again that she hadn't decided to dress more casually.

They entered the Oval Office through the hallway door. She'd seen it many times on television, but actually being there was something quite different, and Denise tried to keep her eyes from wandering. She took in the lush, wheat-colored carpeting, dominated by the presidential seal just to the right of the furnishings, two plush couches facing a coffee table. To the left of these, between the couches and the fireplace, were two leather-covered chairs. Woven somewhere in this carpet, she knew, were quotes from four presidents and also from Martin Luther King, Jr. She looked to the right, toward the desk and the windows behind it.

"Mr. President, the DCI and his party," the chief of staff said, and the man standing at the window turned toward them.

"Hello, Leon," the president said, walking out from behind the desk. Denise thought he was taller than he looked on TV, and grayer, but he had a bit of a smile as he extended his hand to DCI, then to DNCS, both of whom were no strangers to this room.

"Mr. President," DCI said with a touch of formality, "may I present Denise Allenson, one of our top NCS people."

His handshake was firm, and she saw a glint in the dark brown eyes. "A pleasure, Ms. Allenson." He gestured toward the sitting area. "Please, take a seat."

The president sat in the chair on the right, the chief of staff on the left. DCI was in the right-hand couch, with DNCS and Denise taking the left. DCI got right to the point. "Mr. President, thank you for taking the time to fit this into your schedule. As I mentioned in my phone call yesterday, we have actionable intel about a high-value al-Qaida target in Somalia." DNCS withdrew a red-bordered file from his briefcase and handed it to the chief of staff, who passed it unopened to the president. He flipped through the first few pages, nodding slightly. Denise wondered why he would give it such short shrift, but then it occurred to her that he'd probably seen it already.

"He wants to defect?" the president asked.

"That's correct, sir," DCI said. "This was confirmed by our C-of-S in Djibouti, who met with the subject two nights ago in Mogadishu."

The president turned to DNCS. "How about that, John? Do you think he's serious?"

"Our man is convinced, Mr. President. Tom Simons has a strong record. He's not easily fooled. If he thinks it's legitimate, I believe him."

The chief of staff, flipping through the file, spoke for the first time since he'd introduced the visitors. "I see the target wants the standard deal. What's the hang-up?"

DCI pursed his lips and sighed. Evidently this part had not been revealed to the White House before now. "He wants to turn himself over to a private American citizen, a man he attended college with in Wisconsin."

"Are you serious?" the chief of staff asked, with more than a little skepticism.

"I am," DCI said. "He said this man is the only American he ever met who was an honorable person, the only one he'll trust to bring him out."

DNCS pulled out another file, more slender and with no red border, and handed it to the chief of staff. This time he flipped it open and glanced at the single page inside before passing it to the president.

"Have we been in touch with him?" the president asked.

"Not yet, sir," DCI said. "I thought it prudent to proceed

with a contact only after your approval of this action. It's not every day that we involve civilians in one of our operations."

"I see he was never in the service," the president said, scanning the document again. "Applied twice for the reserves, turned down both times. Why was that?"

"Medical reasons," DNCS said. "A college athletic injury."

"So I can't recall him to active duty," the president said. "But his brother is serving, is that right?"

"Yes, sir, a West Point man, just promoted to colonel," DCI said. "Commands a base in Afghanistan. Just before that he was on the ISAF staff."

The president handed the file back to his chief of staff. "I may have met him when the ISAF people were here a few months ago."

Denise knew that the International Security Assistance Force was led by the Army general who would be her new boss in a few more weeks. If this Wisconsin civilian's brother had been on that particular general's staff, he must be a pretty big wheel himself. What kind of man would his brother be? Denise would soon be finding out first-hand, and she knew her evaluation of him would go a long way toward determining whether this mission would succeed. If they got over there and he went all to pieces, it could be disastrous. The Horn was not the place to have a disaster.

"What's your plan with this, Leon?"

DCI straightened his tie. "With your approval, Mr. President, we will contact Mr. Hayes this weekend and bring him to Langley for briefing and training. Simons is scheduled to meet with the target next Thursday, the twenty-eighth, to finalize the defection. If that goes according to plan, we would fly Mr. Hayes to Djibouti the next day. The principals would meet on Sunday the thirty-first, presumably in Mogadishu."

"What kind of backup will Simons have at that meet?" the chief of staff asked. "Are we looking at another *Blackhawk Down* if there's a problem?"

DNCS handled that one. "No, sir. Simons and his people will be supported by a Special Forces unit out of Camp Lemmonier. They'll be ready to extract the civilians if something goes wrong."

"Hopefully they won't be needed," the president said. He gave DCI a look that was all business. "I don't want my people to be hung out to dry, Leon. I'll have a word with SecDef about making sure we have enough assets available to get them out if it comes to that."

Denise saw DCI relax, just a bit. "Thank you, Mr. President."

The chief of staff had been looking at the Hayes file. "This fellow studies martial arts. I hope he doesn't get cocky over there and think he's Chuck Norris."

The president offered a slight smile. "I don't know, Bill. Sometimes I think it might be a good idea to draft Mr. Norris and send him over there."

"We'll keep him on a short leash, sir," DNCS said. "Ms. Allenson will be making the contact with him and supervising his briefing. She'll then accompany him to Djibouti and on the mission."

The President looked at her. "I understand you've had experience in that part of the world, Ms. Allenson."

"Yes, sir," she said, trying to keep her nerves under control. The president must have asked about her background when this meeting was scheduled. "I was stationed in Djibouti for a year until just recently, and before that in Sudan."

"Well, take good care of this fellow," the President said. He turned to the DCI. "Leon, mission approved. I'll have the Attorney General's office draw up the papers." The chief of staff made a note on his pad. "Have the Israelis been notified about the tip on Ashkelon?" the president asked.

"Yes, Mr. President," DCI said, "I spoke to Director Pardo personally yesterday morning. According to the source, Hamas plans to strike Ashkelon sometime tomorrow."

"Any ideas about what they're planning?"

"There are a few possibilities, from what Tamir told me when I talked to him again this morning. They could strike the marketplace or a shopping center, but we believe they intend to hit an elementary school, a graduation event."

"Good Christ," the chief of staff said. The President frowned, shaking his head. Denise could sense his frustration. Give the man credit, he'd tried a different approach with The Opposition, but it didn't seem to be working too terribly well, recent events in Egypt and elsewhere notwithstanding. The administration had started falling back on the only means that seemed to work with bullies and fanatics: force.

"Let Director Pardo know we will render whatever assistance he might require," the president said. He stood, with everyone else following suit. "Well, Ms. Allenson, good luck." He extended his hand. "Bring Mr. Hayes home safely."

"I will, sir."

In the limousine on the way back to Langley, they went over the preliminary plan that had been slapped together earlier in the day. As for what would happen when they got to the Horn, Allenson would have to be flexible. Simons would be in charge of the mission at that point.

They pulled into the underground garage. "I'll be taking my leave," DCI said as the limo glided to a stop. He reached across the passenger cabin. "Denise, good luck. I'm sure you'll do well."

She took the hand, shook it, and said, "Thank you, sir. I'll do my best."

From the curb, she watched the limo drive away. Next to her, DNCS glanced at his watch. "Why don't you call it a night, Denise?"

"That's all right, sir. I have some paperwork to clean up."

"No, you don't. Go home, pack, get a good night's sleep. We've already set up your flight to Chicago tomorrow. Be back here at eight, make the call to the subject, then we'll get you to Andrews. Your flight leaves at ten."

"Perhaps I should call him tonight, sir."

"No, we don't want him to get cold feet and leave town. Don't worry, we're keeping an eye on him. He'll be there tomorrow."

ISRAEL

THE DRONES HAD eyes on the two vehicles from the moment they left the safe house on the outskirts of Ashkelon. On the monitors at the Tel Aviv headquarters of *Sherut haBitachon haKlali*, the Israel Security Agency, technicians and officers watched the white Toyota minivans as they negotiated the Saturday midday traffic, heading east into the city of Ashkelon, some fifty kilometers to the south of the command center. More commonly known by its Hebrew acronym of Shabak, and still known in the West primarily as the Shin Bet, for its Hebrew initials, the agency employed hundreds of people to maintain security within the borders of Israel, utilizing the latest technology but relying more on the human element. Its operatives were among the most highly trained security personnel in the world, often drawing recruits from the nation's regular military services.

Working closely with the Institute for Intelligence and Special Operations, commonly known as Mossad, Shabak kept a close eye on potential threats already inside Israel, while Mossad worked outside the country, primarily in the Middle

East. Close cooperation was necessary, and although there were the usual inter-service rivalries, they rarely boiled over into problems that threatened the efficiency of the agencies' operations. Surrounded on three sides by enemies who had sworn to push Israel into the sea on its fourth side, the security services had little time or inclination to play political games. Those were left to the men and women of the Knesset, who did that job quite well.

One such joint operation was about to come to fruition, hopefully with success. Alerted two days ago by the American CIA, Mossad had swiftly notified Shabak of an imminent terrorist attack on Ashkelon. Potential targets were identified and security measures were stepped up. Surveillance on suspected Islamist operatives and sympathizers was increased as well. Within twenty-four hours Mossad had provided them with the intelligence they were hoping for: a known Hamas courier, seen three days earlier meeting with mid-level officers of the terror group in Gaza City, was spotted in a town on the coast south of Ashkelon. Other departments were working to answer the question of how the man had managed to get into Israel undetected. Shabak agents had the courier under surveillance when he was seen entering a known Hamas safe house. Within a few hours, several other Arab men had found their way to the house. Listening devices planted in the house overheard everything, although the terrorists' Iranian-supplied detection sensors had found nothing.

After consulting directly with the Prime Minister's office, the decision was made to allow the terrorists to launch their operation. It would be risky, as this would require Shabak to intercept the men well before they reached their target, but this was deemed less risky than raiding the safe house itself. They could not be sure lookouts in the neighborhood would not tip off the house about incoming security teams, giving the terrorists a chance to escape. Too often, Shabak agents and local police had invaded such a house, finding only weapons and the clutter of residents who had left hurriedly. This time, they would capture the terrorists en route to their target, while simultaneously striking their headquarters.

The list of potential terrorist targets had been reduced to one as the listening devices revealed their plan. Golda Meir Primary School would be holding a ceremony at one o'clock, honoring its sixth-graders for completion of a special summer program. Some one hundred fifty people would be in attendance, about a third of them children. There would be a security presence anyway, of course, but on this day it was reinforced by policemen in plain clothes to avoid tipping off the terrorists with an increase of uniformed officers.

The men and women of Shabak were used to dealing with terrorists, and there was no such thing as a permissible target for the Islamists to hit, but this one was especially troubling. Many of the agents had children of their own, and as with any Israeli parent, a terror strike against children was their worst nightmare. Their training helped force this fear back, but dialed up their diligence a few more degrees. This terror strike would be stopped at all costs.

All routes to the target were plotted out. It was anticipated that the terrorists would split their vehicles and approach from different directions. The location of the school helped the Shabak agents in this case, because it was located in a largely residential area and thus the vehicles would have only a few options. Plain clothes agents and unmarked cars were positioned carefully along all possible routes. Uniformed police and military security teams were kept in reserve, far enough away from the routes to avoid suspicion but close enough to allow for quick response times should they be called upon.

The decision had been made to stop the vans before they got within a kilometer of the school, so ambush locations had been set up in advance. To avoid as much collateral damage as possible, the two most-traveled routes were carefully blocked off by the early-morning arrival of utility and construction crews, causing traffic to be re-routed. Announcements had been made on the radio and internet about the detours, which were fairly common. Motorists with destinations not close to the school would choose detours that would take them well away from the ambush locations. Those innocent drivers who chose to come closer to the school would be politely but firmly kept out of the way.

As the vans made their way into the city, the Shabak teams kept in touch by cell phone and encrypted walkie-talkies, avoiding police-band radios in case the terrorists were monitoring those frequencies. Constant adjustments were made as the enemy vehicles were tracked, allowing security personnel to be moved away from areas that would not come into play and toward the ambush points. The net was being efficiently and quietly closed.

There had been some heated debate as to how the enemy vans would be stopped. Some within Shabak argued that a visible police presence and order to halt would prevent any tragedy if someone had mistakenly identified the vehicle and it turned out to have innocent civilians inside. Others said that would needlessly put uniformed officers at risk. A compromise of sorts was agreed upon, with the use of utility vehicles to form roadblocks. Civilian vehicles would slow to a stop, terrorists would not. That would make the decision easier for the men in the field.

David Eisner took a final swig of water from his bottle and checked the display on his smart phone again. He and his partner, Levi Rosenberg, were parked in their nondescript gray Toyota utility van along a side street, perpendicular to one of the likely terrorists' routes. The truck's doors displayed the logo of a landscaping service, but the vehicle itself was built with reinforced armor plating and bullet-proof glass. The logo, one of many used by Shabak, was a magnetized sign that could be moved from vehicle to vehicle depending on mission requirements.

The waiting was the worst part. Eisner and his team would likely be in combat very soon, and he was grateful this would not be his first time, nor would it be for any of his men. He trusted in his training, which had gotten him through many tough spots, going back to that first time, during his Army service. He and his buddy Ehud had been manning a checkpoint in Gaza when two Palestinian boys, both about fourteen, walked by. They were wearing long caftan tops, and on such a hot day that didn't seem right to Eisner. When one of the boys brought out an AK-47, Eisner and his partner were ready, dropping to a crouch and cutting the boys down with bursts from their own submachine guns. There had been more than a few firefights since then.

Eisner's phone chirped with a text message. "Red One is heading our way," he said to Rosenberg, using the code name for the lead Hamas van. "ETA, three minutes." He keyed the transmit button on his multi-purpose cell phone, activating the radio function. "Team Two, this is Team Leader. Take your positions. One target en route, ETA three." An answering series of clicks indicated the other four pairs of men in his unit were ready. On the opposite curb of their side street, the engine of a large dump truck roared to life.

On their vehicle's dashboard, a video screen flicked to life, displaying a drone's overhead view of the neighborhood. Five green dots indicated the positions of his team, two of them in vehicles, including their own van, the other three inside or next to buildings, providing a cross-fire pattern. Two sniper teams were set up on the rooftops of three-story apartment buildings, flanking the street leading to the school. A back-up pair was situated further down the block, ready to engage the terrorists if they somehow got through the roadblock that was about to appear in their path. The two pairs on foot were armed with anti-tank weapons as well as submachine guns.

Eisner exited the utility van and went around to the passenger side, opened the cargo door and began preparing the weapons while Rosenberg kept one eye on the screen. "Here they come," he said. "Five hundred meters." Eisner waved to the men in the dump truck, and the heavy vehicle trundled out into the street, coming to a stop at an angle with its nose pointing in the direction of the oncoming enemy van. In the large box of the dump truck was half a load of dirt and gravel. The two Shabak agents climbed down from the cab, the driver going to the back of the truck to unhitch the rear gate of the box, while his partner took a position near the front, crouching with his M-4 at the ready. Across the street, the nearest anti-tank team was in position. Their orders were to take the terrorists alive if possible, but Grossman wasn't going to risk any of his men in an extended firefight that was likely to end with the enemy committing suicide anyway.

The neighborhood was calm. Police in plain clothes had quietly evacuated the homes and shops for a three-block radius around them. Eisner was still on alert, though, in case a civilian had somehow been overlooked.

His phone chirped and a voice said, "This is Balad. I have

contact. Target confirmed, heading our way, just made the turn. Three hundred meters." Taking his weapon from Eisner, Rosenberg scrambled out of the passenger seat and crouched at the back end of the van. Eisner keyed his mike. "This is Team Leader. Engage on my contact." Clicks came quickly in response.

He saw the van now, moving at normal speed for this neighborhood. The driver started slowing the vehicle as he saw the dump truck up ahead. It would not fool them very long. He hoped the other units were closing in from the west, to choke off that potential escape route should the terrorists try to turn around and retreat.

The van slowed, but then swerved to the right, coming right at Eisner and Rosenberg. Eisner opened fire, stitching the front of the van with a five-round burst, shattering the windshield. The van lurched back to the left and slammed into the dump truck. The cargo door slid open and two men jumped out, both armed with AK-47s. The first had hardly taken a step before a sniper cut him down with a perfect shot to the chest, throwing the man back into his comrade.

Eisner shouted at them in Arabic to lay down their weapons and surrender, but to no one's surprise the answer was a hail of gunfire from the inside of the van, through the open side door and the windshield. Rosenberg put a three-shot burst into the second terrorist as the man took a step toward them. The Shabak agent at the front of the dump truck leaned over the hood and fired back through what was left of the windshield. Two more men leaped from the side door and were killed instantly by the ruthlessly efficient Shabak fire.

When the fourth man went down, no more shots came from within the van. Eisner shouted for his men to hold their fire, and they waited for a tense half-minute. There were five Arabs inside the van, and four of them died in the hail of gunfire that started with Grossman's first shots. One was wounded in the legs and right arm. Support units, who had closed on the scene with the first report of contact, now deployed to cordon off the neighborhood, search the van for weapons and explosives, and give medical attention to the surviving terrorist and Eisner's team. Rosenberg had been nicked in the left thigh by a stray round, but he'd be fine. Everyone else came through without a scratch.

The demolition experts quickly concluded that the enemy had not been carrying explosives, which was consistent with the intel they'd picked up from the safe house. This was to be a small-arms assault, turning the school into a shooting gallery. The terrorists would then scatter or, if trapped, fight it out with security forces. It was evident they had not prepared for the possibility that they might've been under surveillance and funneled into an ambush.

As Eisner busied himself with wrapping up the operation, part of his mind wondered about that. Hamas was not normally quite this sloppy. Through much experience, Shabak had learned not to underestimate its enemies. They were highly motivated, cunning, and utterly ruthless. This mission today seemed less than their best effort. Why would that be? Could it have been merely a diversion? No, there were no indications of other activity elsewhere in the country today. Vigilance was, as always, very high. If something else was going on, Shabak would know, and word would have gotten to Eisner and his men.

Eisner watched the attendants shut the doors of the ambulance, knowing what would happen next to the prisoner. He would be treated, stabilized, and then the questioning would begin. He would talk, eventually. They almost always talked. Shabak's interrogation methods were very efficient. Those methods would probably cause many Americans and Europeans to get very squeamish, but things were different here. They had to be. Eisner wished that were not so, but it would be a long time before things might change. Maybe his grandchildren would see it.

The captured terrorist was a teenager, not much older than those boys Eisner and his buddy had killed in Gaza so many years before. The thought of it brought a pang of sadness to him; Ehud had been killed in Lebanon in '06, and sometimes he missed his old friend very much. "What's the matter?" Rosenberg said, pulling Eisner's thoughts back to the here and now.

"Something about this isn't quite right," he said. "I can't quite put my finger on it, though."

"I know what you mean," his partner said. "Let's talk it over in the debrief when we get back."

Eisner turned back to his waiting men and ordered them back to their vehicles, back to their headquarters. The mission would be analyzed, mistakes would be pointed out, improvements suggested. He would write a report, and they would go back to training for the next one, because there would surely be a next one. But as he discussed it with Rosenberg on the way, they agreed on their perceptions of the mission. It didn't seem to them that the enemy had planned this very well. Their security had been sloppy. They had not brought any explosives, and although it was not easy for them to bring those kinds of things into Israel anymore, Eisner knew it could be done. It was virtually a suicide mission, and while that was common, he knew that Hamas and Hezbollah weren't normally this careless. It was almost as if the mission had been designed to fail.

CHAPTER TWENTY

WISCONSIN

JIM WAS ZIPPING his overnight bag shut when the house phone rang. His first thought was that it was Gina, but he didn't think he'd given her the house number. Maybe Annie. The call last night hadn't gone well. He probably should've told her in person, had considered it, but he just didn't want to face her. She'd asked him if there was someone else, and he said yes, he'd met someone. What the hell, it wasn't as if he and Annie had any kind of understanding about being exclusive. He'd brought it up once, a couple months ago, and she'd said no, she wasn't ready yet. And now she was upset?

He looked around his bedroom. Everything was in place, neat and orderly, just like the rest of the house. He'd spent two hours cleaning that morning, after getting in an early workout at the gym. There was no way he would leave the house in any kind of disorder, even though nobody else would see it. It just wasn't his way, wasn't the warrior way. Discipline and order, that was what had gotten him through Suzy's death, had sustained him for these past few years, what would save him from going crazy, or at the least getting old and fat and sloppy. Well, he'd get old anyway, but—

The phone kept ringing. He reached for the bedside extension, cursing himself for not carrying that same discipline into his love life. Why should dealing with women be any different? He vowed then and there that from now on, it would be. He pushed the green TALK button as he brought the phone up to his ear, but he stopped halfway. The screen said UNKNOWN CALLER. Damn, he should've checked it first, let the machine take it. Probably another telemarketer.

"Hello?"

"Is this James Hayes?" A woman's voice, mature, all business, unfamiliar.

"Yes."

"Mr. Hayes, my name is Denise Allenson. I work for the Federal government, and I'd like to meet with you about a rather urgent matter."

A chill ran up Jim's spine. What the hell could this be? His mind raced. Were his taxes paid? Yes, of course they were, he'd sent in his return six months ago and already had his refund. Then another quick thought: had something else happened to Mark? "Is this about my brother?" he asked, dreading the answer. No, they'd tell him in person, wouldn't they? Maybe not, maybe they didn't do that for brothers, just wives or parents, maybe—

"Your brother? No, it's not," the woman said. "It is a matter of national security."

"So you're not from the IRS?"

The reply came with a hint of humor. "No, I'm with a different government agency. We would prefer to meet with you in person, Mr. Hayes."

"'We?'" He didn't know whether to feel relieved or more apprehensive.

"My associate and I. When can we meet? We're on the road right now, about an hour away. I apologize for the rush, but I tried calling you earlier and left a message."

Damn, he hadn't checked the answering machine when he got home. He checked his watch. Nearly one. He'd intended to have a late lunch here and then hit the road for Marshfield, three and a half hours away. Somewhere in the back of his mind an alarm bell was ringing. "An hour from now works for me."

"Good. Can you suggest a place with some degree of privacy where we can sit down together?"

Jim glanced out the window. It was a warm late-summer day, clear skies, giving him an idea. "There's a park, the town square. I'll meet you next to the statue of Rufus King."

"Describe the statue, please."

"Well, it's a general on horseback, pointing a sword. It's the only statue in the park, so it's easy to find."

"I see," she said, and was there another hint of amusement? "We should be there by two o'clock."

"How will I recognize you?"

"Don't worry. We'll find you."

"Pretty little town," Keith Graham said as they rolled down Main Street. "Nice lakes in this area. Came up here fishing with my dad a few times when I was a kid."

Denise wasn't really interested in the FBI agent's opinion of Cedar Lake or much of anything else. They had a job to do and the sooner they found this Hayes fellow and brought him in, the sooner she could get back to Langley. She hadn't said a dozen words to Graham on the two-hour drive from O'Hare, where he'd greeted her flight from Washington. She'd tried not to doze along the way, even though she was bone tired. The frantic pace of the previous day had crashed down on her when she got back to her apartment that evening. She tried to relax with a pizza and a glass of wine in front of the TV after she finished packing, but it had still been nearly eleven when she nodded off. She was working on only five hours' sleep, a couple fewer than usual.

"How much farther to this park?" she asked.

"A few blocks, if I remember right," the agent said. "We don't expect any trouble from this guy, do we?"

"You never know. My orders are to persuade him to come to Washington with me, tonight."

"And you can't tell me why, right?"

She sighed and then caught herself, hoping he hadn't heard it. "You'll find out soon enough."

There was the smallest bit of a shrug from Graham, but she didn't miss it. He was sending out the same vibe she often caught from men she worked with outside CIA, especially the younger ones. *Who the hell does she think she is? She's a spook? Maybe if we want to infiltrate the Cannes Film Festival.* She looked out the side window. This was the real world. Men and women could work together, but it wasn't always as much fun as it was on *Bones.*

"There's the park," she said. Graham found a parking space and easily pulled the government-issue Ford Taurus to the curb. He switched off the engine and was taking the key out of the ignition when he felt her hand on his arm. "Hey, I'm sorry about…well, it's been a long day already and there's a long way to go."

For a moment, there was doubt in his eyes, but then he grinned, just a bit. "No problem," he said. "Let's go find our guy."

Jim saw the sedan right away. He'd arrived ten minutes early and spent five of them looking over the park and its bordering streets from three different angles. There was nobody standing near the King statue, nobody sitting on the lone bench nearby, and he couldn't spot anybody who was obviously out of place. He was probably being too paranoid about this, but you couldn't be too careful when a stranger wanted to meet you. He'd learned some helpful things about surveillance at Systema camp so why not put them to use?

He spotted them just a few minutes past one. A woman and a man. She'd be the one in charge: she'd made the call and the guy was probably just here to back her up. They just wanted to talk to him, and if it had been some legal trouble he'd be at the police station now instead of in plain sight.

The woman was all business but still striking, reminding him of Elizabeth Hurley but taller, maybe about five-ten, wearing a conservative business suit: gray jacket over white blouse, gray skirt, black pumps, and in between the pumps and the hemline were a nice pair of toned legs. Jim had been around enough dojos and gyms to know the obvious sign of a woman who worked out was well-toned legs. She moved easily, with a sense of confident, fluid motion. If she was in some sort of government law enforcement agency, that probably meant she trained in a combative martial art, maybe Israeli *krav maga*. He couldn't see her eyes behind the sunglasses, but he'd bet she was glancing around, taking in everything. He placed her age at around thirty-five.

The man was an agent, all right. Tall, although a couple inches below Jim's six-four, short hair, conservative suit and tie, carried himself well and he was more obvious in scanning the vicinity. Broad shoulders, probably a weight-lifter, maybe a football player in his younger days. Not a guy to mess with. Right now he'd have to guess they were both FBI.

When they were within thirty feet, Jim stood up, glad that he'd taken a few minutes to stretch out when he used the rest room in the bank across the street. He couldn't imagine that he would have to defend himself, not in broad daylight in a public park, but it never hurt to be prepared.

"Mr. Hayes?" the woman asked, when they'd come within ten feet.

"That's me."

She walked up to him and extended a hand. "Hello, I'm Denise Allenson, and this is Agent Graham. Nice to meet you."

Her grip was firm. Her nails weren't too long, and now that she'd removed her sunglasses, he was close enough to see that she had the slight beginnings of crow's feet around her eyes, but that didn't take anything away from their brilliant emerald green shade.

"If this fellow's an agent, I'm assuming he's FBI," Jim said. "How about you?"

She fished a thin wallet out of her shoulder bag and showed him her ID. "CIA," she said. "Is there some place we could talk, privately?"

"We have a nice coffee shop here," he said, nodding to his left.

"That would be good. I could use some."

Jim drained the last of his chai tea latté, trying to give himself another moment to think. He looked over at the counter, where a pair of fresh-faced, happy young baristas served the afternoon crowd. He wondered if any of them would ever in their lifetimes hear a story as fantastic as the one he'd just heard.

He breathed in deeply, settling himself. Then he turned

back to the CIA agent across the table from him. Graham had excused himself to use the men's room. Allenson was boring those green eyes into him. On any other occasion he would allow himself to be entranced by a woman this attractive.

"So let me see if I understand this," he said, choosing his words carefully. "There's this terrorist mastermind over in Africa, and it turns out he's an old college buddy of mine, and he's willing to defect to our side, but only to me, personally. Is that what you're telling me?"

"That's right," she said. "I know it sounds far-fetched."

"You might say that."

"Look, Mr. Hayes, I was briefed personally by the Director of the National Clandestine Service about twenty-four hours ago. He's one of the top men at CIA, and I know he's not one to waste his time or spend Agency money on a wild-goose chase."

"I've read Tom Clancy; I know the DNCS is a big shot," Jim said. "You're saying that this guy they call Sudika, this terrorist, is really Joe Shalita who went to Platteville with me?"

Allenson took a folder from her shoulder bag and now opened it, turning it toward Jim. He saw the grainy black-and-white photo of a black man with glasses, wearing some sort of turban. "This is the best photo we have of Shalita. It was taken some time ago in Pakistan."

Jim looked closely at the picture, trying to remember Joe from those days long ago in Platteville. Could the well-spoken, polite little Ugandan he remembered really be a terrorist chieftain? It seemed too fantastic to be true. Yet this picture—he hadn't seen Joe in thirty years, but it could be him.

"Look, I haven't seen Joe since we graduated. It might be him, but I can't be sure."

"Have you had any contact with him since then?"

"No. I think he told me he planned on going back home

after graduation, or maybe to Europe. It was a helluva long time ago, you know."

"Were you close friends?"

"Well, we hung out together a pretty fair amount, I guess, but I wouldn't say we were best buddies."

"You must've made an impression on him, because he asked for you specifically."

Jim sat back, shaking his head. Graham returned from the rest room and sat down next to Allenson.

"What do you want me to do?" Jim asked.

Allenson closed the file and put it back in her bag. "The director wants me to bring you to Langley, where you'll be thoroughly briefed and prepared."

"Prepared for what?"

Allenson lifted her eyebrows. "We'll be heading overseas."

"You mean...where did you say this guy is now, Somalia?"

"That's where he is, and so that's where we'll be going."

Graham gave her a look, as close to showing emotion as Jim had seen from him. Jim figured this was the first time the FBI agent had heard this part of the story.

"You're leaving something out," Jim said.

"What's that?"

"The part where you say, 'Should you or any of your Impossible Missions Force be caught or killed, the secretary will disavow any knowledge of your actions.'"

Allenson leaned forward. "Look, Mr. Hayes, this is no joke. This is a critical matter of national security—"

Jim stared right back at her. "Hey, I've got a job here. I've got a big project due pretty soon and my boss is on my ass about it. You want me to tell her I'm taking a few days off to go chasing terrorists?"

"You can't tell anyone about this operation," she said.

"You'll recall that when we sat down here, you agreed our conversation would be confidential."

Jim looked away again, trying to sort it out. On the one hand, it sounded like the most bizarre thing he'd ever heard. Joe Shalita, a terrorist? The guy wouldn't have hurt a fly back then. But that was a long time ago, and people changed, sometimes drastically.

He looked back at the agents, trying to decide if they were legit. He supposed it could be part of some elaborate prank, but who would go to the trouble to hire two people to pull off a charade like this? One way to make sure was to have them take him to the FBI headquarters in Chicago. Did the CIA actually have an office anywhere outside Virginia?

If this crazy story was true, if Joe had turned himself into this Sudika character and now he wanted to defect, then he must have some very important intelligence to hand over, otherwise the government wouldn't be playing ball with him like this. They'd just lure him into a trap and snatch him, send him off to one of those secret prisons he was always hearing about, and that would be that. Why would they need to come all the way to Wisconsin to enlist the help of Jim Hayes?

"So you're telling me this is an officially sanctioned mission?"

The CIA agent nodded. "Mr. Hayes, less than twenty-four hours ago I was sitting in the Oval Office, watching the President of the United States review your file."

"I didn't know I had one," Jim said.

"Everybody's got a file," the FBI agent said. That bought him a sharp look from Allenson.

She turned back to Jim. "This operation has been personally authorized by the president," she said. "Now, I need an answer from you."

"I have to use the rest room," he said, standing up. He really did, but he also needed some space. He felt his heart rate accelerating, and forced himself to calm down and breathe regularly.

In the men's room, Jim took care of his immediate business, then looked in the mirror as he washed his hands. He tried to imagine what Allenson and Graham were seeing when they looked into the eyes he was seeing now. Did they see a guy who was skeptical, puzzled, maybe a bit frightened? That's what Jim saw.

He had to give these people an answer. Part of him was saying he should tell them to get lost, forget it, go solve their own problems. He had a life here in Cedar Lake, a home. He had a job, although lately he'd been wondering if it was one he wanted anymore. He had Gina, or at least a shot at something with her. There was his daughter in Milwaukee, and maybe this guy she was dating would give her a ring, and he'd have grandchildren. That was certainly something to live for, wasn't it?

If he went along with these people, he might never hold his grandchild. What if he went over there and things went to hell and he had to act? Could he do it? Practicing in the dojo or at Systema camp was one thing, coming face to face with a terrorist who wanted to kill you was quite another. Even worse than that terrible morning in the church. Not a spot for an amateur to be in. This was a job for professionals.

Like his brother.

The door opened and a man came in, snapping Jim out of his thoughts. He quickly left the rest room and walked down the short hallway back into the coffee shop. The agents were still in the booth, talking together, no doubt telling themselves that this guy didn't have what it takes.

The flat-screen TV on the wall was showing something that caught his eye. It was the silhouette of a man, standing against a cloudy sky, holding a sword straight out. It was an ad for the Marines, one he'd first seen a few nights before.

Marines in dress blues with M-1 rifles, the Silent Drill Team, stood near a lighthouse, then in Times Square. Jim strained to hear the audio.

"There are those who dedicate themselves to a sense of honor...to a life of courage..." Most in the coffee shop ignored the TV, but at one table, a gray-haired man was staring up at the screen, and a tear was rolling down his cheek. Next to him, his wife patted him on the hand. Had he been a Marine? Where had he been? Maybe Chosin Reservoir, or Khe Sanh.

Mark had been in a lot of places. Bosnia, Iraq, Afghanistan, probably more, doing dangerous things, noble things. Where had Jim been, what had he done? He'd always wondered what he would do when the chips were down.

Like they were now.

He made his way back to the booth. The agents looked at him, and he could see their skepticism. He looked away and gathered himself, then back at them. "You probably know my brother's in the Army," he said quietly.

"Yes," Allenson said. Graham remained silent.

"I tried to get in the Reserves," Jim said. "They wouldn't take me. Bad knee. The Marines wouldn't, either. My country said sorry, you're not good enough. But now it seems the country has changed its mind." He paused, thinking of his father, his brother.

"Okay," he said, looking directly at the CIA agent. "When do we leave?"

CHAPTER TWENTY-ONE

AFGHANISTAN

I T WASN'T IN Mark's nature to take a day off, but today he had to force himself to take it easy. Off-days weren't that common downrange anyway, although he made sure his troops got in as much R&R in as possible. Out here it wasn't like it had been back in Vietnam, when guys could get a couple days' leave and head to Saigon or maybe Bangkok. From what he'd been told, those were wild times. If you were out here, the only city to speak of was Kabul, and that wasn't exactly regarded as a playground. But the medical people were finding out a lot about PTSD and said getting rest and some measure of recreation while deployed was vital. Mark wasn't about to disagree.

It took a lot of self-discipline. Alcohol wasn't allowed, porn stashes were discouraged, although Mark knew better than to think those rules were universally obeyed. He told his company commanders to cut the men a little slack. Every now and then somebody pushed the envelope a little far, and there were consequences. Sometimes serious ones, especially if the offense involved civilians. Fortunately, Mark hadn't had to deal with anything like that during his time as C.O. of Roosevelt. So far.

It was nearly twenty four hours after the firefight at the farmhouse and his headache seemed to be a little quieter. There was an angry bruise on his left temple, but the doc said there didn't appear to be any internal damage. He cautioned Mark to be aware of any concussion symptoms, and made sure Ruiz and the rest of the staff were keeping an eye on him. All in all, Mark could live with the headache. If the bullet had been another inch or so to the right it would've made sure that he'd never have headaches again.

Things appeared quiet in the valley, so Mark set out to make his usual Sunday-morning rounds of the base first thing after breakfast. It was warming up already, maybe to about seventy-five today. Hot, but not Iraq-in-the-summer hot. He'd had enough of that, and up here in the mountains there was usually enough wind to keep it from getting stifling. The air was clear, too, unlike the odor of Iraq—combustion fumes, garbage, Lord knew what else. You got used to the heat, you expected it to be hot all the time, but the stench hit you in the face as soon as you stepped off the plane and it took a while to get used to that. It was much better here, although some villages had their own special aromas, and Kabul's pollution was legendary.

Dealing with the weather was easy, but the culture shock was something else entirely. Mark had been all over the country and sometimes it seemed like he was on another planet, maybe a cross between the moon and Mars, except it was warmer and you could breathe the air, sort of. For that matter, the people were like aliens in many respects. The way they talked, dressed, ate, how sometimes the men wiped their ass with a bare hand, how they treated their women. Mark had wondered many times, during his first tour, just what the hell they were doing here, why they bothered with these people. Clean out the bad guys and move on, that's what should've been done.

Gradually, though, his perceptions changed. Yes, they were a different people, but people were different all over, just more so here, and a lot of it had to do with geography. Landlocked, scarce in resources, the Afghans for centuries had been forced to scratch a living out of hardscrabble conditions that made cotton sharecroppers back in the American Deep South look like aristocrats. When you got right down to it, as tough as his life was, the average Afghan wanted what the average American wanted, the average Brit, Russian, Chinese, whatever. He wanted to make a living and raise his family and live in peace.

Over here, sometimes, it appeared that was too much to ask. Since Alexander's day, foreign armies had moved through these valleys and plains, seeking out not plunder but strategic advantage. Whoever held Afghanistan in those days could dominate the trade routes of southern Asia. These days, it wasn't much different. If America could leave this place in friendly hands, that would not only cut al-Qaida off from its once-secure sanctuaries, but it would give America and the West strategic access to this part of the world for decades to come. Mark looked to the north. Up there, the Caspian Sea basin was one of the world's biggest reserves of oil and gas. The Russians had once controlled that, but not now. It was up for grabs. Mark wondered sometimes if that was the real reason he and his fellow soldiers were here.

Whatever the reason, it was tough, demanding duty. One of the biggest challenges for Mark and his fellow officers was keeping their men, and themselves, focused and healthy. Perhaps more than any other conflict in American history, this war was taking a psychological toll on the men and women who fought it, and their families back home. The isolation over here was a serious problem, but in a curious way, Mark believed it was also a strength. With few distractions, maintaining focus was easier than it might've been in earlier wars. The camaraderie among the men here was stronger than anything Mark had experienced before. From the day you arrived here you looked forward to going home, and you knew that the only way to survive lay with your comrades. If you had your buddy's back, he had yours, and you just might make it home alive. And downrange, you needed to trust your buddies because you sure as hell couldn't trust anyone else you would encounter, not even the men of this land you helped train and mentor.

That was the real tragedy, Mark knew now, after spending so much time here. It baffled the Americans, sometimes enraging them to the point where they did things they would not normally think of doing. No matter how much you interacted with the people here, they never fully accepted you. Not like the Germans and Japanese had done. How many Americans came home from those conquered nations with native-born brides? More than a few, but Mark had not heard of a single American marrying an Afghan woman.

They were here because this job, as hard as it was, as distasteful as it felt, had to be done. The enemy who had come to his country to slaughter his people had come from places like this, using them as sanctuaries for training, breeding grounds for hate. Mark was proud of the work his country had done in Afghanistan, and in Iraq too, toppling brutal dictatorships and giving millions a fighting chance to live in peace, but he wondered where it would all end, if it would ever end.

Mark's headache wasn't being improved by this kind of thinking, so he shoved it aside and moved on, out into the main area of the base. Focus on the little things, he reminded himself. There were people way above his pay grade to take care of the big things.

Camp Roosevelt covered about fifty acres on a plateau near the north end of the valley, offering a commanding view. The Russians had realized its strategic importance when they built the first base here back around 1980. Many of their buildings were standing when the Americans arrived, and the engineers had whipped things into pretty decent shape in the years since. It was still on the primitive side compared to Army posts in Europe or back in the States, or even the big one in Kandahar, but it would do.

There were troops out jogging around the perimeter, and Mark supposed that somebody would rustle up enough guys for touch football later in the day. There would probably be some action around the spider pit; sometimes men on patrol would capture camel spiders, non-poisonous arachnids as big as a man's hand, bring them back to the base and match them up in combat with heavy bets riding on the outcomes. Several men waved at him as they ran by, and a few asked how he was doing. Word had gotten around quickly about the firefight.

He came to one of the lookout posts on the perimeter. Nearby, a group of soldiers was working on the wire fencing. Getting the fence squared away in the beginning had been a bitch, but it had to be done. It was in sad shape when he got here, but Mark knew the history of this base in the Soviet days. They'd been lax about the wire and paid for it one night when the *muj* attacked, rocketing the poorly-secured guard posts and breaching the perimeter. Learning from that lesson, he'd ordered the fencing reinforced and HESCO barriers erected at the four corner guard posts. Mark was glad to see that the four men on duty here this morning weren't sleeping or otherwise screwing around. "Good morning," he said.

One of the privates, a new man, stood up and was raising his hand in salute when the corporal pulled him back down. "Goddamn it, Carson, get down," he said. "You don't salute out here at the wire! You want to show every friggin' raghead sniper on that mountain that we got an officer here?" He turned casually toward Mark. "Good morning, sir," he said, nodding.

"As you were," Mark said, kneeling down in the sand-bagged dugout. "How's it going, Mandli?"

The corporal, who'd been here a few months longer than Mark, took off his helmet and wiped a sleeve across his high forehead. The kid couldn't be more than twenty-five but he was already losing his hair. "Pretty quiet, sir. Some movement out there, but nothing out of the ordinary."

"That's good. Maybe it'll be a quiet day. We could use one of those, couldn't we?"

"Could use more than one, you ask me, sir."

"Can't argue with that. Let's see what we got." The dug-out was shielded by HESCOs, wire mesh containers lined with fabric, then filled with dirt. Some of the smaller FOBs had HESCOs around the entire perimeter, but here Mark had just installed them at the four corners, in the center of the north side, and flanking the entrance gate on the south. Mark hauled himself up onto the ledge of the dugout, looking out over the valley. The view was breathtaking. On the mountainside directly ahead, about two miles away, he could see a small herd of goats, with three upright figures guiding them along. Mark took the binoculars offered by Mandli and zeroed in on them. Looked like one adult man and two boys, picking their way effortlessly along a trail that was probably older than all of them put together.

Mark chatted with his men for a few minutes, then stood up and stretched, enjoying the growing warmth of the sun. An inner voice told him to stay low, beware of snipers, but he figured he'd had his close call for the week yesterday. "Say, Colonel," Mandli said, "could I have a word with you, sir?"

"Sure." They walked a few paces away. "What's on your mind, soldier?"

"Well, sir, we got a new guy in our company, Asian kid, Korean, I think he is…" Mandli stopped, then looked away for a second, biting his lower lip.

Mark had a feeling he knew what was coming. Mandli had a rep for being a stand-up guy, definitely sergeant material. "Speak your mind, Corporal. This is just between us."

The slender young man sighed. "Well, sir, there's some guys in the company, they've been giving Hong a lotta shi—I mean, they've been giving him a hard time."

"Why? Because he's Asian?"

Mandli nodded. "Yes, sir. He's the only Asian in the company. Aren't too many on the whole base, I don't think. Anyway, there's only a few characters doing this, and the lieutenant's been on their ass about it, but last night, well, it kinda got worse, some name-calling, things like that. Nobody deserves that kind of treatment, you ask me. I'm afraid one of these times, somebody's gonna get popped and it'll be real trouble. Besides, Hong's a nice guy, pretty quiet, keeps to himself. Can't say that about everybody in the company, sir, to be honest with you."

"All right. What's your company?"

"Company C, sir. I hope I'm not speaking out of turn, sir. The lieutenant's a good guy. I don't want to say he's not doing his job."

Mark checked his watch. Divine services were starting in

about fifteen minutes at the base chapel, and he knew Winkler would be there. "Don't worry about it. I'll have a word with the lieutenant, and I'll keep your name out of it."

"Thank you, sir."

Around 1500, Mark was finishing up an e-mail to Eddie, wondering how long it would take his son to respond this time. Sometimes it was the next day, usually longer. He owed one to Jim, too. It had been a little awkward last night, talking to his big brother on the phone. Dammit, why should that be? They were brothers, for God's sake. Yeah, Mark had acted like a horse's ass a few times around him, but that was twenty-some years ago. Wasn't it time for them both to get past that? Jim was the older brother, he should take the initiative on that, shouldn't he? Well, what the hell, there was no law that said the younger brother couldn't reach out first. What would his dad have said? Mark knew that almost without thinking of it. He sighed, clicked on the SEND button, and brought up a fresh screen. He'd do it, and when he rotated back home, he'd make a point of visiting Jim, and they'd have a talk.

There was a knock on the flimsy door of Mark's office. "Yeah," he said.

It was Lieutenant Reeves, one of the staff on duty today. "Sir, got a message here from Lieutenant Winkler, Company C." He handed Mark a folded piece of paper.

"Very well, thank you," Mark said. The door closed shut behind Reeves as Mark unfolded the message. *Re that issue you brought up after chapel, the men asked to resolve their differences in the ring. Your presence requested, 1600. Winkler, Co C commanding.*

One of the larger buildings on the base had been converted into a gym, and one of the few thing's Mark's predecessor did right was to keep it in first-rate shape. A fitness nut himself, the guy insisted that all the men have regular PT, to the detriment of their regular training and personal down time. Mark was as much a believer in physical training as anyone else, but he had dialed that back a bit and increased emphasis on doing what they were really here to do. But he appreciated the gym and came over two or three times a week himself.

They had some free weights and a half dozen Total Gym machines Chuck Norris had donated during his last visit downrange. As always, it was a busy place, but most of the crowd now seemed to be gathering around the boxing ring that had been built on the other half of the floor. Two men were in the ring, in opposite corners. One of them was a white guy, solidly built, close-cropped red hair, wearing black twelve-ounce gloves, a tank-top shirt with a biker logo on it, knee-length shorts, and no shoes or socks. The other was shorter, Asian, also barefoot, wearing loose-fitting pants, red MMA-style gloves and no shirt. The kid probably didn't weigh more than a buck-fifty but he was ripped. Mark hadn't seen a physique like that in a while.

Winkler was there, saw Mark and hustled over. "Good afternoon, Colonel."

"What've we got here, Gerard?"

"Well, sir, I discussed the matter with Private Hong, and then with Specialist Rue over there. From what I was able to find out, he's been the one giving Hong a hard time."

"I heard that there were a few guys involved in it."

"Rue would be the instigator, sir. He's been on report once or twice." Mark recalled the name now, seeing it on the weekly reports of disciplinary problems he received from his company commanders. Fortunately, those lists were usually quite short.

"I'd thought Rue was coming around, but things started sliding again when Hong arrived a couple weeks ago."

"Okay, now what?"

"Personal combat, sir. Both men agreed."

Mark sighed. He didn't like this sort of thing, had considered banning it, but it didn't come around very often. As long as it was kept under control and both men shook hands at the end, he'd decided to tolerate it, although he emphasized to his lieutenants that this was not the preferred way to handle disputes among the men. Usually they resolved things themselves with a touch football game, one-on-one basketball, something a little less aggressive, but occasionally it came down to the ring.

"All right. What are the rules?"

"Martial arts sparring, sir, similar to Olympic taekwondo. Two rounds, two minutes each. A punch is worth one point, a kick gets two. Nothing below the belt. No grappling. Sergeant Callahan has some experience with this, so he's the referee."

"I didn't know Rue was a martial arts guy."

Winkler smiled. "He isn't, sir. Says he did some tough-man smokers back home in Wyoming, and I've seen him working out here, sparring with some of the boys."

"What about Hong?"

Winkler's grin got a bit wider. "He wouldn't say, sir, other than that he has some taekwondo background, but another fellow told me Hong's a second-degree black belt."

A bell rang, and a large black soldier in cammie pants and black tee got into the ring, summoned both fighters to the center and started going over the rules. Men had gathered around the ring, two ranks deep now. Mark and Winkler stood toward the back, maybe fifteen feet from the near side of the ring.

Outside each corner stood a soldier holding a white cloth in one hand, a red one in the other.

Callahan moved the two fighters about six feet apart, then signaled to two men at ringside to his left. "Continuous fighting. One point for a punch, two for a kick. Judges, raise the hand with the appropriate color when you see a point. Wave the flag for two points. Scorekeeper, the point is scored when at least three judges concur. Private Hong is red. Timer ready? Scorekeeper ready?" Nods in return, and the sergeant looked quickly at each corner man. "Judges ready?" More nods. "Fighters ready?" Mark noticed both men had mouth guards. Rue had a cheering section, some of the beefier guys on the base, all white, while most of the crowd seemed to be outwardly backing the Korean. Evidently Rue hadn't done a lot to make himself popular.

"*Si jak!*"

It was over in fifteen seconds. Rue stepped in with a right that would've taken Hong's head off if it had been there, but the Korean ducked and weaved with a fluidity Mark had never seen, even in the movies. A leg flashed out and Rue grunted as he staggered backward from the blow to the gut. All four judges shot up the hand with the red flag. Another kick, this one from the other leg as Hong whipped his body around, caught Rue flush in the chest and slammed him back into the ropes. More red flags. Hong timed it perfectly as Rue came back off the ropes on legs that were turning to rubber, and the Korean screamed as one foot rocketed around and upward, catching Rue flush on the right side of his head. Rue's mouthguard spurted out and into the crowd as the big redhead turned a slow, ungainly pirouette and slammed onto the mat.

Callahan rushed over as Hong danced away, perspiration sheening that marvelously cut upper body. The sergeant started counting in Korean as Hong went to the far side of the ring and knelt down, his back to the center. Rue groaned and rolled over as Callahan's count reached five, but he didn't get up. "Rydel!" Eight. Callahan waved his arms and a roar came from the crowd. Hong bounced up and walked calmly to the center, where Callahan raised his right arm, shouting *"Sung!"*

Winkler was cheering and applauding alongside Mark. "How about that, Colonel?"

"Pretty impressive," Mark agreed, pleased to see Rue getting slowly to his feet. The beaten man shook his head to clear the cobwebs, then walked toward Hong, stopped, and bowed. Hong returned the bow as the men cheered, and the fighters embraced. Mark joined in the cheering this time.

He noticed Ruiz beside him. "Got here just in time for the bout," the major said. "Colonel, remember that suggestion we got last week about having martial arts classes on the base? I think we might just have found our instructor."

"All right, see if he's interested."

The fighters were leaving the ring now, both surrounded by fellow soldiers congratulating them. Hong looked calm but Mark could see his eyes shining. Rue was starting to come around. He'd have a helluva headache and probably a black eye in the morning, but hopefully this would be an attitude adjustment for him.

"Didn't you tell me your brother does this type of thing?" Ruiz asked.

"Yes," Mark said. "I've heard he's pretty good."

"Oh, and Colonel, I took a call from the General just before I came over here. He wants you to call him back at your earliest convenience."

"Is it urgent?"

"Didn't say so, sir. His aide said when you've got a moment."

Back at the HQ building, Mark told the commo officer on duty to place the call to the General at ISAF in Kabul. "I'll take it in my office."

The phone rang sixty seconds after he took his seat behind his sparse desk. Through the clicks and pops and hisses that marked typical Afghan telephone service, backed up by NATO security features, Mark heard the familiar voice. "Hope I didn't interrupt your Sunday, Mark."

"Not at all, sir."

"Good. This is a somewhat personal call, but it could develop into something requiring your direct participation."

"All right."

Five minutes later, Mark hung up the phone, still stunned. He sat back in his chair, exhaling slowly, replaying the conversation in his mind. He looked down at the notes he'd been scratching on the pad he always kept handy, then realized they'd have to be burned. Bits and pieces of the phone call kept bumping around. He felt another headache coming on.

His brother was in the middle of a CIA operation, flying to Somalia to meet with some terrorist leader, who had gone to college with Jim back in Wisconsin. Unbelievable as that sounded, the guy apparently wanted to defect, and only to Jim. The General expected actionable intel out of the op and it might involve Mark sending some of his people across the border into Pakistan, or a strike team might even be heading into Iran.

"This is close-hold, Mark. I'm letting you know now because of who's involved."

"The meeting will be in Somalia in a few days. I don't have all

the details yet, but DCI gave me a heads-up because if we get any actionable intel, I may have to send a strike team. If the NCA directs, it might be a cross-border operation."

"DCI told me to get my best people ready. I'll need someone I can trust to be on that team, Mark. That's you. I'm getting two teams ready, one for in-country operations, the other will be for the cross-border strike if it comes to that. We have a special unit for that type of thing. You worked with a couple of them from the Legion. I'll brief you in with them in Kabul if we get that far."

"I know he's your brother, Mark, but DCI assures me he'll be in good hands. He'll do all right."

Mark rubbed his temples. What the hell had his big brother gotten himself into?

CHAPTER TWENTY-TWO

WISCONSIN

I T WAS THE phone call that worried him the most, and wasn't that a laugh? He was packing a bag to go to Africa and maybe get killed, and he was worried about calling his boss and asking for emergency leave. There was a policy about getting that, but he couldn't find his company handbook at the moment, so he would just have to wing it.

The phone was in his hand, but he hesitated, looking back at the CIA agent. Allenson was sitting patiently on his couch, while Spears, the G-man, was looking through Jim's bookcase. "We have to leave tonight?" Jim asked.

"I'm afraid so," Allenson said. "We have a plane waiting at O'Hare." She looked at her watch. "We really need to be going pretty soon, Mr. Hayes."

Jim sighed, then looked at his address book, punching in Lori's home number. Maybe he'd get lucky, get her voice mail, just leave a message and be done with it. There would be hell to pay when he got back, but maybe these people could get him a letter from someone in the government, maybe a Cabinet secreta—

"Hello?"

"Uh, Lori, this is Jim Hayes, sorry to bother you at home."

"That's all right, Jim. What can I do for you?" She actually sounded chipper today. Maybe this wouldn't be so bad after all.

"Something has come up, a family emergency. I have to leave town for several days." There was silence. "Are you there?"

"Yes, Jim, I am. You'll be out of town, you said?"

"Yes, I have to catch a plane in a few hours."

Another couple beats of nothing, then, "Might I ask, does this involve your daughter?"

"No, it doesn't," he said, remembering that he had to make one more call tonight. That one would be a lot tougher. "It's about my brother, actually." That was a bit of a white lie, wasn't it? "I really can't say anything more, but I'll be gone at least a week."

There was silence on the other end, then, "I understand there can be emergencies, Jim, but this is a little irregular…"

"Look, if you're concerned about the project, I've got an e-mail ready to send out to Vicki. She can coordinate my files and keep things going, and call Stacy if she needs help." Vicki Johnson was a customer service rep at the co-op who had also worked with Jim on some marketing projects in the past. She hadn't been in the loop on this job, but Jim had no doubt she could get up to speed quickly, and even though Stacy was home with her new baby, she could certainly give good advice by phone, maybe even come in to help out for a day or so. "I already have the draft done. Vicki won't have a problem."

"Not that I don't sympathize with your problem, Jim, but this is a big project, and I just want to make sure it's done right."

"You have good people working for you, Lori," Jim said. "Just let them do their jobs, okay?"

"Jim, there's no call for—"

"Look, I'm under a lot of pressure here." He took a deep breath. "Let me put it to you this way: if you can't see fit to grant me this leave, then you'll see my resignation waiting in your in-box when you log on Monday morning." There, he'd done it, and his heart was racing a bit but damn, it felt good.

There was another pensive beat or two of silence, and then, "All right, Jim. I'll see you when you get back. Please keep us informed." The line went dead.

He had to breathe deeply to get his shaking hands under control. Not a good sign, he thought. He glanced back at the living room, but his visitors apparently hadn't seen that. One call down, two to go. He'd have to log on to his home computer before he left and send that email to Vicki and Stacy. Fortunately, he'd just spent an hour last night paying his bills, so everything was up to date in that department. He'd have to check with Mrs. Leonard, the widow who lived next door, to have her come in and take care of Spike the cat every day, but it would give her something to do besides harass her grandchildren.

Two more calls to make. He found Gina's number in his phone's call log, called and got her voice mail. Probably in a meeting. He hated to tell her this way, but he left the message, promising to call her in the evening. That left the one to Michaela.

"Hey, Dad!"

"Hey, honey. Working today?" Since graduating UWM in '08, his daughter had been teaching high school history and civics at a private school in the northern Milwaukee suburb of

231

Shorewood, plus assisting with the girls basketball team. Her summer job was at a Boys and Girls Club in Germantown.

"Nope. Day off. How about you?"

"Same here. Listen, something's come up."

The drive from Cedar Lake to O'Hare wound up taking about ninety minutes, just about as long as the flight to Washington. The second-guessing started when they were about a half-hour outside of Cedar Lake, about to cross the line into Illinois. More than once he had to fight off an urge to tell them he was backing out, turn the car around and take him home. Not that he doubted the agents and their credentials. Their story, fantastic as it seemed, sounded oddly plausible. Jim kept up on the news, especially with his brother frequently overseas, so it wasn't hard to believe the CIA was closing in on a high-level al-Qaida operative. But Joe Shalita? Little Joe from Uganda, with his wire-rimmed glasses and pencil-thin mustache, his quiet demeanor and studious attitude?

They hadn't told him everything, of course. For the CIA to play ball with Shalita, and Jim still couldn't believe that was really him, he must have something important to say, and he had to be someplace they just couldn't snatch him and sweat it out of him. That wasn't especially comforting, because that's where Jim would be headed. He'd never been to Africa, but he'd heard some stories about Somalia, had seen *Black Hawk Down*. Nasty place, full of warlords and terrorists and pirates.

Yet, surely, the people weren't all like that. In the next town over from Cedar Lake was a turkey processing plant that employed a lot of Somali immigrants. Jim frequently saw them in the office, applying for service, and saw them around town, too. The men were tall and slender, usually bearded, the woman always in flowing robes, and there was some sort of scent about them, spicy, not unpleasant, but definitely different. They were always polite, and he'd heard the billing department people say they rarely had a problem with Somalis making late payments. He'd heard one of the Plant guys talking about an installation he'd done in one guy's apartment, and all that Somali fellow had for furniture was a card table and a couple rickety chairs, an old black-and-white TV sitting on a box, a couple of rugs and a cot. That was it. But over here, making more money than he'd ever dreamed of, sleeping safe and sound every night on a full stomach, that guy probably figured he was living like a king. The Plant guy said it kind of changed your perspective on things. Jim would certainly have to agree about that. He had the feeling his own perspectives on a lot of things were about to change, and drastically. He just hoped he'd make it back to tell people about those changes

The jet droned eastward into the gathering night. Jim had never traveled on a plane this small. They'd told him this was a Gulfstream IV, pretty fast. Not a bad way to travel. Besides himself and Allenson there were four other passengers, none of whom had been introduced to him. The skeptical FBI agent had dropped them at the terminal, then drove away, no doubt thinking the next time he heard the name of Jim Hayes it would be on a TV news story about the latest American civilian captured and killed by terrorists.

Nice as the jet was, Jim wasn't really enjoying the flight. The two books he'd tossed into his carry-on hadn't been touched. In the overhead bin was the gray leather travel bag that he'd started packing earlier in the day for a one-night trip to Marshfield. Now it held some underwear and socks, a case for his toiletries, and some workout gear. Allenson had told him they'd provide him with all the other clothing he'd need.

He had not been allowed to bring along his laptop computer or cell phone.

Allenson came down the aisle from the lavatory. "Mind if I join you?"

"Not at all." She took one of the two seats facing him. "So what's your story, Agent Allenson?"

She gave him a bit of a smile, and he could see fatigue rimming the eyes. Jim had heard government people in D.C. put in some long hours, and certainly CIA was no exception. Still, she was very attractive. It occurred to him that if this were a movie, there would probably be a romantic spark jumping between them about now. He was pretty sure that wasn't going to happen.

"Not much to tell," she said.

"How long have you been with the Agency?"

"Just over fifteen years."

"You must have started quite young."

That brought a smile, and her eyes twinkled. "Right out of college," she said.

That would put her in her late thirties. "Married? Kids?"

"No, and no. How about you?"

"If the president was looking over my file, you probably did, too, so you know."

She looked away briefly. "Yes, I'm sorry. I'm a little tired."

"No problem." There was silence for a few moments, then Jim said, "So, what happens when we get to Washington?"

"You'll be taken to a safe house for the night, then to Langley tomorrow. You'll be briefed in and then begin your orientation."

"So you guys work on Sundays?"

"We work pretty much every day, Mr. Hayes."

He smiled back at her. "If we're going to be working together, how about we use first names? Call me Jim."

"All right, Jim." She smiled again, this one more genuine, "Tell me about your daughter."

They chatted easily for several minutes. Jim found his anxiety starting to dissipate. She was easy to talk to, made him feel relaxed. If they'd been in a bar, he would've bought her a drink, and some inner part of his male brain would've started thinking ahead. But the first step he took down that path brought an image of Gina to mind. "I'm in a relationship, so please don't take this the wrong way," Jim said. "But, if we have some free time in the next few days, maybe you could show me the town. I've never been to Washington."

Her eyes changed just a bit, and he couldn't decide whether she was disappointed or upset. She glanced at him with a look that could've gone either way. "I have some things to take care of before we land, Jim. You might want to get some rest." She unbuckled her seat belt and walked back down the aisle behind him.

Jim slumped back in his seat, shaking his head. "Way to go," he mumbled, "you're off to a good start in your career as a dashing international spy." He rummaged in his carry-on for one of those books.

CHAPTER TWENTY-THREE

SOMALIA

THE PATIO OF the villa offered a spectacular view of the coast and the Indian Ocean beyond, but Yusuf did not have time to appreciate it. He'd only come out here for privacy and a better cell phone signal. As it was, the transmission was scratchy and intermittent, but even so, Yusuf could hear the concern in Amir's voice. "I do not trust these men, Yusuf," Amir said. "They are competent, and friendly enough, but there is something about them I do not like."

"I understand, my brother," Yusuf said. The Quds Force commando team had arrived the previous morning, giving Yusuf only a few hours to evaluate them before he departed for the north. Heydar had left a captain, Khorsandi, in charge of the unit, which consisted of himself and five other men. There was little Yusuf could do here in Eyl some 800 kilometers away, except to encourage Amir to cooperate with the visitors. "When I return we shall talk. How is the training going?"

"It began this morning," Amir said. "Yesterday they chose the men for the mission. Everyone volunteered, Yusuf. You should be proud of your fighters. Only fifty-five were chosen. The ones who will be left behind are very disappointed."

"Reassure them we will have more work for them." Yusuf said, although he had no idea what he would come up with. A field exercise of some sort might be in order. He was finding it hard to think ahead more than five days, when he was due to meet Simons again in Mogadishu, and, if he was favored by Allah, be delivered from this life he had come to despise.

"I will talk to them this evening," Amir said. "How is Eyl? I have heard many stories about its wealth."

"The stories are true, my friend," Yusuf said. "I will have much to tell you when I return tomorrow." Behind him, he could hear voices coming closer, a man's laugh, and then a woman's, with somewhat less enthusiasm. He glanced back, saw Heydar and their host coming through the French doors— made of glass, and without a scratch on them, unbelievably— along with four young women. "I must go, Amir. We should be back by noon tomorrow."

"May Allah bring you safely back to us, Yusuf."

Yusuf closed the cell phone and turned to his host with a smile. The slender, bearded Somali was grinning broadly, but his eyes weren't as happy. Yusuf was not fooled by Ghedi Mahamud's casual demeanor. One did not become the foremost pirate chieftain in Somalia by being overly trusting of men he had just met. That was to be expected. Although they were both Muslims and therefore ostensibly brothers, Ghedi was first and foremost a businessman, and Yusuf was sure the pirate considered him to be little more than a terrorist. A highly-regarded one, to be sure, but still a terrorist.

But one could do business with terrorists, and so Ghedi had graciously invited them to his home for an evening meal and, it appeared, some entertainment as well. Yusuf would have preferred to return to their hotel in the city, but it would have been bad form to refuse the invitation. Besides, it was clear Heydar was glad to be here. He had a woman on each side and his hands, Yusuf felt sure, were cupped on their shapely rumps.

For the long journey north to Eyl, Yusuf had chosen two of his most trusted men as security for himself and the Iranian major. Enduring the drive to Mogadishu in the SUV was nothing compared to the harrowing flight in the two-engine prop plane, but they'd arrived safely after nightfall. The plane would take them back to Mogadishu the next morning. The bodyguards were in one of the villa's outbuildings now, awaiting Yusuf's permission to go back into the city where they could dine at one of the many restaurants and seek out companionship of their own. He wasn't sure about allowing them to leave even for a few hours, but after all, Mahamud's own security team appeared to be quite competent.

And really, there was no security threat to be seen anywhere here. Eyl was the home base of the Somali pirate industry, and the wealth of ransom money over the years had transformed this sleepy port city into the most luxurious spot in the country. That was a relative term, Yusuf knew, but by Horn of Africa standards, Eyl was a world apart. Villas covered the hills and the Hafun Peninsula. In the city below, restaurants and hotels served the pirate clans and their "guests", the foreign ship crews who had been unfortunate enough to have their ships seized and brought here.

"Is everything all right back home?" Ghedi asked. A gold tooth gleamed in the light of the setting sun over the hills to the west.

"Yes, thank you," Yusuf answered in Arabic, the language

they had chosen for their business dealings. "You have a beautiful view here, my friend."

"It is quite nice, yes. But it is becoming crowded, I think. Many Somalis come here to find work. I am fortunate to have found this location here. Not as crowded as the city, where I used to live."

This place had probably cost more than a few shillings, Yusuf knew, but the pirates had money. Their thievery brought them millions, and it was said that the pirate clans in Eyl had more money than the entire state of Puntland, of which Eyl was the seventh-largest city. Enough to provide the clan leaders with estates like this one, and protection from the Puntland Security Force. It hadn't taken Yusuf long to see why the Western powers did not attempt a military rescue of the dozens of hostages being held down in the city. There were enough fighters and weapons down there to make any invasion a very costly affair. He'd even seen some tanks, hulking old Soviet models that wouldn't last fifteen minutes in the field against modern NATO armor, but in an urban environment like this they would be very difficult to dislodge.

"Did you enjoy the meal, Yusuf?" Mahamud asked.

"Very much so, thank you," Yusuf said. Indeed, the meal had been delicious, *baasto* pasta and *digaag,* a traditional chicken dish. He was glad his host had not served the more common *cambuulo,* a mixture of *azuki* beans, butter and sugar; he had eaten that at the hotel the night before and suffered a bout of flatulence afterwards. Heydar's two helpings had caused him much distress, to Yusuf's secret amusement. From inside the house now, Yusuf could smell the frankincense, which had been burning on a censer. It was not unpleasant, but to one used to the raw frontier life of the camp, it was somewhat pungent. Not as pungent as Heydar had been the night before, though, and Yusuf could not stifle a chuckle at the memory.

"A private joke, Yusuf?" the Iranian asked.

He could not resist. "Our host graces us with the fragrance of *lubaan*, my friend. A bit more pleasant than the hotel, don't you think?"

Ghedi roared with laughter. "I know well the restaurant where you dined last night, my friends. I hope my table has turned out to be somewhat more agreeable for you. And, the entertainment I have provided will be better as well, I think."

Yusuf didn't need to have that spelled out. The Holy Quran did not condone casual sex outside the bonds of marriage, of course, but exceptions could be made in certain circumstances, and in Yusuf's experience those circumstances depended upon the man who was making the decision. He himself had tried hard to remain chaste since the death of his second wife five years earlier. His grief had been intense, but on rare occasions since then he had taken a woman, if only for the release of his tensions. Tonight, though, he most certainly was not in such a mood.

Besides, there was still the matter of their business to conclude. "The ship you showed us today was most impressive, hoogamiye, and I am sure the crew you will provide will be very qualified," he said, making sure to add the Somali honorific for his host. "The price you quoted seemed a bit steep, if I may say so."

Ghedi's eyes gleamed and his gold tooth flashed again. "It is the only ship I have that meets your requirements," he said. "And the men I will send with you are some of my best. I will have to delay some of my own operations while they are gone. Delays cost money, as I'm sure you know."

"One million euros, in cash, hoogamiye," Yusuf said,

shaking his head in dismay. "My superiors did not authorize me to approve a sum that high, I'm afraid."

"It is a bargain at that price. Where else in all of Somalia could you find such a vessel?"

Heydar left the company of the two women. "May I have a word with my colleague?" he asked in his rather stiff Arabic.

He motioned Yusuf over to the edge of the patio, where they stood looking out over the ocean. Down in the harbor they could see the ship they'd toured a few hours before, a Dutch freighter that had been captured three months ago. "It is the best available ship," Heydar said. "None others have the ability to launch the speedboats we will use to assault our target. The ship is also in very good condition, and relatively fast."

"I have been authorized to pay only three-quarters of that price, Heydar."

The Iranian gazed out at the ocean and then sighed. "I believe the balance can be provided by my superiors," he said, sounding reluctant. Yusuf felt certain it was an act. The mullahs in Tehran could have bought a fleet of ships lock, stock and barrel if they wanted to, even though their nation's economy was being squeezed by the West's sanctions.

"Very well," Yusuf said. "I have brought enough for the deposit."

They turned back to Ghedi, and Yusuf approached him with his hand held out. "You drive a hard bargain, my friend, but a fair one. We have a deal."

The pirate broke out some Turkish tea, the local variety known as *shaax xawaash,* to celebrate their agreement. The four women lounged casually on nearby divans while the men drank and talked of the weather and Somali politics. Finally, Ghedi put down his teacup. "My friends, I am sure you wish to retire early to rest up for your journey tomorrow," he said with a wink. "I have taken the liberty of providing you with companionship for the rest of the evening. Major Heydar, I believe you have already met Abyan and Libaxo." He clapped his hands twice, and two of the women unwound themselves from their divan and sashayed almost comically over to the Iranian. He whispered in the ear of one of them and she giggled. The major bade them good evening and allowed the women to lead him toward the rear of the villa.

Yusuf eyed the other two women cautiously. Sex was the furthest thing from his mind these days, and even though they were attractive, he knew he'd have to come up with a way to turn down his host's offer without giving offense. "Hoogamiye, I am honored and flattered by your generous hospitality, but—"

"Oh, they are not for you, my friend," Ghedi said, standing. "They are for my own pleasure. Come with me."

Puzzled, Yusuf followed the pirate down another hallway to a closed door at the end. "This suite I save for my most important guests," Ghedi said. He knocked, then opened the door halfway. "Your entertainment came to me by way of a colleague of mine. Enjoy yourself, my friend," he said with another wink.

Yusuf stepped inside and caught his breath. The door shut behind him, but he didn't hear it. A woman was sitting on the bed, and with a small smile she stood, facing him. She was very tall, very blonde, and the gown she wore was almost transparent.

He was transfixed by her beauty, her alabaster purity, and any reservations he had about what might happen receded very quickly to a small back room of his mind. It had been many years since he'd been with a white woman, and while a small—and getting smaller—part of him said that should make no difference, it did. How long had it been? Amazingly, he recalled, not since his university days, and his long-lost Märta. He had not seen her since his visit to Stockholm the summer after their graduation.

"My name is Ingrid," the vision in white said, walking toward him. She was taller than him by at least two inches, younger by at least twenty years. "I am here to please you." Her English carried a northern European accent, but he couldn't quite place it, so long had it been since he'd conversed with such people.

She stood before him, and he reached out to grasp her full, wide hips. "How is it you find yourself in this place?" he asked as his hands moved up and down, feeling the flesh through the gauzy fabric.

"My husband's yacht was captured at sea by Ghedi's men," she said, and he could hear the pain in her voice.

"Where is he now?" He felt he had to ask the question, if only to be polite, although as his hands explored her, his concern for courtesy was growing less by the minute.

He heard her sigh as she looked away, toward the window. "He was killed resisting the pirates," she said. "Two months ago. His family is negotiating my ransom. But…Ghedi told me I would be released next week if I performed this service for him."

Yusuf's hands came up to her full breasts and he gently tweaked her hardening nipples. "He is a trustworthy man, I think, for a pirate," he said. His thumbs stopped their movement, and with his last shred of dignity he forced himself to step back. "I am sorry," he said. "It is not right for me to take advantage of you. It is not honorable. Perhaps if we just spent some time together here, and talked, I could then tell him you fulfilled your part of the bargain."

She smiled down at him. "Thank you," she said. "But... there is no reason we cannot relax a little bit, is there?"

The woman was truly a vision as the gown slipped to the floor with a whisper. He laid on the bed, naked, his clothes having been removed by her very delicately, very expertly. Whatever resistance he'd mustered was long gone. He felt like a young man again, and his manhood responded in a way that brought him the joy any man his age would have. Now he waited for her, and she climbed onto the bed and lowered herself on top of him. He felt her mound, her downy blonde hair, rubbing against him ever so slightly. Then her lips were on his, and her tongue darted inside. She certainly did not seem to be the typical grieving widow, but Yusuf shoved that irritating thought into a closet in his brain and shut the door.

Their lips parted and she smiled at him, but her green-blue eyes were...different. She continued to move on top of him, just enough to entice him. But something deep within his mind, the part that was ever-vigilant, opened the closet door and came out with a question. "You are magnificent," he said to her, smiling. "Where are you from?"

"Sweden," she said. He could not believe it. Märta's country! An incredible coincidence.

The vigilant part, which did not believe in coincidences, would not leave him alone. "From Stockholm?" he asked.

She nuzzled his neck, tongue flicking over his dark skin. "Yes," she said.

"I was there many years ago," he said. "Beautiful city, beautiful women." He kissed her deeply, his tongue probing for hers, finding it. He pulled back just a bit. "I knew a woman there," he said, memories of leggy blonde Märta flickering back to life, in the greatest summer he'd ever known, before he went back to Uganda and his life started spiraling down another path.

"A girlfriend?" She flicked her tongue over one of his nipples, then the other, bringing a gasp from him. No woman had ever done that to him before.

"Y—yes," he stammered. "We would meet...under the big mushroom." It was funny how one's memory worked. He recalled the odd, cement mushroom, in the square downtown. They would meet there when she finished work and go to dinner or a club.

"I know it. The Svampen," she said with a smile. The tongue flicked the other nipple. "In Gamla Tan."

He could not resist any longer. Reaching down, he grasped her hips and pulled her forward, freeing himself, and then pushed her back downward as he raised his hips just so, his tip finding something moist and inviting, and he sighed deeply as she pulled him inside.

Her lips left his and she raised herself, just a bit, her breasts rising from his chest. His eyes were on them and he reached for them as her hips began to move in the old familiar rhythm, He saw her glance away from him, just a quick movement he caught in his peripheral vision, as her right hand moved from his shoulder and slid underneath the pillow.

Something clicked inside his brain, the one small part that stubbornly resisted the overwhelming sensual overload. What had she said? Gamla Tan...that was the "Old Town" of Stockholm. But the mushroom, that was...where? In Stureplan, not in Old Town. He looked at her. The blue eyes were hard and her hand moved toward his neck.

He caught her by the wrist. There was a hypodermic needle in her hand, the point an inch away from his throat, his carotid artery. There was no passion in her eyes now, only determination. Summoning his strength, he thrust his pelvis upward, raising her up, and as she lurched forward he slammed his right elbow into the side of her head. She grunted, and he hit her again, harder, this time in the side of the neck. She fell off him, and he scrambled to the other side and off the bed. In his pants pocket was the pistol he carried with him everywhere. He leaped for the pants lying in a heap on the floor.

She was on him before he could get the weapon, bringing the hypo down toward his thigh. The needle grazed his skin as he swept it away and found the gun, bringing it up just as she was coming at him again. She stopped two feet away from him and dropped the hypo.

"Who are you?" he demanded.

She just smiled at him and backed away. Her nude body, so supremely beautiful just minutes before, was now the well-trained machine of an assassin. But, Allah be praised, he had not surrendered to her completely. His instincts, which had kept him alive all these years, one step ahead of his enemies, were still strong.

"I will ask one more time: who are you? Who do you work for?"

She cursed him in a language he did not understand. He shot her in the left knee.

"A Russian agent?" Amir said to him the next day, when he was safely back in his library at the camp.

"Yes," he said. "From their SVR." He did not add that her confession came only when he threatened to shoot her other knee. But that's all she said before Ghedi's security team broke into the room and hustled her away.

"But why, Yusuf? The Russians have always supported our

cause against the Jews and the West. Why would they try to kill you?"

Why, indeed? Ghedi had expressed shock and anger at the woman's betrayal. He swore that the woman had indeed been captured on board a yacht, registered to a Swedish owner, just as she'd claimed, but that was what his fellow pirate chieftain had told him when he loaned her to Ghedi for the evening. The Somali was no fool; he would conclude that he had been duped by his colleague, and Yusuf had no doubt there would be retribution. The pirates were thieves, and it was said in the West there is no honor among thieves, but Yusuf knew that among the Somalis in Eyl there was indeed a sense of honor, twisted as it might be.

But that was not his concern now. What concerned him was the inescapable conclusion that someone knew, or at least suspected, that he was on the verge of defecting. But who? If the Russians had truly planted her in Eyl just to kill Yusuf, how could they have possibly known he would come there? The only reason he had was to inspect the ship and arrange for—

Heydar. Of course, the Iranian had known all along they would be coming to Eyl. He was the only one to have known such a thing well in advance. Yet he had been just as shocked and angered as Ghedi last night. Or at least, that's how he had seemed. Yusuf shook his head. To Amir, he said, "I don't know, my brother. It is said that sometimes Russian agents hire themselves out for anyone who can pay their price. We have many enemies."

Amir nodded in agreement. They discussed a few more matters about the camp and the upcoming mission, and then he left Yusuf, sitting alone in his library, a cup of cooling tea in his hands. He had always suspected the Iranian could not be trusted. Did his superiors have an idea of what he was planning to do in four more days? If so, why not order Heydar to shoot him right here? No, that would not do; they needed Yusuf, or at least his men, for the attack on the liner, for their diversion. They would not move on him at the camp.

Yusuf looked around the empty room. He was alone, and now he felt more alone than he had ever been in his life. He could trust no one, not even Amir. Five more days. He had to survive until then.

CHAPTER TWENTY-FOUR

AFGHANISTAN

WATCHING HER PUT on her nylons was almost as sexy as seeing her take them off. One more reason for Mark to admire her beauty. In a land with so much primitive ugliness, it was refreshing to see sophisticated elegance. Better yet, he got to do more than just see it.

"What are you looking at?" The sultry voice with the cultured British accent never ceased to excite him.

"You know very well I'm looking at your legs. And the rest of you."

Sophie Barton, foreign correspondent for the BBC, gave him a sly wink. "That's nice." She adjusted the lacy tops of the nylons at her thighs, snugged up her low-cut panties, then put on her bra. Mark sighed. Those just-the-right-size breasts that he'd grown to desire so much would be out of view for at least another few hours.

"You're sure you have to do this thing tonight?" he asked.

"Well, if I were to call in my resignation right now, I suppose I could skip it," she said, walking into the bathroom to fix her hair and makeup. "But I rather dislike being unemployed, not to mention it would leave me stranded halfway around the world."

"I'd like to say you could bunk with me at my place, but I'm afraid it might be a bit uncomfortable for you."

"When you're out of the Army and back home, then perhaps we can discuss it again."

That kept him quiet for a minute, thinking very hard, but careful not to say anything. She appeared in the doorway of the bathroom and leaned against the wall seductively.

"Cat got your tongue, Colonel Hayes?"

"Just thinking."

"And may I ask, about what?"

"Going home. Wherever home might be."

She came to him, sliding onto the bed across the sheets. Propping her chin in her hands, she looked at him. He drank in the green eyes, the cute little freckles around her nose, her sandy blonde hair.

"Would that be back in Wisconsin, perhaps?"

He smiled. "I haven't thought about it much lately, but yeah, if any place is home, it'd be there. You'd like it."

"You shall have to show me sometime."

He gathered her in his arms and kissed her deeply. Yes, he might as well admit it, he was falling in love with her.

She broke free. "Calm yourself, my good man. Duty calls. You know about that, I'm sure."

"Yeah. Duty."

She gave him a peck on the cheek and got up from the bed, walking to the closet for the dark pants suit hanging there. "The press conference should be done by seven. Give me another hour to file the report, and then perhaps you would fancy a nice dinner?"

"Sounds good. When do you go back to London?"

"Next week. I'll be down in Helmand province for a few days, visiting First the Queen's Dragoon Guards."

"I've heard of them. Good outfit. Isn't that your cousin's unit?"

"Second cousin, from Wales. I hope to see him, yes."

"Can I see you here before you fly home?"

"Well, that depends," she said with that sly come-hither look he'd come to love. "Treat a girl to a nice dinner and maybe a massage later, and she'll probably come back for more."

"You've got a deal."

Kabul was relatively quiet tonight, so they chose a decent restaurant only a couple blocks from the hotel. Mark was in civvies, but he still carried a sidearm. He'd found it prudent to be armed wherever he went in country, the only exception being inside the embassy complex or ISAF Headquarters, which was only a few blocks further down Bibi Mahru Road from where they were dining. The Afghan waiters, accustomed to serving foreigners, were very efficient. Sophie ordered *mantu*, thick, Persian-style ravioli, while Mark chose the lamb.

"I'll bet the city has changed quite a bit since your first visit," she said as they started on dessert. She was having bride's fingers, *asabia el aroos,* slender, syrupy crisps with sweetened nuts, while he had the elephant's ears, *gosh feel,* a deep-fried pastry.

"It's a lot safer now," he said, remembering the first time he'd come to the city, during his first deployment back in '02. "Still a lot of air pollution, but there's a lot more commerce. You would've been hard-pressed to find a restaurant like this back then." The walk over here from the hotel hadn't been too bad. The morning rain had dampened down the pollution, which sometimes was so thick you could see the particles in the air.

Respiratory problems were common among the Westerners here, at least for the first month or two until they got used to it. Mark didn't want to think about what might be growing in his lungs.

"What's it like? Wisconsin, that is. Probably more pleasant than Afghanistan."

He grinned. "Oh, this place isn't so bad. Give these people some peace and security, they can do some great things." That was the standard party line, anyway, and Mark could see Sophie considered it to be about as accurate as he did: not very. "But yeah, Wisconsin is better. Lots of rolling hills, farmland. Quite a few lakes, especially up north. Great fishing. You've got Lake Michigan on the east coast, then the Mississippi River on the west. My brother went to college in a town near there. Said the river valley was beautiful."

"Have you heard from your brother lately?" He'd mentioned Jim to Sophie once or twice, said he was widowed, but not much more.

"Talked to him the other night, after the firefight." Jim's current activities were classified, of course, but just thinking about that made Mark shake his head.

"What's the matter?"

"Oh, nothing. Jim and I don't talk very much. Not as much as we should."

"If you don't mind me asking, why is that?"

Jim finished the last of his pastry, took a drink of water. "Well, it's kind of a long story."

"Perhaps you could tell me back at the hotel."

Later, she lay beside him, running her nails gently through the curly hairs on his chest, a few of which were turning white, he noticed with some irritation. "You asked me earlier about my brother," he said.

"Yes. But you don't have to talk about it if you don't want to."

"No, that's okay. I want to. I think it's time I did."

"All right."

"I was thinking...about the day I left for my cow year at West Point." He saw her cocking her head. "Junior year in the civilian schools," he said.

"You told me once you had a fine time at West Point," she said.

"I did," he said. "First two years especially. They were a bit too fine. I needed an attitude adjustment, and that summer before cow year I got one."

She waited patiently as his memories came flooding back. He'd never talked about it with anyone, hadn't really taken the time to sort it through, but now it came rushing out, and he could see it with a new sense of clarity.

"My first two years were tough, but I played a lot of football, starting fullback by mid-season plebe year. That's worth something on any campus and West Point's no exception. The firsties braced me a lot, but it wasn't too bad." He shifted his weight a little bit, and she snuggled closer, his left arm around her. He looked down, and the sheet was falling away from that cute English rump, a sight that under other circumstances would've started him thinking in another direction. "In the classroom I was fair to middling. You can't really skate through academics at the Point, but I wasn't really putting forth a lot of effort. Then in the spring of my second year, one of my profs got on my case. I got a D on a test and he called me into his office, read me the riot act."

"I'll bet that made an impression," she said.

"It did. He was a colonel, Vietnam vet, went through some really tough combat over there, and he told me I was just screwing around, that I had the potential to be an outstanding cadet, maybe even First Captain, if I would just shit can the attitude and buckle down."

"And did you?"

"It started me thinking about things a bit differently," Jim admitted. "But I still wasn't ready to start toeing the line."

He had a month's leave coming after the semester ended, so he decided to head home before going down to Fort Benning for airborne training in July. One night he went to a Brewers game with some friends from high school, and at a tailgate party a woman about twenty years older than him gave him the eye. So he brought her a beer, and after the game they capped the evening with a trip to a no-tell hotel. One more scene on the highlight reel of Mark's life, and a good one it was.

Jim and Suzy came home at the end of June for a few days, and things were a bit awkward between the brothers. "It was almost like he was jealous of me," Mark said. "I had no idea why he should be. He was two years out of college by then, had a good job and was married to Suzy, and she was a knockout, could've been a stand-in for Jaclyn Smith on *Charlie's Angels.* Then a few days later, my dad was taking me to the airport and I found out what was going on."

It was one of those father-son talks that the son never forgets. He remembered it now and allowed himself to be swept twenty-six years back in time. "You know, I could never get anything past my dad. He was pretty strict, so we never got into any real trouble when we were kids, although Jim was a lot better about that than I was. When I got to the Point, the discipline helped me fit in right away. A lot of the other guys had problems. But when I'd get leave, I'd cut loose a little bit.

The time with the woman at the game, I let things get out of hand."

"It was just a fling, Mark, you were a young guy, those things happen."

He looked into those eyes again, wondering if she meant that to sound as casual as it came out. "Yeah, but that day at the airport, before I got out of the car, Dad said he had to talk to me about a couple things. He said he'd heard about the woman. Darlene was her name. She was a minister's wife from Cudahy, the next suburb over from ours, and a guy my dad worked with was a member there and the word was out about her having a one-night stand with a young guy from an academy. Dad asked me straight out if that was me and I said yes."

"Oh, dear."

"I told him she wasn't wearing a ring, how was I to know? And he said as an officer and a gentleman I should've at least asked. I mean, a woman her age, cruising a party for young guys, I should've figured something might be going on." He sighed. "Dad said they were having problems in their marriage. I certainly didn't help matters any."

She said nothing, but he could tell she was listening intently. He'd never really opened up to her about his past, and wondered now if this was too much, too soon, but he had to tell her the rest of it, maybe because he had to hear it himself, hear it and finally deal with it.

"Then he told me about Jim, why he'd seemed so uptight when he was home. Said he'd applied for the Army Reserve and the day before he came home they gave him the word, they rejected him because of his bad knee. The year before, he tried the Marines, they said no, too."

"Why did your brother want to join up?"

"Because he…" Mark stopped, almost choking up. "My dad

said he was envious of me. At his wedding, the year before, I was his best man, and the word got out that I was at the Point, just finished plebe year and, well, I got a lot of attention from people that night." He thought about telling Sophie about the bridesmaid he'd scored with, but decided to keep that one to himself. "Kind of stole Jim's thunder, although I didn't mean to. I was just having a good time at the reception and hey, people thought it was cool I was a cadet. But right after that was when Jim tried for the Marines."

"And they turned him down, and then the Army too. I can see how he would feel badly about it."

"I never knew, never imagined he could ever be jealous of me. And here I'd made a couple cracks that weekend to him about him missing those free throws in the state final, and how I had a championship ring and he didn't. God, what a horse's ass I was."

"Your father brought that to your attention, did he?"

"He sure did. He got after me about my attitude in general. Said there was more to being at the Point than playing football, that would be gone in another couple years and then I'd be an officer and would have men to command, probably in battle." Even now, all these years later, he could still hear his father's words, as the old Korea vet sat behind the wheel of his Oldsmobile.

"I saw officers come out of West Point who thought they were God's gift to the Army and they learned pretty fast that they sure as hell weren't. Some of them learned the hard way in Korea. They didn't come home and a lot of their men didn't, either. I'm telling you, the balloon's gonna go up again one of these days and you'll be sent overseas. Maybe it'll be the Russians, maybe the Arabs, but I guaran-damn-tee you, they won't give a rat's ass how many touchdowns you scored. When they come through the wire they're gonna

be looking to blow your goddam head off and you'd better be ready or you'll be dead and your men will be dead. You need to get your head screwed on a little straighter, son. You have a helluva future, if you want it. Or you can just keep screwing around. It's up to you."

They were both quiet for a few minutes. Finally, he said, "Things were...different after that. I went off to Benning and it just seemed much clearer to me. I had more sense of purpose."

"And your brother? You haven't seen him very much, have you?"

"No. Not as much as I should, I guess. Mom's funeral in '99. I was in the Balkans when Jim called, said she'd been in a car accident." His voice caught a bit. "She was on her way home from church. She worked at the office. Fucking drunk driver. She lasted two days." He blinked away tears. "Then three years later, Dad's funeral. I was over here, first deployment, got the call he'd had a heart attack, but the next one got him just when my plane was landing in Milwaukee." He sighed deeply.

"I'm very sorry." Sophie had told him both her parents were still living, back in northern England. She didn't know how lucky she was. Or maybe she did.

"You know, I've only seen my niece four or five times in her entire life? She's twenty-five years old, for God's sake. I'm her only uncle."

She kissed his chest, but said nothing. He kept going, the words and feelings finally bubbling to the surface. "Last time was at her mother's funeral, six years ago. What the hell does that say about me, that I can only see my brother at funerals? And now he's—"

She heard the catch in his voice. "What's the matter? Is your brother ill?"

"No. He's...I can't tell you anything. It's classified." He

wanted to tell her, desperately wanted to, but held back. The training, the duty, his oath…"He's going into harm's way," he said finally. "And it's sure as hell not in Wisconsin." Suddenly he felt almost overwhelmed by the fear, the dread that Jim was going to be in trouble, and there wasn't a damn thing Mark could do to help him. He suddenly sat upright, cradling his head in his hands.

"Shh, it's all right," she whispered, holding him.

"No, it's not all right. It's wrong. He's my brother. I've got him and my son and my niece and that's it."

She stroked his hair. "You have me," she said. That brought a smile, and a kiss. "Maybe your brother is doing the same thing you are."

"What do you mean? He's not in the military—"

"I didn't mean that. What he's doing now, I know you can't tell me but it's obviously dangerous. Perhaps he's searching for the same thing you are."

"And what would that be?"

Her green eyes were deep and searching. "I've heard you talk about your work here," she said. "It's more than just being in the Army, doing your job. For you, anyway, it's a lot more than that."

"Somebody's got to do it."

"Yes, that's true," she said. "But while many are called, few are chosen. You've been chosen, Mark. I just have that feeling about you. There's a sense of…well, decency about you that I don't always see in military men. Or civilians, for that matter. Especially civilians."

"Well, I've been called a lot of things, but 'decent' is a new one."

"Have you ever thought about why you do what you do? I mean, the real reasons why?"

He looked away for a second, then back at her. Outside, a siren started to wail. He waited for a second, expecting to hear the crump of an explosion, the rattle of small-arms fire, but it didn't come. He forced himself to relax. He thought of his father again. Not a very well-educated man, but hard-working. Ed Hayes was a little rough around the edges, but he loved his wife and his boys, would do anything for them, and he loved his country, fought for it and risked his life to help people stay free. He stood for something, Never got rich because of it, never became famous, he just did what had to be done, because...why? Then it came to him, so simple, yet so true.

"It's...it's a matter of honor," he said slowly.

She smiled. "You don't know how refreshing it is to hear a man say that."

McLEAN, VIRGINIA

THERE HAD BEEN a time, when Jim was reading a novel by one of his favorite authors like Dick Couch or David Poyer, he imagined himself in the middle of some clandestine operation for the CIA, or in the field with the Marines, or at sea on a Navy destroyer. He imagined how exciting it would be, the challenge of the work, the camaraderie with his fellow agents or sailors or soldiers. Certainly a cut above the rather humdrum life he'd chosen for himself.

Now he was here, working with the CIA at their headquarters in Langley, and he was getting bored. Perhaps *impatient* was a better word. Something was going to happen, he was going overseas, but when? He'd been here three days already, and the excitement of seeing CIA Headquarters had worn off a day or so earlier. He was beginning to miss his house back in Cedar Lake, his cat, the dojo, even the office, for God's sake. And what about Gina? Would the spark die out?

When they arrived in Washington late that Saturday night, they took him to a townhouse in the suburban Virginia town of McLean where he would be staying. He was under strict orders not to go outside without permission. There was an agent on duty with him at all times, sitting in the living room, reading or watching television. So far he'd counted four different men on the detail, all of them young, very fit, polite but not talkative. He sensed they were bored, too, and probably a little frustrated with their assignment, but they were professionals and did their job.

Sunday he spent settling in. The closet in the master bedroom held a selection of casual clothes in his size, and the dresser had a decent supply of socks and underwear, in case he ran out of what he'd been allowed to bring along. There was no telephone. A room set aside as a den held a nice selection of books and a computer with some games installed but no internet connection. Allenson came by around five and they went out to dinner at a quiet restaurant nearby, but their conversation was all business. She filled him in on his schedule for the week, deflected his few questions about her work and background, and drove him back to the townhouse, giving him a brief smile and handshake as he exited the car. The agent on duty was standing in the front door.

He could leave if he wanted to, that had been made clear. Until they were airborne on their way to Africa a few days later, he could pull the plug at any time. All he had to do was tell his minder that he wanted to go home, and arrangements would be made. Within a few hours he'd be back in his own house.

But he knew he wouldn't do that, and, surely they knew that, too.

Monday, Allenson showed up promptly at eight in the morning and took him to the CIA building in the neighborhood known as Langley. It was impressive, but he'd seen it on TV and in the movies many times, so he wasn't awed by it.

Filled with people who all seemed to know where they were going, tight security, meticulously clean, the building seemed to know how important it was. Allenson showed him to a conference room, where he met a few other people. They talked about his background, and asked Jim to detail his martial arts training. When he asked about the mission, they told him that would be the topic of another meeting. After lunch in one of the building's cafeterias he was given a tour. He saw the scale model of the A-12 Oxcart surveillance jet, the successor to the U-2 and predecessor to the SR-71 Blackbird. A plaque said the jet could fly more than three times the speed of sound at 90,000 feet. There was the Directors Gallery, busts of Nathan Hale and President George H.W. Bush, the only CIA director ever to become president. There was the museum, a library with over 125,000 volumes, and so much more. They even had a gym, a very nice one at that, and he was allowed to get in a workout. That, at least, had been refreshing. After that, back to the townhouse and a quiet evening.

Tuesday's agenda included some indications as to what was on the horizon. Already knowing from the day before that the only firearms training he'd ever had was as a kid shooting at cans with a .410 shotgun on his uncle's farm, they told him he would not be handling any guns on this trip. He suspected that would've been the case even if he'd known everything there was to know about guns. Couldn't argue with them on that one. He'd probably wind up shooting himself or someone else.

They went over some very general particulars about the mission. They'd fly direct from Washington to Germany and then Djibouti, in the Horn of Africa, a place Jim had heard of before, vaguely. When he looked it up that night in an encyclopedia at the townhouse, he found out a lot more. That would be the staging area. From there, probably somewhere into Somalia. When would this happen? Well, that was still a bit up in the air. They would know soon enough, and they assured him things would start moving quickly after that.

Over lunch he mentioned that he'd never been to Washington. Denise asked him if there was anything in particular he'd like to see, and he told her about two sites that held a certain interest for him. An hour later he was in a car with his minder at the wheel. It was a hot day, so they stopped by the townhouse first so he could change into some light linen pants and a cotton polo shirt, and he spotted a hat store where he bought himself a straw fedora. A short time later they were in the capital.

They only had a few hours to spare, so he wanted to make the most of them. The Vietnam Memorial was very moving, crowded with old veterans and younger people he assumed were the children of fallen vets, some of them weeping as they touched a name etched into the black granite. He wondered if someday they'd put up memorials for the men and women who'd never made it back from Iraq and Afghanistan. There was a bad moment when he thought of seeing Mark's name on a granite wall years from now.

His second and last stop was the Korean War Memorial. It was too bad his father had never made it here. What would Ed Hayes have thought of the nineteen stainless steel statues of wandering soldiers, their hands clutching their rifles, many eyes looking haunted, peering ahead or to the side in search of...what? The enemy? A missing comrade, maybe, perhaps an end to the cold and pain and brutality. There were a few veterans here, a bit older than their Vietnam-era counterparts. Jim sat on a bench near the Pool of Remembrance and read the inscription on the plaque: "Our nation honors her sons and daughters who answered the call to defend a country they never knew and a people they never met."

His father had done that, his brother was doing it right now, and finally it was Jim's turn. He hoped he'd be up to the task.

The Wednesday morning briefing contained nothing really new. Yes, the mission was a go, but they still didn't tell him when. He got the impression they would know something in another twenty-four hours or so. Until then, he would just have to wait. He asked if he could call his daughter, and Gina, to let them know he was okay. Allenson talked it over with someone by phone, then said fine, and he was given some privacy in the conference room, but had to place the call through an operator. Maybe they were worried about him calling MSNBC to blow the whistle on the whole operation.

Mickey was relieved to hear his voice, but knowing someone was surely listening in, he couldn't tell her much more than what he'd said back on Saturday. Gina sounded happy to hear from him, and concerned, but Jim found himself fretting that whatever spark they might've had up in Rice Lake would be gone by the time he got back from the mission. He promised to get in touch with her as soon as he got back, hopefully in a few days, and they'd get together.

Allenson was waiting at the door of the conference room. "I thought we might go out for lunch," she said. She was becoming a familiar mealtime companion by now, and their conversations tended to steer away from the mission, but on the ride to a ritzy shopping area she called Tysons Galleria she said, "I get the feeling you're a little impatient, Jim." At least they were on a first-name basis now. Jim had been wondering if that would ever happen; if he'd discovered anything about the CIA and its people by now, it was that they were all business.

He hadn't thought it was that obvious, but those people were trained observers, after all. "Well, I appreciate everything you people are doing, and I know we have to wait for…something, but yeah, I could use a little action." He looked at her, then chuckled. "I didn't really mean that like it sounded."

That brought a bit of a smile. "That's all right." She flipped the car's signal arm to the right as the entrance to the Galleria approached, then flipped it off. "Tell you want, I know a little place not far from here, a little more down to earth."

"Sure."

Five minutes later she pulled to the curb. Jim had presumed that McLean wouldn't have anything resembling a rough part of town, but this area was noticeably down the ladder a rung or two from their original destination. Denise led the way to a small bar and grill. "Great burgers here, Jim," she said. "I assume you're a burger guy?"

"With cheese and maybe some bacon, I could be persuaded."

The interior of the Bull Run Bar & Grill had muted lights and a décor that was vaguely Civil War-era. Jim remembered that the real battles of Bull Run had taken place only about twenty miles from here. Since they were in Virginia, he wondered why the bar had adopted the Northern name for the battles, rather than Manassas. He took in the other patrons: three of the booths were occupied, two with couples, one with two women. Two men in suits sat at one end of the bar, with a lone man near the middle.

They took a moment to look over the menus. "I have to use the ladies' room," Denise said. "When the waitress comes, I'll have the special of the day."

Jim had considered that, too. "Italian beef. With the house fries or the potato chips?"

"Fries, please." She slid out of the booth and headed toward the far end of the room, turning left past the bar.

"Hi there, welcome to the Bull Run," a soft Southern-tinged voice said.

"Hi, I'd like—" He froze. The waitress was young, maybe early twenties, but she could've been…

"Excuse me?" she said.

"Uh, sorry. I'll have the bacon cheeseburger, and my friend gets the Italian beef. Fries with both."

"Sure thing. How about something to drink?"

That stumped him. He thought about ordering a beer, but Denise was on duty, and technically he was too, he supposed. "A couple of lemonades, please."

"All right, great. Be back with your drinks in two shakes." She gave him a dazzling smile and walked away toward the next occupied booth. He couldn't believe it. Even from behind, she looked like Suzy, from their college days. His heart started beating a little faster. He took a deep breath and forced himself to keep calm.

He couldn't take his eyes off her, though. As she took another order, he noticed a couple differences from Suzy. She didn't have the Cindy Crawford-style beauty mark on the right cheek like his late wife, and she was a couple inches taller. But otherwise, it was uncanny—the build, the hair, and that smile.

He also enjoyed the view from the rear as she walked toward the far end of the bar. Had Suzy ever worn jeans like that? No, come to think of it, this gal wore them even better—

"Hey, darlin', c'mere." The lone man at the bar grabbed her by the arm as she went by.

"Excuse me, sir. How can I help you?"

"Oh, I can think of a couple ways." Jim zeroed in, all senses alive now. The man was about thirty, and more crudely dressed than the other men in the bar: ball cap, sleeveless tee shirt, jeans, boots. Jim saw a tattoo on his left bicep, two metal studs in the left earlobe. As he turned on the barstool, Jim caught a thin rectangular bulge in the right front pocket of the jeans. Knife, probably a butterfly.

The bartender was on the phone at the far end of the bar. The two men at the near end had stopped their conversation and were looking at the lone man and the waitress. Jim saw their body language; they weren't going to do anything.

"Sir, please, you're hurting my arm."

Jim slid silently out of the booth.

"Now, honey, you been ignorin' me an' that ain't polite. You an' me could have a real fine time together." The waitress tried to pull free from his grip, failed, gasping as he tightened it.

"Let her go."

The man saw Jim for the first time. "Fuck off, dude, this between me an'—"

"Wrong answer." Jim reached for the man's hand and peeled away the pinky finger, twisting it back and around counter-clockwise. The man gasped and the waitress yanked her arm free. "Time for you to go," Jim said. He stepped behind the man and brought the hand around and up, into a chicken-wing hold. He applied just a bit of pressure to the elbow with his left hand and lifted the man off the barstool.

He staggered and Jim saw him reach with his free right hand for the knife. "Don't try it," Jim said, applying a hair more pressure to the hold. The man yelled in pain.

"Hey, man, that hurts!"

"I'll bet it does," Jim said. "Not as much as this, though."

He cranked the arm another couple inches, bringing a scream of pain. "Now, let's walk nice and easy to the door, my friend, and there'll be no need for me to break anything."

The two men at the bar were staring with wide eyes as Jim marched the man past them and out the door. He gave the guy a none-too-gentle shove. "Don't come back."

The man lurched away a couple steps, his left arm dangling, but the right hand went for the pocket and out came the knife. "I'm gonna cut you, man!" He flipped the butterfly knife open and twirled it at his side, shoulder-high, then started to swing the four-inch blade around in a slashing arc. It would've done some damage, but Jim had kept himself relaxed and breathing normally and his Systema training came back to him without a thought. He flowed underneath the slashing arm, guiding it around and back at the man as he fired a left punch into the kidney area and kicked at the inside of his right knee. The man buckled and went down as Jim gently twisted the knife hand, freeing the weapon.

The man was on his back on the sidewalk and Jim had his right knee on the ribcage and left foot pinning down the right arm. The guy's eyes bulged as he realized the knife blade was now only two inches from his own throat.

"Don't play with knives," Jim said, standing up and flipping the knife closed and into his pocket.

"Nicely done, Jim."

Denise was at the door of the bar, along with the waitress. They were both smiling. "What the hell is this?" Jim said. He glanced back down at the barroom bully, who started to sit up, clutching his left arm, forcing a small grin through the pain.

"Congratulations," Denise said. "You passed."

CHAPTER TWENTY-SIX

SOMALIA

YUSUF WAS EXHAUSTED again. Of course he wasn't a young man anymore, but it wasn't so much the physical stress. He was used to that by now, after so many years in the field. No, it was the mental strain. He wasn't sleeping well, often waking with so much racing through his mind that he could not relax, so he would usually rise quietly and go into his office to peck away at the computer. Tonight was one of those nights.

He had returned to the camp late last night from another trip to Mogadishu. The meeting with the American CIA contact had gone well. The two men did not yet fully trust each other, probably never would, but there was enough trust between them now to allow them to work together. Simons told him about the foiled attack on Ashkelon, how his superiors were very pleased and were prepared to cooperate with Yusuf, provide him all the assistance he would need to get out of the country and into protective custody.

And, most exciting of all, they had found James Hayes, and he was working with them. Yusuf tried to conceal his excitement at that news, offering only a smile and a nod. They moved on to a discussion of the particulars. They would bring Hayeu to Mogadishu in three days' time, on the thirty-first of July. The meeting was set for the Hotel Quruxsan at seven p.m. Yusuf had only one additional request: that the Americans find his parents in Nairobi and take them out of the country. At first he'd thought they would be safe staying in Kenya, but the more he thought about it, the more he realized he could not trust the men who would soon become his most bitter enemies. They might not be able to find him, but they would find his parents, and punish him through them. That he could not bear, so he had given Simons a letter for his parents, written in Swahili and containing references only they and Yusuf would know, begging them to accompany the Americans to safety. Simons promised that he would pass his request to his superiors and felt confident they would do what they could.

July thirty-first. They would be cutting things very close indeed, but Yusuf couldn't move the timetable up. Heydar's men were now in the camp, and the training for the ship seizure had begun in earnest. The strike team would depart the camp in three shifts. The first truck would leave on August first, with the second twelve hours later, early on the morning of the second, and the final truck twelve hours after that. The staggered departures were a security measure; one could never be sure of the Americans and their drones and satellites, so they would not make it easy for them by sending the entire force out at once. They would meet in Mogadishu and board the ship on the evening of the third, setting sail just before midnight.

Heydar's chief lieutenant, who Yusuf felt certain was an officer in the IRGC's naval detachment, had plotted out the course of the ship precisely. They would intercept the cruise liner on the evening of the sixth. The attack would commence when most of the passengers were sitting down to dinner and thus a large portion of the crew would be busy accommodating their guests. The seizure of the vessel would be announced to the world by the commandos around midnight. It would be in the middle of the night in Europe, still the previous early evening on the Americans' east coast. Plenty of time for the news agencies to start airing the story, but it would take several hours for the American and British governments to coordinate their response.

The cruise liner would be scuttled before dawn. With any luck at all, Heydar said, no American or NATO naval vessel would be within striking distance of them. They would have to move quickly, but the point was not to hold the vessel for days.

"Well, then, what *is* the point?" Yusuf asked. It was a logical question, and one some of his own people, including Amir, had asked him privately after the Iranians held their first briefing for Yusuf and his officers. A high-profile hostage-taking mission had to be drawn out for at least a few days for maximum propaganda value. The longer they held the Westerners, the more embarrassment it caused for their governments. Eventually the commandos would come, of course, but as Amir had said, they should hold the ship for at least twenty-four hours, maybe forty-eight, before doing what they had to do and making their escape, although escape by then might very well be impossible. But at least they could go down fighting, taking as many of the infidel sailors with them as possible.

Only Yusuf had the authority, or frankly the nerve, to ask their "advisers" such an obvious question. Even though many of his men had come to know Heydar, had even been training with him in his makeshift martial arts gym, the camp's leadership cadre did not trust him or any of the other Iranians who had arrived. And indeed, Heydar had been evasive in his answer. "The Americans and the British will once again be held up for ridicule," he said. "We will show them their people are not safe from us anywhere, even on the high seas."

There was certainly ample reason for their distrust, Yusuf knew. It was becoming very clear that he and his own men were more and more becoming simple pawns of the Iranians. Yusuf did not like this, and he recalled past conversations he'd had with Hamas and Hezbollah men in Gaza and Lebanon. No, they did not particularly like the Iranians, either, but that's where most of their arms and financing came from, so they let the Iranians think they were in charge. Things would be different, they said, when the Zionists were expelled from Palestine and the Americans humbled and withdrawn. The Iranians thought they'd be in control of everything then, but they would find out differently.

Yusuf wasn't so sure about that. Tehran was not spending so much money, taking so many risks, just to stand aside if their clients succeeded. Unlike the Americans, who were pulling out of Iraq even now and would eventually leave Afghanistan, the Iranians would stick around. After all, the great caliphate would need a caliph. He would be the man who had the most firepower behind him, and Iran had more of that than any other Muslim state in the world. Pakistan had a larger nuclear arsenal, or so Yusuf assumed, but not for long. No, Iran was making its case for leadership of the Muslim world, and making it in ways that were perfectly understood: they would do it with their wallets, and if that wasn't persuasive, they would do it at gunpoint.

Yusuf knew from his time in the Aladagh that Iran had a perfect choice for the caliph. Tailor-made, so to speak. The Shi'a would believe that, many of them would anyway, although

Yusuf doubted the Sunni would be convinced that the man in the Aladagh was indeed the Twelfth Imam. But that man would be backed by the military arsenal of a mighty nation, so he would call the shots, as the Americans would say.

Yusuf fretted as he tapped away at his keyboard. It would not be a peaceful place, this caliphate, despite what its advocates said. There would be bloodshed on an unprecedented scale. The first to go would be the Christians still living there. It was already happening, in fact, to the Copts in Egypt. Something had to be done to stop it, all of it. Perhaps, he thought, once the Americans knew about the man in the Aladagh and his plans, they would not only stop that effort but strike back. It would certainly seem the logical thing to do, but Yusuf knew from his time in America that its politicians were anything but logical much of the time. Under their previous president, perhaps something might have been done. Had he not swept the Taliban from Afghanistan and chased Osama into the wilds of Pakistan? Had he not roared through Iraq to depose Saddam? The two Islamic leaders who had been thought to be the most powerful, with all the forces at their command, had been routed, and the Americans had only needed to use a fraction of their arsenal to get those jobs done.

The power of the Americans was awesome; it was frightening to think of what might happen if they truly became enraged and struck back with all their might. He remembered the years just before he came to America, after the Iranians had seized their embassy in Tehran and kept the hostages. The American president at the time seemed impotent, even with such a powerful military force at his disposal. But not the man who challenged him. Yusuf smiled now in the dim light as he remembered the joke from thirty-one years earlier: *What is flat, black and glows in the dark? Iran, after Reagan takes office.* And sure enough, the Iranians released the hostages on the very day that man was sworn in. Yusuf and everyone else in the movement knew that was no coincidence.

He pecked at a few more keys, then took the flash drive from the secret place in his desk. He held it up to the light from his desk lamp. A remarkable device, really, something that was once in the realm of science fiction. So small, yet it could hold so much data. He inserted it into the slot on the face of the computer tower, and began sending files into the drive. Within minutes the transfer was complete. He checked the drive to make sure the files were there, was satisfied that they were, checked it again, and then proceeded to delete the files from the hard drive. It took him a half-hour, but he scrubbed every last byte from the computer.

With the drive in his hand, he stretched, looking around him. Nobody was there, of course. Some in the camp were still awake, probably just those few from the security detail who were on duty, but nobody else was here. Yusuf went quickly to the opposite wall of the room and moved the rug away from the base of the wall. A crack in the masonry had worked its way down from three feet up on the wall, all the way to the base. Yusuf reached into the pocket of his robe and withdrew the knife, the one he always carried with him. It was a Fox British Army Knife, which he had gotten years before on a trip to London. Not as remarkable, perhaps, as the flash drive, but still notable in its own right: made of stainless steel, with a can opener, a marlin's pike and a built-in screwdriver. Its four-inch blade was not ideal for knife fighting, but could do some serious damage to an assailant at close quarters, as Yusuf had proven once or twice. The knife had been with him day and night for years. He hoped the Americans would let him keep it.

He used the blade now to work on a piece of masonry

wedged into the bottom of the crack where it had split in two. It took him a minute to pull the one-by-three-inch piece out of the wall. He took a small rag from another pocket and carefully but tightly wrapped it around the flash drive, holding it in place with a rubber band. Finally, he gently pushed the bundle into the wall and replaced the piece of masonry in the hole.

Was that a noise? He looked back at the doorway. Nobody there, behind the beaded curtain. The window was shaded. He was still alone. Breathing out, he replaced the rug and went back to his desk, shut down the computer, turned off the light and returned to bed. In the darkness, he lay silently, trying to shut his brain down, but he could not. He prayed to Allah that he was doing the right thing.

In the Aladagh, he had been told the broad outlines of the Iranian plan to strike a devastating blow against the Great Satan. No exact timetable had been disclosed, just the general details, which were breathtaking in their magnitude. His cooperation would be vital to the success of the plan. He would be told later what his role would be.

Now, he knew what that was. The seizure of the cruise ship would be a great distraction for the Americans, even though it was a British ship. Surely there would be some Americans on board, more than enough to cause their leaders great concern. They would put much effort into getting more information, then formulating a plan to re-take the ship. No doubt the American president would offer to send in his Navy SEALs, who were much feared by the jihadists. But the British had excellent commandos as well. Given enough time, the Westerners would undoubtedly be able to re-take the ship, and in the early hours of the crisis they would think they had enough time.

They would not.

CHAPTER TWENTY-SEVEN
TEHRAN, IRAN

THE DINNER PARTY was going well. Fazeed had to admire his wife for organizing the affair and carrying it off flawlessly. Of course she'd had plenty of experience doing this, but still, he recognized highly competent work when he saw it. As he watched her chatting with their guests, his heart began to ache. If he proceeded down the path he was contemplating, there was a very good chance he would be leaving this world soon, and he would miss her so, but someday they would be reunited in Paradise. He had to hang onto that belief. It was all that had kept him going in recent days. That, and the hope that he might have the support and counsel of his oldest friend. It was time to discover if that hope would be realized.

He caught Admiral Ralouf's eye and raised an eyebrow. The admiral nodded. Fazeed excused himself from his guests and headed off to the lavatory. After conducting his business there, or trying to—his bladder seemed reluctant to function— he made his way to the small study he maintained as his home office. He busied himself with security, checking to make sure everything was operational, and then there was a slight knock at the door. He looked up to see Ralouf entering, quickly shutting the door behind him.

Fazeed handed his friend a cup of tea he had prepared at the special espresso-style machine he had bought in Taiwan on his visit there a year ago. Ralouf took a sip and nodded. "Excellent," he said. The admiral raised his eyebrows, nodding at the window.

"I just checked the security countermeasures. We may speak freely."

Ralouf nodded again, took another sip, then wandered over to the wall, gazing at the photograph hanging there. The photo showed a group of students on their graduation day from Imam Hossein University. Ralouf sighed and smiled wistfully. "We were so young then, weren't we, my friend?"

"Indeed we were, Rostam." Fazeed remembered it well. He and Ralouf had both entered the graduate program in 1986, when the university opened, and received their degrees two years later, Fazeed in aerospace engineering, Ralouf in military science. That was where they had met and become friends. "We were idealistic, weren't we?"

"We were," the admiral said, "with so much potential, just like our young country. Remember how we used to complain that our fathers were such imbeciles?"

Fazeed chuckled. "We were going to lead our nation to greatness, something they had never been able to achieve under the shah."

Ralouf looked at him, serious now. "What happened to that, Arash? What happened to us?"

"Perhaps a more relevant question would be: What happened to our country?"

"Yes. What happened?"

"Reality happened," Fazeed said. "The war with Iraq. The constant focus on the Zionists. Antagonizing the Americans. Everything."

Ralouf nodded sadly. "And so here we are. A new age is about to dawn, thanks in large part to our hands."

Fazeed sat in his chair, suddenly very tired, but he could not allow his fatigue to overcome his caution. He set the teacup down on his desk. "But will it be an age of enlightenment and progress, or a new Dark Age? That is what we must ask ourselves."

Ralouf took the chair next to the desk. "We have already asked that question, have we not? Now we must determine the answer."

Fazeed looked at his old friend. "What do you believe are the chances of success for the mission?"

The admiral shrugged. "Seventy-thirty, perhaps, if you define it as two successful launches and detonations."

"And overall?"

"Factor in the strong probability of eventual retaliation by the Americans, which our nation will not survive. Therefore I would say it is one in ten."

"I would consider that optimistic."

"You may be right about that." Ralouf sighed again, shaking his head. "How could we have allowed this to happen, my friend?"

"It hasn't happened yet. We still have time."

Ralouf looked at him sharply. "To do what?"

This was where Fazeed knew he would have to take a gigantic leap of faith, or forever hold his tongue. Could he trust this man? Rostam Ralouf was his oldest and dearest friend. They had attended each other's weddings, the naming ceremonies of their children. Ralouf personally delivered the tragic news to Fazeed and his wife on that day when their only child, the son Fazeed named for his father, had drowned, two weeks into his Navy basic training

Fazeed made his decision. He could not do this alone. "Rostam, you have been as a brother to me all these years. What I will ask of you now will be difficult. I will not blame you if you refuse."

Ralouf's green eyes held his own. He knew. "Arash, whatever you ask, I shall do my best to help."

Fazeed let out a deep, tense breath. "You know of what I speak, even before I utter the words."

"Perhaps because I think the same thoughts, my friend."

"I seek your counsel about a very serious matter." There was a heartbeat or two of silence, and then Fazeed said, "Some months ago, I met a man at the marketplace in the city near my base. He was a German, quite pleasant, a dealer in antiquities. We struck up a conversation. His Farsi was very good, which is unusual for Germans."

"I have heard that. Please, go on."

"A week later, I visited a different part of the bazaar. He was there again. Just by coincidence, of course."

"Of course."

"We enjoyed a cup of coffee at a little café, and the talk turned to politics. He asked me about the effect of the sanctions placed upon us by the West as a result of our nuclear program. I gave him the standard response: the sanctions are as nothing to us."

Ralouf smiled grimly. "Which is a lie." They both knew the truth. Everybody knew. Their country was being squeezed a little bit tighter every day, prices rising, money getting tighter, people grumbling. Unemployment was rising as fast as inflation.

"He said that back in Germany they feel them, too, because they import much of the mutton for their sausages from us, and our prices have risen sharply in recent months."

"Serious as that may be, I doubt the Germans will invade us to secure low prices for their sausage meat."

Fazeed smiled at that. "I would agree that is the least of our worries. But my new friend Heinz also said, as we concluded our lunch, that he would be most interested in hearing more of my thoughts on these matters. He invited me to stop by a dealer of rugs and antiquities, where he conducts his business when he is in the city."

"And did you?"

"A couple weeks later, I happened to be in the city again and stopped by the shop. The owner was a very polite gentleman from Turkmenistan, and said Heinz was not there that day, but would return in two days' time. So I went back two days later. Heinz was there. He showed me some things he had just obtained from a trip to the Caucasus. One thing led to another during our conversation. He finally told me that if I ever desired to discuss these matters in more detail, he would be able to put me in touch with certain individuals who would be most interested in my views on certain subjects. Individuals who would be willing to compensate me for my time and trouble, should I so desire. His meaning was clear."

Ralouf looked at the window, then around the small room, finally at the door, and then back to Fazeed. "Did you follow through with that invitation?"

"Not yet. But I return to the base tomorrow, and I have been thinking I might want to see the latest wares in that antiquities shop shortly after my return. What do you think of that?"

Ralouf looked toward the window again, then took a deep breath and turned back to his friend. "That sounds like a very good idea. One never knows what one might find in one of these shops."

Fazeed felt some of his tension melt away. He drew strength from his friend's confident determination. "Very true. Perhaps even answers to questions we have been thinking about, my friend."

Ralouf paused. "We must be very careful. We were rather... outspoken in the briefing the other day. Our friend Jafari was not amused. I have the feeling that VEVAK is watching us. They may also be watching this Turkmen rug merchant."

"I know they are watching me," Fazeed said. "I instructed my own security teams to be alert and initiate countermeasures. I suggest you do the same."

"That is very risky, is it not?"

"Yes," Fazeed said, "but I did not mention any VEVAK involvement. I told them to be on the lookout for heightened surveillance from Mossad, which might very well be happening anyway. They are not to take action unless I give my express permission. So far this has merely been a very good exercise for them."

Ralouf nodded, then stood. "Please keep me posted on the results of your...search." He extended a hand as the general stood. "My wife has been telling me it is time for a new rug."

CHAPTER TWENTY-EIGHT
McLEAN, VIRGINIA

THE DAY BEFORE they left Langley, Jim was briefed about what to expect when they got to the Horn of Africa. For an hour, a very capable young man showed him slides with pictures of the people, the terrain, the cities. He went over maps of Somalia and advised about how to interact with the locals, what to say and what not to say, even how to use a public restroom, if such a thing could be found, which was not likely: "Enter with the left foot, depart leading with the right. Remain silent while on the toilet. Use of toilet paper is acceptable. If another man is sitting next to you, do not look at him, do not converse, do not look at each other's genitals, and especially do not touch another man's genitals."

Jim told him they wouldn't have to worry about him on that score. Nobody else thought it was funny.

He wondered how much of this was necessary. After all, he didn't intend to do any sight-seeing. The briefing before the lecture on culture had finally given him a precise itinerary: fly from Washington to the Air Force base in Ramstein, Germany, refuel there during a brief layover and then on to Djibouti, arriving on the morning of the thirtieth, local time. He'd have the rest of that day to get over the jet lag and then they would head to Mogadishu the next day. The meet with Shalita was set for seven in the evening. They'd be back in Djibouti before midnight and he'd be winging homeward at first light.

It sounded pretty simple, but Jim had a feeling it wouldn't be quite that easy. He was going to ask how many of their operations wound up going exactly according to plan, but decided against it.

At noon on the twenty-ninth he sat down to a private lunch with the CIA Director himself, along with Allenson, in an executive dining room. Jim had seen the DCI on television but was somewhat surprised by how congenial the man turned out to be in person. He asked several questions about Jim's background, and although Jim was pretty sure the Director knew the answers already, he was happy to oblige. They finally got around to discussing the mission.

The Director touched his lips with his napkin, then took a sip of coffee. When he looked over at Jim, his eyes, through his glasses, were more serious. "Jim, I don't have to tell you that this mission has some risks associated with it."

"I understand that, sir. Your people have been very thorough in helping me get ready."

"We don't expect you to have to do anything except show up, basically. When you meet with Shalita, confirm that it's him, as best you can—I know you haven't seen him in some time—and then let my people do their jobs."

"Yes, sir. I do have a question, though."

"Certainly."

"What if it's him, but he backs out?"

The DCI glanced at Allenson, then back at Jim. "Well, we have contingencies planned for different...eventualities."

Jim nodded. "Meaning, you're bringing him out one way or another."

The Director sat back in his chair, offering a hint of a smile. "Let's just say we have contingency plans, and leave it at that, shall we?"

Jim nodded, but he could see how this might unravel. Shalita shows up, gets cold feet, tries to leave. He'll have some men with him, certainly. Jim and Allenson wouldn't be there alone, either. It could get rough, and Jim had a feeling that when things got rough over in Somalia it was a lot worse than here in the States.

The DCI glanced at his watch. "I have a meeting on the Hill coming up, so I have to be going." He stood, Jim and Allenson following suit. The Director extended his hand. "Jim, thanks again for your help. You're doing very important work. I'm sure you'll do well."

"Thank you, sir. I'll do what I can."

In the hallway outside, the Director nodded at one of Jim's minders, who was waiting for them. "Jim, this agent will escort you back to the training area. I'd like a brief word with Agent Allenson."

As the two men walked away, with Jim glancing once back over his shoulder, the DCI turned to her. "What do you think, Denise?"

"I think he'll do all right, sir. He's sharp, and he's in great shape. Takes instruction pretty well, doesn't seem to get rattled. He must have some excellent trainers back in Wisconsin."

"No doubt he does, but as good as they might be, they won't have prepared him for where he's going."

"That's true, sir. He's only been out of the country once, to a resort in Jamaica a few years ago."

The DCI scratched the bridge of his nose. "The White House is worried he might try to be a cowboy over there. What do you think?"

Allenson bristled, then caught herself. Was that just a professional reaction, or was it starting to get personal with her? "May I speak freely, sir?"

"Of course."

"If the White House people were doing this, they couldn't find their asses over there with both hands and a flashlight, as my grandfather used to say. I think Mr. Hayes will do just fine."

The Director smiled. "I think you're right on both counts." He extended his hand. "Good luck, and happy hunting."

Allenson came by the townhouse at four to pick Jim up for the trip to Andrews Air Force Base. Inside, she found him packing his bag. The agent on duty would be driving them to Andrews, and after they left, an Agency-contracted cleanup crew would come in to sanitize the safe house.

"All set, Jim?"

"Yeah, I guess so." He stuffed his toiletries kit into the bag and zipped it shut. As instructed, he was dressed casually, in the same clothes he'd worn on the flight here from Wisconsin. There'd be a change of clothes waiting for him in Djibouti.

Jim looked around the place once. He was just getting used to it, but still he preferred his place back in Cedar Lake. Not for the first time, he wondered if he'd ever see it again. He sighed. In a few hours he'd be over the Atlantic, heading east, a trip his brother had made many times during his career. That reminded him of something else.

"Say, Denise, I wonder if I might be able to call my brother. Not now, but when we get to the base, before the flight."

"I'll see what I can do. Feeling nervous?"

For a second there, he thought she was about to reach out to him, but she held back. "Well, yeah," he said. "I just thought it would be good to talk to him."

"I'm sure we can work something out."

Jim settled back in the comfortable seat and tried to relax. He knew he should really try to get some sleep, but his mind was going almost as fast as the jet. He'd taken a melatonin tablet just after takeoff; that usually worked back home when he needed to get some sleep, but this was different.

The lights in the small cabin had just dimmed, an hour after they left the ground, and the few other passengers seemed to be settling in, some sleeping already, others reading or working on laptops and tablets. No doubt they'd done this before. Out the window to his right was nothing but darkness. They'd be landing at Ramstein in about five hours. He'd always wanted to visit Germany, the country his great-grandparents on his mother's side had emigrated from a century before. Wouldn't get to see too much of it on this trip, though. But there would be other trips, assuming he survived this one.

Denise had followed through. Just before boarding the jet, she handed him a cell phone. "Your brother's on the line," she said.

His hand actually trembled as he took the phone and walked a few paces away from the rest of the people getting ready to board. "Mark, are you there?"

"Yeah, big brother. I hear you're taking a little trip."

"I guess you could say that." He had no idea whether Mark knew what was going on, but he suspected he knew at least some of it. "How are you doing? How's the head?"

"Okay. I got lucky that time." Mark hesitated, and Jim could hear the hiss and pop of the line reaching halfway around the world. "Listen, you be careful, all right? Listen to your people. They know what they're doing."

"I will. Mark...I'm sorry I haven't kept in touch more. Next time you get some leave, let's get together."

"Yeah, we both need to get better with that. Drop me an email when you get home. I think I might get back for a week or so in the fall. I'd like to see the leaves turning."

"Sounds good." Jim could feel himself starting to tear up. "I better go now, we're leaving soon. You take care of yourself, okay?"

"I will. Say hello to my niece for me when you get home. And God be with you, big brother."

CHAPTER TWENTY-NINE
AFGHANISTAN

THE GENERAL LOOKED as fit as ever when he climbed out of the chopper, crisply returning Mark's salute. Behind him was another man, a bit taller, wearing NATO-style *flecktarn*-patterned cammies with no insignia. His dark green beret sported a badge Mark had seen only a few times before, featuring the NATO compass, flanked by wings and backed by crossed sword and trident with a parachute at the top. Mark would've known something was up just by having the General make this short-notice visit, but seeing the visitor with him confirmed it.

The General returned Mark's salute and his handshake was firm, as always. "Mark, I don't think you've met Captain John Krieger."

"No sir." He offered the man a hand. "Captain, welcome to Camp Roosevelt. Mark Hayes."

His hand felt like it was gripping a piece of iron. "Colonel, a pleasure," Krieger said with a slight German accent.

"Sind Sie deutscher, Herr Hauptmann?"

"Ja, aber sprechen wir Englisch, bitte."

"Very good," Mark said. That was just as well, his Academy German probably wouldn't go very far. "This way, gentlemen."

The General made the rounds of Mark's headquarters, saying hello to everyone, remembering the names of every soldier except the recent arrivals, whom Mark introduced. This would almost certainly be the last time the General was here; in another few weeks he would be retiring from the Army and heading back home to take over CIA. After a few minutes, the General said, "Well, Mark, I'd like to tour the base, but I need a word with you first."

"Of course, sir. Step into my sumptuous conference room."

Adjacent to his own tiny office, the room was big enough for a table, six chairs and a white board on one wall, with a map of Afghanistan on another. The General got right down to business. "Mark, I have an update on that situation we discussed on the phone the other night. The DCI and I have been sharing intel lately, as you might expect, and he gave me a heads-up on this one because our people here are likely to be impacted."

Mark glanced at the German, who so far hadn't said a thing since their exchange out near the chopper pad. Krieger was the commanding officer of Unit 7, a very specialized outfit within NATO Special Forces Headquarters. During his time on the General's staff at ISAF, before being given command of Roosevelt, Mark had been read in on the unit's presence in country and a couple of their operations. Mark was familiar with special operators from Army Green Berets to Navy SEALs to the French Foreign Legion's elite troops, but Unit 7's work was at the top of the ladder. Krieger's presence here was deliberate on the General's part. "I take it you're thinking about Captain Krieger's unit, General," Mark said.

"That will depend on the where and the when, but yes." He rose from his chair and went to the map. He ran a finger along the southern quarter of Afghanistan. "For anything down here, or over the border in Iran, if we have to go in hard and fast, I have two of the captain's teams ready to move on twenty-four hours' notice." His finger moved to the eastern valleys. "Over here, in your area, Mark, I have other assets available. I have a feeling, though, that we'll be looking in the direction of Iran."

"Anything specific guiding your thinking along those lines, General?"

The General nodded toward the German. "Last week my unit returned from a mission along the border," Krieger said, his eyes hard. "We took two prisoners, both Takavar operators. To find one in that area is unusual. Our interrogation of the prisoners continues. So far they have not been cooperative, and we may have to employ more...aggressive measures." He looked at the General.

"I'll give you some latitude with that, Mr. Krieger, but only some."

Krieger nodded and continued. "In addition, there have been several more indications of increased Iranian activity near the border. I believe you encountered some Takavar on your mission with the Legion recently?"

"That we did, Captain. Do we have any idea why they're getting so frisky?"

The General shook his head. "Not yet. But something is in the works. I've already discussed this with Captain Krieger here, Mark, but if they go in, I want you to go along."

Krieger didn't move a muscle, his eyes revealing nothing about what the man might be thinking at that moment. Mark looked back at the General. "I'd be proud to accompany the captain's unit on a mission, sir, but certainly not as the commanding officer."

That drew a bit of a smile from the General as he stood. "Very good. Now, Mark, if you don't mind, I'd like to hit the chow line with your men, then take that tour. I'm due back in Kabul by 1800."

"Roger that, sir."

Mark and Krieger trailed behind the General as Ruiz conducted the tour. This was the General's second visit to Roosevelt since he'd placed Mark in command, and Mark was confident everything was in order. Letting Ruiz lead the tour gave him a chance for a private word with the German captain.

"In the event Unit 7 is tasked with a mission, Captain, and the General wants me to come along, I can assure you that you'll remain in command."

Krieger's expression changed only slightly. "We are a very specialized group, Colonel. I'm sure you understand that we are not used to having people tag along with us on our operations."

"I do indeed. I also understand that in this environment, cooperation between units within the coalition is vital to the success of our common mission."

"That has not been our experience, to date at least. My unit is tasked with missions that are quite...sensitive, politically speaking. Missions that NATO considers vital, but about which they might also wish to maintain, shall we say, a certain amount of deniability?"

Mark had to chuckle. "Captain, I'm sure you've been in uniform long enough to know that sometimes things out here get a little messy, and the politicians have a hard time coming to grips with that."

"Indeed. Unit 7 is for the messy ones, Colonel." He stopped and looked at Mark. "If you don't have a problem getting a little dirt on your hands, I'm sure your assistance on whatever mission the General assigns to us would be welcomed."

"Let's hope it won't be necessary."

"We always hope that, don't we? Yet, we get missions."

They resumed their walk, staying a few paces behind the General and Ruiz. "Your English is excellent, Captain," Mark said, happy to change the subject. "Have you spent a lot of time in the States?"

"I was born and raised there, Colonel."

"Really? Where?"

"From what the General tells me, a place with which you are quite familiar: Milwaukee, Wisconsin."

Mark almost fell over. "What part of the city?"

"Northeast side. My father was a professor at UWM. We lived only a few blocks from the campus. I went to high school at Milwaukee Lutheran."

"Well, I'll be...what year did you graduate?"

"'Ninety-two. Went into the Marine Corps, came back and went to UWM, then back to the Corps, OCS."

Mark looked at him again. Krieger was every inch a German, even to his accent. "I wasn't aware NATO special ops took Americans."

"Unit 7 does, Colonel. That is one reason why we are different."

"And the German connection?"

"My family has a long history of military service in both America and Germany. My great-grandfather flew with the Red Baron. His son, my grandfather, was a panzer commander on the Russian Front, survived the war and brought his family to the States in '55. My father served in Vietnam. In our home,

German was my first language. My father was quite proud of our heritage. As am I." This time Mark saw something else in those blue-gray eyes. A sense of camaraderie, maybe? "Perhaps, if we are tasked with a mission together, I'll tell you some of their stories."

"I'll buy the beers."

The General's smile never changed, except when he was quite pleased. This time, Mark noted, it was a bit wider than usual. "Mark, I like what I've seen here," the General said as they walked toward his helicopter. "Very nice job."

"Thank you, sir. I have a lot of good men here."

"Everything squared away between you and Captain Krieger?"

"If you attach me to his unit, General, there won't be any problems."

"Glad to hear it, although I didn't think there would be. Have you heard from your brother?"

Mark had long ago ceased being surprised by what the General knew. "He called early this morning, our time. He was about to get on a plane, he said."

"By now he'll be in Djibouti. I would expect they'll be going in tomorrow."

"General, would this possible cross-border mission have anything to do with that?"

The General stopped and faced Mark. "Some people back in Washington are very nervous about this, Mark. The increased Iranian activity we've been seeing, the asset your brother's mission is concerned with, some don't see a connection. Others do. The DCI does, and I agree with him. If there is, and something needs to be done, it might have serious repercussions for the entire region. I have to tell you, some would prefer that your brother's mission fails."

"As long as he makes it back home safely, sir."

"The DCI assures me he will do everything he can to make sure that happens." He extended a hand. "I'll keep you posted, Mark."

CHAPTER THIRTY
SOMALIA

J IM HAD HEARD from friends that traveling overseas from the States was somewhat jarring. You wake up one morning in your own bed and the next morning you're an ocean away, surrounded by people speaking a different language and flying a strange flag. But those friends had been talking about going to Europe or maybe Asia. He didn't think any of them had ever been somewhere like this.

He'd slept on the transatlantic flight but awoke when they were still a couple hours out of Ramstein. An hour after landing in Germany they were on their way to the Horn of Africa. It was late afternoon, local time, when they landed at Djibouti-Ambouli International and boarded a string of Humvees for the short run to the adjacent base. A Navy lieutenant offered Jim the front seat next to the driver and got in the back.

Jim had never been to an actual military base before and Camp Lemmonier was like nothing he would've expected. His driver, a young Marine from Georgia, filled him in. "We call it 'The Lemon'," he said with a drawl that would've sounded perfect in a country song. "French built it for the Foreign

Legion, turned it over to Djibouti and then we got here right after 9/11. Took some fixin' up, they said. 'Bout five hundred acres now, over three thousand troops. Mostly Marines, some squids—I mean, sailors. Beggin' the lieutenant's pardon, sir." He glanced nervously in the rear-view mirror at the lieutenant.

"Carry on, Marine," the sailor said.

"Uh, anyway, we're fixin' to come up on CLUville over here, sir. You aren't in uniform, sir, so I'm assumin' you're a contractor?"

"Something like that," Jim said. He gestured through the windshield at the rows of low, box-like structures. "Would that be Clueville?"

"Yessir, C-L-U-ville, for Containerized Living Units. What we live in here. Not too fancy, but better'n what we had over in Afghanistan." He stopped at an intersection as a platoon of Asian soldiers in camo fatigues jogged past. "Japanese marines, I think," the Marine said.

"Not quite, Corporal," the lieutenant said from the back. "Special Boarding Unit troops, Japanese Maritime Self-Defense Force. Japan doesn't have a marine corps. Their navy is building a base here, helping out in anti-piracy operations."

"Roger that, sir," the Marine said. A few minutes and a couple turns later, he pulled up in front of a two-story building with unit insignia flanking the double doors. A man in plain fatigue pants, civilian-style shirt and a plain black ballcap was waiting. "This is your stop, sir," he said to Jim. "I b'lieve that fella there will show you to your quarters."

Jim found some unmarked fatigues and t-shirts waiting in his Spartan room. The bed looked small and not too comfortable, but after his long flight it was still very tempting. He would just lie down for a few minutes, just to unwind a bit.

An hour later the phone on the desk jangled him awake. It was Denise, reminding him that chow was about to be served.

Eleven hours of shuteye helped him deal with the jet lag, and the next day was a blur of activity. He met Tom Simons, whom he knew to be the CIA station chief thanks to his briefings at Langley, and they went over the mission again. He got in a workout at the base gym and even sparred a couple rounds with some of the men when he saw them training on a mat and asked to join in. The Lemon, as stark and free of luxuries as it was, seemed to be his kind of place.

But by mid-afternoon he was in the air again, this time on a C-12 Huron, a twin-engine Navy transport plane, heading to Somalia, and he had the distinct feeling that he was going to miss the Lemon even more than he thought.

Jim had seen *Black Hawk Down* and was expecting a city that looked like Berlin in 1945, but what he saw left him bewildered and a little off-center. As they moved into the city along the coast from the southwest, he saw some sections that looked fairly modern and Western in appearance, contrasting starkly with areas that were little more than empty shells of buildings surrounded by rubble. Simons was sitting next to him in the back seat of the rusty Land Rover, and when Jim pointed out one building that looked like something from pre-war Europe, he chuckled.

"The Italians built that. They actually bought the city back in 1905 and ran it until independence in 1960."

Buying an entire city? Jim wanted to ask what they paid for it, but instead said, "In the briefing today they said the government actually controls only about half the city, right?"

"More or less. Fortunately, that's the half we're going to, although the hotel where we meet Shalita is near Villa Somalia, the presidential palace, close to the edge of the federal zone. Things are still pretty fluid. Al-Shabaab holds some of the eastern and central sections, but the government's making some progress, with help from AMISOM." Jim remembered that acronym from the briefing. The African Union had sent troops into the city to help the shaky government root out the insurgents, while Ethiopians marched in from the north. It wasn't as bad as it had been in the '90s, but it wasn't exactly a place you'd want to come to on vacation.

Jim counted eight people in their two Land Rovers heading into the city, including himself. Denise was in the trailing vehicle. Jim didn't feel too great about leaving her back there, but the three guys with her looked pretty competent. Well, hell, who was he kidding? Any one of those three guys could protect her better than he could. Not that she needed protection. He'd seen her working out enough over the past few days to realize that she was probably as skilled in close-quarters combat as any woman he'd ever met and most of the men.

His emotions had run the gamut in the past twenty-four hours. Sometimes he felt like he'd be able to handle anything that was thrown at him over here, other times he felt almost sheer terror. He forced himself to keep his breathing calm. Somewhere down deep inside, he hoped, was a reservoir of courage yet untapped. He suddenly remembered something he'd seen back home, a metal sign on the wall of a bar. There was a photo of John Wayne, and a quote: "Courage is being scared to death, but saddling up anyway."

The streets became busier and more chaotic as they got further into the city. People were everywhere, most of them as dark-skinned as any Jim had ever seen, but there was a scattering of lighter-skinned men who could've been Arabs, and even a few Europeans. Almost all of the women wore shawls

or the full-cover garments they called *burqa*. Jim had been told
with great seriousness that interaction with the local women
was not advised. It seemed that every fourth or fifth man had
a rifle hanging loosely on his shoulder. Most of the weapons
were AK-47s, but Jim saw a few bolt-action rifles that looked
like vintage World War II-era arms. There were soldiers in different uniforms and a few men Jim took for police, but not that
many.

The traffic was unbelievable. Small cars, trucks and SUVs,
almost all of them old, dusty and battered, muscled for position on the streets with motorcycles and a few daring, or foolish, men on rickety bicycles. The few signal lights Jim saw
were dark. At some intersections there were policemen trying
to direct the traffic, and they weren't getting a lot of cooperation. Even with the air conditioner roaring inside their Land
Rover, Jim could hear the honking of horns and shouting of
pedestrians and angry drivers.

"It looks like it wouldn't take much to set these people off,"
Jim said.

"Usually it doesn't," Simons said. "We're getting near the
hotel."

Another few blocks and they came to a makeshift barricade formed by two pickup trucks and an ancient bus. Men in
civilian clothes and carrying submachine guns were loitering
nearby. "Doesn't look like we can get through here, sir," the
driver said.

Simons peered through the windshield, then told the
driver, "Take a right here. We'll try to circle around." The agent
next to the driver lifted a portable radio to inform the trailing
Land Rover.

"The Hotel Quruxsan is five blocks further," Simons told
Jim as the driver started navigating down a side street.

"What's with the barricade?" Jim asked.

"I don't know, but we may have to hoof it for a couple blocks."

"That doesn't sound promising."

Jim knew the meet with Shalita was set for seven o'clock. By his watch, it was now just after six. He had an idea that punctuality wasn't high on these people's priority lists.

They made it another two blocks before Simons called a halt. Another barricade blocked the street ahead, but this one looked unmanned. The driver fought his way into a vacant lot between two ramshackle three-story buildings, with the trailing vehicle coming in next to them. "On foot from here," the CIA chief of station said. "Three blocks and we're in the clear." Jim got out and the heat enveloped him again, this time combined with a foul, gagging stench. Exhaust fumes, rotting garbage, and who knew what else was in there. On the street behind them, a few cars turned away from the traffic jam.

Simons ordered the two drivers to stay with the vehicles, then gathered Jim, Denise and the two agents who'd been riding shotgun. "Stay together, people, stay alert, and don't interact with the locals. The latest word I have is that the hotel is secure." From somewhere in the distance came the staccato popping of small-arms fire.

"Al-Shabaab?" Denise asked.

"We had reports they might be making a push," Simons said. "Not good timing for us. Okay, let's go." He clicked a button on the portable radio. "Backstop, this is Badger Team leader. We are three blocks to the south of the hotel, proceeding code white, plus three. Do you have the rigs?"

A confident voice came back through the device. "Roger that, Badger leader. We have eyes on two rigs plus two. We'll keep the bird with you."

"Copy that. Badger leader out." Simons pocketed the radio and said, "Okay, follow me. Carson, take the six."

Jim was already starting to perspire through his short-sleeved cotton shirt. He was thankful he'd remembered to bring his sunglasses, but they'd told him to leave his boonie hat behind. His passport was in the right front pocket of his olive drab cargo pants, but his wallet was back at the base in Djibouti. Simons led the way onto the street, with Denise next, then Jim, followed by Jones and Bentler, the agents from Denise's vehicle, and then Carson, who'd been in Jim's.

He kept his breathing steady and tried to stay alert, concentrating on the people walking along the street. During the briefing he'd been told that a Special Forces team, code-named Backstop, would be keeping an eye on them. Jim assumed that meant some men on foot and perhaps a drone of some kind in the air, probably "the bird" he'd heard mentioned on the radio transmission.

The few people they passed either averted their eyes or gave them cold, unfriendly stares. Six Westerners moving purposefully along the street probably didn't mean good news to a lot of the people here. Simons seemed to know where he was going, which was good, because Jim would've been hopelessly lost.

They emerged from the side street onto a broader thoroughfare where there was still some traffic. How had they gotten past the barricades? "Okay, there it is," Simons said, gesturing two blocks to the east. A four-story building loomed, its architecture in a style Jim took for something out of Mussolini-era Italy.

The sound of gunfire erupted again, this time closer than before. Denise was looking around intently, scanning the rooftops and upper stories of the buildings. They were getting close to the last intersection before the hotel when Jim heard the growling of heavy engines coming from around the corner. Simons held up a hand and they stopped, then moved over to the wall of the nearby building. Jim fought to control his breathing.

An armored vehicle, snorting and belching diesel fumes, nosed its way around the corner from the left and swung through the intersection, turning back down the street from where the Americans had come. It looked like a tank, but nothing like the powerful Abrams tanks used by the Americans in the films and news footage Jim had seen. This one was smaller, with a long, rather small cannon pushing out of the turret, and it moved slowly and clumsily on its treads. Several men hung onto the turret as the vehicle rumbled past. Some of the fighters had AKs, others long tubes that Jim took to be rocket launchers.

Bentler, standing next to Jim, said, "Russian-made, probably a BMP. Thirty years old if it's a day."

"Here comes another one," Carson said. The second tank followed the first about twenty yards behind, again carrying a full load of fighters.

"Intel said the government was holding this district," Denise said.

"These guys look like government troops to you?" Jim asked. She shook her head.

After the two tanks came three Toyota pickups packed with armed fighters. Some of them looked suspiciously at the Americans, but the vehicles kept moving, although not fast enough, as far as Jim was concerned. Simons motioned them up to the corner. There was more civilian traffic coming, having given way to the military convoy.

Simons was at the curb, waiting for a break in the traffic to cross to the hotel's block, when Jim heard a sound to his left. It was a familiar sound, one he'd heard many times in the dojo: the *thwack* of a stick on something soft.

Twenty feet away, a man was beating something with a three-foot stick. At first Jim thought it was a bag, but then the bag moved, and he saw it was a person wearing a burqa. A hand slid out of a sleeve, trying to ward off the blows. A woman's hand.

"Hey!" Jim yelled, taking a step toward the pair. The man wasn't a Somali, he looked more like an Arab of some sort, and when he heard Jim he turned and glared back at him. Two other men, both Somalis, were leaning against the nearby building, watching the show. One of them had an AK-47 hanging loosely on his shoulder. They showed no expression at all as they watched the beating, but when their eyes turned to Jim, they showed something else: a warning.

"Jim! Don't!"

He heard Denise's warning, but he still took a quick step toward the man and the woman, halting only when strong hands grabbed each of his arms. "Let it go, man," Bentler said in a low voice. "Let it go."

Jim looked at Bentler like he was insane. "Are you out of your mind? That son of a bitch is beating that poor woman!" Another smack, followed by a whimper and a pleading voice. Jim pulled against the agents' grips, but they were stronger than him, younger, and there were two of them and only one of him.

"Hayes, get back here!" That was Simons.

It went against everything Jim had ever known, everything he'd ever been taught, but he reached back to the training he'd gone through in the past week, and the number one restriction he'd been given, reinforced in the last mission brief just hours earlier: *Don't interact with the locals.* He relaxed just enough to allow the agents to lead him back to the curb. Simons glared at him, then led the way across the street to the hotel

Inside, the lobby was like something out of an old Humphrey Bogart movie, but Jim barely had a chance to register the threadbare carpet and tired old furniture when Simons was right in his face. "What the hell were you thinking out there, Hayes?"

"You saw it. That bastard was beating that defenseless woman. Those other characters were just watching the show. Nobody was sticking up for her."

"That's what they do here. They told you that back at Langley, didn't they?"

As a matter of fact, one of his CIA briefers had indeed mentioned the occasional public humiliation of women in Islamic countries, but Jim had brushed it off. It was a concept entirely alien to his thinking. Even now, he could hardly believe what he'd seen. "Yeah, they did," he said defiantly, "but they didn't say you had to be a chickenshit and just let it go."

Denise forced her way in between the men. "Get a grip, both of you. What's done is done. We have to get ready for the meet." She looked defiantly at Simons, then back at Jim. "Jim, remember, this isn't Wisconsin."

"Yeah, I get that."

Simons gave him one more intense look and then went to the desk to talk to the clerk.

Jim was still trying to process what had happened out on the street. He'd heard about such things, although they weren't shown much in American media, probably for reasons of political correctness. Were these people crazy? It was like something out of the Middle Ages. But he had to deal with that by not dealing with it as he really wanted to. The clown with the stick was one thing, Jim could've taken him down easily, but the guy with the submachine gun was an entirely different matter. Jim forced himself to analyze the situation from a tactical viewpoint, as his instructors back home constantly stressed. Simons was right, of course, things would've gone to hell quickly and the mission would've been blown. Jim might've gotten all of them killed right there. As it was, he'd drawn attention to the team out on the street. Word would get around quickly.

Carson was next to him. "Don't sweat it," the agent said. "You get used to that type of thing over here."

"Thanks," Jim said. He looked back at Simons, still talking to the clerk. "I hope I didn't screw up the mission."

"Hey, in this shithole of a city, everything's screwed up."

CHAPTER THIRTY-ONE
MOGADISHU

YUSUF ENTERED THE hotel with his heart hammering inside his chest. He felt more nervous than he had on any of his missions. Early on in his career he had been filled with the flame of Islam, dealing death to the infidels, fatalistically accepting his fate if he should be killed during the mission, ready to be accepted into Allah's warm embrace and be escorted to the feast and the nubile virgins awaiting him. Later, as the flame of his faith began to die down, he did his job more and more because it was a job that had to be done. But things were different now.

In the weeks since he'd made his decision to defect, he had for the first time allowed himself to think of a life after jihad. Not as the right-hand man of the caliph, but as someone who would live out his days in simplicity and safety, perhaps caring for his parents in their waning years. Maybe he would write his memoirs, make enough money to get himself a villa in a quiet place, where he could live out his days in peace and anonymity. It made for a pleasant daydream, but it was still very far away from reality.

The two Somali bodyguards entered the lobby ahead of him, then nodded that it was secure. How could they be sure? One never was completely secure in Mogadishu. But if the Americans wanted to kidnap him, they would've done it by now. No, they were here, waiting in some room above him. He went to the desk. He had scanned the lobby and spotted a man he assumed was one of Simons' American agents, sitting in one of the lobby chairs, pretending to read a newspaper.

"Good evening," he said to the clerk in his best Somali. "Could you tell me the room of Mr. Muncie?"

The clerk checked a ledger in front of him. "He just checked in a short time ago, sir. Room 212, second floor. The elevator is to your right."

"Thank you." Yusuf scanned the lobby as unobtrusively as possible. There were a few men lounging about, including one well-built black man who was definitely not Somalian. Yusuf made him instantly as an American agent. "Oh, by the way," he said, turning back to the clerk, "I noticed some commotion outside. People seem to be hurrying somewhere."

The clerk glanced to the lobby, then leaned over the counter. "There is talk that al-Shabaab is on the move. I saw some of their trucks not long ago."

"Indeed?"

"I would advise caution in the city tonight, sir."

"Yes, it is always best to be cautious. Thank you." He nodded to the clerk and walked toward the elevator, then turned when he was out of sight of the desk for the stairway door he had seen with his earlier glance. With the two Somali bodyguards behind him, he entered the stairwell and began climbing to the second floor.

The last digit of 212 had vanished, so Yusuf missed the room at first, forcing him to double back once he got to 214 and then 216. He knocked twice on the door, paused, then three times, as he and Simons had agreed. He told the bodyguards to wait outside and opened the door to the rest of his life.

The CIA agent was sitting at the writing desk, dressed casually, taking a drink from a plastic bottle of water. He stood. "Good evening, Mr. Shalita. You're right on time."

Yusuf closed the door behind him and glanced around the room. "Is he here?"

"Yes, he is. Please, have a seat." Simons gestured at a threadbare easy chair next to the desk. A queen-sized bed dominated the room. The door to the bathroom was closed.

"I prefer to stand."

"Very well." Simons stood. "Are you prepared to fulfill your part of our bargain?"

"I have been prepared for a long time, Simons. Is he here, or isn't he?"

The American gave him a stare, then said, "Okay, Jim, come on out." The door to the adjoining room opened and a tall Westerner stepped out.

The man smiled. "Well, Joe, it really is you, isn't it?"

Hayes was taller than he remembered, his hair was shorter and flecked with gray, as was his mustache, but it was James Hayes, of that Yusuf was certain. He remembered that voice from so many days in class, and around the table at the college pub. "It has been a long time, James." Yusuf walked over to him and extended a hand. They shook, and then, impulsively, Yusuf embraced him.

Simons cleared his throat, and Hayes stepped back. "Oh, right. Joe, you remember that night at the campus bar, the time that girl was draped all over you and spilled your beer on your lap?"

Yusuf had to smile in spite of himself. "Yes, very well."

"What was the name of the bar, and what happened with the girl?"

"It was the Rendezvous Room, in the basement of the Student Center. Just down the hall from the bowling alley. The girl offered to take me home and wash and dry my pants."

"You might've scored that night if her boyfriend the wrestler hadn't showed up."

"Yes, but he was a football player, not a wrestler."

Hayes looked over at Simons and nodded. "It all checks out."

"Okay, good," Simons said. He extended his hand. "Mr. Shalita, are you prepared to come with us now?

Yusuf took the hand and shook it firmly. "Yes, I am."

Another man and a woman stepped into the room. The man was putting a handgun into a holster at the small of his back, under his shirt. Simons had a portable radio and went off to the side, talking into it. The other man and the woman looked Yusuf over with some suspicion, but James was smiling. Yusuf thought of how frightening it must be for his old college friend to leave his peaceful Wisconsin and come all the way to this city, even now with the sound of gunfire in the distance, closer than it had been just minutes earlier. Truly this was a man of courage. Somehow, he wasn't surprised. There had been something about this American, even back then, that told Yusuf a lot about his character. Allah be praised, he had brought Hayes to this place so that Yusuf could begin to cleanse his soul.

Simons joined them. "We have to move, now. Backstop sees some heavy contact only a few blocks north of here."

The male agent was at the window, his gun drawn as he peered around the edge of the ratty curtain. Another one appeared at the doorway. "Sir, we'd—"

Yusuf heard the sound, so familiar and yet still so terrifying, like a train coming straight at them. He dropped to the floor, pulling Hayes down next to him. The explosion shook the building, lifting him up off the floor and tossing him aside like so much loose change. The lights in the room flickered and went dark.

Someone had a pocket-sized flashlight, the beam cutting through the falling dust from the ceiling. "Come on, follow me now!" It was Simons, and Yusuf felt a strong hand lifting him to his feet.

"You okay, Joe?" He looked up in the dim light to see his old American friend.

"Yes. We must hurry."

Out in the hallway, the Somali bodyguards were long gone. The CIA station chief, with one of his men in front, now had a pistol in one hand and the flashlight in the other as he hurried the group down the hallway. No other doors opened, no frightened faces peered out. They came to the stairwell and the lead agent slammed the door open, gun pointing into the darkness and traversing the area. Simons handed him the flashlight and he scanned the hallway quickly. "Looks clear!"

Another shell came in, this time a bit further away, but the old hotel was still rocked from the impact. That had to be government artillery, Yusuf knew, since he was certain al-Shabaab had nothing larger than mortars, but for the government to shell one of the central districts of its own capital? It was insane, but insanity had been a part of Somalia for a long time. On his last visit Yusuf had seen Somali rebels dragging the crushed body of an Ethiopian soldier through the streets not too far from here, and the civilians along the way were cheering them on.

They pounded down the stairwell and burst into the lobby. People were running past them, seemingly in a panic. At the desk, the clerk Yusuf had spoken to only minutes ago was rifling the till kept underneath the desk, stuffing bills into his pockets. The black American he'd seen in the lobby earlier was near the front doors, holding a pistol. The American who'd led the way down the stairs ran to join him. A hail of bullets smashed the glass in the doors and both men went down.

"Back to the stairs!" Simons shouted. Yusuf turned and saw two figures looming out of the shadows. Two shots cracked from the darkness and the trailing American spun around like a rag doll, blood spurting from one shoulder, his weapon flying away. Behind him, Yusuf heard a grunt from Simons and the sound of a body hitting the floor, but he could not look, could not tear his eyes away from the shadows, because from them emerged two men, holding guns pointed his way and at the remaining Americans. Yusuf recognized the first man immediately.

Amir stepped aside, his weapon trained steadily on the woman, and behind him came a voice that brought Yusuf a sinking feeling of despair even before the man stepped into the dim light.

"Well, Yusuf, I am very disappointed in you," Heydar said.

CHAPTER THIRTY-TWO
AFGHANISTAN

THE FIRST TIME Mark met with the Pakistani colonel in charge of the border checkpoint, he was not impressed. That had been two months ago, and he was even less impressed now.

"Colonel Barazani, I know the Taliban insurgents are infiltrating through your checkpoint," he said again. "They have been observed by our scouts, by the Afghan National Army and by our aircraft. Why are you denying this?"

Across the empty desk, the pudgy colonel sat placidly in his chair, twiddling his thumbs. His black beret covered what was probably thinning black hair, but he made up for that with a bushy mustache. On his right sleeve, Mark noted a few qualification insignia and badges, starting at the top with the wings of a para commando. This guy certainly didn't look like a paratrooper or someone from their Special Services Group. The border checkpoints in this region were manned by a paramilitary force, the Frontier Corps, composed of local tribesmen, but commanded by regular Pak Army officers. Mark had heard that a billet with the FC wasn't exactly an elite posting, and Barazani wasn't doing anything to counter that impression.

The Pakistani colonel shot a stream of rapid Urdu at his interpreter, a young lieutenant. "The colonel, he says that your men are mistaken," the 'terp said. "Our checkpoints are secure. It is only permitted for authorized travel across the border."

Mark motioned to Captain Richards, who handed him an iPad. Mark touched a couple buttons and turned the screen to face the Pakistani. "Colonel, this video was taken three days ago by one of our drones. You can clearly see a group of ten armed men walking right through your checkpoint into Afghanistan. Please note that two of them are carrying RPG tubes." The column, in fact, looked very similar to the one Mark and his men had ambushed several days back, only a few miles from here.

Barazini stared at the pad, and for the first time Mark saw a flicker of unease in those piggy eyes. After a moment he shot another indignant-sounding stream of Urdu at the 'terp. "The colonel says that checkpoint is not his. This must be some-where else on the border."

Mark had been pretty sure this would be the colonel's reaction, so he pressed another pair of buttons. The picture zoomed in on the guard post. The drone had gotten a good angle and even from several thousand feet above, the resolution of the shot, enhanced by the computer, was impressive. "You will note, Colonel Barazini, that this guard post is exactly like the one you have out there." He pointed out the window toward the small building where two of Barazini's guards stood, smok-ing cigarettes. On the side of the building was a word painted in Urdu above the number 24. "Even right down to the number on the side of the building."

Barazini took a quick glance at the picture, then looked

away. This time he waited a few seconds before rattling off a sentence to the 'terp. "The colonel says he will investigate this, if the date and time of this you can provide to him."

Richards produced an envelope, and Mark passed it along to the Pakistani. "We took the liberty of making a digital copy of the video. In addition to the time and date stamp on the video itself, we have written the information down. The video also shows six other such incursions dating back two months. We have included the dates and times of those. All through this checkpoint."

Barazini glanced at the envelope, then tossed it to his aide standing behind him. Mustering as much dignity as possible after having been busted so completely, the colonel stood, and Mark did also. "When can I expect to know the results of your investigation, Colonel?"

"Perhaps a week. Perhaps more," the 'terp translated. He was getting more nervous by the minute.

"I'm sure I don't have to remind the colonel that his government and the government of Afghanistan, which is represented by Captain Zadran here, have an agreement to prevent illegal border crossings like these." The ANA officer standing next to Richards offered a broad smile. Zadran had grown up in this region and was fluent in Urdu, so Mark would be able to question him later about the accuracy of the Pak 'terp's translation. He had the feeling it would be pretty solid. "If I am not satisfied by your investigation, Colonel, I will have no choice but to report this to my superiors in Kabul. They might very well order me to be, shall we say, more energetic in my efforts to secure this border from the Afghan side."

When Barazini got the translation from his trembling lieutenant, his eyes grew wide and then bored into Mark. He spoke again in Urdu, this time without taking his eyes off the

American. Mark's knowledge of the language was pretty limited, but he did understand the words *mera lund lay moon main.*
The young 'terp coughed and said, "The colonel...he says he
is an officer in the Army of Pakistan and...ah, he will not be
threatened by you."

The 'terp had not translated all of his colonel's words,
which was just as well. Mark got the gist of it, including the
invitation to perform a certain sex act upon the colonel's person. In return, he just offered a thin smile. "I'm not making any
threats, Colonel. But you have heard of our Predator drones,
of course. They are under the control of soldiers who are not
under my direct command. If they are ordered to attack a
Taliban column that is approaching your checkpoint, well, who
can say where exactly that missile might strike?" Mark spread
his hands helplessly. "The operators are highly skilled, but
from such distances, controlling a missile is not an easy thing
to do."

Behind him, Richards cleared his throat ever so slightly.
The adjutant was well-versed in Mark's moods by now and he
knew when to signal his boss that he was getting close to a line
that probably shouldn't be crossed. Mark took the hint.

"Colonel, I am grateful for your time and hospitality.
Please extend my regards and those of my government to your
superiors. I look forward to meeting with you again. Soon."
When the 'terp finished the translation, Mark extended a hand.
Barazini hesitated, then gripped it firmly. Mark's grip was just
a little firmer. He saw with a bit of pleasure that the Pakistani's
eyes flared slightly. Then Mark released the hand and whipped
his up into a parade-ground-perfect salute.

Outside the hut, the sun blazed down, and even here at
six thousand feet, it was warm. Mark headed off toward the

waiting Humvees, Richards and Zadran on either side. "Okay, Bill, how'd I do in there?"

"Well, Colonel, maybe you pushed him a bit too far on the drone thing."

"Yeah, maybe, but maybe it's time we threw the fear of God into these characters. Or at least the fear of getting a Predator missile up their asses. It's like the NVA and the Ho Chi Minh Trail all over again."

"If I recall my history, Colonel, President Nixon did something about that, didn't he?"

They'd reached the command vehicle. Mark turned to his adjutant. "How old are you again, Bill?"

"Thirty-one, sir." Christ, the man only knew about Vietnam from the history books. Mark himself had been pretty young back then, but he'd talked to a lot of vets who'd spent time in the Land of Bad Things, including a few who'd gone across the border into Cambodia in '70. Many of them thought that if they'd been allowed to really take the gloves off, and if Congress had displayed any balls, South Vietnam would be alive today. From his own studies back at the Point and since, Mark wasn't totally convinced of that, but since coming out here he was starting to see the old vets' perspective.

"Well, look it up when you have the time," Mark said. "Let's head back." They would overnight at FOB O'Neill and head back to Roosevelt the next morning.

Mark rode up front in the second Humvee, with Richards at the wheel and Zadran manning the top-mounted machine gun. Richards drove in silence for about fifteen minutes, then asked the question Mark should've known was coming. Richards was an inquisitive guy, and would go far in the Army, provided he asked the right questions, and more importantly knew when to ask them. "Colonel, d'you think we'll ever go across the border? Into Pakistan?"

"We've been doing that for a while now, Bill, with the drones."

"Well, yeah, but I mean on the ground."

Mark considered his answer carefully. He knew full well that back in Kabul, the General's safe at ISAF HQ held detailed plans for incursions into various sections of what the Pakistanis called their Federally Administered Tribal Areas, especially North and South Waziristan. Everybody knew the Taliban and al-Qaida were thick as fleas on a dog over there, doing whatever they pretty much pleased to the locals, using the area as a safe haven that was only occasionally penetrated by American drones for targeted assassinations. Even more rarely, secret missions involving Special Forces teams had sent Americans over the border for recon and the occasional hit. But's that's as far as it had gone, and Mark knew it wouldn't go any further. Not under this administration for sure, and likely not under its successor, either, whoever and whenever that might be. "I doubt it, Bill," he finally said. "We've got our hands full on this side of the border."

"There'd have to be a helluva buildup if we were to make a major push into there, wouldn't we?"

"I'd say so." Mark remembered one planning session with the General and other members of the staff, when they'd tossed around contingencies: using airstrikes with manned aircraft, increasing the number of SF incursions, and finally up to large-scale conventional operations with infantry and armor. The problem was the terrain, very mountainous with few roads, certainly not optimal country for armor. To really do the job right would require infantry, a lot of infantry and lots of helicopters, more than they had available in theater even with

Iraq winding down, and everybody around the table that day knew it would never happen. Back in '70, Nixon had the balls to go into Cambodia, even over-ruling some of his top advisors, but this was a different time, different war, and definitely a different president. Still, it was better to have a plan than not have one, just in case, so they drew one up and put it in the safe. Mark supposed someday it would either get burned or leaked to the press. He imagined himself seeing it on *60 Minutes* around 2040 or so, with Lara Logan interviewing old ISAF officers.

"How many, do you think, Colonel?"

"Tell you what, Bill, let's just not go there, okay? If we can just keep the lid on over here long enough for the ANA to get up to speed, then we can all go home."

"Roger that, sir. This is my third deployment, and it would be nice to be stateside for a long time."

Richards was on his third deployment? Mark had to think a minute about his own. How many now? Counting Desert Storm, then the Balkans...seven. Damn, that was a lot, even spread out over twenty years. No wonder he was starting to think more often about getting out, going home, doing something else besides soldiering.

But what that something else might be, he wasn't too sure. Well, maybe it was time to start thinking about that. But in the last few days he'd been thinking more about his brother, not about himself. He'd heard nothing since Jim's call, two days ago.

FOB O'Neill wasn't a luxurious place, but then very few places in Afghanistan could be classified that way, so it was still a welcome sight as Mark's Humvee caravan came around the bend in the road. To someone trained in the Cold War era, the HESCO walls looked pathetically flimsy. The FOB would be helpless against a Soviet-style armored assault, and Mark didn't even want to think about air attack. Over here, thankfully, he didn't have to worry about enemy tanks and aircraft. The best the Tals could come up with were mortars and the occasional "technicals", old pickup trucks with machine guns mounted in the box, which were troublesome enough.

They rolled through the front gate and pulled to a stop in front of the main HQ hooch. Like most firebases, they'd built up and around an abandoned Afghan compound that would've been the home of an important family back in pre-Soviet days, perhaps even a warlord. Now it was home to a company of Americans trying to help the Afghans enter the brave new world that many of the natives didn't seem to want.

The FOB's C.O., Lieutenant Williams, was waiting for them. Mark dismounted and returned his salute. Williams was relatively new in country and still pretty formal, but that was okay. Mark was willing to relax discipline to a certain extent but he still wanted his men to pay attention to the little things. If they started ignoring those, pretty soon they'd start ignoring the big things.

"Welcome back, Colonel. How did it go?"

"About as I expected, George. Anything new come down the pipe?"

"Yes, sir. Urgent message for you to contact ISAF right away."

That wasn't a good sign. Mark hustled to the comm shack, trying to think of anything from the latest intel brief that might've indicated trouble, something he might've overlooked. The on-duty comms sergeant was expecting him. "I'll get you connected in just a minute, sir."

Thirty seconds was all it took for Mark to doff most of his

gear. He wished he could ditch the helmet for his trusty old field cap, weather-beaten as it was these days, but out here, where there could be incoming mortar rounds any time, you had to stay covered with Kevlar. "Here we go, sir," the sergeant said, handing Mark a telephone-style handset.

"Colonel Hayes."

The voice on the other end was scratchy but readable. "Stand by, Colonel, I'm connecting you with the General." This can't be good, Mark thought, and that was confirmed a few seconds later.

"Mark, are you there?"

"Yes, sir."

"I hate to be the bearer of bad news, Mark, but your brother is missing."

There was a knock on the door of Mark's hooch about ten o'clock that night. "Colonel, it's Richards."

"Yeah, come in."

The young captain came in carrying a paper plate covered by a napkin and a tall metal drinking cup. "Sir, I noticed you weren't at evening chow, so I brought you a sandwich."

"Thanks, Bill, I appreciate it." Mark took the plate and cup, setting them on his metal desk next to the laptop. The hooch wasn't anything special, maybe a dozen feet square. The desk, a couple chairs, and a cot were the only furnishings. Mark didn't spend much time in here anyway, except in his rack, and saw no reason to get anything bigger or fancier. A couple shelves on the walls held some books and two pictures, one of his son, the other of Mark and his parents on the day he graduated from the Point. "Have a seat," Mark said.

"I don't mean to intrude, sir." Mark saw him glance at the

computer screen. "Begging the colonel's pardon, but if I might ask, bad news from home?"

Mark couldn't bring himself to look his captain in the eye, afraid that his self-discipline would break. Sometimes it was hard, very hard, to lead these men, to deal with the isolation and the privation, the constant danger. But he had to do it. The men needed him, and even more, he knew he needed them. "My brother," Mark said.

"Damn, I'm sorry to hear that, sir. Is he all right?"

Mark sighed. "He's got himself in a bit of a jam. It's touch and go at the moment." He shot a quick look at the younger man. "Nothing illegal," he said, forcing a small smile.

"I didn't think so, sir. He's your brother, after all."

"What do you mean by that?" Mark said, a little too sternly.

Richards didn't flinch, though. "In a positive sense, sir. I would find it hard to believe that any brother of yours would get into that kind of trouble."

"Well, if my folks were still alive and heard that, I'm sure they'd consider it a compliment."

"Absolutely, sir."

They sat in silence for a minute. Mark took a sip of milk from the cup. He was hungry, but he couldn't bring himself to eat right now.

Richards cleared his throat. "Well, sir, I'll leave you to your sandwich. And I'll say a prayer for your brother tonight."

Mark looked at him in surprise. "I didn't know you were a praying man, Bill."

Richards looked slightly embarrassed. "I guess you could say I wasn't, until I came here."

"How's that?"

The captain sat up a little straighter. "Permission to speak freely, sir?"

"Certainly."

"I noticed that you attend the Sunday services regularly. I decided to check them out. A lot of people here told me they did the same thing after they got here. Because of you."

"I'm not sure I follow you, Bill."

"Colonel, I might be speaking out of turn here, but everybody here has a great deal of respect for you. It's not just how you go out on patrol with the men, or check on the little things like how things are going at the gym or in the chow hall, or when you ask guys how things are back home. It's the way you carry yourself, the way you…well, sir, dammit, you're one helluva fine commanding officer and it's an honor to serve with you."

Mark felt his eyes get a little wet. "The honor is mine, sir."

Richards nodded at the computer. "I'd heard you had a brother. If you wouldn't mind, I'd be interested in hearing more about him. What kind of man is he?"

Mark looked back at the screen, into the past, at a picture of two boys. "You know, Bill, right about now I'm thinking that my brother is the bravest man I've ever known."

CHAPTER THIRTY-THREE

SOMALIA

JUDGING BY THE light starting to filter in around the shutters of the window, dawn was breaking. Jim wondered if it would be last daybreak of his life. He automatically looked at his wrist for the time, but the watch wasn't there. They'd taken it from him, along with his passport, before shoving him into this room sometime in the middle of the night. He had no idea where Denise and Joe had been taken but he had heard their voices, briefly, just before they had cut the rope binding his wrists and pushed him inside.

He took off the filthy blindfold slowly, only to find himself in near-total darkness.

He forced himself to breathe steadily, and gradually the terror began to subside. After a few minutes he'd been able to search his surroundings. Hard dirt floor, walls of some type of masonry, a wooden door—locked, of course, but he'd forced himself to test it anyway—and the one window on the wall opposite the door. Thank God for small favors, there was a straw mattress of sorts on the floor, covered by a couple of rough blankets. In one corner was a metal pot for waste, although unfortunately there was no cover.

He leaned against the wall, collected himself, and went over everything that happened in the hotel, in fact everything since they'd landed at the airstrip. Maybe he shouldn't have reacted to that bastard beating the woman; that had drawn unwanted attention to the presence of the Westerners in the hotel. But surely they wouldn't have started an artillery bombardment over that, would they? Well, everything he'd seen and read about these people had led him to believe many of them were seriously out of whack, and certainly nothing he'd seen in the last day or so changed that impression, so who could say?

Okay. He was being held by people who were terrorists, of course, but exactly who were they, and did it make any difference? Yes, it did, it had to. There were all kinds of terror factions and rebel groups over here, with different motivations and goals, strengths and weaknesses. None of them could make the United States military work up a good sweat, one on one, but they didn't operate like that, did they? No, they fought Americans by going after their weaknesses, chief of which was the desire to preserve innocent life.

Like his.

But how innocent would they think him to be, anyway, and why would they care? He had been with the CIA people. They might very well refuse to believe he wasn't CIA himself. They would know he had been there to help Shalita defect. No, come to think about it, there would be precious little reason for them to release him. Yet they hadn't killed him outright. There had to be some reason for that.

They would know, or would find out, that Denise was CIA. With a shudder, Jim realized that meant her treatment was not likely to be gentle, even if she was a woman. And they didn't think much of women over here anyway. No, they weren't going to cut Denise much slack. As for Joe, they certainly weren't going to cut him any slack at all. He was a traitor to the cause, so Jim was pretty sure his old African friend wasn't going to live very long, and what time he had left wouldn't be pleasant.

After Jim had spent a couple hours in the darkness, it began to sink in: he was quite probably never going to see his home again. The thought sent a long, cold shiver down his spine, and he couldn't stifle a sob. Why had he ever allowed himself to get talked into this?

The grief and fear caused him to slump onto his side, and after a few minutes the fatigue took over, pulling him down into sleep.

Later, watching the light begin to seep under the shutter over the window, he still felt the fear and sadness pulling him back down. This time he resisted. He pushed back with the power of prayer, not the panicky, quick pleas he'd muttered during the long, bumpy ride here in the back of a truck, but a serious prayer for strength.

He'd fallen away from his family's Lutheran faith during his high school and college days, found it again after marrying Suzy, then allowed it to wane once more over the past few years. But there was still something there, and he wanted to find that spark now, fan it into a flame. There are no atheists in foxholes, he'd always heard, and he was finding out now that was for damn sure true.

He sat in the hot, dingy room, closed his eyes and let his thoughts coalesce into three words: *Please help me.*

Time had no meaning anymore. He blocked out the sounds from outside, kept his focus, relaxing his body as he opened his mind. He could hear his own heart beating now, his slow breathing. A calmness seeped into him. The fear was almost a visible thing, slowly receding, something was pushing it away.

It was a broom. The fear became water, swishing underneath the bristles of the broom, moving toward a light. His vision pulled back, and he saw shoes, old brogans that seemed familiar, cuffed gray pants, and there were hands on the broom, workingman's hands.

His father's hands.

Jim saw Ed Hayes as plain as day, just as Ed was back when Jim was a boy. Pushing the water out of the garage, as he did every spring after washing the floor. Jim looked down, saw something beneath him. His first bicycle. It was the day he would take his first ride without training wheels.

Ed swept the last of the water outside and faced his son. *It's time now, Jimmy.*

I don't think I can do it, Dad. I'm scared.

No need for that, son. I'll be there with you. His father smiled at him, reached out, and his face shimmered just a bit, changing into someone else's, familiar yet not, kind, reassuring. *Touch my hand, son.*

Jim reached out, his little hand trembling, and touched…

The vision dissolved like mist. Jim was still in the cell, and he was awake and alert, holding out his hand, and it was not trembling now.

He felt calm, at peace, and as he breathed it seemed as if every breath brought him a little more confidence. He might never again see his house again, train in his beloved dojo or pet his cat. He might never again hug his daughter, or cradle a grandchild, or feel Gina's touch, but he would not surrender to his fate. He would shape it, as he suddenly realized he had been shaping it for the past six years.

A warrior does not give up without a fight, and somehow, by God, he would fight.

CHAPTER THIRTY-FOUR
SOMALIA

THEY CAME FOR him sometime mid-morning, the same two men who had brought him breakfast a few hours ago, some sort of broth with a few vegetables, hard dark bread and a bottle of water with an Arabic label. They were Middle Eastern in appearance, early twenties, dressed in nondescript shirts and fatigue pants, with one guy incongruously wearing a Boston Red Sox cap. Jim got to his feet and stood with his hands raised. The Red Sox fan came in first, leveling his AK-47 at Jim. Another armed man appeared behind the first in the doorway. The first guy said something to Jim, motioning with the gun to the door. Jim took some cautious steps toward the doorway, keeping his hands visible. He forced himself to smile, and the second guy's eyes narrowed.

There was a hallway with two more doors on the right, the same side as Jim's cell, and three on the left. At the end was a larger door. When they opened it the sun blazed in. He shaded his eyes with his left hand, making sure to keep the right held shoulder high, palm facing outward.

They were facing what appeared to be a central square, with low, one-story buildings around the perimeter. Behind them was a wall about ten feet high, looking like it had been built with the same material as the buildings, probably some kind of bricks made out of mud. There were men walking here and there, some standing and watching them. Every one of them had an AK, some held casually, others loosely from the shoulder by a strap. They didn't look nearly as tough as the troops Jim had seen at Camp Lemonnier, but Jim knew it would be dangerous to make that assumption.

Everyone in motion stopped when they got sight of the tall American, and they stared. Some looked curious, most hostile. There were a few dark-skinned Africans, but most were Middle Eastern, all with beards. Some looked to still be in their teens, while a few showed some gray. How to deal with those stares? Show no fear, Jim told himself, but that wasn't easy, because he was starting to feel the first tendrils of something stark and cold reaching into him. It was worse than what he'd felt the night before in Mogadishu while being hustled at gunpoint through rubble-strewn buildings with artillery shells crashing nearby, then shoved roughly into the back of a truck, blindfolded and tied to his seat.

He was led to a long building and pushed inside. It appeared to be some sort of conference room, maybe a chow hall, as it had some rickety-looking metal tables and chairs, now moved to the sides along the walls. At one end hung a black flag featuring a yellow circle in the middle and Arabic writing above it. Jim recognized it from news broadcasts: the banner of al-Qaeda. The writing was the *shahada*, referring to Allah as the only God and Muhammad as his prophet. Beneath it were three men, sitting in chairs. A dozen feet away were three empty chairs facing them. Jim was shoved roughly down into the chair at the right end.

There were open windows on the long sides of the building, and between the sunlight coming in and the naked bulbs hanging from the ceiling Jim got a good look at the three men. The one in the middle was clearly in charge. Middle Eastern, with a thin black mustache, he wore olive drab military fatigues bare of any insignia, his pants bloused above combat boots. The man to his left was dressed similarly, but the one on the other end looked like most of the men Jim had seen outside, who'd been wearing any number of clothing combinations, mostly fatigue pants but shirts that ranged from long-sleeved tees to caftan-style tops that reached down to the knees.

Two armed fighters took up station at either end of the seated men, and Jim sensed the presence of more behind him. He was surprised his wrists weren't bound, but that didn't make him feel much better. There was a slight commotion behind him, and he saw the seated men look past him. The middle one smiled and gestured to the two empty chairs. Jim turned his head just enough to get a glance backward. It was Joe. He'd been roughed up. Two men in fatigues similar the two in front dumped him hard into the middle chair.

"One more," the man in the middle said in English, and a few seconds later Jim heard murmurs coming from behind. Denise Allenson was shoved down into the empty chair. Her hair was askew, there was a bruise on her right jawline, and she was clutching the front of her shirt, holding it together with her left hand. Jim could see a few limp threads hanging from the upper buttonholes.

The man in the middle smiled and said, "Well. What am I going to do with you now?" Jim couldn't place the accent, could've been from anywhere in the region. He wasn't experienced enough to know a Palestinian from an Egyptian or anyone else.

Jim swallowed, fighting the fear, but he had to say something, had to show these bastards that they hadn't beaten him. With an effort, he said, "Who are you?"

"Ah. You are…" The man pulled Jim's passport out of a thigh pocket of his pants. "James Hayes. American. Why are you in Somalia, Mr. Hayes?"

"I had some vacation time coming and decided to see the sights."

"Not a wise choice," the man said. "I am Major Heydar. This gentleman to my left is Captain Khorsandi. And to my right, Amir, who is now the commanding officer of this camp."

"If he's the commander, how come you're doing the talking?" Something told Jim he shouldn't antagonize this man, but he figured they were way past that by now.

"Amir's English is not very good, unfortunately. He has asked me to conduct these proceedings."

Denise spoke, in a strong and defiant voice that Jim was pleased to hear. "You have no right to keep us here. We are citizens of the United States, and you have no legal authority to detain us. I insist that you allow us to contact our embassy in Djibouti."

"Miss…Allenson, is it? Yes?" Heydar asked, still smiling. "You and Mr. Hayes are Americans, yes, but you are also spies and so will be tried on charges of espionage against the people of the Islamic Republic of Somalia. As for Mr. Shalita, here, he will be tried on a charge of treason."

Joe had his hands bound behind him and his head was down, but he tried raising it now. Jim could see it was a real effort. They must've worked him over pretty good, judging from the swelling on this side of his face. "Treason...against whom?" he managed to say, with an effort.

"*Harakat ul Shabaab ul-Mujahideen,*" Heydar said. Jim remembered that from the briefing in Djibouti. Al-Shabaab, a terror group affiliated with al-Qaida, had control of much of southern and western Somalia.

Jim didn't have much hope that a trial over here would be anything close to a trial back home. Their only chance was to drag this out long enough for some sort of rescue mission to reach them. "Look, Major Heydar, we don't know what's going on here, but maybe—"

"Do not...waste your breath, James," Joe said. "Heydar is—" The man behind Joe whacked him with the butt of his rifle. Joe groaned and slumped to his left, nearly falling off the chair.

"My old friend Yusuf has become very cynical," Heydar said. "Apparently he has lost faith in our cause. There could be only one reason he was in Mogadishu, talking to the American CIA. It is most fortunate for us that I saw the boy Ayan coming into your quarters that one evening, Yusuf. At first I thought it was because, well, perhaps you are a *khaneeth.*" Whatever that word meant, it caused some commotion in the men behind the prisoners. Heydar held up a hand for quiet. "It would have been better for you if that had been the case. Ayan did not want to tell me what you talked about, Yusuf, but eventually he did. So, I had a conversation with some colleagues of mine in the SVR. I was hoping that the woman would finish you in Eyl. That would have made things much more convenient. But, here we are."

Joe groaned and shook his head. Jim read between the lines; whoever Ayan was, he must have given up Joe and somehow this Heydar character found out about Joe's plans.

They followed him to Mogadishu, using the diversion of the shelling to snatch them. Since they hadn't shot them right then and there, they must have something else planned.

Heydar started talking again, some nonsense about their cause and the greatness of Allah and the inevitable triumph of their jihad. Jim started tuning him out, thinking past him, trying to come up with a way out of this. He hoped, prayed, Denise was doing the same. She had a lot more experience at this kind of thing, but her indignant demand to be allowed a phone call hadn't gotten very far. Jim hoped that wasn't the only idea she had.

If Simons had survived and gotten out of the hotel, maybe he was in Djibouti right now, planning a rescue. Surely most, hopefully all, of their backup team had made it back. Jim had to put his faith in those men, in the troops at Camp Lemonnier. Certainly they had a quick reaction force for just this type of situation.

But, it had only been fifteen hours or so since they'd left the hotel. The intelligence people weren't magicians. They needed time to figure things out, find out where they were, put a mission together. Jim remembered reading that the bin Laden mission took months of planning and training. Well, they certainly didn't have that long now. He couldn't imagine spending more than a few days in this hellhole, much less months, waiting for a rescue that might never come. He suspected that this Heydar guy wouldn't want them around that long, either.

What did they usually do with hostages like them? The Iranians had kept the embassy hostages for over a year back in '79 and '80. They eventually came home. But that was a long time ago, and now it was likely they had only days, not months. There would be some sort of show trial, maybe, and they'd put it on the internet, and then…

He knew what would happen then. There would be a guy behind him wearing a hood, holding a big knife. Jim would feel the blade against his neck, and then agony greater than anything he could imagine. And back home, people would see it: Gina, Mickey—

His breathing was shallow now as the dread began to envelop him. He had to fight it, had to fight them, he couldn't let that horror happen. But what could he do?

He remembered something from the last time he'd heard a news story about a prisoner being executed by these bastards, a thought he had then. It was a long shot, probably the longest of long shots, but what did they have to lose? Especially now that Heydar was talking about a trial.

"The trial will be this evening," the major said, "after evening prayers."

Jim sat up straight, summoning his courage. "Why bother?"

Heydar looked at him, and Jim could sense Denise was as well, but he didn't want to break eye contact with the terrorist. "What did you say, Mr. Hayes?"

"You heard me. Why bother with a trial? Everybody here knows we've already been convicted. Stop screwing around, Heydar, and let's get down to business."

Heydar's eyes narrowed, but he looked intrigued, not angered. He thought he was holding all the cards. Well, maybe Jim had one or two to play yet. "What do you mean, Mr. Hayes? What possible business could you hope to transact with me?"

"I'm offering you a proposition."

Khorsandi, who'd been silent so far, said something to Heydar in a language Mark couldn't understand. Out of the corner of his eye, though, Jim saw Denise paying close attention. Heydar said something back to the captain, apparently mollifying him, because both men now looked back at Jim. He wondered if it was true that the guy they called Amir didn't know much English. He didn't look too comfortable up there, and Jim hit upon something else, maybe another card to play.

"What is your proposition, Mr. Hayes?"

"First, let's stop pretending that Amir there is in charge. You're running the show here and everybody knows it."

Heydar stiffened a bit at that, but Jim was looking for Amir's reaction, and he got what he hoped for. Amir sure as hell understood what was going on and didn't like it. Whether that meant he wanted to deal with the prisoners more quickly, or he didn't like being pushed aside by Heydar, Jim couldn't know for sure, but he was gambling for the latter. It could be their only chance was to play these guys against each other.

"All right, Mr. Hayes," Heydar said, sounding more serious now. Good. He had been directly challenged and he didn't like it. Part of his little charade had fallen apart. "You are in no position to demand anything."

"I'm not making any demands. I'm offering you a challenge. You and your people here."

They didn't expect that. "And that challenge is what?"

"Jim, don't—"

"Shut up, Denise!" He glared at her, then turned back to Heydar. "Don't pay any attention to the woman. She's just along for the ride. The men will decide things." That puffed them up a little. Jim knew from his reading that this was a macho, paternalistic culture, with little respect for women. They also had inflated opinions of their own prowess. "From what I have heard about your movement and your culture, your men consider themselves to be great warriors, isn't that so?"

"That is true," Khorsandi said, speaking in English for the first time.

"We're kicking your ass in Iraq and Afghanistan because we have bigger guns than you do, and we've got planes and missiles and all the hardware money can buy. But one on one, man to man, you think you're better than any American, isn't that right?"

Behind him, he heard muttering. He didn't know how many men were in the room right now, but there were more than a few, and obviously some of them knew some English. One of them shouted, "I keel American peeg!" Others shouted in what Jim presumed was Arabic.

Heydar held up a hand, and the yelling settled down into a few whispers, but Jim sensed a restless energy behind him. He'd struck a nerve. He sensed Heydar felt it, too, but he was doing a good job of holding his composure, better than his buddy the captain. But Heydar was in a bind now. He was obviously a military man, maybe Egyptian or Syrian or whatever, but he'd had training, probably real-world experience against Americans and maybe Israelis, so he would know how tough the Americans really were. But he couldn't admit that to these men here. Jim knew from his reading that they had a twisted sense of honor. Defending their manhood was everything to them. Now it was being challenged.

"Tell us what you have in mind, American." Heydar wasn't so friendly now.

Jim stood up slowly, expecting to be pushed back down or clubbed. He was taller than anyone else here, although Heydar was close, probably about six-one. Jim looked straight at the major and said, "I can beat any man in this camp, hand-to-hand." He took another risk, looking slowly around. There were about forty men in the room behind him, and every one of them looked like they were ready to kill him. "I don't need a fighter jet or a tank or even a rifle. I'm not a soldier or a marine, but I can still beat you. Man for man you're no match for us and you know it."

The room went perfectly still. He looked back at Heydar and played his last card. "Here's my challenge: I will fight any man in this camp. In fact, any *four* men. If I win, you allow us to go free. If I lose, do with us as you wish."

The shouting couldn't be calmed by a mere gesture now. Jim was shoved from behind, but he held himself back, giving only a withering glance back at the man. Heydar stood and held up his arms, shouting something in Arabic, and the men fell silent. If he pulled a gun and shot them all dead right now, he would lose whatever respect these men had for him, and Jim had the feeling they didn't have all that much to begin with. Heydar could not afford to back down. Amir appeared to be enjoying Heydar's discomfort.

"All right, American," Heydar said. "You obviously do not think much of these men and their abilities. I have trained many of them in the martial arts. They are formidable fighters."

"Yeah? Well, let's find out. We have a saying in America: put your money where your mouth is."

The room was silent, but the tension was thick. There was whispering behind him. Enough of the men back there knew enough English to translate. Heydar was on the spot, and there was only one way to get off it.

"Very well."

CHAPTER THIRTY-FIVE

IRAN

F AZEED SAW THE statue when he stopped to look through the shop's display window. The bronze Cyrus the Great, fifty centimeters tall, was facing slightly to the west. The all-clear signal. The Iranian general allowed himself to exhale and fought an urge to glance behind him. Despite what his security officer told him, he found it hard to believe he was not still under surveillance.

Two weeks ago his team had spotted a possible VEVAK unit in the city, but after a few days they had left. Apparently; one could never be sure about the secret police. Fazeed would've preferred to take a little more time, but he could not. Tomorrow he was scheduled to fly to Oman for a regional security conference that would begin the following day. His wife was already en route, having left Tehran a few hours ago. Habibeh had called him on her cell phone as she was about to board the flight to Muscat, reminding him to send in payment for their electric bill, as she had forgotten. That innocuous request told him that her dear friend Dorri Ralouf, the admiral's wife, was with her, just as planned. As the plane was taxiing down the runway for takeoff, she sent him a quick text message. Now, he had to trust that they were in the air, almost at their destination.

Fazeed and Heinz had discussed the plan just a few days ago over coffee in the shop's back room. The general would meet Habibeh in Muscat and then slip out of their hotel, dodging his own aides, and make their way to the German embassy. Admiral Ralouf, flying to Oman from his base at Bandar Abbas, would accompany his own wife to the French embassy. The Raloufs' twin daughters, studying at university in Paris, would be taken into protective custody by French security police when their parents were safe.

Fazeed knew that even if he and Ralouf both made it to Muscat, they would not be out of the woods until they left their hotel. The timing would be crucial; the VEVAK agents accompanying the Iranian delegation would lock down the hotel as soon as even one officer went missing. Fazeed had used the internet to scout the terrain, so to speak; the embassies were both less than two kilometers from their hotel. If for some reason they were unable to hail cabs, they would walk, and if necessary, run.

But first, Fazeed had to meet with Heinz here tonight and deliver the information he'd promised. If he didn't, it was possible the Germans in Muscat would refuse to grant asylum to him and his wife. That had not been stated, but Fazeed was taking no chances. Earlier that afternoon he had downloaded a number of top secret files onto a flash drive, which was now tucked safely inside the left-leg cuff of his civilian trousers. Defeating the security protocols on many of the files had proven more difficult than he anticipated, but in the end he was confident he had enough to make believers out of the Westerners. What they did with his information would be out of his hands. He would pray to Allah that they would act on it, and quickly. The ships were at sea, and every hour they got many kilometers closer to their targets.

Inside the shop, the Turkmen owner, Yaghoub, was talking to a couple near a display of rugs. A young man was on the other side of the shop, studying a case containing rare books. Yaghoub saw Fazeed as he entered, but did not acknowledge him. The general was immediately on alert. It was not like the Turkmen to ignore a customer. His senses ratcheted up and he walked calmly over to a wall display containing swords and daggers.

He would wait two minutes for Heinz to appear, and if he did not, Fazeed would leave the shop and return to his base. That was their backup security protocol. The Cyrus statue might be correctly positioned, but that did not ensure complete security. So far they had met here three times, and each time the German had been waiting for him. But in the event he was not there, even if he had been delayed for some completely innocuous reason, Fazeed's instructions were to wait only two minutes. The general glanced at the clock behind the main counter as a trickle of perspiration worked its way down his back. There was one other protocol that would come into play in the event of an emergency, but so far Fazeed had not seen that signal.

"An interesting piece, is it not?"

It took every ounce of discipline in Fazeed's body to avoid a nervous reaction to the young man's question. Fazeed nodded and offered a courteous smile. "Indeed. A Mongol scimitar, thirteenth century."

"You know your swords, sir. Are you a military man yourself?"

Fazeed had to proceed with extreme caution without being rude. "I have some knowledge in that area, you might say."

The second hand on the clock ticked past Fazeed's one-minute mark. Out of the corner of his left eye, he saw Yaghoub leave the couple and take two steps closer. The Turkmen reached under the counter and placed a shiny object on it, causing a slight clacking sound. Turning his head only a couple inches to the left, Fazeed pretended to look at another sword next to the scimitar, but instead he glanced quickly at the object on the counter.

A knife. Fazeed knew it was a *karn,* a steel dagger with ivory handle, made in Iran circa 1800. It was also the emergency signal. The shop had been blown. His mind raced. What about the statue? The signals sent conflicting messages. But perhaps Yaghoub had adjusted the statue earlier on Heinz's order, and then suddenly, perhaps just minutes ago, received a call from the German, or some other indication of trouble, and had not had time to move Cyrus.

It made no difference. Yaghoub never took an item out of his display cases unless a customer specifically requested it. There could be no doubt. Fazeed had to get out, now. To the man next to him, he said, "Excuse me." Turning to Yaghoub, he asked, "My friend, the book on Darius the Great, has it arrived?"

"I'm sorry, no. Perhaps next week."

"Very well. I'll see you then." Nodding to the Turkmen, who averted his eyes, Fazeed took a step toward the door.

He felt a hand on left his arm, heard the distinctive sound of something sliding on leather. "Just a minute, General."

His reaction was instinctive and instantaneous. He picked the dagger off the counter and in one motion whirled and plunged it into the man's stomach. The man's eyes bulged as he gasped, doubling over. A pistol fell from his left hand and clattered to the floor. The woman at the rug display screamed.

Fazeed stooped quickly and picked up the gun, slipped it into the outside pocket of his coat and walked purposefully to the door, looking straight ahead, ignoring the shocked rug customers. He exited the shop and turned right, took five more steps and turned into an alley. The city's bazaar district was a typical warren of side streets and narrow alleys. Having explored it often, Fazeed was quite familiar with it. He could only hope that the men who would soon be pursuing him would not be.

It took him five minutes to find a shop where he could buy a dark gray short jacket, replacing the tan sport coat he'd been wearing, and another shop nearby produced a cheap straw fedora. The sport coat went into a trash barrel, and he ducked into a small café, entered the restroom and slipped the flash drive from his trouser hem. He dropped it in the toilet, relieved himself, and flushed.

Looking at himself in the mirror, he considered his options. There weren't many. He had no way to contact Heinz, and the German had probably been arrested already. His staff car, which he'd driven himself from the base, was parked about half a kilometer away from the shop, and to get there he'd have to take a roundabout route to avoid going past the shop again. Undoubtedly VEVAK agents had the car under surveillance.

His only hope was to get back to the base and fly from there to Muscat. Although the base was primarily the home of a missile regiment, there was an airfield with a small squadron of Russian-made MiG-29 fighters. Fazeed was qualified on the aircraft. At least half the squadron was on alert at any given time, so there would be a jet available for him, fully fueled... and armed. Oman was well to the south, across the Gulf, but the border with Turkmenistan, to the north, was much closer. He could make it in twenty or thirty minutes, and the largest airfield in the country was in Ashgabat, just across the border. On the other hand, Iran and Turkmenistan had good relations, so he could not trust the Turkmen government to grant him asylum. Perhaps he could go east, to Afghanistan, and find an American base. He might even be able to make it to Bagram, although that would be at the edge of the MiG's range...

This was pointless! He was wasting time. Get to the base, get into a cockpit and get in the air. Then he could make a decision. He pulled his cell phone from the inside pocket of his new jacket and punched in a speed-dial number. First he had to warn Ralouf. The admiral was not scheduled to fly to Oman until the next morning. Fazeed could not be certain VEVAK would not arrest Ralouf, or at least question him, before then. The friendship of the two men was widely known. No, they would come for him, perhaps were already watching him, waiting for orders.

A recorded voice answered. *"This is Admiral Ralouf. Please leave a message."*

Fazeed waited for the beep, then said, "Alas, Babylon," and hung up. It was the code phrase they'd agreed upon, from an old American novel they'd both enjoyed in their student days, warning the recipient to take every precaution and advance his departure if at all possible. Fazeed knew their phones were secure devices, or so their respective security teams had assured them. But how secure was anything in Iran? The secret police had their tendrils everywhere.

Next he hit the button that speed-dialed his security chief at the base. "Colonel Rajaei."

"This is General Fazeed. Condition Blue. I am in the city. Send a helicopter for me. I will be waiting at the soccer field next to the elementary school."

"Are you all right, General? Do you need assistance? I have three men in the city this evening, on personal business."

Fazeed considered that option, then discarded it. It was a large city and the men could be anywhere. By the time they got to a central location it would be too late. Fazeed stepped to the wall of the rest room, cocking an ear to the small upper window. In the distance he heard a siren. No, he would be better off on his own, and the fewer people who knew about this, the better. "Negative, Colonel. I will make the rendezvous by myself." He had to make it sound convincing, so he added, "An attempt was made on my life. I'm sure it was a man sent by our friends to the west. We have rehearsed this, remember."

"Of course, General," Rajaei said. An assassination attempt on the commander of a missile regiment could very well be the opening move in an Israeli attack. "I will have the helicopter sent immediately."

"Very good, Davood. Initiate the appropriate security measures. No one is to enter or exit the base, starting now. Except for that helicopter."

"Understood, sir. I will see you soon." Fazeed signed off, pocketed the cell phone and left the rest room.

Fazeed stood near a tree at the southeast corner of the school's small campus. The cab had dropped him off three blocks away, and the general had wound his way through the neighborhood of small homes, apartment buildings and shops, doing what he could to throw off any pursuit. He was becoming increasingly agitated; he was not trained in this, and the men hunting him were. His only hope was the helicopter.

He looked at his watch again. Nearly thirty minutes since his call to the base, about forty-five since he'd left the antiquities shop. He'd heard more sirens, but they didn't seem to

343

be getting closer. Where was the damned chopper? He would wait another five minutes and call the base again. Could Rajaei have betrayed him? No, it was not possible—

From behind him, in the direction from which he'd come, he heard a siren, two sirens. He began to perspire more heavily. But what was that? The helicopter! Yes, it was coming! He looked out at the soccer field, where children were playing a match. What would the pilot do when he saw them? Would he hesitate? No, they were trained in this type of situation: come in fast and if it was a "hot" landing zone, there was a gunner on board to deal with resistance. But the gunner would not fire on civilians.

He looked to the west, in the gathering twilight, as the beat of the helicopter's rotors grew louder. From behind him, so did the sirens. There it was! Coming in low, running lights off, just as they'd drilled. But the children, some of them didn't see the helicopter. Many heard it, they were halting their play and looking skyward. Some were still playing.

Fazeed looked down the street behind him. Three blocks away, a police car turned the corner and headed toward him, lights flashing. Another was behind it.

The general drew his pistol and ran onto the field, shouting at the children. "Run! Clear the field!" He fired two rounds into the air. That got their attention. Some of them screamed in panic, but they all began to run, all except one, a boy who had the ball. Intent on the game, he was the last to notice anything happening. He was near midfield, and Fazeed saw the helicopter coming in fast from the west, over the school and now the sideline of the field, pulling up into a hover as it prepared to land. The side door was open, and an airman was leaning out, shouting at the boy to clear the landing space.

He heard the screech of braking vehicles behind him,

shouts from the policemen. He had fifty meters to go. The boy knelt down with the ball, terrified, as the helicopter hovered above him. The pilot, realizing the boy was frozen in fear, moved the aircraft several meters to the west, away from the boy, and began to descend.

Fazeed felt something buzz past his head just as he heard the crack of the gun from behind him. A divot exploded from the ground to his right, then another. The helicopter was ten meters above the ground now, coming down dangerously close to the child, but close enough to give the general a chance to escape the gunfire behind him. The gunner at the door readied his machine gun, hesitated, tilted his head as if receiving an order in his helmet's headset, then fired a burst past Fazeed toward the police. Another airman appeared in the doorway, waving at the general to hurry.

More police cars roared to a stop on the street flanking the field on the east. Men poured out and began firing. Two rounds came close to the boy, who looked up in fear. He was about twelve years old, and for a moment Fazeed thought he looked just like his own son at that age.

Fazeed was now under fire from two directions, and the boy was going to get caught in the crossfire. The general angled toward the boy and ran to him. "General!" the airman in the door yelled. "No! This way!" The machine gun chattered again.

Fazeed reached the boy and swept him up into his arms, turned and ran for the helicopter. Fifteen meters. Ten. Something sparked off the windscreen of the helicopter. He could see the pilot flinching. The helicopter had touched down, but now began to rise as the roar of the rotors increased.

The general felt something slam into his right leg and he staggered, falling to the turf, twisting so that he landed on his left shoulder, not on the boy, who was crying now. The helicopter was maybe eight meters away. The pain rushed through Fazeed's body, like nothing he'd ever felt. He looked frantically toward the helicopter. More rounds were hitting it now, and the airman beside the gunner was knocked backward by a hit to his helmet.

Fazeed reached out toward the helicopter as two rounds struck him in the back. His hand fell to the turf, but he held onto the boy with his right, shielding him. Yes, he was so much like his son, wasn't he? His last thought was the joy of knowing that he would now be with his son again.

CHAPTER THIRTY-SIX

SOMALIA

THE GUARDS WHO escorted him to the cell block were in ugly moods, and Jim was careful to do nothing to antagonize them, although he held himself erect and walked with purpose. He could not afford to show any fear to these people, not now. They put him back in his cell, but they didn't lay a hand on him.

The door opened a minute later and Denise was shoved inside. The captain, Khorsandi, was in the doorway. "Compliments of Major Heydar," he said with a salacious smile. "Enjoy the woman while you can. After you are killed by his men tonight, it will be our turn to enjoy her."

"*Surmayye a'raasac!*" Denise snapped at him. The captain laughed and stepped out, the door slamming shut behind him.

Jim reached out to her, but she turned on him with cold fury. "What the hell are you doing?"

"What do you mean?"

She stepped closer, letting go of the front of her shirt. He couldn't help noticing she wore no bra underneath. Had they taken it from her before? He sensed this wasn't the time to ask.

"You deliberately antagonized them in there. Setting yourself up for some ridiculous sort of tournament? How could you be so stupid?"

"Hey, wait a minute—"

"No, *you* wait. You're going to get us all killed, you idiot!" She turned and took a couple steps away, holding her hands to the sides of her head. "My God. And I thought you'd be safe to take on the mission. I stood up for you, for God's sake!"

"Take it easy, Denise. I had to do something to buy us some time."

She faced him again, her anger only slightly cooled. "Jim, we train for these kinds of contingencies. There are protocols. Some things you can try, other things you can't. Or shouldn't, anyway. Challenging your captors to a duel is certainly on the don't-ever-do-this list."

"It looked to me like Heydar was setting the protocols in there. What was your idea? You demanded he let us call the embassy. That went over real well, didn't it?" That brought a huff from her and she looked away again. "And what ideas do you have, exactly, about—"

She cupped a hand behind an ear and nodded toward the door. It took him a moment, but then he got it: she thought the cell might be bugged. Okay. He took a deep breath to calm himself. "What did you say to Khorsandi?"

"It was Arabic for 'there is a shoe on your head.' They consider that a big insult." She said it with a tight smile. That was a good sign.

"Who are those guys, anyway?" Jim asked.

"Heydar and Khorsandi are Iranians, and I'm sure they're officers in Quds Force. Very hard cases. Quds operatives do the dirty work out in the field for the Revolutionary Guard."

"What are they doing all the way over here, in Somalia? Are they working with Joe's people?"

Her anger was gone now, but maybe it hadn't been real anger at all, just an act for anyone listening in. Either way, he was glad to see she was focused. They'd have to make some kind of escape attempt eventually and that was way outside his skill set. He had no illusions about their eventual fate; even if, somehow, he could beat four of these guys—and why didn't he say three, or even two?—there was no way Heydar was going to let them walk out of here and hitch a ride back to K50.

"Shalita is a very big wheel in al-Qaida, and we've had some indicators in recent months that Iran is stepping up their support of these networks. That surprised us at first."

"Why?"

"Because Iran is strongly Shi'a and al-Qaida is largely a Sunni operation. Remember your briefings back at Langley, Jim. They tend not to get along real well. Even before the founding of Islam, the Persians and Arabs were at each other's throats more often than not."

"That seems to be changing now."

She went over to Jim's makeshift bed and sat down, leaning back against the wall. The front of her shirt came open a bit more and Jim forced himself to look away. He sat down next to her, but kept a respectful distance. "I picked up on some things when I was posted to Djibouti in the last year or so," she said. "They're working hard at their nuclear program, but they're not just sitting around otherwise. Iranian activity with Hamas and Hezbollah has increased. They're also showing up more in Iraq and Afghanistan. We see their fingerprints in Egypt. They're major players over here."

"I've been following the news about the nuclear thing,"

he said. "They're still, what, two years away from getting the bomb? Three?"

She shook her head. "No, they're much closer than that. Some of us think so, anyway."

He was surprised at that. "That's not what we're being told."

"You're not in Wisconsin anymore, Jim. Welcome to reality."

"Well, what the hell," he said, "why not let the truth out? People need to know this, a lot of them would get upset if they knew these characters were that close."

"Exactly. There would be demands that something be done, and a lot of important people don't want to go in that direction. There's an election coming up in just over a year, remember."

"But we can't just let them have the nukes, can we? For God's sake, they could hit Israel, they could hit our troops. My brother's base!"

She looked at him wearily. "Jim, we don't make the decisions on policy. That's up to the politicians. We just try our best to find out what's going on, then let them know."

"And you've told them about how close they are?"

"Of course," she said. "But, you know, after the Iraq WMD mess, some people don't listen to us very much."

They were quiet for a long minute. International politics. Weapons of mass destruction. Things were a lot simpler back in Cedar Lake.

"Can you beat them?" she finally asked.

"I don't know," he said. "Depends on who they pick. Depends on the rules."

"We don't know a lot about Heydar, but his name came up when I was in Djibouti. He made the 2000 Olympics in taekwondo, so if he's training these men here, they won't be pushovers."

Jim couldn't remember the name, but he hadn't paid much attention to the martial arts competition back then, since he hadn't yet resumed his own training. "Did he win?"

"What?"

"Did he win? In Sydney?"

She thought for a minute. "No," she said at last. "Got beat in the opening round, I think. And as far as rules go, don't expect any breaks. You may have to kill those men, Jim. Are you prepared to do that?"

She was looking at him so intensely it almost hurt. He looked right back at her.

"Yes."

Jim awoke with a start. Some kind of noise from the window, he didn't know what, but as his eyes adjusted, he could see they were still alone in the cell. It was a bit darker, must've been getting on toward late afternoon.

He was lying on the bedding, Denise next to him, curled up with his left arm around her. They had talked a bit more and then just sort of nodded off. He must've gone down first, the fatigue finally overcoming the tension and fear.

That question she had asked: Was he prepared to kill the men he would have to fight? He'd said yes, without any hesitation, any fear. Now, in the dusty, hot quiet of the cell, he thought about that. Could he really do it? In all his years of training, as realistic as much of it had been, he had never killed anyone, of course, never even seriously hurt anybody. He'd read a lot about it, but that was in the abstract. The reality was right here and now.

It was enough to make most men give in to the terror, but Jim realized that not only was his fear receding, he was actually looking forward to the challenge ahead. Now that was a curious thought, wasn't it? But maybe not. Six years of hard training and study had delivered him here, where things were no longer abstract or artificial. His fate, his destiny, was waiting for him just beyond that wall.

One of his favorite books was *In Search of the Warrior Spirit,* and he had memorized one memorable passage: *The warrior within us beseeches Mars, the god of War, to deliver us to that crucial battlefield that will redeem us into the terrifying immediacy of the moment…We long for the encounter that will ultimately empower us with dignity and honor…*

He had thought all along that he was doing all this for Suzy, for her memory, so that if he was ever tested again, really tested, this time he would come through. Now, though, he realized that it was something much deeper. The men out there were intent on taking his life and the lives of his friends, and from here they would move against other innocents. Eventually they would come to his own country again, maybe even to a small town in southern Wisconsin. They had to be stopped, and in the last ten years a lot of men and women, including his brother, had stepped forward to do just that. Now it was Jim's turn.

He'd once read an essay by a former Army Ranger—what was his name? Grossman, that was it— about the three types of people in modern society. Most people are sheep; nonviolent, peaceful, just wanting to go about their business. A few are wolves, the sociopaths, who want nothing more than to kill the sheep. And protecting the sheep is the third type, the sheepdog. The sheep don't like the dog, really don't trust him; he looks a lot like the wolf, after all, he's big and powerful and, when necessary, violent. But the sheep know that when the wolf shows up, only the sheepdog stands between them and death.

Jim knew what type he wanted to be. And right now, the wolves were just beyond that wall.

Next to him, Denise stirred, muttering, and snuggled closer. He must've been whispering the lines that he'd recalled from the book, but she was still asleep. He couldn't resist reaching up and stroking her hair, ever so slightly, not wanting to wake her. She stirred and moved, rolling slightly toward her back, and Jim watched the front of her shirt slide ever so slowly away from her breast. In spite of the circumstances, the sight of her nipple roused a heat inside him.

He considered reaching over to pull the shirt back into place, but if she woke up right then, it wouldn't look real good. Better to just leave it be, look away, think of something else.

Yeah, sure. Even with her hair out of place, no makeup and at least twenty-four hours removed from a shower, she was still strikingly attractive. How could CIA use women this good-looking as covert operatives? Well, they'd evidently done it with that Plame woman. As he thought about it, he realized their looks would bring them some advantages. Men were pretty much the same all over. A guy was much more likely to let his guard down around a beautiful woman as opposed to a plain one.

She sighed and squirmed a bit against him. She was waking up, but before he could do anything, she had rolled to her right, on top of him, and then her eyes blinked open, their faces only an inch apart She came fully awake and pushed herself upward slightly, giving him a view that in other circumstances he would've considered spectacular indeed.

But he just said, "I think you need a different shirt."

She smiled, leaned close to his ear and whispered, "After you beat these guys, be ready to move."

CHAPTER THIRTY-SEVEN

AFGHANISTAN

K RIEGER HANDED THE binoculars over to Mark and pointed to the west. "That patrol is very regular," the German-American said. "Every day, they pass the checkpoint at 0900 going south, 1200 going north, 1500 south, and 1800 going north again."

The border crossing was manned on the Afghan side by two squads of border police, occasionally augmented by ANA regulars. On the other side, Mark could see the Iranian guard posts. On the road that roughly paralleled the border on that side, three vehicles, two armored cars similar to Humvees and a larger truck, stopped and two soldiers from the nearest guard post went over to have a word with the man in the front passenger seat of the lead vehicle. After a couple minutes, the guards stepped back and saluted, and the small convoy started up again, heading south.

"What about nighttime patrols?" Mark asked.

"Maybe two per night. Usually only one."

The orders had come down from ISAF just a few hours after the General and Krieger lifted off from Roosevelt two days ago. Contingency plans were quickly dusted off and some-body in the spook house deemed it more likely that Iran would be the scene of some action rather than Pakistan, so Krieger's Unit 7 was sent here, to Farah province. The Provisional Reconstruction Team in this sector, based in the city of Farah, was a U.S. team, but overall the Italians were in charge of this province, which was part of Regional Command West. Most of their people were based in Herat province, to the north, but there was an Italian captain now assigned to the unit to act as liaison. Along with Mark, who had arrived here this morning, the roster now numbered twenty operators.

"We won't be inserting at this checkpoint, though," Mark said.

"No. When this patrol is well south of us, we will cross the border about ten kilometers to the north, assuming that we get a mission."

"I have a feeling we will," Mark said. His phone call from the General just before dawn had been short, and there was no further word about Jim in Somalia. Mark tried not to think about that, but it was impossible. Krieger had asked him to coordinate available air assets, and Mark was grateful to have something to keep him busy. Within the next couple hours a squadron of helicopters was due to arrive at their potential jumping-off point, a large FOB to the north. Those birds would have to be serviced and prepped for a mission and their crews would have to be fed and housed overnight. In addition to that, Mark was working with Air Force and Marine fixed-wing commands to have fast-movers on standby, just in case they needed help getting out.

The fact that he had only twenty men told Mark that their target, whatever it might be, wasn't expected to be very big. Using the NATO unit also meant it would not only be top-secret but of high political sensitivity. The last thing any-body wanted now was a war with Iran, but apparently some people very high up the food chain felt there was something across the border over there that might be worth taking out. It would be a big risk, no doubt about it. Somebody back in Washington would have to grow a couple of big brass ones to issue a go order on something like this, which was why Mark thought it likely they'd be ordered to stand down within the next forty-eight hours. There weren't a lot of big brass ones inside the suits in Washington these days, at least when it came to Iran. Popping an elderly terrorist in Pakistan was one thing; going across the Iranian frontier after a high-value target was something else again.

What he really wanted to do was go to Djibouti to help with the search for Jim and his team. He'd asked the General about that and was told no. There were plenty of assets over there to conduct whatever mission was called for, and the last thing they needed was someone riding along whose professional judgment might be in question due to having a relative in harm's way. Mark understood all that, but if he'd been allowed to go he would not have hesitated.

"I need you with Unit 7, Mark," the General had told him. "Krieger and his men are pros, but they're not directly under my command. I want someone with them who represents ISAF." Undoubtedly the General had used a good portion of his considerable horsepower to make that happen, and Mark wasn't about to disappoint him.

Krieger looked at his wristwatch. "We should be getting back," he said. "Considering the air assets we've been given, our options for a target area are limited. We should start planning the most likely scenarios, yes?"

"Sounds good to me," Mark said. He took one last look

across the border, into Iran. The mountains in the distance loomed large. "The Aladagh," he said. "There must be something in there that's going to be worth risking the lives of a lot of men."

"Undoubtedly, Colonel. Perhaps we can figure out what that might be."

Night was starting to fall. Mark buttoned up his heavy coat against the cold. The elevation was not quite as high as it was back at Roosevelt, but it still didn't take long for the heat of the day to dissipate, and the space heater inside the tent was hopelessly outgunned.

"The Aladagh range," Krieger said, pointing down at the map of eastern Iran. "What can you tell us about this area, Baris?"

The Turkish sergeant, short and rather swarthy with an unruly shock of black hair, traced a finger down from the Caspian Sea south and east toward the Afghan border area. "They are not as high as the Zagros in western Iran," he said in accented English. "In the north, from the Caspian, they are called the Elburz, then the Aladagh. The region is known as Khorasan, now divided into three provinces. Here is the major city, Birjand. The ethnic mix is mostly Persian, but many Pashtun also. It is on the Silk Road, the ancient trade route. Today there is much movement of opium from Afghanistan through here."

Krieger turned to a British lieutenant who served as the unit's intelligence officer. "Nelson, what about nearby military installations?"

The Brit was slender and looked like a guy you might see throwing darts at a country pub after a day tending sheep, but Mark had already found out he knew his stuff. "Nearest

Iranian Air Force base is here, at Mashhad International Airport." He indicated a city in the extreme northeast. "They have an F-4 squadron, about ten aircraft, plus a tanker and a couple small transports. As for the Army, there is a caserne near Birjand, with about five hundred troops, a dozen tanks, and most important for us, a squadron of attack and transport helicopters. I would estimate that they could put troops on the ground anywhere along this border region inside of four hours after an alert. But for anything we might be doing in this region, our main concern should be their special forces. Recent intel indicates that a unit of their Takavar is based somewhere in this region."

"Do we know what unit?" Mark asked.

"We think it is 7-Tip 65 Nouhad," Nelson said. "Said to be the best they have. Are you familiar with that unit, Colonel?"

"I was on a mission with a French Foreign Legion platoon a few months ago," Mark said. "North of here, in Herat. We were interdicting an opium route used by a local warlord to move his product into Iran. Just this side of the border there was a firefight with some of the warlord's fighters, backed by a squad of Takavaran."

"What did you gather about their capabilities?" Krieger asked.

"They didn't go down easy," Mark said. "They're not at the level of top NATO units, but mainly because our equipment is better and we can count on better logistical and tactical support in the field. I've heard their training is first-rate, but even if we're on their turf, our biggest advantage should be our combat experience."

Krieger nodded. "Gentlemen, I think we can assume that if we get a go order for a mission, it will involve a strike against an HVT. We might further assume this Nouhad unit will be nearby."

"That will make things interesting," Nelson said.

The briefing lasted another half-hour, during which Mike Marolda, the captain in charge of the helo detachment, offered his insights. Mark was gratified to have the Night Stalkers on board. The 160th Special Operations Aviation Regiment (Airborne) had delivered the SEALs to Abbottabad, not to mention a ton of other ops around both theaters since 9/11. Mark had met Marolda during his last Iraq tour and he was a first-class pilot. He'd brought three Black Hawks and three Apaches with him. If Unit 7 was going across the border, they'd have some of the best aviators in the world carrying them.

Mark visited the FOB comm shack after the briefing, asked if there were any messages for him, and was told no. The General had promised to keep him apprised of the situation in Somalia. No news is good news, Mark thought as he went back out into the Afghan night. Only this time, he didn't think it was true.

He looked to the southwest. Thirty-five hundred miles in that direction, his brother was in trouble, and there wasn't a damn thing Mark could do about it, except offer up a prayer. He gazed up into the night sky and the vast pantheon of stars. "God, I know you're watching over Jim right now. Please bring him back home."

CHAPTER THIRTY-EIGHT

SOMALIA

JIM AND DENISE had been brought trays of food along with bottled water. They ate in silence. The crusty bread wasn't much better than what he'd choked down earlier in the day, but there was brown rice and some sort of meat, probably mutton, she said. No utensils. Somebody had actually been thoughtful enough to provide small towels so they could clean their hands. After the meal they were led to a latrine, more primitive than anything Jim had ever seen in the States, but he presumed they were standard issue over here.

Back in the cell, he said, "Now, about that new shirt." He slipped his own over his head and handed it to her. "It's a little big for you, and it's not in the best of shape, sorry."

She took it with a smile. "It'll do." She looked at him, and he turned around. When he turned back after the rustling was done, she was tying the hem of the shirt into a knot, snugging the shirt as best she could to her body, leaving a few inches of midriff. "How do I look?"

"Under the circumstances, pretty terrific," he said. He gestured at her stomach. "Will they get upset about that?"

"Probably, but we're way past that by now, aren't we?" She gave the shirt one more adjustment, revealing another half-inch of her toned abs. "They'll be coming pretty soon," she said.

"I suppose so."

"Listen, Jim, I have to apologize for what I said before. I know you thought what you were doing was for the best."

"That's okay," he said. "I can understand how you must've felt."

She stepped closer to him. "Don't get yourself killed, all right?"

He reached out to her, and she came into his arms, hesitantly, but then she wrapped hers around him. "I'll do my best," he said. "You might want to start thinking of a better way for us to get out, just in case."

"I'll do my best," she said with a little laugh. Then she looked up at him, and came closer.

The angry shouting started as soon as Denise came around the corner into the yard, with two armed fighters in front of her, two behind her, then Jim and two more men.

A year ago he'd watched a TV series about Spartacus, the Thracian warrior who'd been sold into slavery and became a gladiator in the arenas of the Roman Republic. Jim vividly remembered the episode where Spartacus was led into the arena for the first time, facing a fight to the death. Now he knew how the man must have felt. Every man here wanted to see Jim die.

But Spartacus, a man Jim considered to be the embodiment of courage and honor, had survived that fight and went on to lead a rebellion that nearly toppled the Republic. A dose of gladiator courage would come in handy right about now.

Words came to Jim from somewhere deep in his past, from a source infinitely better than Spartacus: *Even though I walk through the valley of the shadow of death, I will fear no evil, for Thou art with me.*

Dozens of men, probably well over a hundred, ringed the open area in the center of the camp. The sun was dropping into the low hills to the west, and it was starting to cool down. Several torches had been placed in holders along the walls of the three buildings forming the sides of the courtyard. Trucks were parked at each corner of the open end and their headlights were turned on. Ahead of him, three lines of men blocked the way. Beyond them in the gathering gloom were the far reaches of the camp. On the left side was a small wooden platform just large enough to hold a man setting up a video camera on a tripod.

Joe was there, sitting in the middle chair of three that had been brought out from the chow hall. He actually managed a slight smile when he saw the Americans. Jim sat down in the chair to Joe's left, Denise to his right.

"Joe, are you all right?" Jim asked.

His old friend's dark brown eyes looked pained, and one was puffy and swollen. "Don't worry about me, James. Are you ready for this?"

Jim had competed in dozens of tournaments and before every one of them, he'd felt nervous. This tournament would be unlike any he'd ever experienced, but all things considered, he felt good. The decision to give Denise his shirt wasn't just for her; he wanted the men out here to see that he wasn't soft and pudgy as they probably assumed an American civilian would be. He'd spent some time in the cell stretching, getting limber and working up a sweat, and now the evening air felt cool on his bare chest and back. His knee felt fine, thankfully.

If that went out on him now, he'd be in real trouble. Of course he was in real trouble anyway, but he needed everything firing on all cylinders for as long as possible to survive what was to come.

"Well, I'd rather be sitting in my house watching TV right now," Jim said, "but I'll be okay." He actually felt rather calm. He kept his breathing steady, trying to block out everything beyond what was waiting for him in the arena. He wasn't normally a man who prayed a lot, but he'd done more praying in the past twenty-four hours than he had in months. Hopefully God wouldn't consider it to be too little, too late.

The African looked like he was about to break down. Jim could hardly imagine the pressure he was under. All these years as a leader of men like this, and suddenly he was a prisoner, just as he was on the verge of freedom. Jim put his hand on his old friend's shoulder. "Listen, Joe, we're gonna get out of here, okay? We'll find ourselves a quiet little bar somewhere and have a couple beers. We have a lot of catching up to do." A wry grin stretched Joe's parched lips. "Oh, sorry, I forgot Muslims don't drink."

"It's okay, James. I will have an iced tea." He clasped Jim's hand with his own, unable to keep his shoulders from shuddering. But then he straightened in his chair, his strength returning. Jim could see the change in his face. Just moments before, there had been fear and anguish crowding the lines in his black skin. Now, Jim saw courage and determination. The little Ugandan's power seemed to flow into him. Jim removed his hand, and it was almost like breaking an electrical connection.

"I must tell you, I have seen Heydar training some of the men," Joe said. "They appear to me to be proficient."

"I guess we'll find out pretty quick." He saw the rows of men at the far corner of the courtyard part, and the two

Iranians came into view, followed by three other men, all three stripped to the waist. Two of them looked to be shorter than Jim, but one was tall, broad in the shoulders, and scowling. Of course, Jim thought, there's always one of these guys in every dojo, a weightlifter who thinks he can translate that kind of power into what is a totally different kind of training. But if the rules allowed grappling, that guy might be real trouble.

"Have you seen them do any ground work, Joe?"

"You mean, wrestling?"

"Yeah, MMA-style, that kind of thing."

"I do not know of this MMA, but yes, I have seen them do something like wrestling, and the large man there, Mahmoud, is very good. He is Syrian, was once one of Assad's bodyguards."

"Terrific."

Heydar stepped out into the center of the courtyard. Jim saw another pair of men following Mahmoud, and they had their arms full with something wrapped in what appeared to be heavy sheets of some sort. The Iranian major began to speak to the crowd.

"He speaks in Arabic," Joe said. "He announces this series of challenge matches. He thanks the many volunteers who offered to kill the American, but he has chosen these three."

"Well, that's a bit of a relief. I offered to fight four."

"Do not think Heydar the fool, James. Undoubtedly if you defeat these three, he will be the fourth."

The Iranian went on, drawing cheers from the crowd. "What did he say?"

Joe cleared his throat, glancing at Denise, who had stiffened in her seat. "Heydar says the fighter who defeats you will be allowed to use the body of your woman in full view of the camp. Then she will be killed."

Jim looked over at Denise. He still felt the softness of her lips on his, delicate and tender. "I wouldn't think your religion would allow that, Joe."

"Of course it does not. 'Fear God and respect women.' The fourth Sura. But Heydar twists the words of the Prophet, peace be upon him, to suit his own purposes."

"Imagine that." Jim stood up. "Well, looks like it's just about showtime."

Joe stood and offered his hand. "God be with you, James."

"Thanks, I'll need all the help I can get." He took a step to Denise, and her eyes were wet. Maybe these characters needed to see how an American man treated a woman. He extended a hand. She took it gratefully.

"Good luck, Jim. Do what you have to do."

"Thanks, Denise. Thanks for everything." He looked at the enemy fighters, then back to her. "When we get back, I'll buy you a drink at that bar in McLean."

"You're on," she said with a smile.

Heydar motioned Jim to the center, and the first Arab came out from the other side. The guy was young, maybe early twenties. He looked excited, maybe too excited. Heydar looked calm and confident. "Mr. Hayes, this is Abdul, from Iraq. He joined our cause to help fight against your people when they invaded his country."

"I suppose he would rather have taken his chances with Saddam and his boys."

"Joke while you can, Mr. Hayes," Heydar said. "Abdul is one of my best students, and he has no love of Americans."

"Well, I'm touched. Let's get on with it. What are the rules?"

Heydar gave him that same magnanimous smile he'd had earlier in the day in the chow hall. "The rules, Mr. Hayes? My men can choose a weapon from those they've trained with, or they may choose to fight with the empty hands. You may try to defend yourself as you please,"

The two men with the rolled up sheets laid them on the ground at one side of the yard and pulled away the cloth with a clattering sound. Jim saw a scattering collection of familiar martial arts weaponry. Abdul went over to the nearest stack and picked up a pair of *nunchaku,* then walked confidently back to the center, whipping the two connected short sticks around, behind his shoulders and over his head.

Jim watched him carefully. The first thing he noticed was that the weapon was a cheap one, easily available on martial arts websites around the world. Two rounded sticks, probably oak, about fourteen inches long and connected by a short chain. In his *kobujutsu* class back home, Jim used a version of the weapon that was custom-made of polymer, easy to hold and maneuver, connected with a short, tough rope cord. He went over to the weapons and looked them over. He'd hoped there would be a sansetsukon; the three-section staff would have given him a big advantage against everyone but the most highly-skilled opponent, but it was rare enough in America and so he wasn't surprised there wasn't one here. He chose a pair of nunchaku similar to Abdul's. They would have to do.

The men were cheering Abdul as he showed off for them. Jim hefted his weapon. It was in decent enough shape, and used properly it could deliver an impact of about twelve hundred pounds to something fragile, like a man's wrist or his temple. But it could be used for other things, too, and he wondered if Abdul knew about those. Heydar was a taekwondo stylist, and back home Jim knew that TKD people, as competent as they were at empty-hand fighting, generally didn't do much weapons training. Certainly not as much as he did in his classes. Now he would find out whether all that practice would pay off.

They met in the middle of the yard, with Heydar about fifteen feet away. Jim was flipping his nunchaku like he was not very familiar with them. It would be better to really warm up with them first, go through some of his *buri* techniques, but he didn't want them to think he knew what he was doing. It would be a risk, but it might just give him an edge in this first bout. Abdul took a stance right out of a cheap Hong Kong movie, feet splayed apart with the right foot back, knees bent, left hand pushed out, right hand holding the weapon, twirling it easily.

Heydar yelled *"See jak!"* and Abdul charged, screaming, pulling his right hand back to deliver a mighty killing blow. As his body twisted to the right, his left arm extended outward just a bit more, and Jim sidestepped to his right, whipping his weapon around Abdul's left wrist. As the outer nunchaku swung around, Jim grabbed it with his left hand and cranked them apart, generating hundreds of pounds of force through the chain into the Iraqi's fragile wrist. Jim heard it popping just before Abdul's scream changed in pitch.

Twisting the weapon further toward him, Jim forced Abdul down onto his right knee. He gave the wrist one more crank, producing another shriek, and then released the left nunchaku, bringing the weapon up and around behind his head with his right hand and delivering a strike into Abdul's exposed, naked ribcage. The Iraqi staggered to his right, pressing into the ground with his right hand, his weapon now useless. Jim's weapon came around again, his motion hardly slowed by the rib strike, and this time he brought it swinging around Abdul's neck. With the chain planted on the right side of the Iraqi's throat, Jim grabbed the left nunchaku and cranked on the windpipe. The screaming stopped, and there was utter silence from the crowd. Jim heard the choking, saw Abdul's eyes bug out and spasms wrack his body. It only takes eleven pounds of pressure to collapse the human trachea, Jim knew, about three times that to crush it completely. He applied a little more. The Iraqi gagged, and Jim released the grip and stepped back. Abdul convulsed once, twice, then lay still, his breath producing a hideous rasp.

Keeping his own breathing ever under control, Jim turned to Heydar, who was staring in something approaching disbelief, and said, "All right, I'm warmed up now. Who's next?"

CHAPTER THIRTY-NINE
AFGHANISTAN

"COLONEL HAYES? CAPTAIN Krieger wants you over at the comm shack on the double." Mark jumped off his cot, dropped the Vince Flynn novel he'd been reading and trotted behind the sergeant. There was a group of about ten men inside the comm shack, eyes trained on a flat-screen TV set up on a platform at eye level. Krieger was standing in the midst of the troops and he motioned Mark to join him.

"What's going on?" Jim asked. The picture showed what appeared to be an open yard of some sort, with men milling around the perimeter. Not the best light, and Jim could tell by the slight stuttering of the image that it was an internet feed. As remote as they were, the outpost had a connection with the nationwide fiber-optic system installed a few years before by the Chinese.

"We got word from ISAF that there was something happening on an al-Qaida website," Krieger said. "They think it's from Somalia."

"The boys at the Puzzle Palace are on the ball," Jim said.

He knew that the massive, secretive National Security Agency back home constantly monitored numerous websites favored by terrorists. This same feed was surely being watched right now at CIA headquarters in Virginia, and probably also the Situation Room at the White House.

A man wearing military fatigues walked into the middle of the yard from the upper left, and from the right came another man, taller and bare-chested. Mark's heart almost seized up. "That's my brother," he said.

"The man on the right?"

"Yes."

The tech turned up the scratchy audio feed. An Arabic speaker in the crowd started translating. When the officer doing the talking mentioned the woman captive, the camera panned to the right and zoomed in. Sitting in two chairs were a short black man and a taller white woman. The translator hesitated, then said, "If he loses, they're going to rape the woman right there." Several of the watching men hurled curses at the screen, some of the vilest epithets Mark had ever heard, and that was saying something. The stakes had just gotten a lot higher.

Another tech at the comm console yelled, "Colonel Hayes, are you here?"

"Yeah."

"Call for you, sir. ISAF HQ."

The crowd parted as Mark slid his way through them to the desk, keeping an eye on the screen. The tech handed him a phone handset. "Colonel Hayes."

"Mark, are you watching this?" came the familiar voice, now tense with concern.

"Yes, General. Is it a live feed?"

"We got the word from Langley not too long ago, and yes,

they think it's live. There are birds in the air from Lemonnier right now, looking for that place, and there's a strike force spooling up. If your brother can hang on, they might have a shot at a rescue."

Mark tried to recall a map of the Horn of Africa in his head. "General, it's about eight hundred klicks from Djibouti to the Mog, isn't it? It'll take Lemonnier hours to get boots on the ground."

"We have somebody closer than that, Mark. Twenty-sixth MEU is aboard USS *Kearsarge* off the coast."

Mark's heart slowed down. Having a Marine Expeditionary Unit in the neighborhood was always a good thing, and for damn sure it was a very good thing right now. "Thanks, General."

"Don't thank me, Mark. They were down near Kenya helping out with the cyclone that hit a few weeks ago. They moved closer to Somalia in advance of your brother's mission, just in case. I want you to hang up now, Mark, and pull for your brother. Tell Captain Krieger we hope to have a package for him in the next twelve hours."

"Roger that, sir."

Mark had barely handed the phone back to the tech when there was movement on the screen and the watching soldiers let out a yell. He muscled his way through them back to Krieger. "What happened? I didn't catch it from that angle."

"Your brother took down the first fighter," Krieger said, and Mark could hear the respect in his voice. "Using nunchaku. He's fast, your brother. Very good."

"That's your brother, Colonel?" a young officer next to them asked. "Shit fire, he's good. You taught him well, sir."

"I didn't teach him anything like that, Lieutenant. This is all him." He felt a surge of pride like he'd never felt before.

Two men emerged from the perimeter and dragged the first fighter away. Mark couldn't tell if the man was dead or alive, but he was certainly out of commission. The officer in charge motioned to another bare-chested man, who went over to something piled on the ground and picked up a long staff.

"Oh oh," the lieutenant said. "Dude's got himself a bo."

SOMALIA

Yusuf had never seen anything like it. Occasionally some of the men watched movies of Asians battling in the martial arts, but their own hand-to-hand combat training had always been much more basic, perhaps using knives or the occasional spear. He seemed to remember something from his university days about James doing some training. Evidently he had kept up with it. The Ugandan felt the first tickling of hope within his breast. They might yet have a chance. The crowd, shocked into silence by Abdul's quick defeat, was now coming to life again, giving a rising cheer to the second fighter as he went over to select his weapon.

"Who's this next guy?" the woman, Allenson, asked.

"His name is Farid, he is Saudi. A true believer in jihad, a graduate of one of the best madrassas in Riyadh."

"Is he any good?"

"I know that he has been on two operations since he arrived here several months ago. He performed...competently." He couldn't tell the woman about how Farid had been one of the men who'd rounded up the children at Katabolang. Perhaps later, if they got out of here.

Farid picked up a long staff and began twirling it around,

but he was not showing off as Abdul had done. He appeared to know exactly what he was doing. James went to the weapons and picked up two shorter sticks that looked like police batons. "What did he choose?"

"They're called tonfa," Allenson said. She had a grim smile. Not for the first time, Yusuf wondered if there was something personal between her and James. But she did not appear to be afraid, either for herself or for him.

"They are much shorter than the staff," Yusuf observed, watching Jim grip the weapons by their handles, twirling them around in tight circles. "How can James defend himself with them against something so much longer?"

"I have a feeling he knows how to do that," she said. "The bo is longer but it has its limitations. If Jim can get inside his reach…"

The two men squared off, and then, oddly enough, Farid, with the bo tucked behind one shoulder along his right leg, bowed to James, who returned the gesture. The Saudi swung the bo around to his front and dropped into a stance with the weapon held at what almost appeared to be port arms. James was holding onto the tonfa by the grip handles, which were perpendicular to the main shaft. He held the shafts tightly up against the undersides of his forearms, and Yusuf could see how the shafts extended out a few inches from the handles. Farid began circling James, who maintained a distance of about ten feet. The crowd was louder now, many beseeching Farid to kill quickly.

Farid launched himself at the American, bringing the bo up and around toward James's head, but it was blocked by the left tonfa. The blow would surely have broken James's arm had it connected with flesh and bone instead of the wood. Farid brought up the rear end of the bo in an uppercut, but once again it was blocked, this time by James's right tonfa, swinging downward and knocking the shaft aside as James stepped in closer. Then the left tonfa came around almost too fast for Yusuf to follow, striking against Farid's right hand where it clutched the bo. Yusuf could hear the awful crack of delicate bones and the Saudi screamed, but it was cut off quickly as the right tonfa rocketed around in a tight arc and swung outward, its back end connecting solidly with the Saudi's left temple. Farid staggered, dropping the bo, and collapsed to the ground.

AFGHANISTAN

A roar erupted from the soldiers as the second fighter fell. "Fuck me!" the lieutenant exclaimed. "Did you see that?"

Mark had seen it, but could hardly believe his eyes. He'd done his share of hand-to-hand training over the years and had seen a lot of men doing it better than he could, but this was way above that pay grade. He thought of Hong back at his base. Maybe he would drop in on the Korean private's next class.

"Most impressive," Krieger said, and Mark heard an excitement in his voice that hadn't been there before. "Mark, was that the General on the line?"

"Yes, and he said to expect a mission package in the next twelve hours."

"Excellent. Now, if somehow your brother and his people can be extracted…"

"The Marines are right off shore."

Krieger gave him a triumphant look. "Then your brother must hold on until they get there."

A shout brought their attention back to the screen. "Look out!"

SOMALIA

Jim was starting to feel it now, the tension of the first bout and then the next starting to drain him. Time to dig a little deeper. He stepped back from the fallen fighter and started to relax just a bit, keeping the breathing even, and then out of the corner of his eye he glimpsed something coming at him.

The impact was like being hit by a truck. He flew backward, the world turning topsy-turvy, and his rump hit the dirt hard, but the training with the Russians took over and he curled his back, tucked his head and completed the roll, coming out on all fours. He felt something go in his bad knee. He'd dropped the tonfa from his left hand, but still had the right one, and here came the big man again.

Trying to regain his breath, Jim rolled to his left at the last second as the Syrian crashed down onto the dirt with a grunt. Jim got to his feet quickly. The last thing he wanted to do was get into a ground-and-pound situation with this guy. Mahmoud reached out for Jim's leg, but Jim whistled his tonfa down and clipped the Syrian's thumb. He yelled in pain and rolled away.

Jim knew he should try to finish this guy as quickly as possible but he didn't want to get close to him on the ground, even with a weapon. Once Jim was on the ground the weapon would be pretty much neutralized. He looked for the other tonfa. There it was, about fifteen feet away, and he made a move for it, but the Syrian was quick, on his feet again, cutting him off.

Mahmoud was more cautious now, and he was shaking that right hand. Jim was sure he'd gotten a good hit on the thumb, enough to break it, but maybe this guy's pain tolerance level was high enough to shake that off. If he tried to grab with that hand, though, or use it as a fist, it would hurt like a bitch. Jim hoped he wasn't left-handed.

The Syrian circled warily. Jim was down in *zenkutsu dachi*, the standard weapons stance, left leg forward with the knee bent, right leg back, weight evenly distributed, his left arm down to protect the lead leg, right hand back with the tonfa, ready to deploy. He moved enough to keep the big man from getting an angle on him. His knee was starting to hurt but he pushed the pain away. Stay focused. No fear.

The Syrian would come after him again, he'd have to, trying to get inside the tonfa. Jim was taller by about six inches but his opponent was built, probably outweighing Jim by ten or fifteen pounds. Well, size and strength were important, but skill and leverage mattered more.

Mahmoud feinted, then shot in low, going for Jim's legs. Jim splayed his legs backward and outward in a sprawl, catching the man's impact diagonally on his thighs, and brought the tonfa down hard on the back of the grappler's neck. He grunted, his grip loosening, and Jim wrested his legs away from him and came around to the man's back. His first thought was to get away, but no, the Syrian had almost gotten him that time, Jim couldn't afford to take too many chances, so he brought the tonfa around the front of his throat and gripped the free end with his left hand and pulled back hard.

The Syrian bucked like a raging bull, but Jim wrapped his legs around the fighter's waist and held on, cranking the tonfa with everything he had. The man gagged out a raspy roar of pain and fury, pulling at the weapon, and Jim thought he was only seconds away from choking him out when Mahmoud threw an elbow backward, connecting solidly with Jim's left ribcage. He cried out in pain, letting go of the tonfa with his left hand, and the Syrian shrugged him off, onto the ground.

Jim was on his back, trying to breathe through the pain in his ribs, when the Syrian came at him again. Jim rolled to his right and there was the tonfa. He grabbed it, felt a looming shadow and came around with his right hand, thrusting the tonfa straight up. The hard wooden knob at the front end of the shaft caught the man right on the Adam's apple. Jim felt it go deep into the throat, heard something inside snap once, twice. The larynx, then the hyoid bone that protected the windpipe, thin and brittle like a turkey's wishbone. The Syrian seemed to hang above him momentarily, eyes bulging, tongue out, and then he rolled slowly to his right with a horrible gurgling cough, collapsing onto the ground as Jim got his leg out of the way just in time.

Jim sagged backward, then heard Denise shrieking, "Get up, Jim! Get up!" He knew he had to, if another guy rushed him while he was on the ground, he knew it would be over. His strength was fading. "Get up!" she screamed again. But the voice, it sounded different.

It sounded like Suzy's voice.

He got back onto his feet, staggering a bit, and looked around. Nobody was coming at him. The men on the perimeter looked stunned, angered, but none of them were stepping into the arena.

AFGHANISTAN

The cheering was loud now, soldiers were giving each other fist bumps and high fives, but Mark was tense. His elation at his brother's stunning victories evaporated when he saw him struggle get up. Jim had to be exhausted, and it looked like his bad knee was giving him trouble. He couldn't possibly last much longer.

Mark shoved his way to the comm console. "Anything more from Kabul?"

The sergeant pulled his headphones off. "I'm monitoring the nets, sir. Lemonnier has a Predator with eyes on the target. *Kearsarge*'s birds are in the air. ETA, maybe fifteen minutes."

"Can you get any real-time video from the drone?"

"I'll try, sir."

Mark made his way back to Krieger and relayed the news. "Fifteen minutes," the German-American said. "I'm not sure your brother has that much time, Mark. He has fought incredibly well, but he's only a man."

CHAPTER FORTY

SOMALIA

J IM HAD TO go to one knee. If they charged him again, he
would be virtually helpless. Then he felt someone beside
him.

"Water!" Denise yelled at Heydar. "Give him some water!"
Jim felt her steadying grip on his shoulders. He reached up
with his free hand and touched hers, and it was almost as if
he felt strength flowing from her, into him. Why had they let
her leave her chair and come to him? Jim saw what might have
been a look of respect in Heydar's eyes, quickly replaced by a
hard glare.

The Iranian motioned to one of his men, who tossed a
water bottle. It rolled toward them and Denise snatched it up.
Thankfully the cap had stayed on. She unscrewed it and held
the bottle to Jim's lips. "Not too much," she said. "Slow down."

He drained half the bottle, then poured the rest onto his
chest and shoulders. The water cooled him slightly, and he felt
some energy returning. He stood up. "Thanks," he said.

"Hang in there," she said. "They've made a serious mistake. Hopefully it won't be long now." Through his fatigue

and pain, he couldn't quite understand. Mistake? He looked around, wondering what the hell she was talking about. The lights from the trucks blinded him for an instant.

It hit him like a jolt of electricity, and he felt a surge of hope pushing back his fear and pain. The lights. He looked up, saw the stars overhead, and hoped someone, or something, was up there watching.

The Iranians were shouting now for Heydar, and some of the other men began taking up the chant. "He looks pissed," Jim said.

"You can beat him," Denise said. "Here he comes. I have to get back to my seat."

"If you can find a gun, that would be a big help."

The Iranian major was advancing on him now, flexing his arms, then windmilling them with some dynamic stretching. The cocky smile was returning. When he was within ten feet, he began slowly circling. "You have fought well, American," he said. "Much better than I expected. My men did not fight smartly."

"A credit to their sensei," Jim said. He moved, too, hanging on to the tonfa, keeping Heydar out of kicking range. Taekwondo stylists emphasized kicks, and Jim noted that Heydar had not removed his combat boots. That would slow him down a little. On the other hand, getting hit with a booted foot going full blast would end the fight. This wasn't *Walker, Texas Ranger,* where Chuck Norris could deliver a roundhouse kick that barely fazed the other guy.

But Jim still had the tonfa, and Heydar knew it. "Why don't you drop that weapon, American? Fight me hand to hand, man to man. Just our skills matched against each other."

"I don't think so," Jim said. Man, his ribs ached. He had been able to use some of his Systema breathing techniques to expel the pain, but not all of it, and his knee was feeling more tenuous by the minute. He'd have to finish this guy the first chance he got, assuming he got one.

Maybe he could create his own chance. Heydar was talking again. "I look forward to fucking your woman. American women are not compliant like Arab women are. She will be—"

"Right behind you, Heydar." He nodded toward Denise, sitting again but behind the Iranian now, and when Heydar flinched just a bit and glanced back, Jim attacked. He stepped in and bought the tonfa around for a crushing temple strike, but the Iranian reacted just in the nick of time, stepping in himself and bringing his right arm around in an outside-inside block that caught Jim on the inside of his forearm. The force of it broke Jim's grip and the tonfa fell away. Heydar stayed with the turn, coming around for a turning side kick with the left leg. Jim had barely an instant to react, coming down with his left forearm in a scissors block that deflected the kick just enough to avoid full impact, but the Iranian's boot still grazed Jim's left side and he cried out as the ribs lanced him with pain.

Jim broke contact and staggered away. The tonfa was gone, his one advantage, and Heydar knew it. He attacked with a roundhouse right kick to the side, and Jim moved to block it but the leg feinted the kick to the side and came up to the head, the toe of the boot cracking into the side of Jim's head. He fell back, seeing stars, but shook it off, thankful that he had instinctively turned his head just enough to avoid the full impact, and here came Heydar again with a combination of kicks and punches. Jim blocked the first two but the third got through, a solid punch that connected squarely with Jim's breastbone.

Jim tried to shake off the shot but he couldn't, he was gassed. The crowd was roaring louder than ever. He sensed Heydar coming alongside and here came a fist up into Jim's gut. With almost the last energy he had Jim was able to relax enough to absorb the blow and force it out through his breathing as the Russians had taught him, but his vision was now blurry and he couldn't focus well. He felt Heydar's arm coming around him in a headlock.

The men were chanting in Arabic now, but some were shouting it in English, "Kill him! Kill him!" The forearm tightened on his throat. He heard Heydar laugh. Jim reached up to grab the arm but he didn't try to pull it away, just loosened it so he could turn his head to the left, into the crook of Heydar's elbow, enough to clear the windpipe. There was an escape from this hold; he'd practiced it in the dojo, but what the hell was it? His brain was getting foggy. He glanced down at the ground, saw Heydar's booted left foot next to him. The arm was starting to tighten.

He didn't know where it came from, but suddenly he remembered with perfect clarity. He brought his right foot around and stomped as hard as he could on Heydar's instep. The Iranian yelled in pain and surprise. Jim reached up with his right hand to the left side of Heydar's head, inside his left thigh with his left hand, and twisted clockwise.

Heydar's hold broke, and he twirled around to his right. Jim pulled the head down, brought it into a guillotine hold and pulled upward quickly and hard. Heydar gagged. Jim reached deep inside himself, deeper than he ever had, and the energy came boiling up on command. Some of it came out in a ferocious kiai yell, but most stayed right where he wanted it, in his thighs and butt, into his abdomen and up into his shoulders. All that work on his core, the endless planks and situps, pushups and pull-ups, everything came together. Jim heaved again, putting his core into it this time, feeling the adrenaline surge into his muscles. The energy flowed through him and into his adversary, to the delicate vertebrae in the neck. Jim felt them pop, heard the ugly sound along with a choking whimper from Heydar as the rest of his body seized up, shuddered, and went limp. Jim released the grip and the Iranian dropped lifelessly to the ground.

Jim dropped onto his good knee again, drenched in sweat and covered with grime. He felt his remaining energy draining away. He was more tired than he'd ever been and damn if the Iranian captain was coming for him. Jim tried to get up but couldn't. Through his bleary vision he saw the Iranian's angry face and saw him reaching for a sidearm, but then there were two sharp cracks from somewhere and two red spots bloomed on Khorsandi's chest as he fell back.

CHAPTER FORTY-ONE

AFGHANISTAN

MARK HAD NEVER felt such a surge of raw emotion as he did when Jim dropped the officer. How in the hell had he done it? Men were slapping him on the back; word had spread quickly that the Colonel's brother was the American who was seriously kicking terrorist ass for all the goddamn world to see. If Jim lived through this he'd never have to buy a drink the rest of his life.

"Brilliant!" Krieger shouted into his ear as he pounded him on the shoulder. "Your brother is a master!"

"Holy Christ!" someone yelled, and the men hushed quickly as the video jerked a bit and picked up another man in fatigues walking toward Jim, reaching to the holster on his right hip. Mark's emotions took another roller-coaster dive. Then came two tinny cracks through the speaker and the man with the gun jerked once, twice, and fell backward.

The camera swung to the right and there was someone with an AK-47, and he opened up on the men at the far end, where the officers had gathered. The woman dashed out into the arena and grabbed Jim, pulling him backward. Now the picture zagged around wildly, showing men running pell-mell, bringing weapons up and firing everywhere. The audio was drowned out in screams and gunfire. The camera jolted hard and pointed upward. Something was moving up there, moving fast.

"Choppers!" a soldier yelled, pointing at the screen. "Here they come!" Lances of bright light came down from the blackness and cut through the running men like a scythe through wheat, sweeping around toward the camera, and then the picture went black. Static sizzled through the speaker.

SOMALIA

Jim had no idea what was happening, but whatever it was, it was very loud and very dangerous. Denise had him by one arm, leading him away, screaming "Stay low! Stay low!" Another hand gripped his other arm and they picked up speed. It was suddenly darker as the headlights on the trucks winked out. Something buzzed past his head, then another. Two of the terrorists were firing their AKs wildly up into the sky and suddenly they were ripped apart by fiery beams of light. Tracer rounds, coming from above. Jim heard the roaring pulse of helicopter rotors. A man appeared in front of them and brought up his rifle. Jim grabbed at Denise to pull her out of the line of fire, but as the man's fingers fumbled on the trigger guard another round snapped past Jim and the top of the man's head disappeared in a blur of pink and red.

"This way!" It was Joe, and Jim felt pulled to the right, and there were men rushing past them. They rounded a corner and now the gunfire was behind them. The sound of the helicopters seemed to focus in one spot. Jim risked a glance back, and over the low top of the building, he saw men sliding down zip lines from the hovering helos. The cavalry had come over the hill.

They burst through a door and into a dimly-lit building. "In here!" Joe led them through a beaded curtain and released him. Jim saw a chair in front of a desk and collapsed into it, trying to clear his head. Denise, next to the doorway, had somehow gotten hold of an AK. Joe was over at the far wall, on his knees, clawing at something on the floor.

There were shouts from the hallway and gunfire ripped through the curtains. Jim threw himself off the chair onto the floor. Denise hugged the wall, and the hail of bullets stopped. She came around with the gun when a man appeared in the doorway, another of those goddamn Iranians in green fatigues. How the hell many of them were there? He had an AK and was swinging it toward Denise when he spasmed forward, eyes going wide as blood spat from his mouth. The Iranian staggered a step, dropped the rifle and collapsed onto the floor. Denise kicked the weapon away and shot him twice in the back, just above a dark splotch on his back.

Another man appeared in the doorway, an African like Joe, holding a bloody knife. He dropped the knife and held his hands up as Denise trained her rifle on him. "No shoot! I am friend!"

"Amir...my brother..."

Jim looked at Joe, and he was slumped against the wall, one hand on his stomach, blood seeping through his shirt. "Yusuf!" The African bolted past Denise and knelt next to Joe, saying something in yet another foreign language. He embraced Joe, weeping.

Jim tried to get up but his knee gave out. Ignoring the pain, he crawled over the dirt floor to the two men. Joe saw him coming and reached out one hand. "James, my old friend," he said softly in English, and coughed "You are alive. I am glad."

"Stay with us, Joe The good guys are here."

"James, this is Amir, he has been...a brother to me. He...is the one who shot Khorsandi."

The African looked at Jim, tears streaming down his face. "I shoot him," he said, forcing the words out in English, "to save Yusuf, to save friends of Yusuf."

"Here, James, take this," Joe said, reaching over with his other hand. He pressed something into Jim's. It was a computer flash drive. "Give this...to your CIA."

"Hang in there, Joe, we'll get a medic in here for you."

"No...James..." Joe's eyes unfocused a bit. "Allah calls to me." He squeezed Jim's hand, then reached for Amir. "My brother...go with the Amer...icans...it is Allah's will."

"Peace be upon him, and upon you," Amir whispered. "I do as you say, brother."

Joe looked past Jim, and his eyes widened. "I see...how can this be?" His mouth curled into a smile, and then his head slumped back.

"Joe. *Joe!*"

Jim sat back hard, ignoring the pain in his knee, the pain everywhere. There was another shout from the hallway, but his one was different. "United States Marines!"

"In here, Marine!" Denise answered. "CIA! Americans!" She carefully set the rifle down and stepped back. A heavily-armed man came in, wearing a uniform Jim knew very well indeed.

CHAPTER FORTY-TWO

IRAN

" IVE MINUTES TO target." Mark checked his gear one more time, and once again it was all in order. Across from him, Nelson, the British lieutenant, mouthed something that Mark had no chance to hear over the roar of the Black Hawk's engines. Might've been *Bloody well fun,* or something like that. Nelson had been in the Special Air Services before volunteering for Unit 7. Nothing but the best for this outfit, and SAS was certainly one of the best.

Three of the Night Stalkers' Black Hawks comprised the strike force, escorted by four Apaches. Behind them, orbiting just inside Afghan air space, an AWACS radar plane, radio code Zeus, kept an eye out for Iranian air assets. So far, everything looked clear ahead. What they would find when they reached the target might be another matter.

The advance planning they'd done over the previous few days meant they were able to get airborne within ten hours of receiving the mission package. Mark had managed to get an hour in his rack, which he needed badly; he'd hardly slept at all the night before after the stress of watching Jim in combat.

They'd picked up the Predator's video feed after the terrorists' camera went dark, watched the raid in real time, and although there was no audio, Krieger and the other Unit 7 men kept up a running commentary. Mark tried hard to keep up with it but he couldn't stop thinking about his brother, wondering whether he'd survived the assault. It was near midnight when the phone call came from ISAF, with the General himself delivering the news. Jim had made it out, injured but not seriously. The female CIA agent had also made it, but the defector had been killed.

Not, however, before giving them intel, and from what the General said, it looked like valuable intel indeed. Maybe not the treasure trove the SEALs had recovered in Abbottabad, but certainly a prime collection, and from that had come the mission package for the cross-border strike. There was a high-value target here in the mountains, valued enough for the White House and NATO to give the order for Unit 7 to go in. Mark had sat in on the briefing the General gave to Krieger and his officers by radio. This HVT might be the key to preventing all-out war between the U.S. and Iran. Mark knew from long experience that the General was not one to exaggerate, so what he said was sobering indeed.

The tactical challenges of the mission were enough to keep the men's minds on their preparations, but the strategic implications weren't very far behind. Mark didn't spend a lot of time wondering about the political implications. If they failed, if they were killed or captured, the Iranians would have an enormous propaganda victory, their biggest over the West since the failed EAGLE CLAW mission in '80, the attempt to rescue the hostages in Tehran that had gone so horribly wrong. And if the General was right, the political fallout would be nothing compared to what would follow.

Well, that left only one option, didn't it?

Marolda was piloting the lead Black Hawk, with Krieger and his squad aboard, and the Night Stalker captain was in overall command of the helos. His voice came over the headset. "Target in sight. Raven Flight, engage."

"Raven One, copy." The three other Apaches acknowledged. Mark couldn't see them, but he knew the attack birds were now roaring ahead to take out the three anti-aircraft gun emplacements that were shown on the satellite photos of the compound. The fourth bird was backup on the AA attack but would also hunt for vehicles. "Hellfires away." Mark could envision the missiles launching from the pods, zeroing in on the gun emplacements with laser-guided accuracy.

"Wolf Pack, up and at 'em."

Mark removed his headset and strapped his helmet on, flipping down the night vision goggles. The inside of the helo became an eerie green world. He and his five men would take zip lines down from the side doors as the bird hovered about twenty feet up. Their target was one of two small buildings that seemed to be living quarters. Krieger's team, Wolf One, had the other building, while Wolf Three was designated to mop up what was left of the security detachment after the Apaches had done their work. Over the roar of the engines Mark heard the crump of explosions.

The Black Hawk dove down and then heeled back into a level hover. Mark's stomach barely had time to recover when he was at the door and down the line, the rope slipping hotly through his gloved hands. He landed on gravel-covered ground, brought his M4 around and headed for the building twenty-five meters away.

A man appeared at the doorway in front of him and Mark dropped him with a three-shot burst. He flattened against the outer wall with Nelson on the other side of the doorway. The Brit tossed in a flash bang grenade, and the men averted their eyes from the dazzling burst of light. Dust flew out of the door from the concussion of the blast. "Go! Go! Go!" Mark shouted, leading the way inside.

They cleared the two-story building inside of five minutes, bringing down one other man, dressed in robes but trying to bring an AK into play. Nelson double-tapped him with calm efficiency. Three others were taken alive, their hands zip-tied behind them. Outside, the Black Hawks had veered off to avoid any incoming fire while the Apaches buzzed angrily overhead. The defenders' gunfire, sporadic to begin with, dribbled away into an occasional crack, then nothing. The distinctive pops from the raiders' weapons continued for a few seconds, and then silence descended over the compound, except for the crackling of fires at the AA sites and the motor pool and the sweeping roars of the Apaches.

"Building two, clear!" Mark said into his pencil-thin microphone.

"Building one, clear!" Krieger's voice. "Perimeter is secure!" came a third voice with a French accent. Lieutenant LeClaire, in charge of Wolf Three.

"We have Cochise," Krieger said. "Wolf Two, gather what you can and head to the rally point. Disembark in ten minutes." Mark ordered his men to make another sweep through the rooms, taking anything that looked like it might have intel value. There was one room that looked like an office, with a couple of laptop computers. They'd be coming along. Another raider filled a pouch with documents from a small file cabinet.

Out in the courtyard, Mark turned off his NVG's. The burning gun emplacements along the perimeter provided plenty of light. He saw Krieger and his men coming out of the other building, leading four men dressed in robes that looked like sleeping clothes. LeClaire and his men were near the perimeter

"I have three," Mark said. "Which one is Cochise?"

"He's with this group," Krieger said. "Time to find out which one." The four men stood before him. One or two looked defiant, the others were trembling. Mark couldn't have picked out the HVT; they had no photographs, but had been told he was definitely the youngest of the mullahs. Krieger faced them from two feet away, his weapon at the ready. "Which one of you is al-Qa'im?" he asked in Farsi.

None of them said a word. Krieger repeated the question, again got no response, and then he drew his sidearm, a Luger, and pointed it at the head of the man on the far left. "I ask one more time: which one is al-Qa'im?"

One of the men stepped forward. He appeared younger than the others; his beard was entirely black, but his eyes were the bluest Mark had ever seen in this part of the world. In the flickering light they almost appeared to be glowing. "I am he." Krieger pointed the Luger at the man's head.

"Swear before Allah that you are telling the truth."

"Only Allah, blessings be upon him, knows my heart, infidel."

Marolda's voice crackled through Mark's earpiece. "Wolf Leader, this is Eagle One, Zeus reports inbound aircraft, ETA thirty minutes. We have to bug out, right now."

"Take them all," Mark said. "We'll sort them out when we're out of Indian country."

Krieger holstered his weapon, rather reluctantly, Mark thought. "Eagle One, Wolf Leader, acknowledge exfil now. We have seven prisoners."

"Gonna be tight for them on the ride out of here, Wolf Leader."

"Too bad for them, they're used to flying first class." Krieger passed the word to the raiders and they prepared for the inbound Black Hawks. Mark took one more look at the prisoners, wondering which one of them was worth the risk of starting a war. Then again, he thought, this guy might just be the key to preventing one.

CHAPTER FORTY-THREE

PACIFIC OCEAN

THE RADAR OPERATOR stared at his computer screen, but in vain. The contact had disappeared, assuming it had ever been there in the first place. "I am sorry, Captain," the harried sailor said, "but I swear it was there a few minutes ago. Very faint, but it was there."

Nariman put a comforting hand on the radar man's shoulder. "Keep a sharp eye, Rahimi. Notify me if you get another contact, surface or air."

"Aye aye, Captain." Resigned, the operator glared at the screen. Nariman returned to his bridge, where he had an unimpeded 270-degree view of the vast Pacific. Aft of the ship, the sun was dipping below the horizon, and to the east he could see the first stars and planets becoming visible. One of them was Venus, he knew. Two and a half millenia earlier his ancestors had used the very same stars to navigate their tiny wooden sailing ships across the Aegean to a rendezvous with destiny. Now he was doing the same.

He had not seen such vast emptiness in his twenty-four years in the IRGC Navy. Of course, his open-ocean experience was quite limited. Until taking command of *Lion of Aladagh,* his time had been spent aboard vessels no larger than the Thondar class missile boats, with maximum range of only 800 kilometers. This was much different. Instead of venturing out into the Arabian Sea and back to Bandar Abbas, he was sailing halfway around the world.

Fortunately, he could fall back on the experience of one previous voyage on this ship, to   Bangladesh and back, but even alone on the Indian Ocean, he had never felt as tiny as he felt now. He looked to the east. Still more than fifteen hundred kilometers away was the coast of the Great Satan's homeland. By this time three days from now, if it was Allah's will, they would have reversed course for the long return voyage home, to the brave new world that would have been created to a significant degree by his ship.

As the days went by, especially since they departed Japanese waters, Nariman had been thinking about that more and more. He would not give the command to launch the missile; that would fall to another officer on board. But he, Nariman, had the responsibility to sail the ship to the launch point. So, what would happen would be at least partly on his hands.

The lives that would be lost, by the thousands, perhaps the millions, they would be his responsibility too. He had not been told the name of the target, but since the missile had a nuclear warhead, it would obviously be a city. San Francisco, or perhaps Los Angeles, cities full of infidels and crawling with depravity, but even so, the thought did not allow him to sleep well at night. Thus he had taken to spending more and more time in the night walking about his ship, joining the night watch on the bridge, talking with his sailors. They did not speak of the result of the mission, of course, and in truth many of the sailors, those who were not officers, were not supposed to know exactly what was going to happen. But Nariman had no illusions. Scuttlebutt had been part of every voyage of every ship since ancient times. His ancestors who had sailed the ships of Xerxes across the Aegean knew what they were going to do when they got there.

The Quds Force men, though, they certainly knew, as did the engineers who were in charge of the missile and its lethal payload. They all kept themselves largely apart from Nariman's sailors, as much as it was possible to do on such a small ship, but word got around. The difference, he noted, was that the commandos who formed the security detachment were looking forward to the event, and boasted about how they were going to usher in a new era, that of the Twelfth Imam. Such talk unsettled Nariman the more he heard it. It was a good thing, he thought now, that early in the voyage he had met secretly with his senior officers. In the event of a certain order from Tehran, he told them, they might need to deal with those commandos, and so they had come up with a plan.

Two miles away and one hundred feet below the surface, three uniformed men huddled over a plotting table and examined a series of photographs. Around them other men went about their duties with quiet efficiency, but there was none of the idle chatter that had occasionally been in evidence just a few days before. Even the sounds of the submarine itself seemed different somehow, more focused, as if the vessel knew that she was no longer on a training mission.

"What do you think, XO?" the oldest of the three men asked. Silver eagles were pinned to the collar points of his blue uniform. Gray flecked his dark hair, but his ice blue eyes showed no sign of age. He had already made up his mind, but he wanted confirmation.

"It's definitely our bogey, Skipper," the executive officer, Lieutenant Commander Wallace Hemple, said. He indicated the first photo, printed out only minutes before. The high-resolution camera in the boat's photonic mast had taken a series of shots just before the captain had ordered it down, and the computer had touched them up nicely, providing a view as clear as if the two vessels had been only a hundred yards apart at high noon. "The configuration of the ship matches the imagery we received with the mission package," Hemple said, pointing to the two photos that had been downloaded several hours earlier. "And our new shot clearly shows the flag on the mast here, and the name on the bow."

"They've got balls, I'll say that for them," said the third man, wearing blue and gray digital cammies. "Flying their own flag, way out here, heading in our direction." The Iranian tricolor was clearly visible. Lieutenant Steve Schaal, commander of the SEAL detachment, squinted at the picture. "Damn, these optics are good, Captain. If we enlarged this I'll bet I could read the script on the red and green bands."

Captain Dennis Carpenter allowed himself a tight grin. "It's not Farsi, Lieutenant. It's in Kufic, a form of calligraphy. It says 'God is great' a total of twenty-two times."

"You've done your research," Schaal said.

"'Know thy enemy'. Technically they're not our enemy right now, but that might change pretty soon." He straightened up, reaching for the coffee mug that had been resting on the table. Printed in blue on the white mug was USS NORTH DAKOTA SSN-784. He took a healthy swig, and it was hot and good, but what he really needed was some sleep; he'd managed to sneak a few hours shortly after the first alert message came in, but nothing since he'd received the mission orders at 0400 Things had moved swiftly after that. Literally; they'd been at flank speed for several hours on a course to intercept the bogey, slowing only long enough to take the SEALs on board after they'd parachuted into the drink from their aircraft. Carpenter wasn't too fond of stressing his engines like that, but the boat had performed beautifully. Now they were slowed to a more comfortable twenty-five knots, matching the target.

But now the waiting was over. What happened next would be largely up to the Iranians.

"How much time do we have, Wally?" Carpenter asked.

"At his present speed, the bogey will be within maximum range of their best missile in about four or five hours, Skipper."

Carpenter checked his watch. "Full dark in about two hours. We'll start moving into position then. Lieutenant, you'd best prepare your men."

"Aye aye, Captain," Schaal said, and headed aft. The maneuver would be dicey, but one they'd practiced before. In fact, they'd been scheduled for exercises in the Philippines with another SEAL team and Filipino marines in a few days, exercises that would likely have included this very type of evolution. Now they would do it for real. Carpenter would move *North Dakota* directly astern of the target and the SEALs would exit the boat underwater, deploying their Combat Rubber Raiding Craft from the boat's Dry Dock Shelter. There were several ways to board a ship on the high seas and this was not the easiest, but there were no suitable assets available from which to stage a heliborne assault. It would be easier to deploy the men and their small craft from the surface, but Carpenter was not about to expose his boat to Iranian small arms fire or RPGs if he could help it.

"XO, make sure Sonar is paying close attention to the

bogey. If he hears any signs of machinery beyond what he hears now, that'll be the bogey getting the launcher ready. We won't have time to get the SEALs aboard. We'll have to take him out ourselves."

"Understood, sir. I'll get the forward torpedo room busy."

"Have them prepare a full spread, Wally. I don't want to miss this bastard if I have to shoot."

Nariman checked in with his bridge officer, the navigator and the helmsman. The ship was relatively new and largely automated, so a large bridge crew was not necessary. All was well. The officer of the watch, a young lieutenant who had sailed with Nariman on his previous command, nodded respectfully to the captain.

Major Nafisi appeared on the bridge, which was part of his evening ritual as well. After their supper and evening prayers, the commander of the Quds Force detachment had taken to spending an hour or so up here with the captain. Nariman did not consider him a friend, but when they were not talking politics Nafisi was a fairly agreeable companion on these nocturnal visits. They went out onto the bridge wing.

"It is a fine evening, Captain, is it not?"

"Yes, it is, Major. The weather has been cooperative so far."

"Undoubtedly it is the will of Allah, blessings be upon him." Nafisi leaned out on the railing, showing no signs of the seasickness that had bedeviled him and his men for the first week after they had departed Bandar Abbas. "Two days, Captain, to our rendezvous with history?"

"Somewhat less," Nariman said. He checked his watch and did the calculation in his head. "Forty hours, weather permitting." At present speed, they would be at the launch point in less than half that time. Then Nariman would order the ship to reduce speed and sail a meandering course that would eventually take them back to where they needed to be. In the captain's mind, those last several hours would be the most dangerous of the voyage. It was a big ocean, with a lot of room for a ship to loiter, but ships that changed course for no apparent reason tended to draw attention, if anybody was watching. And Nariman found it hard to believe the Americans would not be watching.

The major turned his attention back to the captain. "Any further suspicious radar contacts?"

"Possibly one about an hour ago, but it may very well have been nothing."

"That would be three in the past twenty-four hours, would it not?"

The captain was instantly wary. "That is correct, Major."

"Interesting, don't you think?"

"The sea is a strange place, Major, especially all the way out here. It is not like our home waters. There have been mysterious things throughout history that have supposedly been seen by sailors. I would say it might very well have been a whale, if anything."

The major grunted and looked back out the forward windscreen, to the east. "Any further radio transmissions from home?"

"Just the standard response at 1800 hours to our check-in. No change in orders."

The QF major nodded. "That is good. We are much too close now to turn back." He breathed in deeply, then smiled. "Think of the glory that will be ours when we return home, Captain. We, and our comrades on *Star of Persia*, will be the harbingers of a new age."

Nariman said nothing. He had known since the day they

boarded that Nafisi was a true believer. Nariman, on the other hand, considered himself to be a pragmatist. One had to be careful about expressing such views, though, and the captain was a careful man. He did not tell the major, for example, that he was becoming more certain that theirs was a suicide mission. The Americans could not possibly be so dense as to allow Iranian ships to sail so close to their shores and launch nuclear missiles, could they?

"Are you all right, Captain? You seem...tense."

Nariman forced himself to relax. "I am fine," he said, but he had to change the subject. "I assume, Major, that all is in readiness, with regard to the weapon?"

"Indeed it is, Captain. The launch team will be conducting their pre-launch tests in the morning. We will be ready by this time tomorrow."

"We will need another twenty hours or so beyond that to reach the designated coordinates."

"It is better to be ready well in advance, don't you agree?"

"Of course. I'm sure we will be. The launch team members are highly competent."

Nafisi gazed to the eastern horizon, now barely visible as the night grew. "Imagine, Captain, the Great Satan is out there, almost within our reach."

"Yes, he is," Nariman agreed, but he did not add they were now within the Great Satan's reach as well.

Lt. Schaal made his way through the narrow corridors of the submarine to the captain's quarters. He had a lot to do and not a lot of time in which to do it, but if the skipper wanted to talk to him, that took priority. And like the great majority of sub drivers he'd met, Carpenter was a straight shooter and commanded respect. They'd worked together once before, but that was just a training exercise. This was the real thing, about as real as it could get. He knocked on the door.

"Come in." The SEAL slid inside and shut the door behind him. Carpenter was sitting at his small desk, looking at the trio of photos on the bulkhead. Schaal took them in quickly. On the left was a pretty young woman in a cap and gown, on the right a young man wearing a Naval Academy basketball uniform, and in the middle an attractive, fortyish woman standing on a beach. His family, no doubt. Schaal thought about the picture of his own wife and baby boy that was tucked away in his gear back aft. Before every mission he looked at that picture, trying not to think that he might not ever see them again. He imagined the captain was thinking the same thing.

"You asked to see me, sir?"

The captain turned in his chair to face the visitor. "Yes. How's it going with the mission prep?"

"We'll be ready when you give the order, Captain."

Carpenter tapped the file on the desk. "To say I'm concerned about this would be an understatement, Steve. COMSUBRON feels pretty sure there's a nuclear weapon on board that ship. I know you and your men are qualified to do a lot of things, but I wonder if securing a nuclear weapon is one of them. This whole mission was put together pretty quickly and I know your team was the closest, so here you are. I want an honest assessment from you: if there's a nuke on board that tub, can your people handle it?"

"Yes, sir," Schaal said without a trace of hesitation. "We've been training recently for just this type of mission. The word is that if things in a certain South Asian country start going the way of Egypt or Libya, we might have to go in and secure certain places. I'm sure you can guess which country that might be."

Carpenter would know there was a very short list of such nations. He nodded. "Very well. In the event that ship gets to a certain point, and it's getting pretty damn close, my orders are to do everything I can to secure the target and seize the weapon. Preferably without it going off."

"Don't worry about that, sir," Schaal said with a tight grin.

The captain glanced at his watch. "If he stays on present course and speed, you launch in one hour. If you run into any trouble on board that you can't handle, I'm afraid I can't provide you any backup. I'll have to put a torpedo into him. You'll have very little time to clear the target."

Schaal knew the captain was being honest. His men were very good at what they did, but they weren't trained to board and seize a hostile vessel under fire, and if the skipper was foolish enough to surface close by, the Iranians could cause serious damage to the submarine. The SEALs held no illusions about what they would encounter once they got on board. There were hard men over there and they would fight to the death. But he and his team were veterans of Iraq and Afghanistan and knew all about how to deal with hard men. "Understood, sir. If we get in a bind, don't hesitate to fire, even if some of us are still aboard."

"Let's hope it doesn't come to that, but if it does, the code word is 'Buster'. You've got five minutes from that signal and then I give the order to fire." The captain hesitated. "My orders are also very clear on another point: if your mission fails and any of you are taken prisoner, I will not negotiate with the enemy. I will send him to the bottom."

"I'm sure you won't have to worry about that, either, sir." Schaal had been fighting these people for a long time and had never heard of a SEAL being captured by them. He and his men would not be the first. Schaal knew that the skipper was under a lot of pressure. If the SEAL assault failed, and the sub somehow could not sink the enemy vessel, Washington would have no choice but to take it out with an air strike, quite possibly with a missile, and he wouldn't put it past them to use a nuke themselves. That ship would not be allowed to launch on the homeland.

The phone on the bulkhead buzzed. Carpenter glanced at the SEAL, then picked up the handset. "Captain." His eyes betrayed nothing as he listened. "Very well, I'm on my way."

The talk turned to other things, gently prodded in that direction by Nariman. They came around to history, a favorite subject of their evening visits. Once again, they debated the strategy of Xerxes the Great and his invasion of Greece in 480 B.C. Nafisi returned to his thesis that even after the delay at Thermopylae, the Persian Navy had failed Xerxes at Salamis. Nariman countered that the Army should have easily smashed the Greeks at Thermopylae, making the battle at Salamis unnecessary. "A paltry three hundred Spartans held off the mighty Persian Army," Nariman scoffed, warming to the subject.

"And your mighty Persian Navy was tricked by Themistocles, sailing right into the Straits where their superior numbers were negated," Nafisi countered. "Why did the admiral—"

"Excuse me, Captain." It was the radio operator, in the doorway to the bridge, saluting. He had a paper in his hand. "Message from headquarters, sir. Your eyes only."

"Thank you, seaman," Nariman said. He pulled apart the single-page message, which had been folded and stapled shut. He first looked for a mark in the upper left corner. Yes, it was there, very unobtrusive, looking like a smudge from a finger, but distinctive enough that Nariman recognized it. He breathed a little more easily. His executive officer had read the message and was making his preparations. The captain read the brief text.

"What does it say?" Nafisi asked.

"The mission has been aborted," Nariman said. He handed the paper over to the major, who ripped it from him.

"There must be a mistake. Have your man authenticate it!"

"He has done so," Nariman said. "That is standard procedure with any Code Red communication, Major, as you well know." He turned to the hatch leading back into the enclosed bridge.

"What are you doing?"

"I am going to order the helm to change course."

In the gathering dusk, Nariman saw a movement at the major's hip, then the click of a pistol being cocked. "You will maintain course, Captain."

"On whose authority?"

"On mine, and the authority of the Supreme Leader. I am taking command of this vessel as of now. We will continue the mission."

Nariman faced the major. "I have seen no such orders. I am in command. You will hand me your weapon and stand down, Major."

"Or what?"

"Or I will have my officer shoot you dead." He nodded to his right. An ensign was at the corner of the bridge wing, pointing a Kalashnikov rifle at the major.

Nafisi looked at the armed sailor. "You are making a mistake, Captain. When we return to Iran you will be shot as a traitor."

"I think not," Nariman said. "I have received a lawful order to abort the mission and return home. Now, hand me your weapon. You are under arrest."

"My men will take this ship!"

"They will not. They are all under arrest, even as we speak. Is that not so, Ensign?"

"Yes, sir," the ensign said. "Lieutenant Commander Souroush has things well in hand below."

"Very good," Nariman said, allowing himself to breathe easier. "Now, Major, your pistol, please."

Within minutes, *Lion of Aladagh* began a leisurely turn to the south, and then to the west. Five hundred yards to the north, a mast rose slightly above the three-foot chop of the sea, invisible in the dark. Through the powerful night-vision optics, Carpenter watched the Iranian vessel closely. After a few minutes, satisfied that the target had changed course, the captain gave an order. Moments later a coded message burst from the radio mast up to a satellite and down to COMSUBRON One at Pearl Harbor. From there it would go quickly up the chain of command for the U.S. Navy in the Pacific and then to Washington. Carpenter flipped up the handles of the periscope and nodded to a sailor, who pressed a button that started the 'scope and mast sliding downward.

"XO, pass the word to the SEALs. My compliments to Lieutenant Schaal, and inform him that it appears they'll be able to stand down. I'll be back there shortly."

"Aye aye, sir."

Carpenter took a deep breath and exhaled slowly. He could almost feel the level of tension in the control room go down a few degrees. They would stay on station for another twenty-four hours, just to make sure, and his sonar men would stay alert, as would the men in the torpedo room. But, hopefully, it would just wind up being a very realistic drill.

He started aft, to where the SEALs waited. There would be another mission for them someday. He wished it were not so, but that was the world they all lived in. Perhaps his grandchildren, yet to be born, would live in a better one. Until then, Carpenter and men like him would sail on, doing their best to create that world.

CHAPTER FORTY-FOUR
DJIBOUTI

THE BASE HOSPITAL at Camp Lemonnier was not that large, but it was like every other military hospital Mark had seen, a place of organized chaos. His left shoulder throbbed, but he had already taken one pain pill on the flight here and didn't want to pop another till late afternoon, if then. He would tough this one out, as he had so many others, but damn, it was getting harder to do that.

Why hadn't they known about the Iranian quick reaction force? Someone back at the spook farm in Kabul had screwed up on that one. They'd been loading the prisoners onto the Black Hawks when Raven One spotted the company of motorized infantry moving up through the valley to their west, right along the planned exfiltration route. The Apaches went in hard after them, providing cover for the Black Hawks to run the gauntlet, but Mark's bird took fire from the ground and the pilot's desperate evasive maneuvers had saved the bird but roughed up the passengers. Mark had yielded his seat and the safety harness that went with it for one of the prisoners, and found himself tossed violently against the bulkhead, banging

his left shoulder hard. The doc back at the FOB put him in a
sling and said it was possibly a torn rotator cuff

They made it back with only light casualties among the
raiders and the helo crews. That was the important thing. The
prisoners all made it to Afghanistan as well, but they would
be repatriated quickly to avoid unnecessary political problems
once they had undergone interrogation. The high value target,
who'd admitted to being al-Qa'im after some rather energetic
questioning by Krieger, would be staying for a bit longer.

Mark had been able to get breakfast at the FOB after the
mission debrief, then got a lift to Bagram and caught a special
CIA jet to Djibouti, arranged by the General. He hadn't even
had time to shower and change into a clean uniform, so he
didn't smell real good right now and didn't look real pretty,
but he didn't care. They were used to that here anyway. There
was someone he had to see and it wasn't going to wait.

Jim eased himself out of the hospital bed and tried flexing his
leg. The nurse, a tough-looking Frenchwoman, had warned
him that he wasn't ready yet to put any weight on it. The surgery that morning had gone well but Jim was facing some
rehab time when he got home. Right now, though, he had to
use the bathroom and, by God, he was going to do that on his
own, so he slipped on the robe and reached for his crutches.

Getting up was an exercise in agony. Every part of him
hurt, not just the repaired knee. There were bruises all over the
place. Two ribs were cracked but there'd been no damage to
internal organs. He'd never had cracked ribs before and he'd
always been told they were a real bitch. Whoever told him that
was certainly right on the money.

He cripped slowly to the bathroom, took care of business,
and emerged to find a tall, rough-looking soldier standing in

the doorway to the room. For a moment Jim didn't recognize him, until the man took off the scruffy patrol cap and his eyes hit on Jim and lit up, he knew.

The brothers hugged each other as best they could without inflicting further injuries. "Damn, Jim, it's good to see you," Mark said. He wiped his eyes with the back of a hand. "Good thing the men back at my base can't see their C.O. right now."

"They'd think it's just fine," Jim said, wiping his own eyes. "Where the hell have you been? You're carrying about half of Afghanistan around with you."

"Not just Afghanistan," Mark said. He pointed to Jim's bandaged leg. "Did the knee go?"

"Yeah. Meniscus tear. They fixed that up this morning, but the doc here says I'm a serious candidate for a knee replacement when I get home."

"Well, you've known for a long time that was coming, haven't you?"

"I suppose, but I wanted to put it off as long as possible. I gotta get back into the bed. You wouldn't believe how sore I am."

"Oh, I think I would." He took Jim's arm and helped him around to the bed, got him settled in, and took a chair.

Jim pointed at Mark's sling. "What's with the arm?"

"Shoulder," Mark said. "Probably a rotator cuff."

"Hope the other guy looks worse."

"It was a helicopter, and it has a few holes in it but not from me," Mark said.

Mark stared at his brother for a few seconds, the memories racing from memories childhood to manhood and all they'd been through in their lives. There hadn't been much time to get together in recent years but right now he felt that everything Jim had endured, Mark had been right there with him

"I watched the fight," he said at last. "Damn, Jim, I've never seen anything like that. How the hell did you ever get in that jam in the first place?"

"It's a long story. How much time do you have?"

Mark grinned. "My boss tells me he wants me to take a week's leave, but I'm heading back to the base day after tomorrow. While I'm here I'll have them look at the shoulder. Maybe we can get a room together."

"I have to warn you, the nurses here are mostly French but they're not exactly Brigitte Bardot lookalikes."

"That's okay," Mark said. "There's a woman back in Kabul that would put all of them to shame if they were."

"Your eyes lit up, little brother. You want to tell me about her?"

"She's British and she's great and I'm gonna ask her to marry me." There, he'd finally said what he'd been thinking about for a while now. It felt good.

Jim grinned broadly. "That's terrific. If you need a best man, let me know."

"You'll be at the top of the list. Now, tell me that story."

They talked for the next two hours. Jim got emotional when he described the death of his old African friend, and had to take a moment to compose himself. "He wanted to come out," Jim said huskily. "Put all that shit behind him, the killing and the torture, all of it. He never made it."

All Mark could do was nod. How many men had he known, Iraqi and Afghan, who'd wanted to turn their lives around? A lot of them, and some had made it. Others hadn't. Shot, blown to bits, or just disappeared. It was a damn shame. But a lot of Americans had died over the past ten years or so to give those people a chance. That was a damn shame, too, but maybe, just maybe, it would all be worth it.

The nurse came back, said something about the room needing some air, and opened the window. Jim just laughed, but Mark said he really should be checking in with the base commander and maybe rustle up a shower and a clean uniform someplace.

When the nurse left, Mark stared at his big brother. "I always knew you had it in you, Jim," he said, his voice cracking.

Jim blinked and looked away for a second. "Mark, I—"

There was a knock at the door. Mark turned and saw a gorgeous woman flashing a hundred-watt smile at Jim. He'd never seen her before, but he'd seen many like her: *Agency.* "Hope we're not interrupting anything," she said.

Denise Allenson came into the room, with Tom Simons behind her. The CIA agents looked none the worse for wear except for the bandage on Simons' forearm. When they'd parted the day before, after the helicopter ride from *Kearsarge,* Denise told Jim she'd come to the hospital later to check on him, but the combination of the fatigue and the pain medications had knocked him out for several hours. When he finally awoke again, it was late at night. They'd wheeled him into surgery first thing this morning. Now, he was surprised by how glad he was to see her.

Simons gave him a firm handshake, Denise a hug that lasted a little longer than he expected. Her eyes were shining when they met his.

"How are you doing?" she asked.

Jim glanced over at Simons, who was talking with Mark.

"I'll live," he said. "Right now I'm pretty sore and my leg hurts, but at least we're alive."

"I'm heading back to Washington," she said, "but I hope we can get together sometime."

He grinned at that. "This was my first and last covert mission. I doubt we'll ever be working together again, Denise."

She cocked her head slightly. "I wasn't talking about work," she said, raising an eyebrow just so.

Simons looked over at them. "Jim, we can't stay, have to get back to the embassy and finish Denise's debrief. But first I want to fill you in on what's been happening since you got back here."

Jim sat down on the bed, grateful to rest his throbbing leg. "Okay."

Simons went over and closed the door, then turned back to them. "First things first. The Marines rolled up Shalita's camp and we have the surviving fighters in custody on board the *Kearsarge*. A lot of them will be in Gitmo pretty soon. I expect the intel we get from them and the files we found in the camp will be very valuable. More importantly, Jim, the flash drive Shalita gave you was beyond valuable." He looked at Mark. "Colonel, the mission you went on after that HVT was based partly on intel from that drive, although I'm authorized to tell you it was put in motion thanks to information we gleaned from an Iranian defector in Oman. Adding it all up, from what you two men achieved, along with Agent Allenson here and your strike team, Colonel, we were able to spike a planned attack upon the homeland that would have had extremely serious consequences. You three had an important role in saving a great many American lives."

That took a moment to sink in with Jim. He could see Mark had accepted it almost as a matter of course. Well, that was pretty much the nature of his work, wasn't it? For Jim, though, it was a helluva lot more important than a telecom marketing campaign. Then he remembered a question he'd wanted to ask ever since the night before. "Denise said they made a mistake, back at the camp," he said. "It was the lights, wasn't it?"

Denise had a crafty look in her eyes. "They moved the fight out into the open. Heydar wanted to show off for the whole camp. When Jim challenged him, his reputation was on the line."

"He should've just kept it inside the main building," Simons said. "Outside, they needed extra lights for the TV camera. That was enough for one of our surveillance satellites to spot them. We vectored in a drone and there you were."

"If you'd just picked a fight with him first thing, indoors, it would've been all over for us," Denise said. "A smart move, Jim. I assume that was your plan all along?" Her raised eyebrow showed she was a little skeptical.

"Believe me, I'd love to take the credit, but we got lucky on that score."

"Did they see Jim's fight back home?" Mark asked.

Simons grinned widely. "They certainly did. Jim, I think when you get back to the States you might have to hire a public relations guy." From a thigh pocket on his cargo pants, Simons pulled a folded piece of paper and handed it to Jim. "This is from the online version of USA Today."

Jim unfolded the paper and the headline leaped at him: ONE MAN AGAINST TERROR! *Unarmed Civilian Beats Al-Qaida's Best.* Below that, a surprisingly clear photo, apparently lifted from the video, showing him using the tonfa to block the overhead bo strike from the second fighter.

"It's been all over CNN and BBC," Denise said. "Haven't you been watching?"

"Well, to be honest, no," Jim said. "I wasn't really awake until a couple hours ago." In fact, he was starting to feel a bit woozy. "I'd better lie down," he said. He lay back on the bed and Denise carefully lifted his bandaged leg, placing it carefully next to the other.

"Jim, you take it easy for a while, I'll head over to the base headquarters," Mark said. "What time is dinner around here?"

"Hell, I don't know. Five, maybe." He was getting more disoriented by the second. Christ, the leg hurt. "Can you find the nurse, please? I think I need a pain pill."

Simons promised to come by during the evening, and Mark put a hand on Jim's shoulder and squeezed. "See you later, big brother."

Denise turned back to him when they'd gone. "I'd better let you get some rest," she said. "I'll get the nurse on my way out."

He took her hand. The emotions that had buffeted him the past couple weeks were rocking him pretty good right now. He really liked this woman, and he knew the feeling was mutual. But he also knew it wasn't going to go any further. She had her life at Langley and he had his back in Wisconsin, whatever that might turn out to be now.

"You're pretty special, Denise. I'm glad I got to work with you."

Her eyes changed ever so slightly, the affection tinged with regret. "So am I." She touched his cheek. "I fly out tonight, Jim, so I guess this is goodbye. Call me when you get back home, okay?"

"Yeah, sure." The room was starting to twirl a little bit. He had to focus on her eyes, her face, and those lips as they came closer and closer.

It was amazing what a hot shower and clean underwear could do for a guy. Top it off with a new uniform and it was just about the closest thing to heaven since his last evening with Sophie. Mark felt good as he walked down the hospital hallway to Jim's room, despite the pain in his shoulder. He'd been doing a little more thinking, and things were starting to fall into place. But he needed to talk them over with his brother first. Needed to talk about a lot of things, in fact.

Jim was sitting up in a chair beside the bed, watching television. Mark knocked at the doorway. "Looks like you're feeling better."

"I am, and you look like a new man," Jim said, grinning. "Everything except for the hat, that is."

Mark laughed, pulling off the battered old patrol cap. "We've been through a lot together. It'll have an honored place on my mantle when I get home."

"When will that be?"

Mark sat on the edge of the bed. "Well, my tour here has another six months to go. I'll be rotated back stateside, and then I'll have to decide whether to pull the pin or go for my star. If I do that, it'll mean another couple years at least. Then, if I get the star, I'll have to put in another two or three. I'd probably find myself back over here somewhere eventually."

"My little brother, the general."

"Yeah, it has a ring to it. But I've been thinking about a different type of ring. Sophie—that's the girl I mentioned before—she works for the BBC. She told me she could probably get transferred to their bureau in the States. New York, or maybe Washington."

"She's been dropping a few hints, has she?"

Mark laughed. "I guess she has. I'm just starting to pick up on them." He told Jim about the security firm his old West

Point roommate had back in Virginia. "I just sent him an email a little while ago, asked him if his offer is still open. If he says yes, I'll look him up when I get back there and see what there is to see. I have two weeks' leave coming, so it'll be sometime soon."

"Sounds like a plan." Jim's eyes flicked back to the TV screen. Fox News was about to air a special on Jim's fight in Somalia. Mark pulled up another chair and they watched. A nurse came in to ask about dinner, and in a few minutes they were eating from trays.

During a commercial break, Jim shook his head and chuckled.

"What's so funny?" Mark said, chewing on a piece of Salisbury steak.

"Remember how we used to eat like this back home, watching *Kung Fu*?"

Mark laughed. "Hell, yes. Remember Dad's favorites? Never missed *Gunsmoke*."

"Or *Adam-12*. Hey, remember him watching *The Bob Newhart Show* with us, and what he said about Suzanne Pleshette?"

Jim was laughing too, now. "Yeah. 'Boys, if a schlub like Newhart can get a hot number like her, imagine what you boys will be able to do.'" They traded stories until the show came back on. Bret Baier introduced a guest commentator and Jim dropped his fork onto the tray. "Well, I'll be damned."

Mark saw the distinguished, silver-haired man on the screen and asked, "You know that guy?"

"Yeah. He's our master instructor in weapons." For the next fifteen minutes, the master expertly dissected the combat footage. Toward the end, Jim pushed his tray aside and sat with his head in his hands, fighting to control his breathing.

He felt Mark's hand on his shoulder. "Easy there, Jim. Hang in there, it'll pass."

"What the hell was that?" The shakes were calming down, but he was still scared. Watching the fight had brought it all back with an almost overwhelming rush: the terror, the stress, the fatigue and pain.

"You took a helluva beating, Jim, but sometimes the psychological part of it is worse. It'll get easier as time goes on. You just have to stay on top of it, and don't be shy about talking to somebody about it when it gets bad."

"Does this—does this ever happen to you?"

Mark's eyes were glistening, remembering way too many dark nights and bad dreams. "Yeah. It does."

They sat side by side in silence, watching the show wrap up. Political pundits were offering their take on it, but there was nary a word about Mark's mission. Jim brought that up as the show closed. "They didn't say anything about your mission. Can you tell me where it was?"

Mark hesitated, then said, "Iran. My unit went in for an HVT. High Value Target."

"And you got him?"

"Yeah, we did."

Jim shook his head. "Hell, man, from what Simons said, he must've been a pretty big one. People should know about that."

"I have the feeling you won't hear anything about that for a long time, if ever," Mark said. "Iran is a very sensitive subject for the politicians right now."

"But what Simons told us about the mission saving a lot of lives, what about that?"

"Jim, our people are saving lives every day over here.

418

Sometimes just one or two at a time, sometimes a whole lot more. It's what we do."

Jim clicked the remote and sat back in his chair as the TV went dark. "You don't know how many times I've wished that I was over here with you."

"Well, here you are. Your wish came true."

"I mean, with the Army, or the Marines maybe, some branch, where I could do my part. This damn knee..." He almost slapped it in disgust, but held back at the last second.

"Hey, you've been doing your part. Keeping the home fires burning, keeping the faith."

"Yeah, sure, farting around with TV commercials and ad campaigns for cell phones and internet service." Jim pushed his tray aside.

That was almost too much for Mark. His brother didn't know how good he had it. Safe and sound back home, a safe warm bed every night, nobody shooting at you, no IEDs to watch for on the road to work. "Hey, you want to talk about wishes?" Mark stood up and took a step to face Jim. "If I had a buck for every time I've wished I was back home, working a job somewhere, I'd be a rich guy. Sometimes I wonder what the hell I'm doing here, in the Army, when I could be back home, with my son—" Mark's eyes teared up and he turned away, not wanting his big brother to see him like this, but then he felt a hand on his shoulder.

"It's okay, Mark." Jim turned him around a bit, slipping an arm around Mark's shoulder. "I guess...maybe we've both been looking for something more."

Mark took a deep breath, calming himself. "For just a second there, I thought you were a typical civilian, big brother. Living the easy life back home while we're over here, doing the heavy lifting to keep everybody safe. But you chose to come over here. You volunteered. Just like all of us."

Jim sat down on the bed. "Sorry. The leg."

"It's okay," Mark said, sitting next to him. They were silent for a minute, then Mark said, "You know, Dad told me something before I went away to the Point, and I've never forgotten it. 'Live a life of honor,' he said. We heard it all the time there, quotes from MacArthur."

"Yes," Jim said. "'Duty, honor, country.' Good words to live by."

"They've worked for me so far."

Jim massaged his repaired knee. "I've thought about Mom and Dad a lot lately."

"I have, too," Mark said. "I'll always feel bad that I wasn't there when they died."

"It couldn't be helped," Jim said. "They were both very proud of you."

"Well, they felt the same about you, I know that for a fact," Mark said.

"Yeah, maybe Mom did, but I don't know about Dad."

"Come on, Jim, he was always proud of you. That night after the state championship game, he could hardly sleep, he felt so bad for you."

"Get outta here."

"I'm serious, man. A week after the game, Dad was having a beer with some guys after bowling and some clown said something about how you should've made that free throw and Dad put him right up against the wall."

Jim looked at his brother. "Are you serious?"

"Hell, yes. I heard him telling Mom about it, and he ordered me to keep quiet. Didn't want to give us the idea that losing your temper was okay. But he stood up for his son. Later on when I was playing football, he'd remind me of how you played, how you were a leader on the team, how they never would've even gotten to State without you. That inspired me."

Jim shook his head, and he couldn't help smiling. "I think a lot about how they lived their lives. Pretty quiet lives, really, but you know something? They lived them honorably."

"Yeah, they did," Mark said. "Maybe, when you get right down to it, that's about the best you can say about someone."

"People seek that out in different ways," Jim said. "Most do, anyway. If you hang in there, you can find it."

"It's worth the effort," Mark said.

"Yes," Jim said, "it is."

CHAPTER FORTY-FIVE
WISCONSIN

THEY'D TOLD HIM that his return to the States would be hush-hush, but when Jim walked out of the terminal at Dulles there was a large crowd of reporters and dozens of other people, many with signs welcoming him home. Some of the signs looked professionally-designed, and he wondered briefly if certain people in Washington had decided it would make someone else look good if the conquering hero was properly hailed.

But, what the hell, he crutched up to the waiting microphones, said a few words about how glad he was to be home and to have been able to serve his country. The CIA handlers were waiting with something less than complete patience, so he backed away and started toward the idling car when a pretty blonde woman holding a microphone with an NBC tag said, "Mr. Hayes, do you think your experience sends a message to terrorists?"

He was tired and hurting and just wanted to get home, and he let his better judgment slip. He stopped and said, "Yeah. Don't mess with the U.S."

If he'd had any hope of quickly fading back into a quiet life in Cedar Lake, that remark made sure it wasn't going to happen. It was late that Friday night by the time Jim got back to Cedar Lake, jet-lagged beyond belief. He'd slept the last couple hours from O'Hare in the back of the CIA car, then lay awake for two hours in his familiar but somehow strange bed, his cat Spike purring contentedly next to him, before sleep finally came.

The next morning, when he opened his front door to get the morning paper, they were waiting for him. TV trucks with their satellite dishes pointing to the sky, reporters and camera operators jostling for position, and outnumbering them all were the people with signs and flags. Yellow tape tied into ribbons festooned almost every tree in his neighborhood, something he hadn't noticed the night before. A roar went up as he appeared, unshaven and bed hair and all. He gave them a quick wave, retrieved his paper and stepped back inside.

After a shower and shave he felt a little better, only to discover there was no milk in the refrigerator. He decided to grab breakfast at the coffee shop downtown, then stop by the gym to use the Jacuzzi before going to the supermarket. His knee was sore but he was sure he could still use it to drive safely. How to deal with the horde outside, though? He called a friend, a fellow student at the dojo who was also an editor at the local weekly paper.

"Sam, how do I deal with all these reporters outside?"

"You have to give them something, Jim," was the advice. "Go out there, be polite, answer a few questions and then say you have to go. Just don't get carried away." There was a laugh. "What you said last night in Chicago, well, it sort of fired them up."

"Yeah. Thanks, Sam. I owe you an interview. I'll give you a call Monday to set it up."

Later that afternoon, he made his phone calls. Mickey first, of course. She burst out crying, and when she had calmed down they talked for a half hour. "I'm coming down there, Dad," she said, and there was no changing her mind. So much like her mother. She'd throw an overnight bag together and be there in a couple hours.

Two other women deserved calls, and he'd been thinking about them all day. What he'd shared with Denise in the past couple weeks was something he was still processing, would always be the best part of an extraordinary experience, but that's as far as it would go, he knew. He had his life here—wherever that was going to go now, for he knew things would never be the same—and she had hers, with CIA at Langley and in whatever exotic locales she was destined to serve. He dug out the card she'd given him, called the cell number and got her voice mail. Somehow that sealed the deal for him. He hesitated, then said he'd gotten home safely and hoped they could stay in touch.

Gina answered on the first ring.

He got another hero's welcome when he arrived at the telecom Monday morning. Even Lori gave him a hug; it was a bit awkward, but sincere, and he thought that maybe she wasn't quite the ice maiden he'd always taken her to be. Many of the other women fussed over him for a few days, and two of them even asked him out, invitations he politely declined.

The guys back in Plant hailed him as the returning conqueror, and it was a good feeling to have, harking him back to that night in high school when he'd made that shot at the buzzer for the sectional championship. They insisted on throwing him a proper welcome-home party at a local bar Friday night after work.

But that didn't go so well. Someone had bought a DVD of the fight—to Jim's amazement, one of the news networks was hawking them over the internet—and they asked him to give a blow-by-blow account. Hey, no problem—but when the video started, it was like someone had shut the lights off, and when they came on again he was back in the cell, with the heat and the stench and the terror. He heard the latch on the door again, the creak of the hinges, and this time he knew they'd shoot him, so he threw the first thing he could find at them.

The pitcher hit the restroom door and shattered in a kaleidoscope of glass and beer. Jim blinked once, twice, and then said, "Please, turn it off." He went home, and kept the lights on all night long, and the dreams, the ones he hadn't had for a few nights, came back in full force.

The next morning he was tired and grumpy, but at least the reporters weren't there anymore. Things had calmed down on that score, thanks to new events that had grabbed their attention elsewhere. Jim had never thought he'd be happy to hear about another political scandal or another celebrity meltdown, but they'd taken the heat off him, at least. He was out in his garage just after lunch, thinking about taking his bicycle out for a long-overdue spin, when through the open doorway he saw a gold Nissan Juke pull into the driveway. You didn't see too many of those, and in fact the last one he'd seen was a few weeks earlier up in Rice Lake.

The woman who emerged was even more beautiful than he'd remembered, her dark hair set off by the midriff-baring white sleeveless top, red shorts accentuating the toned legs. "Hi, Jim," Gina said.

The pain in his knee and ribs was suddenly gone.

EPILOGUE

WISCONSIN

JIM'S FIRST BIG surprise on Christmas Eve was that Gina was able to beat the snowstorm. Things hadn't looked good on the radar that morning, with winter's first big blast lurking over Minnesota and heading his way, but his phone rang just after six a.m. and she said she would be on the road as soon as she got showered and dressed.

"Are you sure about this?" Jim asked her. "I'm worried about this storm coming in."

"I can beat it, if I don't hang around talking on the phone very long. I don't want to be alone on Christmas, Jim." Gina's boys were spending their holiday break in Italy, visiting their grandparents.

"Okay, but promise me you'll turn back if it gets too bad."

She laughed. "Jim, I've got four-wheel-drive. We're used to the winter up here, not like you people down south." Jim had to give her that. Winters up in the far reaches of northern Wisconsin were often more severe than down in Cedar Lake, near the Illinois line. He'd heard people up north refer to his area as the "banana belt" of the state.

He fretted all day, staying busy by cleaning the house from stem to stern, but stopping every fifteen minutes to check the weather on the computer. It was cold in Cedar Lake with an inch or so of snow on the ground, but so far it had been a mild winter. That looked like it was about to change.

Well, that would be fitting, wouldn't it? A lot of things had changed in the past few months. His knee zinged him a bit as he jockeyed the vacuum cleaner around the living room. The surgery was five months past now, and the knee was in good shape. Fortunately, it had only been a meniscus tear, small potatoes as far as knee problems went. The orthopedist told him that a total knee replacement was in his future, but not for several years. Sooner, if he kept up the martial arts training. He considered that for maybe about fifteen minutes. Would he have it at sixty-five, or sixty? He was back in the dojo two weeks after his return home.

By then the media frenzy had died down. He turned down every interview request that came around, no matter who it was from, and some of them weren't very happy about it. His patriotism was questioned by a rep from a right-leaning network; another from the left side wondered whether the men Jim had fought over there were even worthy opponents. "I wonder if you're as tough as they say you are," the man sputtered. Jim thought briefly about inviting him to come down to the dojo, strap on some gloves and go a couple rounds, but decided against it.

The topper, though, came from a woman who hosted a prominent network morning show, who all but offered to go to bed with him if he'd allow himself to be flown to New York for an exclusive interview with her. "I'll make it worth your while," she said, before he hung up on her.

Life in Cedar Lake went on, his included, but it was

different. People recognized him, most with a friendly wave and hello, a few others with what almost seemed like fear. A handful had a different reaction. A month after his return he took a Saturday and went to Madison, just to knock around at some stores and then catch a movie. On the way home he stopped at a roadhouse to use the restroom and decided to have a quick beer. Two burly guys in leather were shooting pool, asked him if he was the guy in the video, and challenged him to come outside and show them how tough he was. Things might've gotten out of hand if another pair of patrons, a husband and wife, hadn't intervened. Shorter and leaner than the pool players, the man had nevertheless told them in no uncertain terms, in a voice that brooked no disagreement, that they were to let this man have his beer in peace or they would answer to two former Marine Corps sergeants.

As he put the vacuum cleaner away, a thought of Gina caused him to smile. Since her surprise trip down they'd seen each other every other week, usually at a town halfway between Ashland and Cedar Lake. He'd become pretty familiar by now with places like Marshfield and Stevens Point. For Thanksgiving, he made the six-hour haul up to Ashland and enjoyed the holiday weekend with Gina and her sons, who were home from college in Duluth. He stayed at a local hotel for that visit, although he knew they weren't fooling the boys.

Right on time at three o'clock, the gold Juke rolled into his driveway just as the snow was starting to come down. The storm had diminished as it swept across Wisconsin and now there would be just enough to make for a postcard-perfect Christmas Eve. As they sat in front of the twinkling tree later that evening, sipping hot chocolate, the only thing missing was a fireplace.

"This is a very nice home," Gina said, "but you need a fireplace."

"I was just thinking the same thing." This wasn't the first time that had happened. It was almost like they had some sort of extra-sensory connection. That was intriguing, and sometimes a little worrisome. It was a lot like what he'd had with Suzy.

He hesitated, then said, "Maybe someday we'll find a better one, with a fireplace."

It hung there in the air, and he felt her tense just a bit, reclining there in his arms, and then she snuggled in a little more. "I think I'd like that," she said.

The second big surprise was about ten the next morning. Jim had just put the turkey in the oven, and Gina was telling him it was way too big, and he said he liked turkey leftovers, when the doorbell rang.

"Are they early?" she asked as she filled the dishwasher with the day's first load.

Mickey and her boyfriend weren't due till one o'clock. "Maybe it's that morning-show bimbo again," he said as he went to the door.

Gina laughed. "Take her into the bedroom. I'll get the camera, we'll make a fortune from the tabloids."

He opened the door to see a man and woman standing on his small porch. He recognized the woman's face from the news. He recognized the man's face, too.

"We were in the neighborhood, thought we'd drop in," Mark said.

Jim was in the kitchen, rummaging through the refrigerator for the whipped cream. He had just enough room for one more piece of pumpkin pie. From behind him, he heard a familiar mushy swoosh. "Looking for this?" Mark said.

"That isn't the last piece of pie, I hope."

"Nope. One more." Mark held out the whipped cream can. "Don't pile it on, now."

Jim snatched the can from his brother. "That's what Mom used to tell me. But now this is my house, my pumpkin pie, and by God it's my can of whipped cream." He aimed at the pie, pressed the plunger, and got only a few flecks of cream and some compressed air.

Mark stopped laughing long enough to spoon a big dollop from his pie slice onto Jim's. The brothers chuckled as they forked away, walking together into the dining room. Ahead of them, the lights blinked merrily on the tree and the three women sat on the couch, Mickey in the middle, flipping through yet another photo album. In one of the chairs, Mickey's boyfriend Ian was losing his battle with turkey hangover.

"Anything happen here since you got back?" Mark asked.

"Well, membership at my dojo has gone way up. And people recognize me. When Gina and I go out, the drinks are always free."

"Yeah, but I mean something really serious." He gave Jim a concerned look. "Any threats? You know what I'm talking about."

Jim sighed and said, "You heard about the *fatwa*." Two months after his return, a Muslim cleric in Saudi Arabia had issued a fatwa, an Islamic legal pronouncement, calling for Jim's execution. That had led to some secret and fairly tense meetings with the FBI, who said they'd provide Jim with protection, but he asked them to be discreet about it. A month or so later they'd told him nothing seemed to be happening, so whatever surveillance they were doing backed down. At least that's what Jim assumed, but he had no illusions. Someone was likely to be keeping an eye on him for the foreseeable future; he could only hope they were the good guys, and go about his business.

"I had a couple meetings with some FBI people," Jim said. "Nothing ever came of it."

"I met with the General in D.C. when I got back into the country," Mark said. "He told me CIA was taking it seriously, so he called in a favor and got you some extra backup. Over and above the FBI's people."

"I've never noticed anybody," Jim said.

"You won't." Mark finished his last bite and set the plate and fork on the table. "The girls are hitting it off," he said.

"Yeah. Mickey likes them both."

"That's good," Mark said. "One of them will be her new aunt in a few months." Mark had made the announcement at dinner: he and Sophie would marry in August.

"The other one will be her step-mother one of these days," Jim said.

That brought a look. "Is that official?"

"Not yet," Jim said. "But I just made the decision." He hoped Gina would agree with that decision, but he had a feeling she would. The night before, when he'd presented his Christmas gift to her, he could sense a little disappointment when she opened the box and found a diamond necklace, not a ring. But she got over it very quickly, judging by her passion later on.

"Good job. And speaking of good jobs, I have a proposition for you."

"Yeah?"

Mark took one last swig of milk from his glass. "I'm leaving the Army, Jim. Six months from now, I'll be out. As of the first of July, I'll be an executive vice-president of Odin Security Services."

"Is that your old West Point buddy's company? The one you mentioned over in Djibouti?"

"Sure is. I'm meeting him in Chicago in a few days to finalize things, but it's a done deal. He's opening a branch office in the Midwest and wants me to run it."

"Congratulations. Sounds like a good move."

"It will be. It'll be tough to leave the Army, but it's time, I think."

"Well, you've put in what, how many years?"

"It'll be twenty-five this spring, since I graduated the Academy and took the oath." He sighed. "I'm sure there will be times when I wonder if I should've stayed in. I think about that star. But then I think about all the paperwork that would go with it."

"If you've already made the decision, then you know the time is right for a change," Jim said, setting his plate down next to Mark's. In the living room, the girls whooped with laughter as Mickey pointed at a photo. "I've been thinking about making a change, too. I was sitting in that cell over there, and I kept saying to myself, 'If I get out of here alive, I'll be happy to live a nice quiet life back in Cedar Lake, working at the telecom.' But you know what?"

"You're not satisfied with that anymore," Mark said.

Jim looked at his brother in amazement. "Yeah, that's right. How did you know?"

Mark looked back with very serious eyes. "It's what you did over there, Jim. You made a difference. Now, nothing else seems to measure up."

Jim looked away, past the women in the living room, past the Christmas tree, to someplace far away, a place filled with

fear and doubt but also with a sense of purpose, of honor.
"You're right," Jim said. "It's not the same." He hesitated, then
said, "I've been offered a book deal. I've turned down everything else, didn't want the publicity, but this is different. It's
not about the money, although it would mean a pretty good
piece of money, enough to retire on if I wanted to, but when I
looked it over, I thought about how there are a lot of guys out
there like me, wondering if they can make a difference somehow, wondering if they ever could rise to the challenge."

"I'll bet you've been getting some mail," Mark said.

"Yeah, somehow my email address leaked out so I got tons
of that before I changed it, and sacks of the paper stuff. It's
starting to let up, but I still get several letters every day."

"What kind of letters?"

"Lots of offers. Personal appearances. Jobs, even." He
grinned, then lowered his voice as he leaned slightly toward
his brother. "Some of the letters from women are really
something."

Mark grinned right back. "With pictures?"

"Yeah. But they go right in the trash." His grin faded. "A lot
of the men's letters are pretty moving. The stories they tell...I
had no idea. Especially the ones who've never been in the service. How they're searching for some kind of meaning in their
lives. Even beyond religious faith."

"Jim, one thing I found out fast in the Army is that people
need leadership, they need inspiration. If they get that, they
can accomplish some pretty remarkable things." He rested a
hand on his brother's shoulder. "Write that book. Be a leader,
be an inspiration. Even if the guy who reads it is inspired to
just lead his own life a little better, be a better husband and
father, a better man, you will have made a difference in his life,
maybe a big difference."

Jim thought about that. The mail he was getting from all over the country certainly showed that people were looking for something, were hungry for it. So many of them thanked him for what he'd done, for standing up for his country. Many of them were veterans, welcoming him to their brotherhood. That meant a lot to Jim, more than he ever would've imagined.

But underlying almost every letter was a sense of foreboding. Not too many people seemed to be convinced by the TV pundits who assured them that things were calming down. There were more Heydars out there, lurking in the shadows, seeking to tear down, to kill and destroy. They would only be stopped if people of honor stood up and said no, and were ready to back that up with action if and when the words failed.

"Okay," Jim said. "I'll do it."

"Great," Mark said. "When you get done with that, though, you'll be looking for something else to do. This company I'm joining does a lot of good work, teaching people how to stay safe, providing security for companies and individuals. We do a lot of work with martial arts masters, putting on seminars and things like that. Now, about that proposition I mentioned. I'm going to need some help in running this security outfit. Somebody I can trust. I can only think of one guy I want to work with. Interested?"

Jim looked at his brother and held out his hand.

AUTHOR'S NOTES

The seeds of *Quest for Honor* were planted some years ago. I was watching a news report of a man captured by Islamic extremists somewhere in the Middle East. In front of a video camera, he was seated on a chair, his hands bound behind him, and he stared ahead with hollow, frightened eyes. Flanking him on both sides were hooded men armed with submachine guns. One of them rambled on with his manifesto, stating the alleged crimes of the West for which this man was about to pay the ultimate price. The prisoner said nothing, but in his eyes one could almost see a final, desperate plea: Please help me.

And, no doubt like many others who were watching, I asked myself a question: What would I do if that was me?

It is not a comfortable question to contemplate. The great majority of us here in the West go about our daily lives meeting challenges that are usually somewhat routine. For many, the biggest is deciding what to wear to work that day, or how to occupy our time if we have the day off. Occasionally we will face more serious challenges, such as finding a new job, or dealing with a serious illness, financial hardship, or a rebellious child. Rarely do we encounter situations that are truly life-threatening. For that, we can thank the men and women who guard our streets and our shores, who put their lives on the line every day to keep ours safe. As George Orwell once said, "People sleep peaceably in their beds at night only because rough men stand ready to do violence on their behalf." We go about our lives knowing that if push ever does come to shove, we can make a phone call and within minutes there will be armed, trained men and women to deal with whatever threat we face. It is a comfort we tend to take for granted.

But what if we could not make that call? What if there was no reasonable hope that help would arrive in time? What if we were truly on our own, facing people like the hooded men in that video, and our very survival depended on what we would do next?

I began studying the martial arts in 2001, well into my forties. At first it was a way for me to spend quality time with my teenage son, who had started training in the Korean art of *taekwondo* several years earlier. Besides, who wouldn't want to be like one of those people on the movie screen, bringing down the biggest and baddest bad guys with stylish kicks and nifty punches? But like everybody who has ever begun training in martial arts, I quickly discovered that I was not going to be Bruce Lee in six or seven easy lessons. No matter what art you decide to study, it takes long hours of arduous practice and dedication to achieve proficiency, and years to attain mastery. In truth, the training and education never stops. In taekwondo we have a saying: as color belts (lower ranks), we are learning how to learn; as black belts, we are learning.

As the years went by I expanded my training to include the arts of *isshin-ryu karate,* Russian *Systema,* and *ryukudo kobujutsu,* the study of Okinawan weaponry. I have also dabbled in *jiu-jitsu* and hope soon to take up the study of *krav maga,* the formidable close-quarters combat art taught to the Israeli military.

So little time, so much to learn. Along the way the training has opened up huge vistas, and I began to study what I and others call the "warrior ethos". What does it mean to be a warrior? Does it mean fighting, combat, sowing death and destruction upon one's enemies? Or is it something much more subtle, more enriching and empowering? I believe strongly that it is the latter. The warrior ethos embraces a code of honor, and that in itself is a subject worthy of study, for without honor one can never truly be a warrior, in the truest sense of the word. Indeed, the concept of honor, as was once known and accepted in this country, seems to be diminishing in importance, much to the detriment of all of us, in my opinion.

So it was that I decided to write about men who are trying to define their own sense of honor in the midst of today's tumultuous world, and who find themselves facing the ultimate challenge. The Hayes brothers, so different from each other and yet so similar, face their challenges in environments that are, at first, vastly different. Safe in his small Wisconsin town, Jim searches for meaning after the love of his life is violently taken from him; in the mountains of Afghanistan where death and terror lurk almost everywhere, Mark strives to keep his men alive while protecting the innocent Afghans in the villages near his base, all the while wondering what will be left for him to do when he takes off the uniform for the last time. And Yusuf, a man of noble birth who is trying to throw off a murderous ideology of hate, decides to grasp whatever honor might be left for him after years of bringing pain and destruction to others.

The concept of honor, as it relates to the individual and the group, has changed over the centuries, like virtually everything else. My great-great grandfather was a Civil War veteran, and I would imagine that if he was out in public with his wife on an evening in the 1870s and she was insulted by another man, he would've demanded satisfaction from the offender and quite likely gotten it, either in the form of an apology or a physical confrontation. His peers would congratulate him on his defense of his wife's (and his own) honor and the law would almost surely look the other way. Nearly a century and a half later, I would likely be thrown in jail if I punched out a guy in public, even if he had called my wife the vilest slur possible, and would probably also find myself on the receiving end of a lawsuit. Many would call this progress, but sometimes I wonder; while we certainly can't have people going around assaulting others over perceived (or even real) slights, at the same time we have seen a skyrocketing increase in rude and uncivil behavior, perhaps because there are no consequences for such conduct anymore.

We see this not only in our own towns and cities but among nations. Increasingly we see armed movements, ranging from terror groups to whole governments, brutalizing their own people and oftentimes their weaker neighbors, in large part, I think, because they know that potential adversaries with the strength to resist them will act only in rare cases, after the most egregious transgressions against their own people. And even then, the offender is likely to avoid the full force of his adversary, who will prefer to rely on diplomacy and economic sanctions to restrain the offender's behavior.

On my favorite website, Art of Manliness, author Brett McKay published an in-depth study of honor in late 2012. In his summation, McKay makes a convincing argument that "honor is more powerful than rules and laws in shaping human behavior."

Without honor, mediocrity, corruption and incompetence rule, Honor is based on reputation, and when people stop caring about their reputation, and shame disappears, people devolve into doing the least they can without getting into legal trouble or getting fired. This leads to mediocrity, corruption and incompetence.....As society has become more complex and anonymous, and the bonds of honor have dissolved, we've had to rely more and more on obedience—rules and regulations—to govern people's behavior...We must be policed by an external authority to check our behavior in the absence of honor...Honor acts as a check on narcissism, creates community, creates meaning.

Here's hoping that we can rediscover honor, as people and as a society.

ACKNOWLEDGMENTS

Nobody ever writes a book alone. It is a collaborative effort, for the writer has been inspired to write by someone, trained by someone else, supported by another, critiqued by still more. My inspiration for this book came from my grandfathers, James L. Tindell and Alvin Carpenter, who lived lives of simple dignity and honor and set high standards for their sons and grandsons to follow. They left this world some years ago but I have faith that we will be reunited someday. My father, James J. Tindell, continues to set high standards for me and my brothers as he enjoys a well-deserved retirement in Arizona, watching golf and baseball with his Yorkie on his lap. I have also been blessed with strong women of honor: my grandmothers, Leona Tindell and Meta Carpenter, both daughters of German immigrants, and my mother, Sandra Tindell, who is living proof that saints do indeed walk the earth. Last but certainly not least, my wife Sue, who has been my greatest supporter as an author (as well as a sharp-eyed but fair critic). She also takes me along on many of her travels around the world, for which I am very grateful, and she can open up new vistas for you as well. Look her up at www.travelleaders.com/ricelakewi.

Most certainly this book would not have been made

possible without the assistance of my peers in my critique group, who reviewed and helped revise *Quest for Honor* from start to finish. Each of them are fine authors in their own right: Donna White Glaser, Marjorie Swift Doering, Marla Madison and Helen Block. Check out their books on www.amazon.com.

A special thanks to a good friend and fellow black belt, SFC Keith Graeme, U.S. Army National Guard and Afghan War veteran, for lending his expertise to the chapters involving Mark Hayes and his troops. His expertise in the dojo has also been most helpful for me on my martial arts journey.

Cover art by Damonza, and book trailer produced by my son Jim Tindell, who is destined for major accomplishments in the field of cinema, and that's not just a proud father speaking.

I am also indebted to these writers and historians for their work, which made my research most interesting and pleasurable:

Honor: A History, James Bowman

If Not Now, When? Col. Jack Jacobs (ret.) and Douglas Century

In Search of the Warrior Spirit: Teaching Awareness Discipline to the Green Berets,

by Richard Strozzi-Heckler and George Leonard

Living with Honor, Salvatore Giunta

Never Without Heroes: Marine Third Reconnaissance Battalion in Vietnam, 1965-70,

Lawrence C. Vetter Jr.

On Combat: The Psychology and Physiology of Deadly Conflict in War and Peace,

Dave Grossman and Loren W. Christensen

Outlaw Platoon, Sean Parnell

The Outpost, Jake Tapper

This Man's Army, Andrew Exum

War, Sebastian Junger

The Warrior Ethos, Steven Pressfield

Warrior Mindset, Dr. Michael Asken, Loren W. Christensen, Dave Grossman

and Human Factor Research Group

Warriors: On Living with Courage, Discipline and Honor, Loren W. Christensen

The Way of Men, Jack Donovan

http://www.artofmanliness.com/2012/10/01
manly-honor-part-i-what-is-honor/

Made in the USA
San Bernardino, CA
30 August 2014